Death Among Brothers, Book Two

The Kirishitan Problem

Death Among Brothers
Book 2

The Kirishitan Problem

a novel

Marc Charles

The Ross House Press

Published by The Ross House Press,
an imprint of Canopic Publishing

Canopic Publishing
389 Lincoln Ave.
Woodstock, IL 60098
www.canopicpublishing.com

Designed and edited by Phil Rice

All illustrations used are in public domain.

First Edition

ISBN-13: 978-0-9971695-7-7 (alk. paper)

Dedication

This book is dedicated to four people. One I have known for over forty years. She is my better half, my partner, my sunshine, my nurse, my heart. She is my Sako. A better wife a man could not have. She still makes it all worthwhile.

When cancer gets its claws into you, family rallies and does their best to cheer you up. Friends are different. Most don't know what to say. It is not their fault. What do you say to a man diagnosed with stage IV cancer? Most tend to become quiet. Jim Van Evera, L.K. (Doc) Richardson, and Dave Easton bucked the tendency.

Jim Van Evera has been my home teacher for years with the LDS Church. He has been steadfast and faithful in his honoring of that calling. He has provided me peace of mind and been my balm of Gilead in troubled times. I thank him for it.

Doc Richardson is nurturing by profession. I met him as a Farmers Insurance agent in Los Angeles. But before that he was a combat Navy Corpsman taking care of Marines. Marines have heroes too. They are called Navy Corpsmen. Doc Richardson has been a good friend and kept me grounded in my attempts to complete this book and defeat the beast.

The fourth person I never met, and I will not meet on this plane. He passed onto a greater reward last month. His name was Dave Easton. He was a Korean era Marine combat veteran and author of *Leatherneck Sea Stories*. We shared the same publisher in Canopic and we corresponded via email. Throughout my illness he provided me with Marine stories and tidbits of information to brighten my day during the dark times. We were both Marine Security Guards. He stood watch over me though he never met me. He was a good man.

Acknowledgements

There are people who I must thank for their efforts in putting this book together. Without their help the second volume of the *Death Among Brothers* series would never have happened.

The first is Michelle Charles. Michelle is a voracious reader. For that purpose, I have used her as my beta reader. She devoured this book when it was in its infancy giving me germane recommendations throughout. She did so while balancing motherhood, grandmotherhood, working in her own business and keeping my younger brother, Doctor Raleigh Charles out of trouble (no easy task). For her efforts I am thankful.

Tom Tyner is a professor at Middle Tennessee State University in Murfreesboro, Tennessee. He has been a family friend for years. He is the person who originally introduced me to my publisher, Phil Rice of Canopic Publishing. I asked Tom to edit this book after I had corrected it several times, to include a reading of it backwards. I actually thought Tom would have little to do. What Tom returned to me was a Herculean effort in turning my ramblings into prose. It was a humbling experience. I am now sure that I would receive a failing grade in his class. He is an expert in what he does and if you enjoy *The Kirishitan Problem*, it will be in large part due to his efforts. I thank him profusely.

Phil Rice published my first book, *Death Among Brothers: A Samurai Comes of Age*. Although we had a rocky start, the finished product is one that anyone would be proud to hold their name. That is in large part due to Phil's acumen. I have done many things in my life of which I am proud. I have been around the world several times, dined with a king, briefed Congressial committees twice, seen the chaos of a beggar's moon in Kathmandu, and led Marines in just about every clime and place. Of the things I've done, and the accolades received, *Death Among Brothers* wins me the most respect. I find that slightly troubling. But it is probably more of a reflection on the quality of the book Phil published than the values of the world we live in today. Phil deserves some serious kudos if *The Kirishitan Problem* lives up to the standards he set with *A Samurai Comes of Age*.

Pamela Charles read the first two chapters of *The Kirishitan Problem* immediately upon their construction. It was her honest critique that gave me hope that I might be onto a good story during the two cancer filled years that followed when writing was the furthest thing from my mind. Thanks Pam.

I would also like to thank four martial artists. John Bartusevics, Captain USMC (Ret.); Chuck Potter, former Marine and retired Law Enforcement Officer; Sylvester Lopez, First Sergeant USMC (Ret.) and Dean Stephens, Master Sergeant USMC (Ret.). All the above gentlemen hold impecable credentials in the martial arts. I do not have room enough here to list their accomplishments.

Captain John Bartusevics USMC (Ret) is a Kyoshi in Isshinryu Karate and a legend in Marine Corps martial arts circles. He studied under the master of the system, ran several dojos and was a whispered legend in the Marine Corps in close combat and martial arts circles. The man that taught me to fight (really fight) learned from John. Despite several debilitating operations, John still trains and expands his gargantuan knowledge in the arts. His latest endeavors are to train with legends Hanshi Fumio Demura in kobudo and Hanshi Minobu Miki in Iaido.

Chuck Potter and his brother were household names in Judo in San Deigo before he joined the Corps. He kept up his training through out the Corps, later as a police office and eventually as an instructor at the Police Academy. He retired

8

from law enforcement and still assists at a Vista Judo dojo despite battling the cancer beast for the fourth time. Chuck is a linguist and speaks not only Japanese but the Hogen tongue of the Ryukyuan people. I borrowed on his language skills for this book.

Sylvester Lopez and I were dojo mates in the early seventies at a not open to the public dojo tucked behind the Close Combat office on Marine Corps Recruit Depot San Diego. It was run by the Close Combat Non-Commissioned Officer-in-Charge, Gunnery Sergeant Jones. Sylvester was recently promoted to Sixth Degree Black Belt in Isshinryu by his long-time Sensei A. J. Advincula.

Lastly, I need to mention Dean Stephens whose photographic memory on all things Okinawa Kenpo, especially Master Seikichi Odo, have proven very useful to my writing career. Dean taught me how to use a bo in my driveway one summer's day in North Carolina in the late 70's and has been a source of martial knowledge ever since. He still teaches in Idaho.

I know I've left some people out that helped me with this book and I'm sorry. The fact that I finished this book at all is a miracle. The first book took me one year to write. This one took three years. You can thank cancer and the plethora of drugs and hormones that tamed the cancer but fried my brain and emptied a lot of my memory. I will try to remember those I forgot and pick them up in the last book of the trilogy, *The New Shogun*.

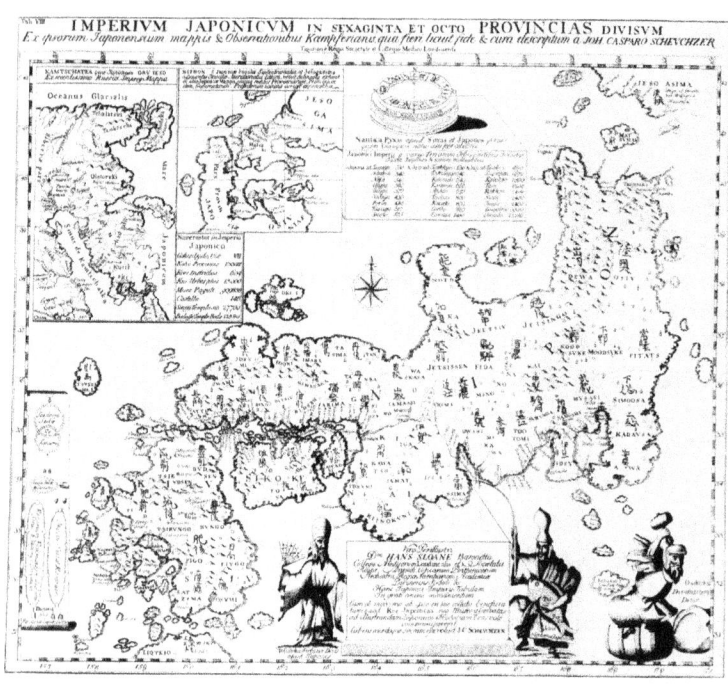

Contents

Principal Characters
Listed Alphabetically

Akane: Sister to Saito and daughter of Diamyo Matsukara of Shimabara.

Aya: Farm girl sold into a brothel at 13 to keep family from starving. Moved to Deshima Point to service the foreigners. Caught the eye of Dom Joao Procurator of the Portuguese. Married her due to her ability to learn languages and business. She has no love for her husband as he is sadistic. She has honored her position and made both her husband and herself wealthy due to her shrewd business dealings. She is the owner of the Jaded Princess one of five waterfront inns serving bad food, watered drinks, soiled doves, and games of chance. She is gambling her life on getting Mei's new urushi nuri to China before her husband or the evil governor find out about it. She has little heart and is ruled by profit. She hires Hideki as her bodyguard (yojimbo) and is flustered with is unwillingness to ignore evil and protect only her. His adherence to bushido provides friction to their relationship.

Chiyo: Japanese girl living at Buddhist temple that housed Yasuke. She wants to be Yasuke's girlfriend and eventually marry him. She and her whole family are abducted and sold into slavery.

Hachiro: Headman of the Ryukyuan village and brother to the Nigan or root kami.

Doi: Wako pirate and friend of Jobu.

Dom Joao: Procurator of the Jesuit order and owner of the black ships that ply their trade between Japan and the rest of the world. He is a sadistic lover and married to Aya. He keeps different wives in each port to look after his holdings.

Father Sebastian: An ordained priest of the Jesuit order who is also Japanese. While working to help his flock, his primary allegiance is to the Church.

Gon: Poor nephew to Jiro from Wajima. Jiro has taken him in

13

and taught him a trade. He is shy but wants to marry Mei.

Gotou: Mother to Aya.

Hai Yang: Assassin for the Golden Hatchets triad.

Hasebe: Father to Aya.

Heizo: Historical character and governor of Nagasaki. Called Bad Heizo by all. Merchant by social status. Avaricious and petty. Knows how to make money. Keeps the foreign goods flowing in Japan. Currently interested in getting Dom Joao and his Jesuits out of Japan and bringing in the Dutch. Has a nefarious association with the Wako pirates and slave trading.

Hidetada: Second shogun in the Tokugawa shogunate. Son of the founder Ieyasu.

Iai: Fast drawing of the katana, striking the opponent, and returning the sword to the scabbard all in one motion.

Ichi: Headman of Aya's village.

Imo: Wako pirate.

Jii: Grandfather to Hideki and Nagamasa. Raised both when his own son and daughter-in-law were killed. Newest member of the Roju (lesser body of the Tokugawa government).

Jiro: Urushi nuri artisan from Wajima, Japan, who settled on Mount Tara outside Nagasaki. Married to Momo with daughter Mei.

Jobu: Leader of the Wako pirates that raid a village next to Aya's and take prisoners.

Kuro Lobo: The Black Wolf is Dom Joao's number 2 man. He likes inflicting pain almost as much as he likes killing people. Kuro is a proponent of the Destreza Style of sword fighting. He takes pride in killing samurai in the pit.

Matsukara Saito: Proponent of the Suio style of fencing. Senior student of Hamada Sensei. Son of daimyo Matsukara of Shimabara.

Musashi Myamoto: Famous Japanese swordsman. Believed to have killed 61 men in duels. First real instructor to Hideki.

Mei: Daughter to Jiro and Momo. Lives on Mt. Tara. She has perfected new uses for the lacquer ware (urushi nuri) taught her by her father. Her artistry will make her rich.

Midori: Second in command of the Five Families of Ninja and friend of Myo the leader. Accomplished ninja sent to Kyushu by Jii to investigate the threat of the Kirishitans. Has taken a job with Aya playing the samisen and singing as well as cooking. Befriends Yasuke, a teenage Ryukyuan boy who becomes key to Aya's urushi nuri plans.

Momo: Kirishitan (Christian) owner of a mountain-top inn on Mt. Tara. Mother to Mei. Widow to Jiro.

Neh: Slang expression at the end of a sentence inferring agreement. Much like "yes" after a statement in English.

Nigan: The root spirit of the Ryukyuan village. The headman might make a decision, but he always asks that the Nigan bless the enterprise.

Shiro: A young, Japanese Kirishitan. A charismatic leader of the Kirishitans in Nagasaki. The faithful attribute miracles to him.

Tahei: Heizo's number two. Samurai and leader of the militia and therefore Magistrate of Nagasaki. A thug leading thugs.

Taro: A courier for a local service in Kyushu and old friend of Jiro and Momo's.

Tatsu: Bartender at the Jaded Princess. Confidant and admirer of his boss, Aya. Former samurai.

Tengu: A creature of Japanese lore with the face of a bird and body of a monk thought to be disruptive.

Yagyu Jubei: Eldest son to Masanori (current counselor to the Shogun Hidetada) and inheritor of the Shinkage-ryu school of fencing. Deadly swordsman who has been used as a legal assassin by his father to eliminate challengers to the Tokugawa regime. Friend to Hideki since Hideki saved him from an inglorious death in an Edo jail last year. He is attracted to the Yoshinobu willingness to do right no matter the cost.

Yama: Wako pirate.

Yasuke: Ryukyuan youth, raised at a Buddhist temple. Now living in Aya's chicken coop. Makes a living selling flutes and kids' toys he makes himself.

Yoshi: Ninja of the old school. Uses haragai (seeing through the darkness) a technique thought extinct. Friend of Hideki.

Cobbled together an allegiance between the Yoshinobu and the Five Families of Ninja. The Five Families now work for the Yoshinobu exclusively. Adept in the dark arts of the shinobi no mono.

Yoshinobu Hideki: Grandson to Masahige and brother to Nagamasu. Eighteen year old on a warrior's pilgrimage. Has studied with the two greatest swordsmen of the era (Myamoto Musashi and Yagyu Jubei). Currently traveling with Jubei to Kyushu. He has had to become a left-handed swordsman in a country that labels "different" as freaks. This journey is about him coming to terms with his handicap and growing as a man.

Yuki: Nagamasa's wife and mother of Yoshisune (baby). Daughter of Hittori Hanzo, leader of the shogun's metsuke (spies). Both samurai and ninja.

Death Among Brothers, Book Two

The Kirishitan Problem

I

Urushi

"Did I ever tell you how my father taught me to make the cuts?"

Mei looked down from her ladder as young Gon made a sign not to answer. "No Otosan, how did you learn?" Gon rolled his eyes in disbelief.

"I was sure I had told you. Oh well, maybe not. It is a good story, worth repeating," Jiro nodded towards the youngsters. "In Wajima, when I was just old enough to go to the trees with my father, he placed me on a ladder next to a tree, tied a pot in place, and made a horizontal slice in the bark. Soon, the beautiful white liquid began to seep down the bark and into the pot. He then told me to mimic everything he did. He carved five more horizontal slices above the first one so the liquid was flowing. Then he told me to do the next tree. Of course, I was eager. I tied the pot in place and made a slice high on the bark above it and proceeded to slice five more below it." Jiro's natural jolly face broke into a wide grin. "You guessed it; I got the white liquid all over my hands, tried unsuccessfully to rub it off on my clothes, and even got some on my face as I tried to brush the sweat away. In just a few moments I felt like my skin was on fire. It was burning and itching and turning a bright red that changed to splotches of black. It itched and burned at the same time. The more I scratched, the worse the itch became. In no time, I was miserable."

"Oh no, Father, how bad for you," Mei said.

"That is the yin and the yang of the urushi tree, my children.

The sap provides us with a living, but it can also extract miserable revenge if you are not careful," Jiro warned, turning to point his small cutting knife in the direction of the young people. "You must always be on your guard with the trees. You never know when they might turn on you. The yin is wonderful and beautiful to behold; the yang, not so much."

"Yes, Father, you have taught us to be careful in all things regarding the urushi," Mei said.

Jiro nodded, knowing his Mei was always careful. He looked over at Gon and shook his head. Either Gon would become more careful or he would not. Either way, Jiro knew he'd done all he could for the young man. Taking him in from a distant relative up north in Wajima would have been all that was expected of a kinsman, but Jiro had made him an apprentice. Jiro had taken Gon into his house and made him one of the family. Now his wife was plotting for Mei and Gon to marry. Gon was not Jiro's first pick for his only daughter, but out here on the mountain there were not too many picks available.

"The trees can be harsh teachers. When you have your own children Mei, you will not be allowed to hold them until we know if they are sensitive to the urushi. We will have to find a wet nurse to care for the child because your touch and your milk will have been tainted with the poison in the tree," Jiro warned.

"Yes, Father, I know the warnings. I will not know the joys of motherhood until the child is two years old. Then we will know if he is sensitive to the urushi or not."

Jiro nodded in agreement with his daughter's statement.

Mei yawned. This was about the one hundredth time she had heard the story. But she was a dutiful daughter and hid her yawn in the shadow of the tree. Jiro transitioned to this reminiscence as if the subject had not changed.

"Later, my mother packed my arms, hands, and face in hot wet cloths to relieve some of the pain. However, it took almost a month before I could function again. To this day, I remember now to make the first slice just above the pot and continue upward to keep the sap off my hands."

"A wonderful story, Otosan. We will remember it," Mei said.

Gon whispered under his breath, "You know we have heard that story hundreds of times."

In an equally conspiratorial tone, Mei chided, "One more time will not hurt us, and he likes telling it."

Gon turned away mumbling about the stupidity of old people.

Mei watched him wander off to the cart and sighed audibly. The thought of that whining, timid, indecisive boy becoming her husband sent shivers up her spine.

"Thinking of someone better?" Jiro asked.

Mei almost fell off the ladder. She had not heard her father approach. Then she frowned as she looked after Gon. "He is not much, Father. He certainly is not half the man you are. But he is likely all I will find out here in the mountains so far from the city."

"Do not be too hard on him. I was not much of a man either until I married your mother."

Mei tilted her head toward her father. "What do you mean? You were the third son of a Wajima lacquer ware family. You struck out on your own because life would not provide much for you there. You heard sailors talk about the urushi trees near Nagasaki so you walked for three months and started a new life. I would say that required quite a bit of courage and stamina," Mei defended.

"Oh, all of that is true. But I did not really start making anything of myself until your mother bought a lacquer ware bowl from me in the marketplace. Being a good merchant's daughter, your mother tried to get the bowl for half price. But once I extolled the value of our fine Wajima lacquer ware, she became a believer in the bowl and in me. Until you are married and responsible for others to feed, you do not know what you can achieve. You and your mother made my struggles worthwhile."

"Well, now you are a well-respected artisan and you may be trading with the Sung and the big noses," Mei said.

"Only if Father Sebastian comes through with introductions; if not, I will have to take that bandit Heizo's offer and work for nothing this year." Jiro spat on the ground as he spoke the Nagasaki's governor's name. "Just think, that worm was once a Kirishitan like us."

"No Father, he was never like us and he was never a Kirishitan. He believes more in silver than he does in Jesu," Mei corrected. "What kind of a man starts life as a Buddhist, converts to Kirishitan to further his business, then renounces both to become a Shinto Abbot? He has no soul."

Jiro smiled at his daughter's rebuke. "I may open the door to other lands with our lacquer ware, but it will be you who keeps us there. My lacquer ware is good, but yours is better and the designs you have created has everyone talking. Even the foreigners want to know how you do it. I will never tell and neither should you. Don't even divulge it to your future husband, whoever he may be. Your gift is our family's heirloom." Jiro couldn't help but laugh at his own words.

Mei looked around the stand of urushi trees and the forested ridge above. She knitted her brow.

"What troubles you, daughter?" Jiro asked.

"The mountainside has grown strangely quiet."

Jiro turned toward the ridge above. "That is strange," he said.

"You do not think the beast is prowling with so much daylight left, do you?" she asked nervously.

"This would be the first time," he said. "But we will take no chances. Both you and Gon take the cart back to the inn and lock yourselves and your mother in tightly."

"Why here and why now? What could we have done to disturb a forest tengu?" Mei asked.

"I do not know. These last six months have been unlike any I have experienced. A tengu killing innocents; whole families disappearing at night; strange noise in the dark and no noise during the day; it is all very strange. Hurry now. You and Gon get back to the inn."

"You come along too," Mei said.

Jiro smiled warmly. "I will be along. I want this last pot of urushi oil or we won't have anything to show Father Sebastian."

Mei stared straight into his eyes. "Get the pot and get home quickly Father. I want you at my wedding, whenever it is."

"I would not miss it for the world Mei-chan," Jiro said, using the baby ending on her name. He still thought of her as his baby girl. But she was a grown woman, and three years older than 16-year-old Gon. He was very proud of how she turned out. He now had someone to carry on the family business and take it beyond his capabilities. He was an artisan. Mei was an artist.

In a business where one bowl could take six months to produce, you had to be good or starve. He was good enough. He had learned the craft from his father. Fortunately, his family had been known for their fine skills. But patience taught you hunger. Jiro had learned both early.

First, you had to season the wood for the bowl; unless you were throwing it from clay. If wood, then you had to carve it and sand it to perfection. Once it stood on its own as a functional and presentable bowl, Jiro had learned to apply several base coats of raw urushi oil known as arami. Then he had to dry and polish each coat. Sometimes ten or fifteen coats were applied. When exposed to heat and humidity, the spirit of the oil would breathe air through the poisonous white sap. The arami would solidify as it breathed in the air, pushing the liquid to its skin giving it a wet and polished look that valued by all. The bowl would be transformed from a functional vessel to a work of art. Once the arami dried, the coating was like armor. You could drop the bowl from great heights and it would not break.

All this, he had taught to Mei. But she had taken his skill further by discovering that heating the arami at low temperatures and then filtering it through old kimono cloth removed the bark and debris to produce a much finer finish and one that was a deep, darker brown.

Her next great discovery came while the surface coats were still drying. Mei placed small intricate designs on the outer bowl in white paint and the drying arami absorbed it into the finish. The effect made the white design look like it was part of the bowl, not a cheap add-on. The same thing could be done with gold leaf and finely sliced pearl. The results were astonishing. Mei's lacquer ware made the Wajima products look boring and plain. She was also experimenting with adding dyes to the arami to produce new colors. The techniques Mei discovered would make her rich—if that bastard Heizo did not get involved. That bloodsucker and his Hakata relatives were a blight on all honest traders in Nagasaki. He would have to devise a way to get his wares to the Nagasaki shippers without Heizo taking a slice of his profits. Father Sebastian had better come through with some introductions fast or all was lost this year.

Jiro waved to Mei as she and Gon pushed the cart along the dirt trail between the trees. Once she was out of sight, he spun back toward the ridge line above. He could feel something out there. It was watching him. He would stay to get the last of the urushi oil but more importantly, to keep himself between whatever was out there and his beloved Mei. From inside his jacket he pulled out his small, razor-sharp knife, climbed onto the short ladder and willed the white, sticky liquid to flow faster.

Once it was filled, he placed the top on the small pot and tied it in place. The whole thing went into a leather pouch hanging at his waist. Then Jiro climbed down the ladder and strained his ears to hear any sounds. Nothing. No birds chirped, no crickets sang, no cicadas called. It was strange. Jiro had lived his entire life in forests and had never heard one this quiet. Even the eerie stillness of the eye of a typhoon that Wajima residents feared seemed noisy compared to this. Perspiration broke out in the small of his back.

Jiro was turning back to the ladder when a great roaring wail tumbled down the ridge. Jiro froze. He had heard that identical sound three times in the last six months. All had been at night and the result was dead people. Now he was hearing it with one more hour of daylight left and it was coming for him. Jiro almost wet himself. Then he thought of the picture of his daughter waving to him as she left the trees. He found the strength to turn towards the noise, reach into the leather pouch with his left hand and untie the strings with his right. Once untied, Jiro stood like a statue, urushi oil in his left hand, the small knife in his right. He convinced himself that he would meet the demon here, in his urushi trees. But fear overcame his paternal instincts. He was not a fighter. He was an artisan.

Jiro turned and started making quick even steps down the path that Mei had taken. When the roar came this time, it was much closer. Jiro did not want to stop. He wanted to run faster and keep running until he could close the thick wooden doors of the inn behind him. But if he ran, the urushi oil would leak out of the pot and onto his hand. He did not want that. Besides, he needed the oil for Father Sebastian. No, he did not want to stop. He knew he was too far from safety. The beast only killed individuals. It had not taken multiple lives as far as he knew. If he could stall it for even a few minutes, Mei would make the safety of the inn. No, he did not want to stop. But he did. He stopped and turned slowly, and wished he'd kept running.

There, in between two of his large urushi trees, just ten paces distant, stood a giant demon tengu with a fiery red face with white streaks and a great long nose. He towered over Jiro and was clothed in a flowing white kimono pulled off his shoulders and hanging at his back like two huge wings. His white hakama pants, white leggings and white toed socks set off the color of his body. Below the red face and down into the white he was black. The contrast was terrifying. Most terrifying of all were the huge golden claws in his right hand. Those claws were open and coming for him.

Jiro knew in an instant that he was going to die here among the trees that he had planted over twenty years ago. He was not going to drink at Mei's wedding, nor bounce her babies on his knee. He was not going to know the comfort of Momo's futon again. This was a tengu demon summoned by some hateful person to persecute the Kirishitans. The small cross he wore around his neck made from his own urushi attested to his religion. Momo had wanted him to convert to her religion. Now, it was going to be the death of him. This demon had been summoned and it would not leave until it had tasted blood. The long-nosed demon raised its head skyward and blew a long blast from a huge conch shell suspended from a red rope over one shoulder. The roar was almost deafening.

The demon took two steps toward Jiro, raised its golden claws and stopped.

Jiro had done the unexpected. He had thrown the pot of urushi oil and hit the giant in the bare chest. The white arami marred the black chest and red face. The tengu looked stupidly at Jiro for several moments and tried to brush off the white oil with its free left hand.

"Bad mistake, demon," Jiro said aloud. It was the last words he spoke. The giant tengu's golden claws raised and lowered with amazing speed and ripped Jiro open from left shoulder to right hip, exposing his internal organs. Jiro died before he hit the ground. With his last thoughts he wondered if a demon tengu would be sensitive to the yang of the urushi oil. He hoped so.

II

Jiyu Waza

Hideki tried to blur his vision. It was not as if he was trying to obscure his sight, he just needed to not focus on any one thing. His opponent was larger, stronger, and much faster. He knew from experience if he focused on any one thing he would be in trouble.

That damned eye was the most troubling. You were drawn to it. It was mesmerizing, drawing you in, demanding attention, and lulling you so that the lightning fast blade could cut you down. The eye itself felt like a weapon. It could cut through a man and lay open his soul.

It was much like the man in front of him holding his bokken in a two-handed, blade forward stance. There was no light in that eye. Usually you could tell a lot about a man by looking him in the eye. Not so with Jubei. The eye was like everything about the man   dangerous. He wielded a glance from that eye like a weapon.

Most men could not hold Jubei's gaze. Hideki knew he had to stay away from that eye.

Hideki had to slip into mushin. For the first two months of his musha shugyo he had been the pupil of the man in front of him. Yagyu Jubei had once been the fencing instructor to the shogun. He was expert in the famous sword style of Yagyū Shinkage-ryū. He had volunteered to accompany Hideki on this, his first warrior's pilgrimage. Jubei had been a good friend to Hideki and his Yoshinobu family since Hideki had saved his life in an Edo jail the previous year. But despite his previous year-long training at the hand of the deadliest duelist in Japan, Myamoto Musashi, Hideki's body bore the welts and bruises caused by Jubei's bokken from twice-a-day practice sessions as they travelled south to Kyushu for the winter.

"Drill or jiyu waza?" Jubei asked.

Hideki knew the question was coming, so it did not break his journey into mushin. "Jiyu waza."

A slight move of the head was the only indication Jubei gave. This session would not be to memorized ritualistic steps known as kata. Jiyu waza meant attacks just like real life. Jubei would not hold back.

When the attack came it was an overhead strike. Once the motion was committed downward Hideki reacted without thinking. This was the essence of the bushi warrior—the ability to move into and out of mushin at will. The "no mind" of the warrior was not easy to obtain. It required years of training, but Musashi sensei had drilled Hideki in its use.

"There are faster and stronger opponents all around," Musashi would say. "Use mushin to defeat them."

Hideki had not seen his sensei in over three months. Not since the audience with Shogun Hidetada where the bird woman had tried to kill him. During the first two months of his warrior's pilgrimage he had tried to adjust himself to his new teacher and learn the techniques of Shinkage-ryu. In so doing, Hideki had repressed many of Musashi's teachings. That had cost him many painful nights as he slept on bruises.

But recently he had started remembering his drills with Musashi. More importantly, he had started adding to them. After the Fox Gang and the Bird Woman had captured and tortured his right hand with flaming bamboo splints under his fingernails, Musashi had taught him to be a be a left-handed swordsman. The leather glove that enclosed his fingers on his right hand allowed his fingers to work somewhat in unison. But for all intents and purposes, Hideki was a freak. He was now left handed; left-handed swordsmen were an oddity and usually scorned. Whenever he felt depressed about what he had been and what he was now, he remembered Musashi sensei's words about fighting a left-handed swordsman.

"The man was not good, but he almost killed me." Hideki's surprise had been met with the explanation that, "Left-handed swordsmen do not move like everyone else. Everyone grows up learning to fight right-handed opponents. This man almost defeated me because everything is backwards with a left-hander. It was only through mushin that I survived," Musashi said.

Now Hideki slipped into mushin because it was the only way to defeat Jubei.

Hideki moved forward and slightly off angle from the overhead attack. He was not quick enough to get out of the way of the descending blade so he brought his hands up and in front of him and reversed the blade, so the tip was trailing over his left elbow and down past his shoulder. The degree on the blade had to be just right—too far back and his left elbow was exposed. Too far forward would leave his left shoulder the target.

"Thawk," the sound of the two wooden bokken crashing together exploded in the little clearing near the road. Hideki had executed the move flawlessly and the hardwood blade of Jubei's bokken was passing down his defense and away from his body. An instant later, Hideki turned his right wrist down, and the tip of this defensive block made a deadly arc as he executed a retaliatory overhead strike to Jubei's head. Jubei barely had time to react by using Hideki's tactic of stepping slightly to the right, reversing his sword to protect his shoulder and elbow. Another "thawk" and several more exploded in rapid succession as each swordsman went from defense to offense in a blink of an eye.

Jubei finally broke the chain by striking to the side of Hideki's neck. Hideki struck the sword just as it was to reach its target and stepped in to ride the impact toward Jubei. Had it been a real blade, Jubei's right arm would have been severed at the bicep.

"Matte!" Jubei exclaimed, surprised, recognizing the wound. "You have improved, Hideki. It was if you were knowledgeable of my moves before I made them. This improvement is not from my teaching. Is this Musashi?"

"I do not really know, Jubei. I may have just gotten lucky."

"I do not believe so. I believe it was from Musashi. I think you have used mushin," Jubei accused. "I may have given him too little credit in the past. Your reaction time is halved when you are in mushin. Can you attain it at will?"

"Most of the time … if I don't let things distract me."

"Then your skills will one day exceed mine," Jubei admitted. "I have never achieved it. Maybe you will teach me."

"I'm not ready to teach it. I am not sure how I obtain it myself. But if I get to where I can teach it, you will be my first pupil."

Jubei nodded. "It is enough."

Gathering up their traveling gear, stowing their practice swords in their blankets slung over their backs and returning their real swords in their belts, Jubei and Hideki moved toward the road and their southern journey.

"Come. Let's hurry while there is still light. I do not want to be sleeping in this forest tonight. I have heard strange stories."

Hideki looked to that murderous eye. It was not like Jubei to be worried about anything.

They walked steadily, the dust from the road rising up to powder their ankles at every step. They were traveling through the mountains. The tall pine trees were thick and came right down to the road on both sides.

"Do you hear that?" Hideki asked.

Jubei looked at his companion with arched eyebrows. "You mean the fact that there is no sound?"

"Exactly. No birds, no insects, no nothing."

Hideki slowed his walk and scanned the left side of the road where the trees began. "An entire squad of infantry could be upon you if they were hiding in the trees," Hideki worried.

Jubei scanned the trees to the right. "You are expecting an infantry attack?"

"I don't know what to expect, but the natural sounds of the forest stopping all at once might signify there was something or someone about."

"Well you are correct about the trees offering good cover

very close to the road, and these long shadows would cover movement," Jubei agreed.

Both men shifted into the center of the dirt road, continuing to scan the trees on their respective sides. They froze in their tracks as a low and guttural howl emanated from back in the woods somewhere. The echoing effect made it hard to tell where the terrifying noise emanated.

"By the Buddha, what was that?" Hideki asked, placing his left hand on the sword hilt in front of his right hip.

Jubei was quiet as he listened for the last sounds of the howl. "I do not know, but it was too loud for a wolf and certainly was not a bear."

"You traveled these roads before. Have you ever heard anything like that?"

"Never," Jubei confessed.

"Then I think we better pick up the pace. I don't want to sleep in these woods with that thing around," Hideki offered as he walked more quickly.

"Agreed, but I would surely like to know what that was."

"Hopefully we do not find out tonight," Hideki stated.

The two quickened their pace and Hideki felt a trace of perspiration on the small of his back. The combination of the pace and consternation over the unknown howling elevated his heart rate.

The howl came again, this time much closer. It caused the hair on Hideki's neck to stand on end. The howl was followed by a human scream cut short.

Hideki was torn between going to the poor soul's aid and breaking into a run away from the menacing sounds. Jubei solved the problem.

"You have heard enough death sounds to know we could not help him," he said.

Hideki agreed, and they both pushed off at almost a run.

"I believe we are safe tonight," Jubei volunteered.

"What do you see?"

"If I'm not mistaken, I see a flickering light around this right-hand curve ahead. It could only be made by a small intense fire, maybe a forge," Jubei said.

31

Hideki strained his eyes seeing the general location that Jubei had indicated, but could see nothing but trees. Sometimes Hideki thought Jubei's one good eye was worth two of his. As they came around the bend, the shape of the wooden building came into view. The fire that Jubei had seen was in the back of the structure. The front of the structure, just off the road, had makeshift benches out front for travelers to rest on. Hideki noticed the sign above the opening to the building declaring this a traveler's rest stop and inn. Hideki also noticed a cross carved into the building just below the painted sign. They moved to the benches and sat down after removing their katanas from their belts.

"Irashimasu," came the cry from the interior of the shop as a middle-aged woman in a commoner's dark blue kimono stepped off the wooden platform of the building and onto the sand floor of the entrance. When she stepped down to the sand, she stepped into wooden getas. She bowed three times as she moved to her two new guests.

"Conbanwa, samurai-sama. You are traveling late. May I offer you refreshment?"

As was often the case, Hideki spoke for both. "Yes, obasan, some tea and something to eat would be well received."

The woman bowed again and retraced her steps to the wooden platform that was the building floor. She returned shortly with a large lacquer tray, complete with ceramic teacups and lacquer dishes filled with sliced radish and pickled plums. These she set between the samurai on the bench, careful not to touch either of the men or their swords leaning on the bench next to their legs. Hideki could tell from the steam rising off the liquid that it was hot. He blew on his tea slightly and used the movement to scan the woods on the other side of the road. Despite his perspiration and the hot brew, he felt a chill. Something evil was out there.

The old woman backed off a pace, waiting for her customers to sample her wares.

Hideki brought the tea to his lips and sipped. He let out a loud sigh and smacked his lips. "Oishii desu," he complimented the woman. "This is very good."

The woman bowed again, "Domo, samurai-san. It is a local brew. We're very proud of it."

The woman's gaze went to Jubei's face. A man of few words, Jubei sampled a radish by plopping it into his mouth with his eating sticks, chewed, and grunted.

"High praise from my companion," Hideki volunteered, "who does not say much."

The woman nodded her understanding, bowed again, and started to move back to the building entrance when she stopped, turned, and spoke. "Samurai-sama, will you be traveling on tonight?" she asked, then realizing the impoliteness of her inquiry, continued quickly. "I would very much like you both to stay here for the evening. We have a nice bath that my daughter has heated, and I will provide you dinner for free. We have some very nice fish," she added nervously.

"Oba-san, we had planned to push on this evening," Hideki lied. When the disappointment showed on her face, he added, "Does your wanting boarders have anything to do with that beast we heard earlier?"

The old woman bowed again. "You heard the roar of the beast earlier?"

"We heard something," Hideki said. "But we could not identify it."

"Neither can we," said the woman. "Other than it is a beast and it seems to prey on those on the road at night."

"A demon?" Hideki asked.

"We do not know. We only know that it takes lives after we hear the howling."

"Who has it taken and how did they die?" Hideki inquired.

"There have been six, the latest one being my husband."

"I'm sorry for your loss, but how did he die?" Hideki persisted.

"His body was found not one ri from here back in the woods near his urushi trees. He often journeyed to his trees for his lacquer ware business. I found him slashed asunder from shoulder to opposite hip. He was laid open as if he were nothing more than a chicken to be cleaved," she said with a sniffle.

Hideki looked over at Jubei, who betrayed no emotion. He looked back at the woman. "What have the authorities done?"

The woman gave a nervous laugh. When she spoke, it was with contempt in her voice. "The authorities have done nothing that I can see. There are two laws here. One is for the government and one for Kirishitans. We fall into the latter, which means we get no justice at all."

"I see," Hideki said. But he did not see. Bushido demanded equal justice for all. Had not his older brother, Nagamasa, demonstrated that as magistrate in Edo by running the first public trial and purging the police department of corruption?

Jubei spoke for the first time. "Have all the victims been Kirishitans?"

The old woman bowed again. "Hai, samurai-sama, they were all Kirishitans."

Hideki picked up on Jubei's line of thought. "What do you think of a beast that attacks only Kirishitans?" he asked his companion.

"Maybe it is a tengu and not a demon," Jubei mused.

"That is what the new monk at the old temple says," Momo volunteered.

"That would make sense, if you believed is such things," Jubei added. "A tengu is associated with the old ways of Shinto, especially the mountain monks who embrace Shugendō as a way to gain spiritual power. I could see a tengu siding with the Shinto temple."

"I think I'd prefer to be indoors tonight. I don't mind admitting I'm curious about this beast," he said. "Maybe we'll hear from it again before morning."

"Oh no, samurai-sama, do not say such things. I told you, anytime we hear the beast, one of us dies," Momo said. "If you see a tengu he will kill you. No one can look one in the eye and live."

"I must admit to being both frightened and thrilled," Hideki said. Then, turning to the woman, "We will be staying the night. Please tell your daughter to prepare our baths."

III

The Beast

Hideki requested that he and Jubei see the rest of the building.
Momo was only too pleased to oblige.

"We would like to look at the outside first," Hideki said.

The woman bowed her understanding, collected the empty
dishes, and retreated to the inside of the building.

Both Hideki and Jubei picked up their swords and started
around the outside of the building.

"Very thick wood," Hideki observed.

"Yes, someone knew what they were doing," Jubei agreed.

As they moved around the north side of the building,
they could see that, with the exception of the front part that
was now a roadside tea house, it was a substantial two-story
building. Two thirds of the house and the back had two small
balconies that opened into sleeping quarters. As they moved
around to the rear of the building, there was a second entrance.
Adjacent to the house was a large stone kiln.

"Someone was very clever," Jubei remarked. "The fire and
kiln serve two purposes. It heats whatever they are baking in
this contraption, and if I'm not mistaken, it heats the water for
the ofudo."

Hideki was impressed. He was more impressed
when he saw what looked to be portion of a small pool
protruding from the building. "This must be where they fill
the bath from outside," Hideki guessed, as he picked up the
wooden water bucket and glanced around for a well.

"If we were trying to keep Yoshi out, this would worry me."

Hideki laughed. "Yes, this would provide little challenge for our ninja friend." Then changing the subject, Hideki asked, "How do they heat the water inside?"

Jubei moved the bucket aside and lifted the wooden cover on the small pool. "I think these metal rods must extend into the kiln. The heat travels down the metal through the brick into the pool and heats up the water."

"Have you ever seen anything like this?" Hideki asked.

Jubei shook his head. "Never."

"I knew this pilgrimage would be educational, but I am hearing and seeing things that I never expected. So instead of carrying water from a well or a stream to heat it in a tub and then carry it to the bath, they carry the water directly to this outside part of the bath and it is heated by the fire from the kiln. I'm impressed."

"I think you will see a lot in this part of the country that will be new to you. Nagasaki and Hakata are old trading ports. Foreign ideas and inventions have been flowing into Japan through these cities for years. Nagasaki's Deshima Island is where we first saw firearms. Oda Nobunaga was the first to make full use of them on the battlefield. I guess we have the Portuguese to thank for an abundance of dead," Jubei stated. "Maybe all new ideas are not good ideas."

"Well, I like this idea," Hideki said, looking at the bath.

After touring the rest of the outside of the building, Hideki and Jubei reported to the entrance and called for the proprietress. Once they had taken off their straw sandals and beat the dust from their tabi socks, she showed them the rest of the interior. As they moved upstairs they were met by a younger version of the proprietress. She introduced her daughter Mei. Mei had been busy rolling out the futons for their guests in one of the rooms upstairs. There was one other member of the house. Jubei and Hideki were introduced to a young man of shy ways. His inability to speak even the briefest greeting and his constant low bowing made the two samurai dismiss him as of no importance and no threat.

"Thank you for staying, samurai-sama," she said. "We don't usually get honored guests."

She was young, about half the age of her mother. Her

long black hair was tied in a bun held with leather strips. Her kimono was a dull brown, and she had tied up the sleeves with a silk cord to allow freer movement as she worked. She talked to both samurai, but her eyes stayed on Jubei.

"Momo-san, I noticed a yumi and arrows above the main entrance downstairs. Was your husband an archer?" Hideki asked.

"He was good enough to provide us with rabbits and the occasional deer. The bow that you saw was his. It is a family heirloom, passed down through generations of his family," she explained, choking on her words at the end. "It was the only thing my husband brought with him from Wajima."

"The yumi is the weapon of the samurai," Hideki left his statement hanging in the air between them.

"My husband was not a samurai," Momo said. "The family tradition says that one of his ancestors saved a great lord from drowning. The bow was a reward."

Hideki nodded his understanding. "I know this is going to sound unusual, but could you move the sleeping material down to the first floor?"

"It will be warmer and much more comfortable up here," Mei said.

Jubei smiled at her. It was the first time Hideki had seen him smile during the trip.

"Mei-san, it would be more comfortable up here, but my companion is correct. If we are going to defend this building tonight, we need to do it from the first floor."

Momo thought about it for a minute and understood the utility. "Daughter, please do as they say."

"Hai, Okasan," her daughter bowed. "I will do it now. Gon, come and help me." Gon seemed eager to do anything that Mei requested.

Jubei watched her as she gathered up the futons and moved gracefully down the narrow stairs.

"We sleep upstairs and leave the downstairs for business. I run the tea house and Mei runs the kiln, and we both pitch in if we have guests in the inn," she said.

"What do you produce in the kiln?" Jubei asked.

"You ate off of them tonight," she said. "My husband was famous for his lacquer ware. Mei is trying to keep the tradition alive."

"How is business?" Hideki asked.

The woman shook her head, "Since that beast has taken to killing Kirishitans on the road, I get very few customers stopping here. Mei has sold some of her work in Nagasaki, and one of the largest houses has hinted of a consignment, but so far it is difficult."

"While looking at the kiln, we noticed what looked like musket barrels running out of it and into what I assume was the outside portion of the bath. Is that how you heat the bath water?" Hideki asked.

"Yes, my husband used to sell his lacquer ware in Nagasaki. Many of the large stores had the same arrangement. I believe the concept came from the Portuguese fathers. You will see many wondrous things Portuguese fathers have brought to our land from all over the world."

Hideki was a little surprised when Jubei took up the questioning.

"Do the Portuguese fathers have much influence here?"

Momo bowed. "Oh yes, they have been here for many years and many of the people have converted to Jesu."

"You follow him as well, do you not?" Jubei asked.

"Yes samurai-sama. Many of us do here."

"So who do you owe your allegiance to?" Jubei continued. "Is your first allegiance to the church of the Portuguese fathers or to the government in Edo?"

Hideki looked at his friend, wondering why he was pursuing such a line of questioning. Was this an inquiry from his father, Yagyu Munenori, the Chamberlain to Shogun Hidetada?

Momo considered the question, bowed her head and spoke. "For things of the land, I listen to the government. For things of the spirit, I listen to Jesu."

Jubei would not let it go. "If what one said conflicted with what the other said, which would you choose?"

Momo was truly uncomfortable now. So she covered her mouth with her hand and giggled slightly. "Oh samurai-sama, they would not conflict. Jesu tells us to render to Caesar what is Caesar's."

Hideki was lost. "Who is this Caesar?"

"I think he is the shogun of the Portuguese," Momo said.

"Do you followers of Jesu meet?"

"Yes, every week we meet on family day."

"And what do you discuss?" Jubei asked.

"Come with us to Nagasaki and you can listen yourself."

That suggestion shocked Jubei. "I can do that?"

Momo laughed the nervous little laugh again. "Certainly, both of you would be most welcome."

Hideki brought the conversation back to the moment. "Thank you for the invitation; let's focus on getting through the night. Once you blow out your candles tonight, do not light them again, no matter what."

Momo looked confused, but nodded her compliance. The women closed the sliding doors of the front and back entrances, laying wood blocks in the tracks to keep them from being opened. Jubei and Hideki both checked and pronounced them secure. It was several hours after nightfall. Hideki extinguished the paper lantern between their bedding just behind the main entrance. Both men slept with her feet toward the door and their swords by their sides.

"Have you been to one of these Kirishitan meetings?" Hideki asked.

"No."

"Then why all the questions?"

"I'm a curious man," Jubei said. "I'm going to sleep. We still have a long way into Nagasaki."

Hideki's exhaustion won out over his curiosity. He closed his eyes and dreamed of nothing.

He woke with a start. Something had stirred him, but he was not sure what. He was not sure how long he had slept. It felt like only a few moments, but he had no way knowing. He slowed his breathing and strained his hearing and tried to orient himself in the dark. The sound that had disturbed him was of something large moving in the dust just on the other side of the entrance of the building, which was just four arms lengths away. It did not sound like a human walking. It shuffled along as if under great weight.

The quiet night was shattered by a wild howling coming from the other side of the locked sliding door. Hideki jumped to his feet with his sheathed sword in his right hand. He could not see Jubei in the pitch blackness, but he heard him move. He knew Jubei would not move about unless forced to do so. They had taken the measure of the room before dark and knew each other's responsibility. To move around in a pitch dark room with razor sharp katanas was an invitation to disaster. Hideki also heard soft whimpering from the women upstairs. The only light in the dark room seeped around the loose fitting boards in dim intermittent horizontal lines. The vertical moonlight creep was not strong enough to illuminate the room. But with the moon at its zenith, anyone on the outside would break the pattern as he moved near the wall.

Hideki felt a chill run up his back. He was no stranger to danger, but the thing making that inhuman howling worried him. He silently prayed to Buddha that the walls would hold.

He involuntarily jumped back a step as something massive struck the door and dragged down its length. Hideki could hear large claws biting into the raw wood. A massive shadow blocked the moon light as the howling intensified. Judging by the shadow it cast against the boards, it was almost twice as tall as Hideki. As quickly as it started, the howling stopped. Hideki could sense that the beast was moving around to the side of the building near the high window. Normally the window's height would preclude anyone but a ninja from entry. Certainly nothing as large as the shadow he'd seen could crawl through. But something as large as the shadow could put his head through the paper. Hideki had no wish to come face to face with a demon or a tengu.

He carefully laid the sword and scabbard on the tatami mat next to his futon. He straightened up and reached up with his right hand into the darkness and grasped the yumi and moved it off its pegs. He then repeated the task for the quiver of arrows. He carefully stepped through the bow and strung it. Because the Japanese yumi is so long, Hideki turned it to the horizontal to nock an arrow. Once ready, he took a shoulder-width stance with his left foot pointing at the window. The window disappeared as two razor sharp talons ripped it to shreds. Then a black apparition blocked the moonlight. Hideki pulled the bow back as far as it would go and loosed an arrow into the apparition.

There was a loud, high-pitched scream and a loud thud as the beast fell into the dust below the window. Then it was up and clawing in a frenzy against the wall. Hideki nocked another arrow and waited. Finally he heard the shuffling sound as the beast departed. Everything quieted down.

"Do you want to go outside and see if you killed it?" Jubei asked.

Hideki found himself shaking. "Strange," he thought. He had been in many battles recently but remembered shaking only after the first. "I'll wait here while you go check," Hideki managed in a calm voice that he had to force.

"Not me, it was you who shot it."

"I don't know what came over me. I just felt it was too big for a sword."

"I'd call that good thinking and a very nice shot," Jubei congratulated. "I think we can sleep now."

"Not very likely," Hideki mumbled under his breath. Judging by the moon's zenith, he had initially slept for two hours. It might be all he got tonight.

IV

Jii's Audience

Jii sat on the bench in the prow of the barge. It was manned by
Yoshinobu retainers. One large samurai at the stern poled the
barge along the canal away from the castle and toward the Yoshinobu Edo mansion at the Kanda landing. Jii had removed the
naga-bakama, the bottom half of the kamishimo that was required
attire while in Edo castle. To move, the trailing legs required a
skating motion with tabi clad feet treading on the material as the
hands moved each pant-like leg into position to keep from trip-
ping. It was uncomfortable and ungainly, and Jii got out of it as
quickly as he could each evening. He still wore the upper part of
the kamishimo over his kimono. This upper piece exaggerated his
upper body as the starched cloth wing tips extended beyond the
ends of his shoulders. On the lapels of the kamishimo was the
embroidered symbol of a white hollyhock. It proclaimed to all
that the wearer was part of the Tokugawa family—the shogun's
family. Everyone not wearing it, bowed to it. Jii was great uncle
to the current shogun, Hidetada.

He was the most recent appointee to the Roju, the lesser
counselors to the shogun and the six men charged with
keeping the country running. What he had heard today in
chambers with the Taira, the greater counselors, and the High
Counselor troubled him.

"I want a bath and then an audience with the young
prince," Jii said to his attendant. The samurai grunted his
understanding and turned to give direction to subordinates.
The front of the barge touched shore and the old man lightly

jumped down to the compacted dirt road that met the water's edge. It was a short walk to the imposing Yoshinobu Edo residence. By the time they arrived at the compound gate, the mansion was covered in lengthening shadows.

Night descended quickly in autumn. Before the fire warden could strike his wooden blocks together and call out fire warnings for the hour of the dog, Jii had bathed and was being announced at the sliding door of the section of the vast house that was used by his eldest grandson Nagamasa, wife Yuki, and new baby.

"Jii-sama has arrived and is calling upon Yoshinobu no Kuro Yoshitsune, the new prince of the Yoshinobu," the guard at the sliding door announced, smiling as he knelt and positioned his hands on the wooden border.

"Hai," Yuki called from inside. The door slid back to reveal a large ten tatami room with Yuki and Nagamasa kneeling around a baby swaddled in white. Upon Jii's entry they spun in his direction and greeted him with a bow.

Jii returned the bow while standing and came to a sitting crosslegged position in front of them. Leaning over to catch a better glimpse of Yoshitsune, he asked, "He's not asleep yet?"

"No Jii-sama, he has been asleep and re-awakened. He will doze again later," Yuki said.

"That is good, Yuki-san. A child grows as he sleeps."

Jii reached a finger in front of the baby's face. The little one immediately latched five little fingers onto it. "Look at that, a natural sword grip," Jii exclaimed and laughed.

Leaving his finger for the baby to play with, he turned his attention to the adults. "It is great to have a baby in the family again."

Naga knew his grandfather too well. The old man had raised him and his younger brother Hideki from the time they were orphaned as children. "Something is troubling you, Jii-san. What is it?"

"We are receiving word of much unrest in Kyushu," Jii said.

Yuki looked up quickly, "Is Hideki safe?"

"I do not know Yuki; I have heard no word from him

since he left almost three months ago. That concerns me. I allowed him to go on his musha shugyo because Jubei was to accompany him. My understanding with the high counselor was that his son would send back reports via the metsuke. However, Munenori Yagyu has heard nothing from his son Jubei nor from the spies."

"Well, no news could be good news, right?" Naga asked.

"On its face, you might be right. But little of the other reports we are receiving gives me reason to remain calm. I'm becoming concerned."

"What can we do?" Yuki asked.

"Besides playing with my great-grandchild here, I came to get your opinion on a course of action. I plan to send Yoshi and a team that he deems appropriate to Kyushu to find and protect Hideki."

Naga smiled, "It is about time. While I have no reason to distrust Jubei, I would feel better with our own shinobi no mono looking after my little brother."

"I have every faith in Jubei's ability to protect Hideki, but I too would feel better knowing my brother-in-law had the best ninja available," Yuki said.

Naga turned to his wife. "You count Yoshi and the five families better at ninja skills than Jubei and the metsuke? I would have thought being the daughter of the leader of the government spies and being a trained ninja yourself you would count the government's Iga ninja superior."

"I rate Jubei's skills very high, and the Iga and Koga ninja of the government metsuke forces know their business. But Yoshi has proven his worth in protecting Hideki time and again. They are friends first. And he possesses haragai, an art thought dead to the ninja. Besides, the Five Families now work for Myo. She is Hideki's lover. There are no bonds closer than that. Yoshi with the support of Myo and her Five Families make a daunting force. So, I say send Yoshi as soon as possible," Yuki said.

Naga nodded his head in agreement with his wife. "What is the situation in Kyushu?"

"According to what I heard today, governor Heizo is

petitioning the shogun to expel the Portuguese and the Kirishitan church from Japan. The Portuguese and the Kirishitan church is petitioning the shogun for a personal audience in order to bestow gifts of wild animals, exotic beasts, and boxes of gold upon Hidetada to persuade him to change governors," Jii said.

"That sounds like politics as usual," Naga said.

"It might, if that were all there was. But there are reports of a tengu on Mount Taro killing Kirishitans," Jii said.

The question showed plainly in Yuki's eyes. "Are there such things?"

"I do not know, but something is killing Kirishitans at night when they are alone on the roads. There are reports of wild howling and fearsome screams before each victim is found. It is one of the reasons I want Yoshi down there."

Naga smiled. "This sounds like the kind of crap my brother would get involved with. If there is trouble within a hundred ri, he will find it. What is that saying Yoshi recites to him?"

Yuki giggled. "You mean stepping in cherry blossoms or benjo?"

"Yes my dear that is the one. Hideki is either looking good or screwing up."

"I have not told you the whole story yet," Jii said. "Something is now targeting Buddhist temples. A total of thirty people have lost their lives in most gruesome circumstances. The report said the temples run red with blood. The bodies are slashed open and entrails dragged out."

"How horrible," Yuki said, reaching for her baby.

"No, the worst part is last. Each had their throat crushed as if from huge jaws."

"Are these two different demons?" Naga asked.

"No one knows. The people sleeping in the temple seem to have been killed in a more gruesome manner than the Kirishitans killed on the roads. But we do not have enough information to know anything right now except the Kirishitan and Buddhist populations are crying for help and accusing each other. If the governor can be believed, he needs help from Edo immediately."

"Do we have a magistrate in place? Does he have a police force?" Naga asked.

"The governor has a militia that has been used for policing duties. When the governor first asked for assistance, we assigned a new magistrate. He should be in Nagasaki now. However, we have had no reports from him to date. As you know full well from having started a police force from scratch, it is no easy task," Jii said.

"So, the new magistrate has no troops. Who can he call on for assistance?" Naga asked.

"Normally we would call on the daimyo for help. But Matsukara-sama is new. He replaced a Kirishitan," Jii said.

"It sounds like a powder keg," Naga said.

"That is a good description."

"Should we send some of our police to assist the new magistrate?" Naga asked.

"If Nichi wasn't so large, I'd send him. But I'm not sure the old sumotori would weather the trip," Jii decided.

"No, I wouldn't send Nichi, but I could spare several Yoriki and a squad of new recruits. I would let Nichi pick the men. Since Nichi has reconstituted the police from the Gumsumgumi, my job as magistrate has been easy," Naga said.

"I will consider your offer. I think it wise. The government has ignored Nagasaki and Kyushu for too long. Did you know the governor of Nagasaki is not samurai?"

Both husband and wife's surprise showed on their face. "What is he, Jii-sama?" Yuki asked.

"He is a merchant," Jii said, hardly hiding his distaste.

Naga's mouth hung open.

"Supposedly, his family has traded for years with the Sung and Chosin and have been elevated to their position due to their ability to keep goods flowing into the coffers of Edo and Osaka," Jii explained.

"Jii-san, we need to get Yoshi to Nagasaki as soon as possible. That city is not a powder keg. It is a cesspool," Naga said.

Jii retrieved his finger from his great grandson and nodded at his family. "You are correct. I would never have let Hideki go to Kyushu if I'd known the situation there."

V

Aya

Aya watched the room. It was hard to do. There was movement everywhere. Light from fifty paper lanterns cast shadows along the four wooden walls. The smoke emitted from the whale oil candles wafted into the high roughhewn rafters and mixed with the scent of pipe tobacco, unwashed bodies, old noodles, cheap perfume, and desperation.

This was the Jaded Princess. Aya smiled as she thought about the name. She had always thought it a little pretentious but apropos for one of five teahouses on the waterfront of Nagasaki. Describing the Jaded Princess as a teahouse was pretentious.

They served tea, so that part was true. But the establishment was better known for disgusting food, poor lodging, cheap sake, willing women, gambling, and occasional entertainment. Most patrons would argue the entertainment was about on par with the food.

Tonight was a weeknight, but every seat was taken by male laborers or sailors from the Portuguese, Indonesian, or Sung trading vessels trying to drink enough sake to make the woman at their table look like someone else.

The name fit the circumstances of every woman in the place, Aya thought. Each had been a princess to someone when they were girls—a father or a childhood sweetheart. Now they were all jaded by the life they led. Jaded Princess was apropos because it described the owner best.

Aya did not watch the tables. She knew what went

on there. This type of action had been her life since she was thirteen years old and sold to such a place. She briefly registered on the fake interest the women were trying to muster for prospective clients. She had learned to lie with her eyes too; and with her mouth; and with her heart. She had become what she initially hated when sold by her parents to a talent finder. Although she had been told she was going for a maid's apprenticeship, she always suspected her parents knew better. No one paid two gold ryu for an apprentice maid. Her mother had cried but done nothing to stop her from going. Losing Aya's mouth meant survival for the rest of the family. The two gold coins would feed them for years to come. Life was hard for farmers, especially in lean years.

Aya's attention was on the small tables on the far wall. These were usually the ronin tables. Although these out of work samurai had less money than the day laborers, some still had their samurai pride. Aya smiled to herself. "They would not have that," she thought, "if they had my life."

"Everything as it should be, ma'am?"

Aya looked at the large man behind the plank bar. His threadbare kimono was tied back at the shoulders to allow his powerful arms ample room to work. His hair was held in place by a plain brown hachi maki tied with the knot high on his forehead, as was the commoner's way.

"Quite all right, Tatsu," Aya said giving him a slight smile.

Aya signaled for the barman to lean close. "What do you know of the ronin at table six?" She asked.

The barman leaned away to get a better view. "Oh, him. He comes in about now most nights, drinks one bottle of sake, eats some noodles, and then departs."

"Has he taken any girls upstairs?" Aya asked.

The barman shook his head. "No Ma'am, but they continue to try. They think he's handsome, in a dangerous sort of way. Some are put off by the scarred right hand. But just about all of them have tried to take him upstairs."

"Maybe he does not like women," Aya suggested.

"I don't think I would make that observation around him.."

"Why do you say that?"

"Just the feeling I have. Crippled hand or not, he has an effortless way about him."

"What is this effortless way you speak of?" Aya asked.

"I may be all wrong, but he gives off an air of someone completely at ease with his abilities. You seldom see that in someone so young. My guess is that he is a master swordsman."

Now Aya was interested. "How good can he be with a crippled hand?"

"I have no way of knowing without seeing him draw. But I have seen swordsmen with greater disabilities than his remain dangerous into old age," Tatsu explained.

"So, you think he is a good swordsman?" Aya asked. "He does not waste his time or money on spirits and girls. I wonder if he can be trusted? Does he pay for his sake and noodles?"

The barman stepped back. "Madam, you know me better than that. Everyone pays in here," he said thumping himself on the chest proudly.

"Gomen nasai, Tatsu," Aya apologized. "I was not thinking," she said as she signaled for Tatsu to lean in again.

"I am looking to hire a yojimbo. Can you recommend anyone?"

The barman screwed up his face in thought and twisted his chin with a ham-sized fist. "It would help if I knew what you needed him for. Samurai are hard to judge. Some might not like working for a lady," Tatsu opined.

Aya laughed. "No problem on that score Tatsu. You of all people know I am no lady."

"Never say that," Tatsu objected. "You are one of the greatest ladies I know. Who else would give a criminal a chance at honest work and protect the ladies by paying their doctor bills?"

Aya did not bother to tell Tatsu that both acts were not from charity but based on sound business decisions. This was Nagasaki. She knew firsthand how the big nose's pox destroyed lives. This was not Deshima Point. That was a real hell hole for prostitutes. Only the ugliest or the criminally condemned were sent to the city-run brothels that service the foreigners.

But many of the sailors that frequented the Jaded Princess frequented the same type of establishments in other countries. The doors would not stay open long if the Jaded Princess became infected with the pox. So she placed two Chinese doctors on retainer to monitor the girls' health.

"I'm starting to have trouble at the warehouse with the workers, and I am discerning a shift in the attitude of those around the governor. This is not a good time to be a Kirishitan."

"Ma'am, do not hire a ronin. Let me find you a jutte or gumi man to protect you. You never know what ronin will do. Those samurai do not think like normal humans. They can start drawing swords over nothing and kill a man in an instant, then eat a big supper."

Aya smiled at the imagery. "Thank you, Tatsu, but if my instincts are correct, I'm going to need someone who has the capability to kill, not just lay an iron jutte on a head."

"Killing is bad business ma'am. Once you get started, there is no end to it. Even if you kill the lowest of the low, they have someone who will miss them and then the revenge thing starts," Tatsu said, shaking his large head. "Take my advice as a man who has seen a lot of violence. Do not hire a ronin."

"Well, I do not want any ronin. I'm looking for a man skilled enough that he has nothing to prove, but with a sense of honor. If he takes my money, I want to be sure he will protect me. I don't want him selling out to my enemy because the money is better," she said, realizing for the first time that such a man was exactly what she was searching for. "I want a killer guided by principal."

Tatsu made a ceremony of looking around the room. "I do not think there is much chance of finding such a man here."

"You are probably right, but keep an eye open for me. If you get any prospects, let me know first before you approach the man, okay?"

Tatsu bowed, "As you wish ma'am."

"So how is our star boarder getting along?" Aya asked, changing the subject.

Tatsu involuntarily glanced up the stairs to the rooms

above. "When she plays those ballads on her Samisen everything stops. The men stop drinking. The women get watery eyes. The only bright spot is that the cook stops cooking."

"Yes, we really have to do something about a cook," Aya reminded herself. "Does she ever play lively pieces?"

"Yes. When she does that, the business doubles. Her playing and her voice can turn a dull night into a joyous one. She really is quite good," Tatsu said, letting the idea hang in the stale atmosphere.

Aya smiled to herself. "Are you trying to influence my decision making, Tatsu?"

The barman feigned surprise. "Never, Ma'am. I just think if she is to lodge here, why not make use of her?"

"Tatsu, your instincts are good. But the Jaded Princess is just one of our worries. We are playing for much larger rewards. We have several pieces in play, and it is the most dangerous game we have played. Our opponents will be the governor of Nagasaki, the Kirishitan church, my own husband, and maybe the Tokugawa. We need to find that yojimbo soon before things get out of hand."

Tatsu nodded his head knowingly. "You have the brains and the heart for it, ma'am. Just point us in the direction. The men and I will do whatever you want."

"Thanks, Tatsu; it is always nice to have people you can trust."

The big barman started to blush and started wiping the already spotless bar.

VI

Yamabushi

At first light, Hideki and Jubei unbarred the front sliding door to the inn and stepped outside, prepared for anything. Jubei began checking the tracks in the dust.

"Whatever it was, it was big," Jubei opined.

When they rounded the corner of the building they found nothing except some blood on the ground and massive scratches in the wood.

"Your demon has sharp claws," Hideki said.

Jubei stepped up to the wooden boards and studied the deep marks. "There is something funny here."

"Something funny about a massive beast that carves open Kirishitans on the main road at night?"

"No, something funny about these scratches," Jubei said. "Come look at them."

Hideki stepped up beside his friend and fixed his gaze on the destroyed paper window a head above them and at the two deep gashes above and below the window.

"An animal's claws would leave a furrow. Notice how these slashes leave a deep cut."

Hideki looked at the slashes more closely. "You are thinking a blade?" Hideki asked.

"Or two blades," Jubei said. "Notice how the two slashes are evenly spaced and evenly deep. Nature is seldom so precise."

"So demons don't have claws like a sword?"

Jubei shook his head slowly. "I have no idea, Hideki.

This is my first experience with demons, or tengus for that matter."

"So, a tengu demon may have a right hand made of two sharp blades?" Hideki asked.

"For all I know he may have a right hand made of two sharp blades and a left made of muskets," Jubei stated. "I told you, I have no experience with tengus and demons."

Hideki stepped back. "We don't know much about this beast. But we do know it exists and it is hostile to Kirishitans. Should we leave the women here alone with that thing roaming around?"

"I am glad you brought that up. I plan to stay a few days."

Hideki looked at his friend. "Did you find something that piqued your interest?"

"Oh, you mean Mei, the daughter." Jubei almost smiled. "She is an interesting person. The mother says they are trying to make a deal to export her lacquer ware to China. I guess she has discovered some unique ways to make bowls."

Hideki could not pass up a chance to make his friend uncomfortable. "Is that the only reason?"

"No. I really want to find out as much as I can about the Kirishitans. My father gave me that assignment before I left."

"You have an official assignment?" Hideki asked.

Jubei rested his left hand on the handle of his katana. "I don't know. I am pretty sure that I don't want one. When I resigned my position as the shogun's fencing master, I traveled around the country working for my father. At least I did initially. But somewhere in those two years I started questioning what I was doing."

"What were you doing?" Hideki asked.

"The way I feel now, I was the shogun's assassin," Jubei admitted.

"Assassin? You actually killed people?"

"Oh yes, many of them."

"And you used your ninja skills for this?" Hideki asked knowing that Jubei had mastered both worlds in preparation for taking over the shogun's metsuke ninja spies led by his father.

"No, I used my sword-fighting skills. What better way to

murder than to challenge a man and kill him in a fair fight?" Jubei asked.

Hideki was stunned and intrigued at the same time. "Am I to understand that you went from dojo to dojo on a musha shugyo challenging talented samurai to duels so that you could kill them in the name of the Tokugawa?" Hideki asked.

"Kind of makes you question your faith in bushido, doesn't it?" Jubei commented.

"Why would someone need to be killed?" "The only reason is for being a threat to the Tokugawa," Jubei admitted.

"That does not explain much. How would your father know if someone was a threat?"

"Therein lies the dilemma. After a while, the system seemed arbitrary. Upon reflection, I think some of the men I killed were good men, and most were not a threat."

"That is terrible, Jubei. I may not always agree with my grandfather, but I can always be assured that he makes right decisions, or makes decisions for the right reasons."

"Well, that is why my father and I don't see eye to eye. I am never sure if he's making the decisions for the right reasons. But I was inspired enough by your family to try to heal the breach between us. So when he summoned me concerning the trip, I complied. But nothing had changed. He still sees conspiracies at every turn. He is obsessed with keeping the Tokugawa in power and quashing any possible rebellion."

"So, you have killed innocent men?" Hideki asked.

"Most assuredly … and some very bad ones too, if that helps."

"It does not help much Jubei. I look up to you and Musashi as my two real mentors. My whole life I have studied bushido as the perfect path. Now I find it being twisted and used as an excuse to kill undesirables by the very government my brother and I may lead one day. I am just not sure of anything anymore," Hideki lamented.

"Now you see why both Musashi and I found something special in you."

"Special? I'm the second son. I'm a mediocre left-handed

swordsman. And I'm a cripple with my right. What is special about me?"

Jubei took a couple of moments to answer. "You do not seem to be driven by greed or power or any of the normal things samurai must contend with these days. Your approach is simple. You try to do the right thing, every time. Bushido is your guide, just as in the old stories. You place others above yourself," Jubei said, adding as he pointed at Hideki's right-hand, "And you are a better swordsman crippled than most whole students I have taught."

"What about now?"

"What do you mean?" Jubei asked.

"I mean, are you planning on killing anyone on my musha shugyo?"

"I am to study the Kirishitan problem and make recommendations," Jubei said.

"So, you have no one on your assassination list this time?" Hideki asked.

"There are two names, but I told my father I was finished being his assassin. I will find the men and determine for myself whether they need to be eliminated or not. I am through being an attack dog."

"What made you accept the assignment at all?"

"I think it was the time I spent with your family that changed me. You and Nagamasa and the old gentleman, Jii, are close family. You live by principles, you believe in bushido, but you are practical enough to see that sometimes the rules need bending for the benefit of all. I thought I would try to mend the breach between my father and myself and try to live up to the shogun's admonition."

"I assume you mean the one about finding better men to run the country," Hideki said.

"That is the one."

"What is your impression of the Kirishitans?"

"I have not seen that many, but if I had to judge them by Momo and Mei, I think they are industrious, gracious, and peaceful."

"What about me? What should I be doing while you are

away studying the Kirishitans?" Hideki asked.

"What do you want to do?"

"I want to continue my musha shugyo," Hideki said without thinking.

Jubei nodded. "Then you should do so."

"Is there any place I should go?" Hideki asked.

"You should try Hamada sensei's dojo. He is old now and does not take challenges. However, I have heard that he has several excellent students. The one I'm interested in goes by the family name of Matsukara."

"Any special etiquette I should use?" Hideki asked.

"No, you have done it before. Pay your mon, be respectful, learn, and try not to get yourself killed. I think that would affect my father more than me dying," Jubei said.

"I do not pretend to know the relationship between you and your father, but I cannot imagine my death would trouble him more than yours."

"You are Tokugawa! We Yagyu live for the Tokugawa."

"What sword style does Hamada sensei use?"

"It is called the Suio style. It is somewhat unusual. They keep their guard low and increase the kamae. That distance between opponents can lull you into thinking you have plenty of time. But they train in water and can lunge very quickly on dry land. All their other motions come off that initial lunge. You should survive."

"And when shall I see you again?" Hideki asked.

"There is an inn on the waterfront called the Jaded Princess. Take a room there and I will find you in a few days."

"You are sure you won't need me to help with your demon fighting?" Hideki said with a smile.

"No," Jubei said, the good eye drilling a hole into Hideki's soul. "You are becoming a much better swordsman. You may one day surpass me with your skill. But I will always be a better killer than you. I'm just good at it. I always have been. I always will be. Now go get breakfast. I saw Momo setting it out on the benches. I have to tell Mei that she will have a guest for a few days more."

Hideki smiled, not sure if his friend was staying here for

research on the Kirishitans or on Mei. But it did not matter. Jubei seemed happy to stay, or as happy as Jubei ever got. And now he would have the opportunity to explore new places. He was confident in his ability to protect himself as long as his right hand held up and he had always traveled into new places dressed as a ronin so he could blend. But this time he would be truly alone. He hoped he would stay out of trouble, because unlike other times, he had no one to rely on anymore. With Jubei staying back, he would have no allies.

Hideki studied the steaming lump of white rice sitting in a beautiful red lacquer ware bowl perched in his left hand. It was little challenges like this that still perplexed him. With his right hand he reached down to grasp the contents of another perfectly made bowl. The simple task of picking up a delicate object would have been done subconsciously a year ago. But that was before a power-crazy woman had tried to burn his fingers off by shoving burning bamboo splinters up one nail at a time. Hideki still cringed at the thought of the pain. He wondered what Yoshi was doing today. He missed his ninja friend.

Then he wondered where his ninja lover Myo might be. She had hinted that she was going to accompany him on this journey, but she had not appeared in the months he had been traveling. He smiled thinking of her. They had fallen in love not knowing each other's true identify. He thought her the daughter of a courier service owner and she thought him a ronin. It wasn't until Yoshi had proposed a partnership between her ninja Five Families and his Yoshinobu clan that they were no longer threats to each other.

The Yoshinobu were country samurai with no experience with ninja. The Five Families were ninja with a legitimate country-wide network of couriers. By siding with the Yoshinobu they gained protection from the government metsuke for accepting a contract on Naga and Hideki's life. Normally the punishment would be death. Now the Five Families had one client and protector, the Yoshinobu. The Yoshinobu benefited by having a ready-made national intelligence gathering organization, something they were going to need now that they were in Edo to stay. And in Edo as in any governmental town, knowledge was power.

Hideki banished his friends from his mind and focused on making his fingers work. It was not as hard now; some feeling had returned to the tips of his fingers and the soft black leather glove that covered all but the tips of his fingers on his right hand helped coordinate the strength there. But it was not the same.

He gingerly picked up the brown egg and cracked it on the side of the black bowl. He let the yellow and white viscous contents slide out of the shell and into the bowl. He placed the empty halves of the shell on the tray. The sun was warm on the back of his head, but the wind was cold on his face. The bowl with the egg was raised in his right hand and its contents dumped onto the steaming white rice in the black bowl of his left hand. Replacing the egg bowl onto the tray seated next to him, he shifted his position on the wooden bench and wondered if he was up to the next task.

He transferred the rice bowl to his right hand, reached across, and picked up the watabashi from the tray. Once the sticks were positioned in his left hand, he proceeded to mix the egg with the rice. Then, he reached back across to the tray to pick up a slice of thin, dried seaweed with the eating sticks. This he placed on top of the rice. Using the tips of the eating sticks, he carved out a lump of the now glutinous rice, using the seaweed as a retainer. He raised the bite-size morsel to his mouth, plopped it in, and began chewing his breakfast.

Two months of walking across Japan had given Hideki an appreciation for the simple pleasures in life. His life was made up of little challenges now. He knew this musha shugyo was more about him challenging himself and not accepting the status quo. Learning martial skills and challenging other dojos was secondary. This revelation had been an epiphany. Musashi sensei had been correct. This journey would either be his salvation or his doom. He glanced across the road into the forest and wondered if his doom would be by demon. Demons were not something he'd planned on when undertaking this journey. He'd really made the decision out of boredom.

His grandfather had purpose again and was deeply engaged in bringing good government to the Roju, the lesser counselors of the Tokugawa government. His older brother Naga had a new wife and was focused on rebuilding the judicial system in Edo. Hideki had nothing to do. They had tried to get him to stay in Edo, but Hideki sensed that was because they were concerned for his safety. If he stayed in Edo, he would have no purpose.

Musashi sensei had told him that a warrior's pilgrimage, a musha shugyo, was the way to find his path. So, he had taken to the road with the goal of becoming the deadliest left-handed swordsman in Japan. Over the weeks, as he learned to do trivial things with his right hand again, it no longer mattered whether he attained his goal as a right or a lefthander. That realization had brought him peace. Now he no longer spent hours trying to accomplish little tasks with the damaged right hand unless it involved a martial technique. Then he would spend painful hour on painful hour mastering it. Now he could feed himself using a combination of both hands. It was progress. But he always worried the damaged right hand might give out when needed most. It was a troubling doubt that could nag at him at the wrong time and get him killed. A true warrior had to be able to fight with "no mind."

Jubei joined him and set about eating his rice, egg, and seaweed. From his vantage point on the bench, Hideki could see up the road as it climbed steadily toward the peak. The inn was on a finger and the road to Nagasaki traversed the north edge of the mountain. Everything to the north fell away down the mountainside. Hideki had an unrestricted view up the road for several ri.

"When was the last time you saw a yamabushi?" Hideki asked between mouthfuls.

The question was such a strange one that Jubei's head came up in mid chew. "Yamabushi? I don't think I have ever seen one. I might have seen one when I was a boy."

"Unless my eyes are failing me, I think four of them are coming down the mountain, headed this way."

Jubei looked up the road with his good eye. "You are right.

There are four of them. That's enough to have a temple."

"What do you suppose yamabushi would be doing on this road and in such large numbers?"

Jubei put his head down and continued to eat. "I guess we will know soon enough."

Hideki placed his empty bowl on the tray. As if on cue, Momo stepped out of the inn and retrieved the dishes.

"Excellent breakfast, oba-san. Do you have many yamabushi in this area?"

The woman froze in her tracks and spun to look up the road. "Oh, dear, I don't think we have time to run."

Jubei looked up. "They have been here before?"

Momo bowed, "Yes, samurai-sama, they come to run us off the mountain. The last time my husband returned in time and used yumi-san to scare them off."

"Your husband took on yamabushi with a bow and arrow and survived?" Hideki asked in disbelief.

"Yes, samurai-sama," Momo said. "He was very skilled."

"He would have had to have been," Hideki said with respect in his voice.

The woman was really worried as the four approached the inn. "What am I to do?"

"Momo, let us pay for our breakfast by helping you with the yamabushi," Hideki offered.

"I do not want you hurt. There are four of them this time. There were only two last time. They can be very violent."

"Why don't you step back up into the inn and let us reason with them," Hideki advised.

"Do you really think they will listen to you?" Momo asked.

"Oh yes, Momo-san. They will listen to us," Hideki reassured.

Momo did as she was asked and almost ran to the step up.

The four yamabushi walked into the dirt landing and two took seats on the benches opposite Hideki and Jubei. The other two stood behind their comrade's benches and glared.

The smaller of the two in front demanded, "Who are you and what are you doing here?" As he said this, he tightened his grip on the long naginata between his legs.

Jubei looked to Hideki. "Grumpy lot, aren't they?"

"Smelly too," Hideki replied.

The man opposite Hideki grasped the naginata with both hands, lifted it out of the dirt and brought the gleaming large blade down toward Hideki.

Hideki saw the blade coming at him, but did not move. The only concession he offered the yamabushi was to spread his legs wider. The sharp blade sunk into the wooden bench between Hideki's legs, missing his crotch by less than a hand's width. As soon as the blade sunk into the wood, Hideki pressed the back of the blade deeper into the wood with the palm of his left hand.

When the yamabushi saw intimidation had not achieved the desired result, he stood and tried to lift the blade out. Hideki's hand pressing down would not allow it.

The yamabushi pulled and yanked and finally cussed. "Let go you bastard."

Hideki timed his release superbly. He lifted his hand just as the man yanked the hardest. When the blade released the man went flying backwards, crashing into their table and his two men behind it. All but one went down into a heap.

Momo laughed from the inn entrance. The remaining standing yamabushi recovered enough from the shock of seeing his leader and comrades trying to separate themselves from the pile to spin on Momo and raise his naginata blade skyward. He stopped when he heard the slight click of Jubei's sword being pulled a few inches from the scabbard.

The yamabushi was mad. He was not stupid. The samurai before him had just loosened his sword. If it came out of the scabbard, legend said it would have to taste blood. Something about this one-eyed man dressed all in black sang out "killer." The yamabushi stepped back.

The leader was finally on his feet. He addressed Jubei as the most senior of the two. "Our grievance is with this Kirishitan bitch. Are you going to interfere?"

"No, my traveling companion will settle with you and your friends."

The man's smile was genuine. "What? You don't mean this

boy with the bad hand? He'll be dead before my friends can reach him. I will slice him open like a ripe melon."

"Then slice away, monk. There are only four of you. But if any of you move toward this woman, you die where you stand."

All four of them moved away from Jubei and toward Hideki.

"Thank you for your support," Hideki said to Jubei trying to keep the nerves out of his voice.

"My pleasure. You are here to learn the art of war. There is nothing like learning firsthand," Jubei said.

Hideki knew the sun was on his neck. That placed it in their eyes. Musashi sensei would have liked that. Before they came too close, Hideki stood and drew both swords. The katana went into his left hand and the short wakazashi into his right.

The leader could not wait to right the insolence of being dumped in the dirt by a mere boy. He dropped the tip of the naginata and lunged the large three-shaku blade at Hideki's face. Most of the time, Hideki would try to get inside the man's leading foot. The yamabushi, being right handed, was lunging with his left foot forward. Hideki knew one of the men from behind the table had moved to his leader's right and was almost even with him. If he turned the leader to the right, Hideki would leave his left side exposed. He angled to the right front, deflecting the blade of the naginata to the left and moved his short sword over the top of the man's lead hand. Hideki's wakazashi cut deeply into the man's left thumb. The leader screamed and dropped to the ground holding is hand, out of the fight. Hideki leaped over the man before his comrade on the right could react, covering the distance between them in one leap and bringing the katana in his left hand down in an arc slicing the muscle above the yamabushi's right knee. Blood spurted, and the man screamed, falling to the ground holding his leg. The second was out of the fight.

Hideki continued his sword's arc to the right and was in position for the next yamabushi still behind the table. Hideki took two steps toward his next target and leaped to the table and beyond, bringing the katana down with an overhead strike. This yamabushi was better trained; he deflected Hideki's attack to the right. It was what Hideki wanted. Now Hideki brought up the short sword underneath his left hand and sliced into the back of the man's extended elbow. The yamabushi screamed and dropped his naginata, backing up quickly, trying to get away from the deadly blade.

The fourth yamabushi was uncertain now. He'd seen three of his companions bested by a crippled boy. He dropped his point and advanced slowly toward Hideki. Hideki waited until he was almost in striking distance with the naginata and kicked the wooden bench over and onto the man's sandaled feet, striking unprotected toes. The fourth yamabushi abandoned his attack but kept his grip on the deadly bladed halberd. He cussed and hopped on his good foot. Hideki jumped onto the table again, reversed the katana in his left hand and struck the man on the top of his head with the back of his blade, rendering him unconscious.

"Excellent work," Jubei congratulated. "You left enough to help the wounded back."

Hideki flicked the blood from his katana and wakazashi before returning them to their scabbards. "Yes, the two with cuts on their hand and arm can help carry the leg wound, and the idiot that is unconscious can spell them back up the mountain."

"What you have done is maimed three and embarrassed a fourth. Are they more likely or less likely to want revenge now?" Jubei asked.

"Yes, sensei, they are more likely to seek revenge," Hideki said.

"Exactly. What did Musashi always say? 'When you draw, draw to cut; when you cut, cut to kill.'"

"I just thought that four bodies on Momo's property might be a problem for her and Mei," Hideki said. "Momo, do you feel like tending to their wounds or shall I send them up the hill as they are?"

Momo was still in shock by what she had just seen. She finally collected her thoughts and spoke. "I will tend to their wounds. It is the Kirishitan way."

VII

Yoshi Sleeps High

Yoshi was lost. It was not the first time, but it was the first time
in a long time. He did not like the feeling. He had been given a
shortcut across Mount Tara by a woodcutter. It was the highest
mountain on Kyushu and one that needed to be traversed by
southbound travelers coming from the main island of Honshu.
Most travelers skirted the mountain peak using the road in the
north, avoiding the rugged forests on top. But Jii had made plain
the need to get to Hideki as soon as possible. That is why he
gambled and asked for a shortcut.

Woodcutters were the scouts of the mountains. They
traversed the peaks and valleys in a daily hunt for firewood and
building material and usually knew the lay of the land.

Yoshi knew the risk. Until he'd met Hideki, Yoshinobu
he had lived by the ninja creed: "I live in the dark; I die in
the dark." Any direction from an untried source could be
dangerous. But he had been on the road for almost three weeks
and was anxious to get to his friend. So he had thrown caution
to the wind and asked a woodcutter for directions.

"I should have been more careful with the woodcutter,"
Yoshi chastised himself. Now he would have to waste more
time doubling back. But first he had to make sure he was lost.

Instead of his normal courier disguise, he had decided to
travel as an apothecary. The reasons were many. As a courier,
he had to travel at the shuffling gait that ate up miles but
tended to wear you out over time. This was a long trip. Because
he was traveling all the way to Kyushu and into an unknown

territory, he opted for a disguise that other travelers would trust.

Everyone had need of powders, roots, or teas to heal ailments. And everyone liked to describe their problems to a medicine man. The additional advantage of the apothecary garb was a lightweight wooden chest with small drawers, which provided multiple hiding places for other tools. The chest was held secure to his back via cloth shoulder straps. A blanket roll rode high on top. The canvas roll also housed his ninja sword and an assortment of other weapons.

He wore medium-weight cotton gi bottoms collapsed under knee-high leggings that started at his ankles. Because it was autumn and often chilly, he wore the commoners' han-gappa coat for travel over the top of his faded and patched blue kimono. It was loose fitting with inside pockets filled with all manner of nasty items a ninja might find handy.

Yoshi had eschewed the normal wide triangle straw hat for the more traditional cloth covering with two tails over his ears reaching down to his shoulders. The last piece of his outfit was a walking stick of plain white wood.

"No use putting it off; I have to make a decision," Yoshi told himself. He looked for a spot where the current path the woodcutter had put him on intersected with an animal trail. He knelt down and lowered his tongue to the dirt. He let the dirt cover his tongue and registered the tastes. Then he brushed off as much as he could before he started spitting out the residue in earnest.

"No salt at all," Yoshi said to himself. "No rain in a couple of weeks, so no animal or human has passed this way in some time. The woodcutter either lied to me or I missed the turn off." Yoshi suspected he'd missed the turn. His haragai, his ability to see through the darkness, would have alerted him to danger from the woodcutter. It was true that on occasion, his haragai abandoned him; but not often. He realized he relied quite heavily on the special gift from his now deceased father.

He would have to backtrack and lose more time. That was not what he had wanted when soliciting advice on a shortcut. He wasted no more time fretting; he just turned back down the trail from whence he had come, moving rapidly. The sooner he found the right trail, the sooner he would get to the Buddhist temple.

Half a day later, with the last vestiges of sunlight disappearing in the West, Hideki heard a loud howling somewhere in the forest. It was not really a howling. It was more of an angry growl amplified almost as loud as a cannon across the mountain top. It was the only way Yoshi could describe it to himself. He had heard a cannon once and it was loud. This howling was loud also but somehow more menacing than the cannon. The sound grated on the nerves. It cut to the center of one's being where fears lived. It unspooled those fears and let them multiply a hundredfold. All of Yoshi's muscles tensed and all his senses strained to locate the direction of the hideous sound.

His haragai told him of a serious threat. "By the Buddha, I cannot defend what I cannot see," he said to no one.

He had to know where it was located and where it was going. "It does not sound far," he muttered under his breath. He looked in every direction trying to isolate the source. He simply could not be sure. Then something happened totally unexpected. Yoshi began to sweat. "Yoshi, what is this?" he asked himself. He repeated his father's mantra. "Stay calm! Stay in control! Stay alive!"

Despite his own admonition, the howling began again and Yoshi's head came up. "Where is it?" he asked himself.

But in the trees, sound dulled almost instantly. For some reason this sound lingered just a moment longer than necessary. It felt like another worldly taunt. "Come out ninja! Come out and play, ninja!" it seemed to be saying. It did not sound like anything he had heard before.

What really worried Yoshi was it did not sound like anything in nature. Yoshi had spent most of his life on mountains. Where normal men feared the dark, ninja embrace it. As a child he would be left in the forest for days with only his clothes, his wits, and a tanto. Yoshi knew the rhythms of nature. This howling was not natural.

No more howling. "Is it gone, or just gone silent?" Yoshi

asked himself as he moved to put a tree behind his back. Then he heard a sound he did recognize. It was a human scream of terror cut short by a death blow. Jii had warned him about the tengu reports, but he'd never dealt with a demon before, so he did not know what one sounded like. Could this howling be the sound of the Kirishitan-killing tengu? He did not know, but he knew someone had died tonight in a horrible manner. That much was sure from the scream.

Yoshi was still not sure of his exact location, but from the few stars he could see and the feel of the terrain, he placed himself somewhere close to the summit of Mount Taro. The Daiyu-ji Temple was close, but he wasn't going to find it tonight.

"I don't relish spending a night on the ground with that thing in the vicinity," he told himself. There was only one other option. He chose a large tree with no accessible low branches, reached into this coat and fitted two metal claws to his hands and began climbing. Once into the canopy, Yoshi slung a hammock of hemp netting, strapped off the small chest against the trunk, ate dried fruit and nuts and his last rice ball, finished it all off with water from his bamboo canteen, and waited. When he heard no out-of-place noises, he interlaced his fingers and started chanting in a very low voice.

This was a normal evening ritual. It relaxed him. It also kept his father's memory alive. But right now, he was troubled. That thing out there, what was it? How do you fight a tengu? Does it have a weakness? Can I kill it? Do I want to kill it? If I do kill it, what happens? There were too many unanswered questions.

In this modern world the idea of a tengu killing unsuspecting travelers seemed like a ghost story told to young children to keep them from getting hurt. But that howling sound was real enough. And if he had had any doubts, that death scream cleared them up. Someone had died on this mountain tonight, in a horrible manner, not far from here.

Yoshi was paid to provide intelligence. He was good at his craft. He knew he should be on the ground searching for the tengu, gathering as much information as he could. But he did not move from his lofty perch. He had not seen the tengu and already it frightened him. He would use the kuji kuri to calm his spirit and restore his center. But which symbol to use and which mantra to chant?

The kuji kuri hand weaves of nine symbols cutting were meaningless on their own. Yoshi knew that simply clasping hands in a certain way would not produce any powerful effect. What the hand symbols really do is to serve as keys to the ninja's own memory and mental focus. In other words, the ninja would make a particular hand symbol only to remind himself to access an entire set of associated ideas and concepts stored in his memory. The goal was to enter a certain mindset, which was thought of as a process of opening "energy centers" in the mind and body. This would give Yoshi the spiritual and psychological tools to accomplish the task at hand.

Kuji-kuri or nine symbols cutting is the opening ritual in the majutsuhi's art. To some, the majutsuhi was a magician; to others, a conjurer. Yoshi knew the cutting patterns, the mudras, and the concentration to trace the patterns on nine lines in the air was the foundation of his haragai—the sixth sense that warned him of danger—before it happened. It was a mental exercise just as his katas were a way to physically exercise. As a ninja from the old school, Yoshi knew his mind was his most powerful weapon. "Control your mind, control the thing," his father would say. It had taken Yoshi many years to realize "the thing" was himself. With that demon killing people in his close proximity, the symbols took on a new urgency.

It took a long time for him to settle his nerves enough to focus on the first mudra. He lowered his breathing to almost nothing and traced the first symbol in the air in front of him.

"Rin, for power." Yoshi placed his hands together, the fingers interlocked. The index fingers were raised and touching. Yoshi traced the mudra across the first line in the nine-lined imaginary grid he saw in the air before him. The mudra was dok ko-in/kongoshin-in or seal of the thunderbolt. Then he quietly muttered the mantra, "On baishirammantaya sowak a."

It took him six more times until he felt at peace and

powerful again. Then he moved onto Hyo, the second symbol. Yoshi slowly dissolved the symbol of Rin. Then he carefully moved his hands together, pinkies and ring fingers interlocked. His index finger and thumb raised and pressed together, middle fingers crossed over his index fingers with their tips curled back to touch the thumb tips, the middle fingernails touching. Yoshi traced the mudra down the first vertical line of the grid in the air before him. He focused on the symbol and uttered the mantra, "On isChiyoya intaraya sowak a."

Somewhere between the "To" and "Jin" symbols, Yoshi felt a great peace come over him. All traces of fear vanished. In a flash he knew what he must do. His father had called what he must do the dark arts and warned him to use them sparingly as it was hard to tell who would answer your summons. But Yoshi had not felt this vulnerable since he was a child. These were extraordinary circumstances, and they called for extraordinary measures. So, he moved seamlessly from the last symbol of kuji kuri into an older and darker set of weaves and chants. He unconsciously opened gates of energy at the base of his spine, in his chest and eventually by forcing his tongue into the roof of his mouth as he chanted, into his brain. His calmness changed from peace to dread in seconds. He was immediately uncomfortable and felt totally naked with a sense that he was going to be knocked out of the tree. But he kept chanting and focusing. Eventually the peace returned. When he opened his eyes, and unfolded his hands he realized he had been sweating and the animals and bugs had resumed their nightly chorus. He would live another night. Then he slept.

VIII

Samisen

The samisen player struck the three strings with her bachi and sang several plaintive notes of an old song. She was rewarded by the lull in the activity below in the Jaded Princess. She completed her song and placed the instrument alongside her bedding on the tatami. Now all she could do was wait.

Her patience was answered by heavy footfalls on the stairs. She filtered out other noises trying to detect any signs of danger. She could detect none. She was kneeling when a distinctly male voice uttered, "Sumi masen."

"Hai," the woman answered.

"The proprietress wants to speak with you downstairs."

"Right now? I was preparing for bed," the woman lied.

"She was pretty insistent," the man said.

"Oh very well, tell her I'll be down as soon as I get my clothes on."

"Thank you," the man said and departed.

The woman was fully clothed. She busied herself wrapping up her meager belongings and placing them into a traveler's roll for her back. With the bachi tucked into her obi and the samisen in her hand, she departed the room and made her way down the stairs to the main floor. The room bustled with men eating noodles, drinking sake and women waiting or fawning over them. The woman looked to the large man behind the bar and raised her eyebrows. He nodded slightly toward a table in the corner where one woman of indeterminate age sat by herself sipping tea.

The woman with the samisen moved to the table and waited. "You wanted to see me?"

The proprietress looked over the woman from head to toe. "I see you are wearing your traveling clothes."

"I thought it prudent to be ready. When the proprietress summons me, it can be a prelude to an invitation to leave," the samisen player said.

A tiny smile broke one of the corners of the proprietress's mouth. "You are not new to this. I see it is the way you earn your rice."

"It is how I feed myself, yes. And it is honest work," the samisen player defended.

"Is it honest to come in, reserve a room for three days, play your instrument, sing your songs during the busiest hours, hoping that I would take notice and hire you?" she asked.

"Either hire me or show me the door. Those are the normal two options," the woman admitted.

"I have let you play for two nights now and observed your effect on my business. Your old love songs bring the drinking, fornicating, and gambling in the back to a halt. I think you remind the men of home. But when you play your lively tunes, the drinking, gambling, and fornicating double. Why don't you sit down and have some tea?"

The singer took a seat and allowed the proprietress to pour her a cup of tea. "You may call me Aya," the proprietress said.

The singer bowed her head. "I am Midori."

"Well Midori, would you like some noodles?"

"No thank you. I ordered some my first night."

Aya smiled, "Yes, our cook is really a teamster. He is filling in until we can find a proper cook."

"I think he left a bridle in the noodles," Midori said.

"Yes," she almost smiled. "He is pretty bad. It is a good thing most of our customers are too drunk to notice."

"So how may I be of assistance to you, Aya?"

"I want to hire you as a singer. Three songs a night at one bu a night," Aya said.

"Let's see, you charge two bu per night for room and food. So if I'm making one bu a night, I'll have to find another job to be able to stay here. Do you want me singing for the competition?"

"No, I cannot allow that," Aya said, the almost smile vanishing.

"I thought not. It is one of the reasons I chose the Jaded Princess. Your competitors are bigger and closer to the water. They don't need a singer," Midori pointed out.

"And you think your singing will change that?"

"No, my singing will be an added value. They will come for the food."

"Food? Don't tell me you are a cook as well?" Aya asked, very interested now.

"I happen to make the best ramen and udon in Kyushu," Midori bragged.

"Even if that is correct, you will be singing three songs a night. How will you cook noodles and sing at the same time?"

"You will give me an assistant. She should be someone young enough to learn. You have plenty of farm girls upstairs. Give me one too young to work the tables or someone else that you can spare. I'll prepare the bowls before I sing. If an order comes, she can add the hot broth to the prepared bowls as I instruct her, and your customers will not have to wait. You will eventually get a girl who can be my replacement."

"What if it's a boy?" Aya challenged.

"I suppose a boy would do, if he likes to cook."

Aya liked the arrangement. "You plan to move on?"

"Eventually, I bore easily. Besides, houses with women are full of intrigue. I hate intrigue," Midori said.

"Somehow, I don't believe you. What if I were to tell you I was looking for someone to run this establishment, so I could focus on my other enterprises and you might be that person?"

Midori looked over her right shoulder. "I'd say the big fellow with the brown headband is first in line for that job."

The almost smile was back on Aya's mouth. "You are astute. Okay, how much is this singer and noodle-maker combination going to cost me?"

"Six bu a night for everything."

"Six bu? Are you crazy?"

"Did I hurt your feelings? Gomen nasai. I do apologize. Very well, make it four bu and I get half the price of each bowl of noodles," Midori countered.

There was no trace of a smile now. "You are a snake, Midori. I think you already know how much you are going to make on the noodles and you are just trying to wring more money out of me," Aya accused.

"Maybe, Aya … but it will cost you four bu and 50% on each bowl to find out," Midori said.

Aya burned a hateful stare into Midori. But Midori smiled and Aya relaxed.

"I agree, Midori. I admire your ambition and confidence. If you are as good as you say you are, my cook problem is solved. Now all I need is a good yojimbo. You wouldn't happen to be a master of the blade, would you?" she asked in jest.

"Eyi, no! I can cut a grabby customer with this," she said holding up her bachi. "Why do you need a yojimbo? Does this place get that rough?" she asked, glancing at the customers again.

"Do not fear, Midori. If anyone gets out of hand, Tatsu can handle it," she said, nodding to the muscular bartender. "As I mentioned earlier, I have other holdings, and business in Nagasaki is getting more dangerous by the day. Now there is a demon killing Kirishitans on the roads. I must travel soon, so I will need someone to protect me."

"Oh, Aya-san, be careful. I have heard that yojimbos are not to be trusted and I don't think many would prevail against a demon."

"That is why I'm not looking for just *any* ronin. My yojimbo must be skillful as well as honest and loyal. Once he takes my money, I don't want him being bought by my enemies."

"But how will you know? Won't they all act honest until the bribing starts?" Midori asked.

"I will know him by his actions," Aya stated.

"Oh, I see," Midori nodded. "You will watch for someone who does the right thing not for profit or glory, but because it is the right thing to do."

Aya stared hard at Midori. "You really are an unusual

entertainer, Midori. You see things from a much larger perspective than most. I will have to keep an eye on you."

Midori knew she'd overplayed her hand and attempted to put Aya back at ease. "If so, it is because I travel so much. You learn to quickly analyze situations and people."

Aya tried to smile again. "Probably so, Midori, I can see how quick judgments in your line of work would help keep you safe."

"I will be watchful for a ronin with the specific skills you need," Midori volunteered.

"Thank you. If you find him, there will be a reward for you. But until then, give my customers a song and make it a lively one," Aya demanded. "If I am to pay your outrageous wages, you must increase my sales."

Midori stood, bowed to Aya, withdrew the bachi from her obi, and cradled the samisen on her right hip. Then she started strolling through the busy tables singing and banging on the instrument. All eyes in the place were on her, except the young ronin against the back wall. He sipped his sake and stared into the table.

Midori belted out the song, keeping rhythm on the samisen. Soon most were clapping in time with the music and joining in the song. The sake flowed and dirty hands reached for her at every table. Midori kept singing and playing and mysteriously seemed to know just when to pivot or turn to evade a squeeze.

When the song was over and the clapping subsided, several drunken men rose and started towards her. Midori retreated to the far wall. Her pursuers hesitated. The far wall was where the ronin drank. She hurriedly picked one table and stopped.

"Do you mind if I sit with you samurai-sama?" she asked. "My fans are ardent tonight."

The young samurai looked up from his sake cup. Midori stifled her surprise. "Do I know you?" he asked.

Midori smiled and bowed deeply. "Not unless you travel and frequent these types of inns, samurai-sama," said Midori covering her face partially with the neck of her instrument. "I am a traveling singer. I just started tonight."

"Your performance seemed to please the masses," the samurai said, pointing to the room with his chin.

"I do not think it agreed with you," she said.

The young samurai looked up and managed a little smile. "It was fine. It just reminded me of someone."

"Oh, samurai-sama. You have come to the right place to forget someone, not be reminded of them. There are plenty of rooms upstairs where one can forget."

The samurai's slight smile turned into a frown. "I do not want to forget."

"Then why are you here samurai-sama?" she asked as she canted her head.

The smile was back. "A friend of mine recommended it. I am to meet him here soon."

"Oh, then you did not come here for the drink and the female companionship?" she teased.

"No, I am waiting for a friend. You don't think I'd stay here and endure this watered sake and horrible noodles for anyone but a friend, do you?"

Midori giggled, "No, I do not. But your luck has changed. The proprietress has hired a new cook who starts tomorrow."

"He can't be any worse than the one they have now."

"Oh samurai-sama. She is a great cook. I bet you will be very happy tomorrow. I am so sure of it that I will wager with you."

The samurai gazed closely at the woman's face in the bad light. "You are sure we have not met before?" he asked.

"I am sure we have not met formally," she responded vaguely.

"So, what is the wager?" he asked.

"I will bet that you will enjoy the noodles tomorrow. If you do not, then I will pay for your meal."

"What if I do like the meal?"

"Then you will pay double."

"That is not much of a bet for you. I assume you know the cook, at least by reputation."

"You are correct, samurai-sama. I know the cook. So, let's lessen the damage to your purse. If you like the meal, then you must buy me a bottle of sake. Now, may I sit, at least until my fans go back to admiring their companions?"

The samurai indicated the empty bench with his upturned gloved hand. She took the seat, but kept her hands about her chin, obscuring the samurai's view of her face.

"I am known for my memory and something tells me we have met," the samurai insisted.

"Oh, I would have remembered such a handsome young samurai," she said, batting her eyes. "I am sure you must have a favorite upstairs," she continued, changing the subject.

The samurai's head went back to his sake cup. "I have a favorite, but she is not upstairs."

"I am sorry samurai-sama. You must have a wife at home, please forgive me," she said.

"No, no wife; just a lady in Edo that I want to see again."

"You are in Nagasaki, samurai-sama. She will never know."

The samurai looked at her strangely, "I would know."

"Samurai-sama, how romantic, you wait for the one you love. Is she a princess?"

The samurai smiled. "No, she is no princess, inquisitive one. Her father owns a courier service."

"That is so sad, samurai-sama. Then your family would not approve. She is a commoner and not of your station. Which courier service?" Midori asked.

The samurai's head came up with that question. "Why do you wish to know?

"Do not take offense. I ask because I travel and may know of it."

The samurai relaxed. "He owns the Abe Courier Service," he said.

"Not anymore."

"Pardon me?"

"He does not own it anymore!"

"Did he sell the business?" The samurai asked, surprise in his voice.

"No, he died."

"Died? Are you sure?"

"Quite sure. Your girlfriend is now the owner," Midori said.

The samurai tried to process this latest information then smiled from ear to ear. "That is good news."

"I am guessing you and the old gentleman were not the best of friends?"

"I only met him once, and he seemed fine to me."

"Then why the joy upon the news of his death?" Midori asked.

"For selfish reasons, now she will be able to visit me on my journey."

"Samurai-sama, I doubt she will have the time. Abe is the largest courier service in Edo. She must consolidate the business and ensure all the stations and runners are still loyal to the Abe brand. She will have no time to chase you around the country."

The samarai sighed, "You are probably correct. But it was a sweet thought for a few moments."

"How will you get around the difference in station if you do re-unite smurai-sama?" she asked.

The samurai wasn't listening anymore. He seemed preoccupied. "I do not know," he eventually said. "But if I don't find a way to make some money soon, I will not be able to buy your noodles."

Midori's face brightened. "Oh, samurai-sama, the Buddha smiles on you. I know of a prosperous woman who is looking for an honest and loyal yojimbo."

"Yojimbo? Traditional samurai would not blemish their sword working as a bodyguard and twice as many would not work for a woman."

"Are you one of those, samurai-sama?" she asked.

"Fortunately, no, I have worked as a yojimbo before. And I find some women to be deadlier than men," he said.

"How good are you with your swords? Are you strong?"

"I am good enough," he forced himself to say.

"Well, you seem honest. I can attest to your loyalty. Your lady friend has no reason to doubt you so why should I. Besides, you are good cnough with your swords. You seem to have all the prerequisites. Shall I recommend you?" She asked.

"I appreciate your offer, but let us see what tomorrow

brings. I am waiting here for my companion. If he arrives tomorrow, he will have money. If not, I may ask for your help. Thank you."

Midori stood and bowed to the samurai. "It will be my pleasure to repay your kindness for allowing me to escape my fans samurai-sama," she said.

Then she bowed again, turned and moved through the tight tables while whispering to herself, "It is my duty to help you, Yoshinobu Hideki. We shinobi of the Five Families have only one master now, the Yoshinobu. And as you well know, your lover Myo is my leader and now runs a courier service. Thank goodness for the poor lighting, my makeup, and your melancholy; otherwise, you would have recognized me for sure. When last we met, Myo and I pulled you out of a cave where those Fox bandits had tortured you."

Midori giggled as she moved between the tables. It was something samisen players did. Tomorrow should be interesting. She would have to get a message to Myo.

IX

The Yellow Eyes of Death

Yoshi was alert as he pushed across Mt. Tara. The happenings of last night had shaken him. He would have to be better prepared when he met the tengu again. It was not supposed to attack during the day, and it was not supposed to attack anyone but Kirishitans. "I wonder if the one who died last night was a Kirishitan?" he asked himself.

Yoshi thought he had traversed the peak of Mt. Tara about an hour ago. He had been walking slightly downhill ever since. The path was narrow but well worn. He hitched the medicine chest up higher on his back to preclude the bottom striking him near the spine as his stride adjusted to the downhill movement.

It was obvious that people passed this way. Not only was the path well worn, but human debris discarded by travelers littered both sides of the hard-packed white clay. A geta with the instep strap broken, a paper hat, half of a watabashi, a child's pinwheel with a broken stick, discarded single sheets of paper carried by most samurai for all manner of activity, and assorted trash were strewn haphazardly on one side of the path or the other. People used this path. But it was deserted today. Yoshi had seen no other travelers since ascending the mountain.

Yoshi cast about, his eyes moving constantly. He liked his solitude, but this mountain terrain had trees and a secondary undergrowth of tall weeds, grasses, and bushes that could conceal anything from a battalion of samurai to a large tengu. Yoshi shivered involuntarily. "I'll be glad to see Hideki," he thought. The truth was he would be happy to see anyone who was not a threat. As soon as he thought these words, he saw the Buddhist shrine in the distance. One minute he was staring at trees all around for as far as the eye could see, and the next, down the trail on a point, the Buddhist Hikawa Shrine.

It was not a particularly pretty site. There was the ubiquitous wall around the compound with the Torii gate looking toward the east and the rising sun. The knoll had been cleared of most trees and a simple two-story temple erected. There was nothing ornate about it. It was not designed for show. It was a place for the Buddhist priests to come and do spiritual exercises. The only thing unique about the building was the construction using dark wood, almost the color of leather. But the ends of all beams were painted white. That gave some symmetry to the design and in the morning light illuminated the eastern side of the building as if several candles were glowing. According to the written report handed him by Jii, this shrine, although isolated, enjoyed the patronage of old seaman from Nagasaki to the west, Omura to the south, and Kashima on the north.

"By the Buddha, what is this?" Yoshi asked himself. It was daylight, but his haragai was sounding alarms in his head. Something was not right. Yoshi immediately moved off the path and into the wood. He closed the distance to the building on high alert, moving silently from tree to tree and bush to bush. His running was a soft gait and the motion of his body distorted. Instead of the normal pattern of a running man, he adopted a shorter, step over instep, motion. To the observer it looked like a man running sideways. In essence, he was. Yoshi was stepping through kibi dachi—the horse stance—as he ran. Should anyone come upon his tracks they would see footprints laid out side-by-side. With no toe and heel to give direction, the observer of the tracks would have to guess which way Yoshi traveled. It was not much of a subterfuge, but it did not have to be. To a ninja, it might mean the difference in survival.

The warning was still going off in his head, but he could see nothing. He froze in the shadows and waited. "I'm good at waiting," he thought. "Of all the things I have mastered, I am probably best at waiting." And he was.

When the sun was almost directly overhead, Yoshi approached the shrine. It was dead, literally. There was no movement inside, and the main gates were tied shut with bamboo poles and rice rope. Some official party had been here to close it off as a crime scene. When he got closer, he recognized the marking on the paper attached to the poles as the mon of the Matsukara clan. "So the daimyo's people had investigated a crime." There was no law out here, away from the cities. The daimyo was given authority by the Tokugawa government in Edo to reign over his lands and was charged with control. Any hint of rebellion would be met with swift retribution. A daimyo failing to keep the peace would lose his lands and head.

Yoshi did not wait for permission. He climbed the wall and jumped down into the court yard. The crime was evident. The sweet smell of blood hung in the air. Someone or something had killed anyone in residence here. The bodies had been removed but the evidence of a horrific struggle was everywhere. Shoji screens were lying on the ground, candle holders were extinguished in the dirt where they had been dropped, and the sliding paper doors to the shrine rooms were off the tracks, ajar and shredded.

"Judging from the blood stains, I'd say four or maybe five people met their end here," Yoshi speculated. He spent several hours trying to find tracks of intruders or any sign that a tengu might have left. The daimyo's forces had trampled everything of interest on the grounds. He did find a bloody print in the priest's quarters amongst all the other bloody human prints. He could not determine its origin. It looked like a huge smudged cat's paw. Yoshi shivered. Did a tengu have feet like a cat? He thought they were supposed to be more birdlike, but he could not recall. But why was a Kirishitan-killing tengu killing Buddhists? Yoshi was troubled again. He remembered his chanting efforts last night in the tree and found little solace. His father's admonition haunted him: "Don't use this unless you have to, Yoshi. Sometimes what you summon is worse than what you face."

Yoshi put his medicine chest on his back, but something bothered him. The smell of blood and fear was evident in the compound, but there was something else. It was faint but steady. He moved back into the rooms trying to isolate the odor. It was familiar, yet not. The harder he tried the more the answer alluded him. He gave up and headed down the mountain to Nagasaki.

"I hope I am in time to find Hideki," he said as he picked up the pace. "The government needs Hideki," he said. Then he corrected himself. "By the Buddha, I need Hideki. I only have two friends. I cannot afford to lose one."

By the time he got to the outskirts of Nagasaki, it was late at night. The temple was hard to miss. It had been built just thirty years ago by the Chinese monk Chaonian for the Chinese sailors that plied their trade between Fukian and Nagasaki. Yoshi knew from Jii's description that it was an Obaku-Zen Buddhist building. The lights from Nagasaki below illuminated patches of the garish red walls and gates identifying it to any Japanese as being of Chinese construction. Although late, there should have been lights from the compound visible to the traveler. The gates were closed, and there were no lights anywhere.

"I have got to get closer," Yoshi told himself. "Jii is counting on me to protect Hideki and find out what evil is working here. I cannot do that from the safety of the trees." But Yoshi's haragai was beginning to whisper incessantly in his head. He was heading into danger.

Slowly, Yoshi slipped from his camouflaged position in the tree line and moved from shadow to shadow in the darkness. It was quiet. Had it happened again? Had the tengu managed to get ahead of him and attack another Buddhist compound? Yoshi suspected the worse.

He studied the terrain between his position in the brush to the compound gates. Concealment choices were limited. As he got closer, there were fewer and fewer trees and the underbrush almost nonexistent. With his next step he would be exposed. He paused and strained all the senses. He could hear no movement or normal evening sounds from the temple. Even this close he could discern no other lights or any sounds. It was the hour of the ox, and almost everyone should be sleeping.

But people still went to the benjo at night. They still yawned, cried out with a nightmare, or simply knocked something over during passion. Nighttime in a city was not silent. This Buddhist temple was as silent as a grave.

Yoshi had always heeded his father's words. "Disregard this gift at your peril," he had said more than once. His father had been respected by his clan and other ninja families. He was known as an extremely effective assassin and a respecter of the old ways. His knowledge of the dark arts placed him in a special category among ninja. Yoshi would have to take action soon; the haragai warnings were increasing to alarm level.

Personal safety or the mission, it was always a balance. But Hideki was his friend. He and his family allowed Yoshi to extricate himself from a legal contract the head of the Five Families had coerced upon him the previous year. Now he was the chief advisor for intelligence to Hideki's grandfather, a member of the Roju, a ruling element of the Tokugawa government in Edo. The Yoshinobu were a noble family. Hideki and his brother Nagamasu were cousins to the shogun. Yoshi grew up on a mountain in rags and hungry. They could not be more different. But they shared a common goal. They both wanted to make a better life for the citizens of the country—a country that had been at war for the last 150 years. The Sengoku Jidai or Warring States period had left the country in a mess. Whole sections of the country had been cut off from each other. Villages that had survived the wars lived long enough to starve to death. Disease from the half-buried bodies that populated the countryside had done the rest. Trade had come to a grinding halt, which was why a foreign trading port like Nagasaki was so important for the future. Peace must reign in order for trade to survive, and trade was needed to rebuild the nation.

Yoshi could not help but grin. A year ago he had not ever spoken to a samurai. In fact, Hideki was the first samurai Yoshi had a conversation with in his life. Now he was no longer just an assassin. "Now my young wife and mother-in-law sleep in a nobleman's compound in Edo," Yoshi muttered silently, "and occasionally I influence the country. Not bad for a lowly assassin." Then Yoshi made his decision. "If I am to help my friend, I must take some chances." He would meet this tengu again and try to kill it.

His haragai was buzzing alarm bells in his head now. He could see the reason for the trouble.

"Concealment is not cover," his father used to say. Yoshi was standing at the base of the last tree between himself and a cleared gate area. It was all open ground from his present position to the red gates. Yoshi marked off the distance in his head. It was about 10 paces. "It might as well be 100," Yoshi noted.

"Now I have concealment, but no cover," Yoshi said to himself. A quick glance across the clearing to the temple walls told him he could scale them within five steps, but as he thought this, the haragai buzzed louder. Whatever was threatening his life, it was imminent. His only option was the large tree he was standing beside. Then he smelled it. Blood and something sweet and vaguely familiar. He had smelled it before, but not often. He still couldn't place it. The Haragai was sounding a claxon in his head now.

He slipped on his metal claws and leapt at the tree. With significant effort he was able to hoist his body, working like an inch worm as his sharp claws cut into sappy bark. He was then able to get his leg up over the first limb. He looked down, quickly realizing he had covered almost the height of two average men in one leaping effort. The haragai warnings did not abate. So, he dismissed the first limb as refuge and continued to climb the trunk to the next one. The buzzing stopped. Only then did he look down. He wished he had not.

Out of the blackness below, two large yellow eyes peered up. Whatever they were attached to leaped up the tree and secured a purchase to scramble onto the first limb.

Yoshi started to reassess his refuge. The copper taste returned to the back of his tongue. "Aya, by the Buddha, what are you?" Yoshi asked of the two eyes.

The eyes disappeared and Yoshi lost touch with the demon. He strained all of his senses to capture any information about its whereabouts. It was too dark. The light cast from Nagasaki below did little to illuminate the blackness in the tree.

Then the yellow eyes returned. "You vicious bastard. Are

you a demon?" Yoshi demanded. The thing did not reply. It just made a tremendous leap up the tree trunk toward Yoshi with what sounded like flailing metal claws. The eyes got larger and larger as the beast fought its way up toward Yoshi's limb. Yoshi grasped the handle of his ninja sword from the top of the medicine chest bed roll. He knew if the thing reached his limb, he would have very little ability to defend himself. "How do you kill a tengu?" he asked himself again. The tengu missed.

The thing had failed. It could not sustain its upward momentum long enough to gain a tochold on Yoshi's limb. It slid down the trunk heavily, leaving what Yoshi could imagine would be deep marks in the bark as gravity pulled it earthward.

Then it was quiet. It was so quiet that Yoshi was tempted to climb down and inspect the demon's claw marks and tracks. But he did not. "You are powerful, demon. I know of no animal that could make that leap from the first limb. But you have limits." Just as Yoshi said this, the two yellow almond eyes appeared. It had been waiting at the base of the tree for Yoshi to make a mistake.

"I do not know what you are, but I see you cannot fly and your strength has limits. So, I wonder if you can be killed?" Yoshi asked so only he could hear. Then he reached into his coat for the secret pocket and pulled out a small clay vial with a cork stopper on one end. Then he turned to his medicine chest and withdrew what look like a child's flute. From the drawer below he extracted a long and narrow wooden dart with a needle-sharp tip on one end and several small feathers on the other. Yoshi carefully pulled the cork out of the vial and dipped the needle into the liquid within. Then he carefully replaced the cork and moved the vial to one of the drawers in the chest. Then Yoshi placed the dart into the mouthpiece of the flute. A closer inspection of the flute would reveal holes painted on and real openings at the mouth and on the business end of the blowpipe. Then Yoshi moved into position.

"You have very large and ugly eyes, Mr. Demon. I will try to close one for you. Let me introduce you to Mr. Fugu."

Yoshi moved the flute to his lips, trying to match the motion of the two yellow eyes that seemed to constantly be moving. When he had the rhythm matched, Yoshi exhaled his breath in a burst. The dart left the flute with a burst of air and winged its way to the yellow eyes.

Yoshi almost fell out of the tree when the screaming began. It was a maniacal scream of pain and fury blended with wild thrashing as the demon snarled and clawed toward Yoshi but finally fell to the ground. Its thrashing continued at the base of the tree and then on towards the woods. The screams continued into the brush and away from the temple back toward the Nagasaki lights.

Yoshi took stock of what had just happened. The screams meant he had hit the demon, possibly in one of its eyes. The screams did not sound like the howling he had experienced on Mt. Tara. This screaming was loud and frightening, but it was not as menacing as the howling of last night.

"Is that because the screams sounded more natural?" Yoshi asked himself. Then he dismissed the idea almost immediately. He had never heard anything like these screams either. "No matter. There was enough fugu poison on that dart to kill ten men," he said to himself. "Thank the Buddha I married a good-looking woman who knows her way around poisons."

Yoshi wondered if the tengu was faking injury and waiting to pounce from the dark. He waited a little while longer then made his way down and to the red gates. He knew what he was going to find, but he had to have firsthand knowledge that he could give Jii. Hearsay was one thing. Genuine firsthand intelligence was what Jii expected. It is what he would get.

This scene was different than yesterday's massacre at Hikawa Shrine. This time the bodies lay where they had been sliced open. The stench was overpowering. The blood Yoshi knew. But there was a real odor of something else as well. It was sweet smelling and it made his mouth water. What could do that? Yoshi gave up again. He knew trying to force the memory was a sure way to suppress it. He would remember in time. In the meantime, there was real evil loose in Nagasaki, and his friend and employer was in danger. He wondered if he and Hideki were skilled enough to stop it.

X

The Messenger

Taro began his downhill gait off the crest of the mountain. He involuntarily glanced to the right, scanning the trees as they met the gravel and sand road. If there was to be trouble, it would come from the right. There was no left. The road fell away down into one of the many valleys that threatened to suck the precariously perched highway into its maw several ri below as it traversed Mount Tara. It was a hard climb, but one that had to be made if you wanted to see the rest of Kyushu. Further below, down toward the city, any report of brigands would be met with an immediate dispatch of the militia. Governor Heizo would not tolerate any impediment to trade. Trade was the lifeblood of Nagasaki. Taro was a courier. He carried that lifeblood throughout Kyushu Island, the southernmost island of the four main land masses of Japan. But Taro had crested the mountain. Up here, there was no law. Travelers provided their own protection, and of late it wasn't enough.

Taro's zori sandals slid slightly on the crushed gravel and sand with each step. He leaned back and bent his knees slightly to compensate for gravity and the steepness of the downward slope. He did not want to begin running. Running for a courier was not advised. He knew too many couriers who had ended their careers running. Running led to injuries. Injuries led to farming or working on the docks. Taro wanted no part of either. Farming led to starvation and dock working led to bodies floating in the causeway. Taro usually found being a courier a good career choice. That was before the tengu started killing lone Kirishitans.

Taro was no Kirishitan, but how would a tengu know that? Would he stop and ask? Doubtful! The demon would probably descend and strike with his great claws as he had Jiro. Jiro had been a good man and a good friend. He wondered how Momo and Mei were managing without Jiro. What sort of a devil would awaken a tengu to target Kirishitans? It would be just his luck to get killed by a less-than-discerning tengu. Maybe he should wear a sign of the Buddha around his neck.

Taro chopped his steps more. He couldn't die now. He had a wife and three children to support. They were not really a joy, but they were his. With three healthy children, he and his wife could count on at least one of them taking care of them in their old age. He still enjoyed his wife's futon, even if she was getting a little cranky. She had put on weight she could not lose after giving birth to their third child. It was as if she were blaming Taro. "Damned unfair," Taro thought. "Blame the gods, not me."

Taro had seen some travelers this morning, but none moved alone. The tengu had everyone scared, not just the Kirishitans. The road did not exactly level off, but it became less steep. Taro knew where he was. The clump of trees below and on the left was Jiro's forge and Momo's inn. Momo would have refreshments for him. At least she always did while Jiro was alive. He wasn't sure what he would find this time. If Jiro was still alive, he would know what to do with the information in the courier pouch. But Jiro was gone. "Karma," Taro muttered to himself. "You never know when it is your time to join your ancestors."

With that thought, Taro glanced to the right again. No tengu. "Good." Maybe today was not the day for him to die. Taro knew the message he was carrying for Momo and Mei. Father Sebastian had read it to him in case the scroll in the pouch was lost. The content of the message meant Taro would not be alone when he returned to Nagasaki.

Taro slowed his shuffle as he turned off the road to the short pathway to Momo's inn. Once on the path, he slowed to a walk and began to untie the large straw hat advertising his employer. With hat in one hand, he reached into his grey cotton top, retrieved a cloth, and started wiping his brow and the back of his neck. Although cool in the mountains this fall day, his exertions had caused a fine bead of sweat to develop in those places and down the small of his back. He was going to be here for some time if Momo was up to her old standards of hospitality. He did not want to catch a chill when the perspiration evaporated. To a courier, falling ill ranked close to running into demons and becoming injured. Children had to eat. You can't make money if in bed with a fever.

When he first caught sight of the black-clad ronin sitting on the bench in front of the inn, the messenger pulled up with a sharp gasp, wondering for just a moment if he were looking at a demon.

He was something dark and evil to be avoided. Taro realized the man's one good eye had been on him for quite some time and the messenger instinctively dropped his gaze. The Ronin's black attire would be enough to give someone pause. Even his swords were black. The black tsuba used as an eye patch and the black silk sageo cord that held the eye patch in place and disappeared into the thick jungle of jet black hair pulled back into a stiff bundle at the crown of his head completed the effect. This Ronin's appearance exceeded Taro's normal self-preservation alerts. He did not appear dangerous. He appeared frightening.

Taro moved up to the man just out of sword's length and bowed. "Sumi masen, samurai-san. Is Momo at home?"

That piercing good eye never left Taro as he stated in a matter of fact voice, "Call her."

Taro bowed again, straightened up and faced the entrance. "Momo, it is me, Taro, with a message from Father Sebastian."

The wooden door slid to the side and Momo appeared at the inn's entrance and bowed to Taro from the step up above. "Taro-san, how nice to see you. The message is from Father Sebastian?"

"Hai," Taro responded. "May I come in?" Taro asked, not wanting to discuss Momo's business in front of strangers.

"Hai," Momo answered. Then to Taro's surprise, "Please come in as well, Jubei-sama. This message may affect you too."

Taro hung back, not wanting to step in front of the ronin. The one-eyd devil motioned with his head for Taro to proceed. Taro felt the perspiration in the small of his back again, and it had nothing to do with the weather. "What is worse," Taro wondered, "a demon on the road or the devil in a small room?" This courier job was getting far too dangerous. Maybe he would discuss a career change with his wife when and if he returned to Nagasaki tonight.

Jubei sat where he could face the only entrance to the six tatami room. Taro sat as far away from the evil-looking ronin as he could get and still be in the room. Mei came to the door and bowed to the room before turning sideways to get around Taro. She was followed by Gon. Mei bowed to Jubei and kneeled in the formal manner by folding her legs under her and sitting on her ankles next to him. Gon bowed and kept bowing, kneeling beside and to the rear of Mei. Jubei nodded slightly, acknowledging Mei's bow. Lastly, Momo came in with a large tray. Taro overcame his fear long enough to move slightly toward Jubei to allow Momo space to enter. She placed the tray in front of Taro, but offered a cup of tea to Jubei first. Jubei dismissed the offer with a negative nod of his head.

"I wouldn't wonder that you are not thirsty," Momo said to Jubei. Then she turned back to Taro. "We have just had the noon meal. Please help yourself."

"Domo, domo, Momo-san, I have been thinking about your bento all the way up the mountain," the messenger said, picking up the ohashi, ready to eat.

"Perhaps you could read the message first, and eat later," Jubei suggested.

Taro was hungry enough to protest, but that piercing lone eye jolted him back to reality. He put the ohashi back on the tray.

"Certainly, the job comes first," Taro said, not meaning it at all. He reached into this haori jacket and produced a small scroll. This he handed to Momo.

Momo untied the scroll and unrolled it.

"Okasan, what does it say?" Mei asked excitedly.

"It is good news Mei-chan; Father Sebastian has a buyer

for your work. He asks that we bring all you have to Nagasaki immediately. It says the buyer will remain anonymous until we meet at the church. It further states your prices will be met."

Mei clapped her hands together. "The blessed virgin has helped us in our hour of need," Mei said.

"Yes, we must thank her tonight. But now we need to get all your pieces together on the cart. Gon, you will have to push the cart and accompany us to Nagasaki," Momo said.

Gon's face broke out into a big smile. "I finally get to see the big city."

"Yes, it will be exciting," Mei said. "But we have a lot of preparation. We must wrap the pieces carefully. They must not only survive the cart ride to Nagasaki, but the boat ride to their final destination. I want to use washi paper."

Then Momo turned to Jubei. "Jubei-sama, may we impose upon you to protect us in our journey? We cannot pay much, but I have already lost one family member to that beast. I would hate to lose any more."

Jubei bowed his head. "It would be my pleasure. It will be an opportunity to see the inside of the Kirishitan church."

Taro visibly relaxed. "I have never seen this tengu that took my friend's life, but reports of its sightings are scary indeed. I feel much better knowing we will be traveling as a group and with such a strong-looking warrior to protect us."

"Jubei-sama, how may we proceed to minimize risk?" Mei asked.

"It is noon now. It will take you the rest of the afternoon to pack the cart. I suggest we get a fresh start tomorrow morning. I have been in the presence of this tengu, and it is a fearsome creature. I do not want it to have the advantage of darkness should we meet on the road."

"Sensible, samurai-san," Taro said. "I will stay the night and we will all depart in the morning. That way I can get two terrific meals from Momo.""

"Oh, Taro-san, you flatter me," Momo said, well pleased with the compliment.

Taro reached for his ohashi again but had to scramble out of the way as Jubei rose and strode out of the room.

Once the samurai had departed, Taro looked to Momo and talked in a low tone. "What are you doing with a samurai here? They are dangerous at the best of times, and this one looks to be more dangerous than most."

Mei spoke for her mother. "Jubei has been with us a few days. He has a younger pupil on a musha shugyo who has gone ahead into Nagasaki. He appears fierce, but has been very kind to us."

"I'm with you, Taro-san. I don't like samurai. They act like they are better than the rest of us, and they fight over nothing. And when they fight, someone dies," Gon said.

"Urusai," Momo said in a stern voice, "Quiet. I will have no bad talk about Jubei-sama. He is not only a guest; he is our protector. I don't know why he has chosen to be so," she said, looking at Mei and causing her daughter to blush, "but we are safer because he has."

"That's another thing," Gon said. "He is taking liberties with Mei and she is engaged to me."

"Gon! That is not true. He has taken no liberties and has always been respectful," Mei said.

"He's always asking you questions about the church."

"He is interested, and it is our responsibility as Kirishitans to help him understand, especially since the missionaries have been expelled," Mei said. Then thinking about one of his comments, she added, "Besides, I am engaged to no one."

"Your father as much as promised we would be married," Gon whined.

"Father is not here, Gon, and until you hear me say it, there is no engagement."

Gon looked devastated, as if his worse fears had just been realized. "It just isn't fair. A samurai comes to visit, and you women fawn all over him and forget about the rest of us. I have a good mind to go in there and tell him a thing or two."

"Please don't do that, Gon. While I have not yet decided to marry, I am fond of you and I would hate to see you lying dead on the floor," Mei said.

"Do you think he would kill me for talking to him?" Gon asked incredulously.

"Gon, you saw what his pupil did to four Yamabushi."

What do you think the teacher is capable of?" Mei asked.

Gon slumped down further on his ankles. "It just isn't fair," he lamented.

"There, there, Gon; buck up. There is nothing going on between Jubei and Mei, and there has been nothing decided about a wedding yet."

Gon nodded his head, but got to his feet and moved quickly out of the room, sniffling as he went.

"He isn't crazy enough to challenge that samurai, is he?" asked Taro between bites of rice.

"I hope not," Momo said. "He is very smitten with Mei. He follows her around all the time and continually asks about a wedding." Then, turning to her daughter, "I don't know what is going on between you and Jubei-sama, but be careful. He may seem dashing and dangerous, and I know how that can turn a young girl's head. But just remember, he is of a different class than you. We don't mean much to them and by your own description, Jubei appears a highly skilled warrior."

"Do not worry Okasan. Jubei is interested in the church and somewhat less in my lacquer ware. I am flattered that someone of his status takes notice of me, but life with him would be difficult at best. He barely says anything of himself, and he is like a coiled spring. He is tense all the time. He never relaxes. He looks for threats everywhere. I feel sorry for him. Jubei's is not really a warm human existence. When I marry I want a man that focuses on me and is home every night, just like Father."

"Feel sorry for him?" Taro said, shaking his head. "You might as well feel sorry for a habu or a mamushi."

"Now we're comparing our protector to poisonous snakes. I'll have none of it. I thank you for delivering good news, Taro-san, but you will have to keep your opinions to yourself tonight and tomorrow. Can you do that?" Momo asked.

Taro nodded, "Hai, I can do that. Keeping my mouth closed around that coiled snake will be easy," Taro agreed. "Why give him reason to kill me?"

The next morning, all had had breakfast, the hand cart was loaded and in front of the inn, and Taro, Mei, and Gon were in traveling clothes patiently waiting for Momo and Jubei to come out the front door after locking up. Taro's head came up at the sound coming down the mountain.

"What is it Taro?" Mei asked.

"They should not be here. Governor Heizo's authority stops on the far side of the crest. This is the great lord's land. Nagasaki police have no jurisdiction here," Taro said.

"I have a bad feeling about this," Gon said.

Coming down the grade was a mounted samurai wearing a bugyo's lacquered black hat and an attendant leading the horse by a tether. The attendant, with the six deputies behind, and the three musket men trailing all had to shuffle to keep up with the gait of the horse coming downhill. The attendant was trying to slow the horse with the tether, but gravity was proving an obstacle. The noise was the neighing of the horse being denied its head and the calling of cadence by the senior deputy attempting to keep everyone in step. The clear, crisp fall air carried the unfamiliar sounds down to the inn. Taro and Gon moved behind the heavily laden cart. Mei moved to a spot away from the cart to greet the newcomers. They had to be coming to the inn. There was nowhere else to go for a party traveling as light as they.

The attendant stopped the horse in front of Mei and knelt. The six deputies fanned out to the left, leaning on their six-foot rokushakubos trying to catch their breath. The three musket men moved to the right and fussed with the wicks on their matchlocks to restore fire. The bugyo pointed his long riding crop at Mei and in a commanding voice yelled, "Submit, in the name of the governor! Submit!"

Mei bowed low. "Submit to what, Bugyo-sama? We have done nothing."

"Silence. Everyone in this building is under arrest for violating foreign trade laws of the shogun, and all products are seized as contraband," the bugyo said, raising his crop aloft as if he were going to bring it down on Mei's head. Gon found his voice as he ran around the cart and placed himself in front of Mei. "Do not harm her. The governor has no authority here," he said, mimicking Taro's earlier observation.

"Buka," the bugyo said as he brought the riding crop down across Gon's face, opening a long laceration from forehead and along the nose. Blood flowed, and Gon fell to his knees holding his head. The bugyo grabbed his saddle's horn and leaned forward to deliver another blow to the kneeling Gon. Mei stepped in front of Gon. "No, this is insane. We have done nothing to deserve this treatment."

Seeing his original target now in reach, the bugyo raised his crop for a blow to Mei's head, but an arrow flew across the inn's entryway and into the arm of the bugyo. The bugyo dropped the crop and screamed as the arrow lodged in his right arm half way between the elbow and wrist. Before he could utter another command one musket man had an arrow piercing his throat, the second one had an arrow lodged in his brain extending out his right eye socket. The third musket man jumped away from the grotesque sight of his friend's ruined head. The jump saved his life as the arrow caught him in the shoulder and spun him around, causing him to collapse to the ground writhing in pain.

The six deputies with wooden staffs were frozen with shock. This was supposed to have been an easy arrest of two women and a confiscation of their wares. Now the bugyo had been shot and their most awesome weaponry neutralized. They all took an involuntary step back when a black-clad samurai with an eye patch appeared in the entranceway and stepped down to the path between the benches—a charged yumi at full pull and two arrows suspended from his forward left hand.

The bugyo found his voice despite the blood loss. "Are you crazy? We are on government business. You have killed deputies. Your crimes carry a death sentence."

"Rudeness will not be tolerated," Jubei said flatly.

Something about that matter-of-fact voice and the deadly accuracy of the first three arrows convinced the bugyo the currently notched arrow at full pull would soon protrude from his throat if he did not do something quickly.

"Gomen, nasai," he said, bowing in the saddle to Mei. Then to his men he yelled, "Retreat."

Everyone started backing up when Jubei said, "Take this garbage with you."

The bugyo ordered the dead and wounded to be picked up. "We can't carry the dead all the way back to Nagasaki," the bugyo complained.

Jubei just stared at him. "Your problem, not mine."

Cursing, the bugyo stepped out of the saddle and ordered the bodies to be lashed on. Nursing his right arm with the arrow protruding from it, he led the retreat. Jubei watched them go up the road to the crest and then disappear out of sight.

Momo appeared in the doorway and stepped down with a bowl of water and cloth towels. "How bad is it Mei?"

"It is a face wound, so it bleeds, but it is not too deep," Mei replied as she placed a cloth compress on the wound. "With a bandage he should be able to travel soon."

"My, my, Gon, aren't you the brave one trying to save Mei," Momo praised.

Gon blushed, but it was hard to see due to the blood on his face.

"Yes," Mei said. "I may have to take you more seriously, Gon-san."

Jubei stepped through the yumi, collapsing the bow somewhat and unstrung it before handing it and three arrows to Momo. "Thank you for lending me such an exquisite weapon."

Momo bowed and took the deadly bow and arrows. "It is only exquisite when used by a superb bowman," Momo countered. "You may be in real trouble now, but thank you for saving my daughter."

"Should we continue into Nagasaki now?" Taro asked. "They may be waiting for us."

Momo looked to Jubei. "We will leave as soon as Mei thinks Gon can travel. I do not believe they will bother us anymore. That will probably change once we are in the city," Jubei said.

Momo looked to Mei. "If we don't get these bowls sold, we will not last the winter. I say we go see our anonymous benefactor."

Mei looked up from her ministrations to Gon, "I agree

mother. That thief Heizo was trying to steal my work. We should go."

Jubei nodded his appreciation for the decision. It was time to go to Nagasaki.

XI

Bad Heizo

"This will not do! This will not do at all," the short, fat man said as he paced in the large airy room. He paused long enough to rock up on his toes trying to extend his height to the maximum. It was a useless effort. He gazed out the sliding doors that were moved back to allow viewing of the small garden and the breathtaking scene of Nagasaki Bay below.

The open doors in autumn, like the stretching on tiptoes idiosyncrasy, was designed to reinforce to the governor that he was in control and significant. It worked. The hillside view at the head of the harbor reminded him he was in control of all in view.

The governor turned toward the samurai sitting uncomfortably in one of the western chairs near the mahogany dining table. "I pay you handsomely to control the city. We cannot afford to look weak. I put you in charge of the police, send you off to capture a girl, and you come back wounded with two of my musket men dead. Do you know how this looks?" Heizo asked, his voice rising. "Do you know what happens if that girl's discovery gets into someone else's hands? How could you fail me?"

The man sitting in a chair with his right arm in a black sling was having none of it. "You were not there. There was nothing I could do. He wounded me and killed two men before you could blink."

The fat, little governor smirked. "All this damage was inflicted by an old-fashioned bow? Your men had muskets, and he spanked you and sent you home with your tail between your legs like whipped puppies."

"Like I said, you were not there," Tahei insisted.

"No, Tahei, I was not there. I am just dumbfounded to learn that your skills are so ineffective. I am equally chagrined there is a dangerous man nearby and I know nothing of him. Was he samurai?"

Tahei's reply dripped with sarcasm. "Of course, he was samurai, Governor. Who else shoots rapid-fire arrows from a yumi with deadly accuracy?"

"I am told that the proprietress of the inn you visited was married to a commoner who was quite good with a bow. So, I'll ask one more time, was the man that shot you and killed my men a samurai?" The governor asked.

Tahei's eyes narrowed. "Yes Governor, the two swords in his belt were a dead giveaway. His black attire and a black tsuba covering his left eye emphasized his deadliness. But the real clue was the fact that he put an arrow through my right arm and the eye and throat of two of my men and almost killed a third all in the span of a heartbeat," Tahei said with frustration causing his voice to rise. "You are a member of the merchant class, Governor. I am a member of the samurai class. I don't ask you about trade, so don't presume to question me on matters of battle," he yelled, gripping his short sword tightly with his left hand.

Heizo knew he had gone too far. This wounded subordinate before him could kill him if he perceived a slight to his samurai pride. If he went to trial at all, he would probably receive banishment. It did not pay to antagonize samurai if you were a commoner, even a wealthy one that controlled all the trade in and out of the city.

Heizo was the governor of Nagasaki just as his father before him. His position was critical to Japan and to the Tokugawa government and Edo. All governments ran on money. He had the knowledge, he and his family had the connections, and he kept trade flowing in and out of, heretofore, the only port allowed to trade with foreign countries. But despite his importance, he was not samurai. As a member of the merchant class, he could buy and sell samurai all day long.

They were a dime a dozen in the tea houses and gambling dens he controlled on the waterfront. As the Tokugawa in Edo disposed of daimyo after daimyo in their paranoia to stamp out all rebellion, master-less samurai flocked to the dock area of Nagasaki looking for work.

Heizo had enough money to wage his own war. But that was not the kind of power Heizo wielded. Heizo knew how to make money. That was his importance. Samurai might sit at the top of the social and political hierarchy, but their expertise was not in commerce. Commerce was beneath them. Their idea of commerce was to dig another gold mine. Therein lay Heizo's importance and opportunity.

Heizo turned back to gaze on the sights of Nagasaki below. At anchor, beyond Deshima Point, straight below his garden were two ships still taking on stores. They had the high stern of Portuguese vessels. They would both depart tomorrow at high tide for Macau and Manila where they would trade their cargo of silver, copper, swords, and lacquer ware for pepper, cloves, spices, wax and cinnamon from the first two destinations and ultimately silk, gold, ivory, porcelain, rouge, and aromatic wood from China.

Heizo smiled thinking of the amount of money he would make. He had more money now than he could ever spend. He lived in the grandest house in Nagasaki. He wore the most expensive silk and enjoyed all the niceties found throughout the known world. He had a wife and two children and two mistresses. If he grew bored with the mistresses, he could always get his trading partner to supply him something new. Women were easier to get than samurai. But he was finding it harder and harder to stay interested. His tastes these days ran toward keeping his empire intact.

"You know the damn Portuguese keep cutting into our profits. The clerics keep finding ways to cheat us. I fear we may never see our interest on the silver loaned them last trip," Heizo lamented.

"What do you mean?" Tahei asked. "I was counting on my share."

"Oh, now I have your attention? You heard me. I don't

think the Portuguese can pay. Lobo and Dom Joao are due back in harbor at any time. If they don't have what they owe me, I think it is time we found some new partners."

"New partners; surely you jest. Who can we partner with that gives us access to so many ports? Surely you don't speak of the Sung?" Tahei asked.

"No, Tahei, I do not speak of the Sung. The Chinese ban on direct trade with Japan has not been lifted."

"Then who?"

"I had the Dutch in mind," Heizo said.

"The Dutch," Tahei questioned, "you know them? I remember only one Dutch ship in Nagasaki."

"Correct Tahei, we have had only one. And you recall how the Portuguese howled. But several Dutch ships have called on Hirado, and my uncles there tell me they are ready to take over all of the Portuguese routes."

"How could the Dutch put into Hirado without the Tokugawa approval? Tahei asked.

"Very good question, Tahei," the governor stated. "Makes you wonder what is going on in Edo, doesn't it?"

"Can the Dutch just jump in and take over if the Portuguese lose favor? Can it be done?"

"Oh yes, Tahei. Just as the Portuguese took over from the Okinawans," the governor said. "The Dutch can take over the Portuguese trade, and then we would be free from the dreaded Jesuits."

Tahei smiled. "You dislike them because they cut into your profits."

Heizo turned his short body towards his deputy. "I dislike them because the Portuguese use their religion to control the population. I can deal with sharp negotiators; I can deal with pirates; what I cannot deal with is merchants who wrap themselves in robes of religion that can threaten an uprising. More importantly, I'm counting on the Tokugawa in Edo to feel the same."

Tahei was frowning now. "You have lost me governor."

"Tahei, how can you have been around me so long and have learned so little? Have you not studied the Chinese classics? Do you not know Sun Tzu?" Heizo asked.

"'Know your enemy as you know yourself and your victory will be assured.' Yes, I know the Art of War," Tahei replied.

Heizo smiled. "Then you should know that we are at a crucial junction in our continued existence. We are threatened on all sides," Heizo said rocking back on his toes again. "We could lose everything in a matter of weeks."

Tahei smiled again as he rubbed the pain away in his bandaged arm. "You like the dramatic, Heizo. You should be on stage." It was meant as an insult. Heizo did not take it that way. A big smile broke across his face and he pushed himself higher than ever onto his toes.

"You are perceptive after all Tahei. All of the big stage plays, like the kabuki in Edo or the Bunraku puppet theaters imitate life. Do you see?" Heizo asked.

Tahei threw his good hand up in the air in surrender. "I do not see. How can you say we may be ruined in one breath and tell me life is like a puppet show in the next?"

"Let me help you, my deputy. How is money made in this port?"

"By trading foreign goods for our own," Tahei guessed.

"Good guess, and essentially true. What do the Japanese people need that they do not have?"

Tahei thought a minute. "We need gunpowder."

"True, we do. But it will not be long before we will manufacture it ourselves. What else do we need?" Heizo insisted.

"I guess we need raw silk from China along with porcelain, dye, books, and the sweet-smelling wood."

"Good Tahei. You have been paying attention to the inventories at the warehouses," Heizo commended. "And how do we make money on these items?"

"I guess you buy them cheaper in China than you sell them here," Tahei ventured.

"But you miss another opportunity for huge profits. Care to guess again?"

Tahei was tiring of the game. "No!"

"Taxes and fees are the route to riches," Heizo said.

"So what is in crisis?" Tahei demanded.

"The crisis is that modern Japan has caught up with us. The Tokugawa are in power and the country is generally at peace. The first thing a country at peace starts looking for is revenue. Governments run on money. Our isolation on the southernmost island of the country has kept us out of their minds until recently. Now they are looking at Nagasaki with lust. If the Tokugawa controlled the city, who would make the profits?"

Tahei's head was going up and down in agreement. "The Tokugawa!"

"Correct deputy," Heizo said.

"So, you want to keep the Tokugawa out?" Tahei asked.

"I do not think I can keep them out. Now a second-generation shogun rules over all the land. The days of playing one daimyo against another are gone. A new official magistrate arrived this week along with four yoriki to establish a new police force."

The look of surprise on Tahei's face was real. "So, I'm out of a job?"

"Do not pout, Tahei. Losing that job was inevitable. We must find you another one. If I have a job, you have a job. You just can't play police chief and magistrate anymore. We now have an official one straight from the Tokugawa in Edo."

"What will happen to our policemen? You can't just fire them. They all have families," Tahei protested.

"Do not be ridiculous. We need good men, or we have no power. No, they will move over to become customs officials. The Tokugawa are new to foreign trading, but the Dutch are trying to educate them now. Ever since that English navigator was shipwrecked—Adams, I think—the Dutch have been very close to the Tokugawa in Edo. The Dutch worship the crucified Jesu God of the Kirishitans, but don't practice the conversion of the peasants like the Jesuits. The Dutch government is not run by a church; neither are their trade practices. We can deal with them," Heizo predicted.

"This is all a little sudden and a little hard to understand. The Tokugawa are coming and some are here now. It will take them some time to wrestle control of the trade from your family. But they are preferable to continued dealings with the Portuguese," Tahei attempted to recap.

"Preferable, and inevitable, Tahei. If my calculations are correct, Dom Joao will not be able to pay our interest on the last shipment. That means our profits from the trade must rely on taxes until we can get the Dutch to take over. We will not be able to charge the Dutch the same high-interest because, while shrewd, they lack the greed of our Portuguese partners. They don't try to get rich overnight. They have the long perspective. So they are unlike the Portuguese who promised to pay but never do."

"How do we get the Portuguese out?" Tahei asked.

"That is the tricky part. We can't convince the government to shut off trade overnight. We have to be able to offer a better alternative. We have to play on the Tokugawa paranoia. The entire Yagyu clan sniffs out rebellion and banishes entire families at the least hint of disloyalty. We have to convince the Tokugawa in Edo that the Portuguese and their Kirishitan Church are dangerous and planting seeds of uprising amongst the peasants. The Tokugawa are predictable. They will send in their spies first and their officials later."

"But we already have an official here. You said so yourself."

"Well Tahei, what does that tell you about the spies?" Heizo asked.

"That they are already here?" Tahei ventured.

"Exactly!" the governor said.

"How do you convince the Tokugawa the Kirishitan Church is a threat?" Tahei asked.

"We have to take advantage of their paranoia. This tengu the country folk are so afraid of gives us a good opportunity to eradicate some of our enemies," Heizo smiled. "And I know the Portuguese well. They owe me money. They cannot pay. I will increase the pressure on Dom Joao to the point that he'll go to the church to threaten a work slowdown on the docks or get the gumi to refuse to distribute the goods, like he always does. Either way, we have what we want.

"I get it. If they go to the new magistrate, nothing happens because he has no police and therefore no power. If they go to the daimyo, Lord Matsukara, whatever action he takes will be suspect by the Tokugawa because most of his vassals are Kirishitan. Either way, Edo will be suspicious. If Dom Joao causes a work slowdown via the Kirishitans, then Edo will know they are a problem. That is devious, even for you," Tahei said with a certain amount of respect in his voice.

"Yes, I thought so too. We need to step up our operations. I want the people panicking. We need to expedite things with this new magistrate in town. I don't want him catching on. And try to manage things this time without anyone getting caught or getting any more of my men killed."

"Understood," Tahei said, standing but not bowing.

XII

The Challenge

Hideki awoke early. The single futon had been enough to keep
the cold off while asleep, but now that he was up and about, his
thin sleeping kimono let in the crisp, cold autumn air. He exhaled
his breath into the streaks of sunlight that entered through the
paper windows of his upstairs room to see if it was cold enough
to make his breath visible. It was.

Nature called, so he placed his katana in his right hand,
shuffled his feet into the hotel straw slippers at the door and
headed downstairs. The main floor of the Jaded Princess
seemed deserted. He heard noises coming from the kitchen
area behind the bar but did not have time to tarry.

The cold was more pronounced outside the building. The
icy air licked at his bare legs and made his race to the benjo
more urgent. Several paces behind the main building stood
a large wooden shelter with two doors. Hideki moved to the
left entrance, slid back the door and wrinkled his nose at the
unpleasant odor. It was too early for the benjo Etas to be up
and pouring water on the late-night deposits. He moved over
the shallow trench that cut through the building's wooden floor
and placed his sword on the stand that was within easy reach.
He gathered up his lightweight kimono above his hips and
loosened the fundoshi undergarment that girded his loins, en-
suring the long-unwrapped end did not dip into the filth below.
He squatted and relieved the pressure on his kidneys.

The summer kimono's light-weight belt would not support the weight of his katana. To wash his hands in the trough

outside, he placed his sword between his knees and bent at the waist to reach the water. Thinking of simple pleasures, he tried to decide whether to spend his last coin on breakfast or pay for a lesson in the dojo Jubei had suggested. Either Jubei turned up today or he must find a job. He was out of funds.

"So, this is what it is to be free," Hideki mused. "Jii was correct. Freedom breeds responsibility. I am free as a bird and free to starve if I cannot feed myself."

Hideki moved back towards his room. As he came abreast of the kitchen, he saw the samisen player from last night buying eggs from a thin young man. He slowed to hear their conversation.

"I will pay you for collecting the eggs each morning and delivering them here unbroken," the woman said. "And I want you to fetch enough water to fill that pot over there to half-full. Then I want you to start a fire under it," she said, looking into the young man's eyes to see if he understood. He did. "Very well," the woman stated; then she caught sight of Hideki standing outside the room. She saw recognition on his face and quickly placed three fingers to the right side of her face and turned it toward Hideki.

Hideki recognized the sign taught him by his ninja friend Yoshi and swallowed the words he had planned on uttering.

"Oh samurai-san, please come and meet my new helper."

Hideki moved into the kitchen, noticing the large wooden table against the far wall festooned with knives and long eating utensils. In the center of the room was a square sandpit with a fire strategically placed under a large, blackened pot suspended from a metal tripod straddling the flames. Hideki was about to speak to the samisen player when he saw another two fingers on her chin. He could not remember what that sign meant, but decided silence was usually a good course of action. Instead, he stepped deeper into the kitchen area and waited.

"Samurai-san, this is my new helper, Yasuke." The boy, several years younger than Hideki and noticeably shorter and thinner, looked as serious as his youthful personality would allow and bowed low. "Yasuke desu. Dozo yoroshiku onegaishimasu," he respectfully announced.

"Dozo, Hideki desu," Hideki said in return to the very formal introduction.

"Yasuke is an orphan raised in the Buddhist Temple north of town. The priests there taught him to read and write and he taught himself a trade," Midori said as she moved pots around. "He makes flutes and he had a girlfriend. She was the fair young Chiyo."

Hideki looked longingly at the pot.

"Samurai-sama, have you eaten?" Midori asked as she pointed to the boiling pot over the fire.

"No, I was wondering whether to spend my last sen on an egg or use it for a lesson today," Hideki said.

"No need; keep your money. I Midori, the best cook in Nagasaki, with the help of Yasuke will prepare you a free breakfast," she said winking at Yasuke.

Hideki bowed to her. "I hope your cooking is as good as your singing."

"Oh, Samurai-sama … better! Do you prefer warm or cold?" she asked.

"Warm, please," Hideki decided.

Midori instructed the youth on how to hold the egg on the end of the long cooking sticks without crushing it and how to lower it into the boiling water. Then she directed him to place the cooked rice into a glazed bowl. Then she sprinkled bits of dried seaweed over the top of the rice and placed a pickled radish slice in the center.

"Okay Yasuke, retrieve the egg." Yasuke did so after several aborted attempts and placed the egg on the wooden table. Midori placed a bowl of cool water next to it. Yasuke lowered the egg into the water.

"The sudden cold will cause the egg to contract from the shell, making it easier to peel," Midori explained. Yasuke covered the egg in a plain white sheet of washi paper and broke the shell. It came away easily. Yasuke cut the egg in half as instructed. He then placed the whole semi-egg onto the rice next to the pickled radish. Midori handed Hideki a set of clean watabashi for eating. Hideki leaned his sword against the wall. With the watabashi in his left hand he moved the egg to his mouth and proceeded to eat, making loud smacking noises.

Midori giggled. "That means he likes it," she said, for Yasuke's sake.

"Now get the samurai-sama a cup of tea to loosen his throat," she said. Yasuke complied.

Hideki ate two more large mouthfuls and drank half the tea, before he slowed down to breathe.

"Midori-san, I cannot wait for your noodles tonight. This is an excellent breakfast."

"See?" Midori said to Yasuke.

Yasuke bowed to his teacher. A smile lit up his face.

"Why is he so happy?" Hideki asked.

"Yasuke has learned something new today. He is quite an entrepreneur, normally selling flutes and whistles that he makes himself to passersby. He is on his own. Whatever he earns goes toward his survival. He is now thinking he may be learning something that will better his life," Midori explained. Then to Yasuke,"Go get us some more wood, please."

Yasuke bowed and left through the back entrance.

"He is a sweet young man," Midori said. "He was recently run out of the Buddist temple."

Hideki stopped eating. "It is unusual for Buddhist monks to cast out children unless they have committed a crime."

"It was not the Buddhist monks who cast him out. It seems some yamabushi moved in about six months ago. The Buddhist monks have not been seen or heard of since," Midori explained.

"Some monks can be hard to run out," Hideki opined.

"That is true, but these monks just seemed to have disappeared," Midori said. "I checked myself."

Hideki lowered his empty bowl to the wooden table and placed his eating sticks across the top. Hideki looked at the young woman before him. With her white apron over her light blue kimono and white towel wrapping her hair, she looked every inch a cook. But last night she sang and entertained a full house and looked every inch a samisen player. Hideki knew from experience that she was many things depending on what was required. He knew she was a very skilled ninja. He also knew he owed her his life.

"Midori, the last time I saw you, you were carrying me out of a gold mine. Are you here to look after me?"

The woman moved closer to Hideki and held the three fingers up to her face. When she got close she whispered. "My mission is to find whether the Kirishitans are a threat. But since I am here, I find Yasuke's story all too common. Whole Buddhist families are disappearing at night. The Ryukyuan families have been hit the hardest and they aren't really Buddhists. On the other side Kirishitans are being slaughtered in the mountains by what the locals are calling a monster or tengu or something. I have looked but found nothing. The tengu may just be myth. That is why I moved down to the city and took a job here. The woman that runs this place is a Kirishitan and married to the leader of the Portuguese traders. If I can stay close to her, I may learn something."

Hideki finished the last of his tea. "Jubei and I had a run-in with your tengu in the mountains."

"What is it? Is it really a demon?" Midori asked.

"I do not know what it was, but it was very large, very powerful, and very scary," Hideki shivered remembering.

"How did you survive?" She asked.

"We were lucky. I would not want to meet it in the open at night. We were inside an inn, behind locked doors. I got in a lucky shot with a yumi. My arrow hit it. Whatever it is, it bleeds," Hideki said.

Midori smiled. "My leader is correct about you. You have excellent instincts. But Yoshi was correct about you as well."

"Yoshi?" Hideki asked. "Is he here?"

"Not that I know of," Midori said. "But that does not mean he is not."

"What did my old companion have to say about me?" Hideki asked.

"He said you were lucky."

Hideki smiled. "He is not wrong. In fact, he used to have a saying about cherry blossoms … "

"Or benjo," Midori finished. "He told us."

"You are ninjas. Between Yoshi and Myo, you know me well."

"My leader took you as a lover. She would not do so lightly."

Hideki felt excitement at the mention of the new leader of the five families. "So, what you said last night is true. The Five Families is now being led by a woman—my Myo?"

"It is true, the woman you know as Myo leads us," Midori said. "I am sorry for teasing you last night. But I had to find out if you were true to her. She will expect me to report what I have found."

"I guess it is a good thing that I have been a good boy," Hideki said. "Do you think she will come south?"

"I'm sorry Hideki, I do not expect it. She is very busy. She is consolidating our families to keep up with the work your grandfather has us doing."

"How is Jii?" Hideki asked.

"I do not see him very often, but before departing on this trip, Yoshi told me to tell you he is in good health and ruffling feathers throughout the castle."

Hideki smiled in relief. "Just as long as he does not get himself hurt."

"Your brother Naga and his wife Yuki are doing fine, and your nephew is growing."

Hideki felt nostalgic for a moment, but then steeled himself.

"Thanks to you I can afford a trip to the dojo today," Hideki said changing the subject.

"I have recommended you to the owner. Please come around this afternoon. I will introduce you," Midori said. "I know you are here for the training, but Yoshi said you have a penchant for getting to the bottom of things."

"I will help if I can. I will be back here this afternoon if for no other reason than to gather my belongings as they throw me out. If I don't find a job, I will be sleeping rough tonight. Thank you, Midori, you always seem to arrive in time to save me."

"I would do that anyway. It is a ninja's job to protect the client. And we of the Five Families have only one client, the Yoshinobu. You are a prince of the Yoshinobu. You are a cousin to the shogun. Most importantly to me, you are the lover of my leader. How can I face her if anything happens to you?"

"Well, thank you. I shall see you back here in the hour of the monkey," Hideki said, bowing and moving toward the stairs.

"Hai," Midori said, returning the bow and holding it until Hideki had disappeared. Then she turned to the kitchen chores and thought about preparing noodles.

Hideki approached the dojo with trepidation and excitement. He had done this many times, but the feeling was always the same. As he removed his sandals at the entrance area and brushed his bare feet with his blue cloth from within the folds of his kimono, he wondered how today would end. He stood and stepped up to the main floor of the dojo and removed his katana and wakazashi from his obi. He placed both swords in a katanekake that was part of the wall just off the dojo's highly polished hardwood floor. The sword stands allowed students and visitors a resting place for their live blades during training. The katanekake accommodated the long sword on top and a short sword just below. Both rested in their saya, curved edge upward, visible from anywhere on the dojo floor. A glance at all the swords already at rest in this manner meant that business was good.

As he approached the entrance to the dojo floor, Hideki reached into his flowing left sleeve and retrieved his last coin. This he deposited into a wooden box with a small slot cut in the top. The click of the coin striking others as it hit bottom triggered a nod of acceptance from the stern-faced samurai standing at the entrance of the dojo main floor. He motioned Hideki to the left side of the dojo toward the rear. It was the place of inexperience. Hideki did not take offense. Masterless samurai who showed up unannounced were not particularly welcomed in most dojos. The dojo's reputation was put on the line each time a ronin issued a challenge. The challenger had nothing to lose, except maybe his life. The dojo, on the other hand, had everything to lose if the challenger beat the students and ultimately the master. With the win, the challenger's reputation would grow, but the dojo's fortunes would decline. Who would want to send their young samurai to a school that was defeated by a ronin?

Hideki took his spot and kneeled, sitting back on his

ankles in the formal sazen position. A man of some authority moved to the right front of the room and called, "kyotsuke." Approximately twenty students took up position in order of their seniority, from right to left facing both the man and the small raised area of honor at the head of the dojo.

"Sempai," Hideki thought. Sempais ran the dojo for the master, usually doing the warm-up exercises and monotonous repetition of the basic drills. The master might not appear in the dojo every day. "I hope Hamada sensei shows up," Hideki said to himself.

The sempai warmed up the class and was working on basic overhead strikes when the sempai called out, "kyotsuke" again. All stopped what they were doing, coming to a position of attention, wooden bokken in their left hands, points trailing away from the front of the class. When the command, "Re" came, all bowed.

Hideki bowed from his sitting position as an old-gray-haired man in formal kamashino attire entered the dojo and slowly moved to the raised portion at the front. He stepped up onto the raised portion without bowing and sat cross-legged leaning slightly to the right onto an armrest. He nodded his head slightly to acknowledge the students' bow. "Hajime" came the sempai's command and the students resumed the overhead striking drills. The old man turned his head from right to left, taking in everything within his domain. His eyes stopped on Hideki.

"See anything you like?"

Hideki turned to see a large, well-built young man a few years older than himself in a brown kimono and hakama with a lighter brown jacket. Hideki looked at his face, and then his eyes went to the mon on his lapels.

"The Matsukara clan I think? Are you a student here?" Hideki asked, noting the five-sided Chinese flower designs.

"I have been for some time. Are you here for a challenge?" the man asked pleasantly.

"I have had a good breakfast this morning. I thought I might stretch my luck," Hideki replied.

"They have some good swordsman here. It could end badly," the man warned.

"That is always a possibility," Hideki admitted.

"What style do you practice?" the man continued.

"I really do not have a true style," Hideki said, surprising himself. "I have studied with some fine teachers. I hope a little of all of them rubbed off."

"That is a pity. I think it is better to have a sensei who you can be loyal to and have a style you strive to master. If you spread yourself thin, your expertise will be thin," the man said. "I am Saito," the man said, bowing slightly from his standing position.

Hideki nodded his head as well. "Hideki desu."

"Well Hideki, are you ready to challenge?" Saito asked.

"Yes, but I do not want to disturb the class or disrespect the master."

Saito smiled. "Manners and ambition are an unusual combination in a ronin these days. But do not worry, I have some influence," he said, raising his hand toward the master.

The master at the head of the class also raised his hand and all practicing activity ceased.

"We have a challenge?" The master asked in a frail voice.

"Hai, sensei, this is Hideki and he would like to challenge the Suio style," Saito said.

"No family name?" the master asked.

"I take it he is a ronin and obscures his family name for a reason."

"No matter, this dojo does not stand on ceremony. We welcome all challenges. It is the only true way for a system to grow."

Saito motioned for Hideki to go forward and meet the master. Hideki looked uncertain. Saito motioned again. Hideki complied by standing, bowing, and moving forward to the raised platform and bowing again.

"So what have you learned from your observations of our little school?" the master asked.

"Hamada sensei, I am too inexperienced to pass judgment on such a noble school," Hideki said bowing again.

The sempai on the main floor stepped forward. "Sensei, he is just a youth. Let one of us beat some sense into him and throw him back into the street where he belongs." This was met with a chorus of agreement from the students.

Saito looked at Hideki, then back at his master and waited.

"You see it, don't you?" The master asked Saito.

"Yes master," Saito responded, "I see it."

"Good! Then you are the only one who has a chance against him. Do you accept?" The old man asked.

"I do hereby accept this challenge on behalf of the Suio style," Saito said. All the students moved off the floor and sat down.

"Hideki, is your right hand strong enough for this?" the master inquired.

Hideki glanced down at his partially leather clad right hand and the red stain across his exposed fingertips caused partially by the fire and partially from Yoshi's mother-in-law's potions. "I guess we will find out, sensei."

The master nodded, all sense of honor and propriety met.

Both Hideki and Saito moved to the back wall and selected practice weapons. Saito selected a standard bokken with his name below it. Hideki also selected a standard bokken from one of the many columns without names. Then he picked out a wooden sword of approximate length of a wakazashi. Selecting the second short sword caused some murmuring among the students. The two opponents stepped to the center of the floor facing each other about five paces apart and bowed.

Saito moved his bokken into a two-handed grip with his right shoulder forward, stepping back with left leg. Hideki stood in a neutral stance with his feet shoulder-width apart and the tips of both blades pointing at the floor. The distance between the two opponents was too far for either man to strike the other, but Hideki remembered what Jubei said about the lunge, and suddenly the distance did not seem far enough.

Hideki's mouth tasted like a copper coin. "So, this is what fear tastes like?" he thought. "Will I have enough strength to survive? Will my right hand react well? Is there enough will in my left hand to wield the bokken correctly? Will I remember my technique?" A hundred doubts flashed through his mind. Then Hideki saw recognition in Saito's eyes. "He sees my fear," Hideki realized.

Saito dropped his sword point low and leaned forward toward Hideki. His head is almost as far forward as his sword tip.

"I will not fall for that," Hideki said to himself. "If I go for the overhead to compensate for your low tip, you lunge under me while my hands are raised. Thank you, Jubei," Hideki muttered under his breath, giving credit to his most recent mentor.

When Hideki did not take the bait, Saito exploded from his crouch. The tip of Saito's wooden blade flew towards Hideki's throat.

Hideki knew he is in trouble. He had not thought a man could cover distance so quickly. The tip of Saito's blade was upon him before he could reacted with his short sword. There was no time to react. There was no time to pivot. If he wanted to keep his throat from being pierced by the tip of Saito's sword, he could do but one thing.

Hideki brought the flat of the blade of his wakazashi vertical in front of his face and took the concussive blow on the short sword instead of his throat. With Saito's full body behind it, the strike was powerful. Hideki's fist grasping the short sword is slammed into his chest while the flat of the blade mashed into his chin, splitting the skin and knocking him off his feet. The next thing Hideki saw was his feet above his head as his shoulders struck the floor behind him. He had enough presence of mind to remain in a ball, hit, and rolled backwards into a new standing position, both swords in front of him. He is fixed on his opponent and is barely aware of the warm liquid oozing down his lower jaw and neck.

The Suio students cheered their hero. But Hideki had room for only one voice in his head. "There are always stronger fighters and more skillful swordsmen. Do not compete with their strengths. Make use of their weakness. Use mushin! Flow with your opponent. React to the point that you know where he will move before he does."

Hideki slowed his breathing and ignored the blood dripping from his chin. There are only his swords, Saito, and Musashi in his head.

Saito lunged again. The distance he covered was incredible, but it was in slow motion to Hideki this time. He maintained his neutral position and brought the short sword up neck high and deflected Saito's blade a hand's width off center and to his right.

Saito stopped the penetration immediately, and with a flick of his wrists redirected the tip of his blade up and around Hideki's head to culminate in a slicing motion into the neck area on Hideki's left side. Hideki kept the short sword at neck height and moved it over to the left to parry the strike simultaneously rotating his left shoulder forward, with the tip of his long sword arching up and into the soft tissue of Saito's throat.

Saito dropped to the floor clutching his throat, the bokken forgotten as it clattered to the hardwood floor. Suio students jumped up and surrounded their fallen hero. Saito coughed and attempted to suck air into his damaged wind pipe. Several students started toward Hideki, who assumed a neutral stance with both tips down.

"Matte," came a sharp command from the head of the dojo. Everyone looked to the master. The old man waved Hideki over.

Hideki felt the waves of hatred as he circled the students and moved toward the master. Hamada sensei pointed to a woven cloth mat on the raised portion of the dojo next to him. Hideki bowed and sat. The master kept watch on Saito's recovery. He then waved Saito to join them. Once Saito was seated, the students all sat around the raised portion so they can hear and learn.

"Very impressive, Hideki. Where did you learn to blunt a thrust with the sword blade?" the master asks.

Hideki thought a minute. "I do not believe anyone taught me that maneuver, master. Saito came at me so fast, it was the only thing I could think to do."

The master smiled. "I do not believe thought had anything to do with it, young man."

Saito tried his voice for the first time. It worked but was raspy. "What do you mean, master?"

The old man reached into his kimono and withdrew a dark brown cloth. "You will want to staunch that split. The chin bleeds profusely, even from small wounds."

Hideki bowed his thanks and clapped the cloth on his chin.

"You are an instinctive fighter, Hideki. I have only seen one or two in my lifetime." Then turning to his apprentice, "What did you think, Saito?"" the master asked.

Saito cleared his throat several times before he spoke. "I think if they were live blades, Hideki would still be bleeding from his chin and I'd be dead." This caused murmuring from the students just below. The master raised his hand to stop them.

"What Saito-san says is true. The challenger won the match. Hideki defeated the best we had. His skills are superior."

Hideki bowed low from his seated position. "Domo arigato, master, but I feel I do not deserve such praise. I am sure on another day, Saito could best me."

"Then you do not know your own capabilities. Saito could not defeat you. I could not defeat you in my prime. Why is that, Saito?" the master asked his disciple.

Saito looked at Hideki. "As the master said, you are an instinctive fighter. The lunge is the secret of the Suio style. We practice in the bay to build up strength in our legs to cover great distances. I caught you unaware the first time, but you had the ability to protect your throat with the flat blade of your short sword and to roll away from me to regain proper mai. Once you had the proper distance everything changed. I felt I was then at a loss. You seemed to know my next move before I made it. I can only assume you used mushin."

There was again murmuring from the students on the use of the ultimate samurai mental state.

Hideki chose to ignore the reference to mushin where all is physical reaction with no conscious thought. "What did you mean when the master asked if 'you saw it' earlier?"

Saito looked at his master. "Master Hamada was commenting on your favorable aura. You exude confidence but are humble at the same time. You do not swagger, and you are polite. You are on a musha shugyo, the mark of a student. I would mark you as high born, but travel as a ronin. That is either the mark of a superior swordsman or a fool. I did not figure you as a fool. You and your body appear to be one with the world," Saito said.

Hideki held up his right hand. "I used to be; now I am trying to come back from this injury."

"A fire, I think," Hamada said.

"Yes, master; perpetrated by a very evil ninja woman trying to kill me," Hideki said.

"Why would a ninja try to kill a ronin?" Saito asked.

"I kept getting in her way," Hideki explained.

"Do not pry too far into Hideki's background, Saito. He will tell you if and when he wants to."

"Hai, master," Saito said bowing to Hideki. "Go men."

Before Hideki could respond, the master saved him further embarrassment. "I am curious Hideki; I have seen only one other man fight with two swords. Did someone teach you this?" the master asked.

Hideki paused for a moment. "I had the pleasure and the privilege to be trained by and fight beside the greatest samurai of our era, Myamoto Musashi," Hideki stated.

Hamada slapped his thighs in laughter. "I thought so. Musashi-san is always an honored guest here. You may consider yourself one as well."

Hideki bowed deeply. "Domo arigato, master Hamada."

"Saito, you must take our guest to town and show him the sights. He has done you a great service today," Hamada said.

"What service?" Hideki asked.

Saito rubbed his throat. "Mushin," Saito said. "I had never seen it before or even believed it existed. Now I know better."

XIII

Nagasaki

Hideki and Saito walked toward the center of town. The further east they moved, the heavier the traffic became. It was midafternoon, and Hideki's stomach was grumbling again. The sun reflected off the compacted roadway that split the city and ran along the south rim of the bay. Saito kept rubbing his throat and occasionally grunting as if clearing the airway.

"I have never seen a town laid out in such a narrow fashion," Hideki said as they moved in the center of the dirt road.

"Geography demands it," Saito said. "The mountains in the north and the bay on the south restrict normal growth."

As they moved closer to Deshima Point the chaotic ballet of stevedores and merchants and government inspectors and those jostling for work intensified. Hideki had his head on a swivel trying to keep out of the way of fast-moving handcarts stacked precariously with heavy loads while trying to disengage himself from all manner of aggressive multi-gender and multi-aged sales persons hawking wares that ranged from children's toys to garish kimono cloth.

"Is it always this crazy?" Hideki shouted to be heard.

"No," Saito shouted back against the din of the squeaking wheels, loads striking wooden decks, animals braying, elephants trumpeting, and straw bosses cussing laborers to higher effort. "It quiets down when the Portuguese leave."

Hideki was amazed at the undress of most workers. Few had clothes. The threadbare and ripped kimonos he did see were few and far between compared to the majority wearing only fundoshi. Even footwear was unusual. Dirt mixed with blood and sweat hung like a wet blanket over central Nagasaki.

"This may be the way of the future, but it looks like the pursuit of profit and prosperity isn't enjoyed by the laborer," Hideki said.

Hideki stopped to watch a pathetic, dirty, old man with an obvious broken arm in rags beseeching passersby for a hand-out.

"If I had a coin, I would give it to him," Hideki said.

"It is just as well you do not," Saito said.

"Why? Is compassion outlawed in Nagasaki?" Hideki asked.

"No, but begging is. And so is giving to beggars," Saito said.

Saito grabbed Hideki by the arm and moved him a few steps away as a group of scruffy militia men surrounded the beggar.

"What will happen to him?" Hideki asked.

"The same thing that would have happened to you if you had given him aid. You would be arrested and fined," Saito said.

How does fining a beggar make any sense? He has less than I," Hideki said.

"If he cannot pay, he will work off his sentence on one of the ships," Saito said.

"But he is obviously crippled," Hideki said.

"They will find something for him to do," Saito said. "Come, I cannot afford any trouble with the governor."

"Doesn't the injustice bother you?" Hideki asked.

"Sure, but the world is full of injustice. I choose to accept what I cannot change and fight for what I can," Saito said.

Hideki thought about his friend's words. "That was very wise of you Saito-san. You will go far."

"Right now, I'd settle for some food and drink. That is as far as I want to go," Saito said.

They had taken no more than three steps when they were stopped in their tracks again. Hideki stared with his mouth open as a procession of big-nosed foreigners moved from

Deshima toward the warehouses. They were donned in the strangest clothing he had ever seen.

"Quite startling at first, is it not?" Saito asked.

Hideki was speechless for a few moments. "Are they Portuguese?" He finally managed.

"Yes. See the colorful chap in front with the billowing pants tucked into the light silk stockings?"

"Any of them would be hard to miss, but him above all. I have never seen such a display of color except on a young girl's kimono," Hideki judged. "And the tight-fitting coats would look more appropriate on a woman." Hideki was rushing his words because he had so many new things to comment on and ask about. "They are darker than we are. I assumed they would all be white as they are in the wood block prints."

"They tend to be darker than we, but some are very dark."

"You do not mean that fearsome monster holding the huge shade awning for the leader, do you?" Hideki asked.

"No, I believe he is a slave from the Africas or some such place," Saito said.

"He wears the same color pieces as the others. On them it just looks ridiculous, as if their heads were blooming from a chrysanthemum. On the black one, that looks like a chrysanthemum gave birth to a devil. He is very fierce looking with those scars on his face." Hideki said.

"Yes, I would hate to have to fight him, and I have no idea of his skills. He just looks savage," Saito agreed.

"So, who is under the awning, anyone important?" Hideki asked.

"I think you are looking at Dom Joao Pereira, the Feitor and Controller and Procurator of Far East Trade for the Portuguese government, and behind him Augustine Lobo, called the Wolf. Stay away from him. He is very skilled and is the king of the Pit. They are probably here to negotiate prices for the arrival of the Black Ship at New Year's."

As the crowds swirled around them, each person focused on his or her own goal, Hideki noticed something else. "There are as many children working the dock as adults. Why?"

"Knowing Bad Heizo as I do, I would guess cheaper labor

has a lot to do with it. You do not think our illustrious governor would enact any laws protecting the weak, do you? He especially would not if he thought he could exploit that group as cheap labor," Saito said.

Hideki noticed long lines of men standing beside the ubiquitous employment agency. "Are they waiting for work?"

"Most assuredly so, but I do not think they will find any work this late in the day," Saito said.

"There are three times as many waiting as there are working," Hideki said.

"Yes, it is like this every day. It is worse when we have no foreign ships in port."

"Most appear to be farmers, but some are samurai," Hideki said.

"Unfortunate for sure, but a daily occurrence with the Tokugawa disbanding clans; the samurai must go somewhere to make money and find food," Saito said.

"This city is very troubling to me," Hideki said. "I try to live my life by the tenets of bushido. Bushido does not seem to have a place here."

The pair commenced their trek to the Jaded Princess when a loud, head-piercing wail made Hideki jump back and reach for both swords. "By the Buddha," he exclaimed. "What demon is this?"

"Relax, Hideki. These are elephants and wild beasts from the Africas and other corners of the earth. They are meant for the shogun. The Portuguese are attempting to buy an audience," Saito said.

Hideki released his swords amid smiles from passersby used to the noise. They had to wait as the elephants marched single file across the road, trunk to tail followed by oxen-drawn wagons with lions and tigers and huge bears in cages.

"What would happen if one of those large beasts escaped?" Hideki asked.

"Nothing good," Saito opined.

Hideki could not hide his curiosity. "Can we go see the collection of these strange animals for the shogun?" he asked.

"Sure, they are kept in a large warehouse and a clearing behind the customs building," Saito said.

The warehouse was a huge, red-tile roof supported by large, round, wooden beams. There were no walls. The rolling cages for the predators were moved under the roof, disconnected from the oxen and staged in single file along one side. The elephants were taken to the back of the compound where pools of fresh water awaited their bathing pleasure. The other grazing animals were led to separate pens beside the elephants where seed and grass and various food and water awaited them. It was a well-coordinated dance with everyone doing his job. The only ones out of place were the two samurai.

"This is part of the customs house gentlemen. You must leave at once," a young doshin with a jutte tucked into his belt announced.

The two samurai turned toward the speaker.

"Oh, it is you, Saito-sama. I'm sure the governor would allow you access," the doshin said.

"Thank you," Saito said bowing slightly. The doshin returned the bow much lower.

"What has happened to the large tiger in cage number one?" Saito asked. All three turned to look at the cage in question. In the other four tiger cages, the big cats were pacing back and forth watching everyone. In the number one cage, the cat was lying on its side and panting in the heat. Several foreign men wearing highly wrapped cloth on their heads conferred in a language Hideki did not understand.

Happy to be of service to important men, the doshin responded, "He has been that way all day. He was all right yesterday, but this morning they were afraid for him. You cannot understand anything the rag-heads say, but the director of the facility told me to keep everyone away. He is very sick. They don't expect him to live."

"What do you do with a dead tiger?" Hideki asked.

"Bury him in the garden, I suspect," Saito said.

"Well, they are magnificent animals. I'm not sure what the shogun will do with them," Hideki said.

"I do not think he will accept them," Saito said.

"Why not?" Hideki asked.

"I believe the days of the Portuguese are numbered. The Tokugawa have a reputation for crushing any sign of resistance to their rule. How do you think they feel about seventy percent of Kyushu being Kirishitan?" Saito asked.

"Yes, I see what you mean. But the Kirishitans I have met seem like normal people."

"Yes, most are. But if you were shogun and had a choice of the Portuguese or the Dutch, both could provide the same services and the Portuguese came with a religious component that could possibly threaten your rule, who would you choose?" Saito asked. "Besides, they have already expelled the missionaries. It is only a matter of time until they expel all Portuguese as well."

"How will that affect Nagasaki?" Hideki asked.

"Unknown. It will be that period of adjustment," Saito said.

The Portuguese entourage moved to the clearing where the foreign men who cared for the animals bowed and made signs with their palms together.

"While the colors are interesting, how can a man make such a display of himself? And those tight-fitting things on their legs are almost obscene," Hideki said.

"True," Saito agreed. "But I would not mention that to them. They seem to have a quick temper."

"The swords seem serious enough. They wear two swords like samurai?" Hideki asked.

"The little one at their back is called a dirk or main gauche and they fight with both at the same time. I have watched them in the Pit. They can be quite good. I think the two swords would be bothersome for a while, but I believe their fighting system inferior to ours. They like to make much of their footwork, changing swords strikes and making quick thrusts. The Japanese style is to deal the most serious blow with the least number of strikes," Saito explained.

"What is the Pit?" Hideki asked.

"If you stay here long, you will visit it. It is a Portuguese form of entertainment and gives you a peek into their dark souls."

"I judge from your distaste you do not approve of this Pit," Hideki said.

"You have to realize that the Portuguese look down on us. They see us as barbarians," Saito started. "Our women are good enough to bed, but not to marry. Our clothing is good enough for trade but not for wearing. Our ships cannot compete with theirs and their cannon outrange ours by ri. Even our martial arts are inferior to the West's and they try to prove it in the Pit."

"So, the Pit is a like a Dojo challenge?" Hideki asked.

"In a way. But dojo challenges are often fought with wooden swords. The Pit is always fought with live blades and ends with death."

"Dojo challenges can end in death," Hideki said.

"You are correct. But the whole premise of the Pit sits wrong with me. First, the Japanese that participate are not the best swordsmen the nation has to offer. They are starving ronin like you saw in line today who are given a chance to gain a spot on Heizo's militia. Nothing motivates like hunger or the empty belly of your child."

"Challenging to obtain a position is a time-tested method for samurai," Hideki suggested.

"True, Hideki, but none have obtained a position."

"You mean the governor has no intention of advancing the winner?" Hideki asked.

"No, I mean no samurai has ever won," Saito said.

Hideki was stunned. "How can that be?" Hideki asked. "Surely the Portuguese swordsmanship cannot be superior."

"The Pit was constructed by Heizo and his Portuguese partner Dom Joao to demonstrate western martial skills to Japan. They are very proud of their Destreza style of sword fighting. But the Pit has deteriorated into a charnel house for samurai. There are five foreign swordsmen who compete in the Pit and no Japanese has ever survived against them," Saito said.

"How many have tried?" Hideki asked.

"Almost one hundred."

"Why have one hundred died? Is Destreza that good?"

"It is deadly," Saito opined. "But it is pride that kills our ronin."

"Pride can kill?" Hideki inquired.

"It can if you enter the pit thinking your skills superior to the Portuguese, spending little time studying them. They realize their mistake when the main gauche is embedded in their belly."

"What is a main gouche?" Hideki asked.

"It is the deadly dagger they all wear in their belts in the back. You never see it until it is too late," Saito said.

Hideki did the math in his head. "That means each one has defeated over twenty samurai. By anyone's standards, that is impressive. Their technique must be very good."

"Good enough that they are bragging far and wide that their Destreza is superior to our Kenjitsu," Saito said.

"How long is that main gauche?" Hideki asked.

"Oh Hideki, you have sharp eyes," Saito praised. "The main gauche is shorter than your wakazashi by almost a hands width. Therein lies an advantage of Kenjitsu."

"You are obviously a student of this Destreza. What do you think of it?" Hideki asked.

"I think it is deadly. The Pit is designed for Destreza. Any samurai entering the Pit is already at a disadvantage."

"How so?"

"The Pit is a sunken circle in one of the warehouses. The floor is dirt and the walls are reinforced with wooden boards. On the dirt floor there are four white chalk concentric circles starting in the center and moving outward," Saito explained.

"Why circles?"

"Destreza is a form of fighting using both rapier and main gauche where the opponents move along circular paths to get to each other. The rapier could cut skin if slashed, but it is mainly a thrusting weapon. By moving in circles, the opponent is deceived as to the distance between them."

"You lose track of mai," Hideki ventured.

"Exactly. The rapier deflects the katana and sets up the main gauche for the thrust to the body that kills," Saito said. "Kenjitsu is taught in a linear fashion. We move in and out and side to side. You and Musashi have elevated that to a fine science by moving diagonally as well. But we do not practice against a circling attack. That is why all the ronin in the pit receive multiple cuts on arms, shoulders and legs before the death blows are dealt."

"They play with the ronin before they kill them?"

"Yes."

"Now I see why you are against the Pit," Hideki said. "I have to assume some of the departed were skilled swordsmen."

"That would be a good assumption. They were playing in a game they did not understand," Saito said. "But since I have seen you and Musashi fight, I am left wondering how your two-sword style would fair against Destreza."

Hideki shook his head. "I do not know. As you know, ninety per cent of the fight is in the fighter and not the style. What are the Portuguese like?"

Saito could not hide his distaste. "They have no honor. Winning is everything to them. And if you should ever face the one known as Lobo, be very careful. He likes killing," Saito warned.

"Everyone likes to win," Hideki said.

"You are not listening. He likes the killing. Destreza is his tool. If farming could kill, he'd be a farmer."

"You are telling me he is a killer first?" Hideki said in a question.

"Exactly."

"Thank you for the warning. I shall endeavor not to meet him in the Pit or anywhere else," Hideki said.

"With your sword skills, I think he will seek you out," Saito warned. Then changing the subject, "Are you ready for food and drink now?"

"Oh yes. I have many questions, but food first. I have not eaten since breakfast and that was long ago," Hideki said, rubbing his stomach.

XIV

Yasuke the Flute Maker

"Yasuke? Is that you?" Hideki asked of Midori's apprentice. Yasuke bowed deeply behind his makeshift table laden with all manner of flutes.

"Yes, samurai-sama. I am pleased to see you again," Yasuke said.

"Are you an artisan as well as an apprentice cook?" Hideki asked.

"Yes sir. I used to make these flutes at the Buddhist temple where I lived."

"And the priests there taught you how to write?" Hideki asked.

Yasuke looked at his small sign that he had constructed on a board that said "Flutes" in kanji lettering. Hideki turned towards Saito and winked. Saito nodded and said, "I can read it."

Yasuke looked a little embarrassed. "I was not a very good student," he said. "But I would give anything to see my old teachers again and Chiyo."

"Who is Chiyo?"

"She is the girl I grew up with. We were to be married," Yasuke said with sad eyes. "At least that is what she told me."

"You have no idea what happened to them?" Hideki asked.

"No samurai-sama. As soon as the dirty priests showed up, my Masters and Chiyo's family disappeared. I just know something bad happened to them."

Hideki looked at Saito, a question in his eyes. "That would be the new Shinto priests that are friends of the governor," Saito said.

"And you say our governor has recently converted to Shinto?"

135

"Yes, he participated in fumie earlier this year by trampling on a picture of the hanging Christ," Saito said. "Shortly thereafter he started wearing Shinto robes and announced he had been made a priest in the Shinto religion."

"Did that raise any eyebrows?" Hideki asked.

"We thought it odd. There are no Shinto priests in Nagasaki. How did he get appointed a priest?" Saito asked.

"But then the Yamabushi showed up and you thought it was part of some Shinto ritual?" Hideki asked.

"Exactly," Saito said.

"So, it appears the governor controls his militia, the police in the city, and a band of renegade Shinto priests," Hideki said.

"It would appear so," Saito said.

Hideki turned his attention back to the flutes. "These are well made and sturdy," he praised. "Unfortunately, I seldom have need for a flute. But I always have need for information. Maybe you could answer some of my questions and if I ever have any money I will pay it to you," Hideki suggested.

"Do you have any questions now, samurai-sama?" Yasuke asked.

"No, nor do I have any money. I am here to see the proprietress about a job as a yojimbo. It seems she needs a bodyguard. Do you know anything about that?" Hideki asked.

"I know she has many holdings throughout the city and is considered a shrewd businesswoman. I know she is married to the Portuguese they call Dom Joao. But he is seldom here. I know she spends her mornings at her warehouses but afternoons and evenings here at the Jaded Princess," Yasuke said, using his thumb over his shoulder to point out the inn. "And I know her staff are loyal to her and that she has been good to me, allowing me to sleep in the back with the chickens and sell some of my flutes in front of her inn. She hasn't even asked for a percentage. But I'm going to give her one anyway."

"Well thanks for that information. It may be helpful. But if I am ever to pay you, I must go inside and get that job. We will talk later," Hideki said, and both he and Saito started toward the Jade Princess entrance.

"Make way for the new magistrate," a loud voice proclaimed.

Hideki and Saito turned toward the noise.

"It must be the new Tokugawa magistrate," Saito said.

Hideki counted six policemen accompanying him, not including the one leading the magistrate's horse and moving people back with his voice. Hideki studied the new magistrate. He was attired in indigo with no mon showing anywhere.

"Our new Bugyo refuses to recognize his clan. What do you make of that?" Saito asked.

"I am not sure. It could be he wants to see what support he gets from the citizens before he advertises his clan connections," Hideki said.

"Maybe, but my guess is that it would be the three-leafed hollyhock," Saito said.

"You mean the house of the shogun?" Hideki asked.

"Think about it. It makes sense. If he is directly from the shogun's family he could not very well wear the symbol of the Tokugawa without having everyone bow to it," Saito explained. "I told you the Tokugawa were going to get interested in Nagasaki soon."

"Yes, you did. But I have a feeling he has a clan mon and it is not the Tokugawa," Hideki said.

The group with the magistrate stopped in front of Yasuke's table. "What is this? Do you have a permit to sell here?" the doshin in charge asked.

"Miss Aya lets me set up here," Yasuke muttered.

"Miss Aya is one of the troublemakers in this area," the doshin said to the magistrate. "You wanted to see the city, you can see what we are faced with. This street urchin has no permit and is working for a known brothel owner. She is probably behind on her taxes too. This is as good a time as any to show you how we work," the doshin stated. "You men there, destroy this table and arrest the ruffian, but teach him a lesson first."

One of the jutte-carrying police seized Yasuke and the other backhanded him with his jutte across the mouth. Yasuke screamed and dropped to the sand holding his bloody mouth. A third moved to destroy the table.

"Just a moment please. I was about to buy one of those flutes," Hideki said.

Saito looked at Hideki like he was crazy. "Do not get

involved. You don't know how things work here. It can only go badly."

Hideki answered Saito but was talking loudly enough for the magistrate to hear. "I would like to forget the whole thing and get something to eat, but my grandfather raised us on a saying: *no wrong too small to right; no right too small to defend.* And this is wrong. Bushido demands the protection of the innocent."

"If you interfere we will arrest you," the doshin warned.

"You will try, Mr. Policeman. But you will not succeed. Instead you and your men will receive welts, bruises, and lumps and will be humiliated in front of your new boss. Why not escape the pain and take your bullying act somewhere else?" Hideki asked.

The doshin looked at his three men by the table and his two behind. They were all paid ruffians, used to the rough life on the waterfront. "Big talk for a ronin with a crippled hand and a backwards sword," the doshin managed." Then to his men, "Forget the boy. Arrest *him*," he cried, pointing his jutte directly at Hideki.

Saito backed away from Hideki. "I can have no part in this," he said. "I am sorry."

Hideki moved to the table and selected two shaku hachi flutes made of hardwood. The two men holding Yasuke dropped their prisoner and rushed Hideki with their juttes drawn. One was just a step ahead of the other. He swung his jutte from the shoulder, attempting to hit Hideki by the ear. The blow never landed.

Hideki met the blow. He struck the hand holding the weapon directly across the thumb with the flute. The policeman screamed and dropped the jutte. Hideki continued to strike him in the throat all in one motion. The screaming stopped as he tried to suck air through his damaged windpipe.

His partner aimed a blow to the top of Hideki's head. This Hideki deflected by bringing up the flute in his right hand. As the attacking weapon slid by his shoulder, Hideki used the side of the flute, striking the nose. The attacker's downward momentum supplied the power to the counter. He went down in a gush of red holding his battered nose.

The remaining three charged as one. Hideki moved to the outside of the man on the end. The other two were now impeded by their comrade. This one tried to lunge at Hideki's throat. Hideki parried outside with the flute in his left hand, bringing the right flute up with a quick snap to the attacker's ear. He dropped to the sand with a burst eardrum.

Hideki gave a quick look to the magistrate. He had not moved from the saddle. The remaining two opponents separated and attempted to flank Hideki. Hideki let them set up. They nodded to each other and stepped in at the same time aiming blows to the side of Hideki's head. Hideki looked straight ahead keeping track of the opponents in his peripheral vision. As their momentum brought them close to him, he dropped to one knee as the juttes clanged together above his head and struck each in the groin with a flute. Their hands went to their groins as they doubled over. Hideki took his time rising, walked over and placed the flute on each forehead and pushed them over onto their backs. Next, Hideki lunged toward the doshin holding the magistrate's horse and struck him along the jaw line. The Doshin dropped to the dirt street. Hideki looked up to the magistrate on horseback. The magistrate was looking past Hideki to the crowd that had formed.

Aya walked forward. "What is the meaning of this?" she asked.

"I am the new magistrate. I do not know the police force, nor do I know the city. The doshin here was showing me how things are done in Nagasaki. The demonstration was most educational."

"You have no right to interfere here. All of our permits are in order. And the boy has my permission to sell his wares here. His inventory is covered by my permits. This could all have been avoided if you had asked," Aya said.

"I could not agree with you more madam. I'm sorry for troubling you and your patrons." Turning to Hideki the magistrate asked, "You do know that you could be placed in prison for striking a policeman. What is this boy to you?"

Hideki looked at Yasuke, who had risen from the dirt and was dusting off his knees. "Why we have been friends for almost a day. He helped cook my breakfast, and I am hoping to eat some of his noodles this evening."

"That is it? You would risk prison over a cook? How is that possible?" The magistrate asked.

Hideki tossed the two flutes onto the table. "He is an innocent citizen of your city. You are samurai. You have sworn to follow bushido. How is it you would not risk it?"

The magistrate smiled and nodded his head. "I see. We can count one bushi among our citizenry. How would you like a job?"

"Doing what?" Hideki asked.

"I'm going to need a deputy. I need someone who can handle himself and someone I can trust."

"But you do not know me," Hideki said.

The magistrate pointed to his five policemen sitting in the street. "I can see that you can take care of yourself, and anyone who believes in bushido the way you do can be trusted."

Hideki looked towards the Jaded Princes and saw Midori. Then his gaze when to Aya. "I believe I have a job offer already. If it does not come to fruition, I may look you up."

The magistrate nodded. "Do that. I will be at the jail," he said as he turned his horse and walked back toward the center of town.

One by one, the policemen stood and staggered after him. Hideki moved to Aya. "Midori tells me we have business to discuss."

Aya did not smile. She just gestured toward the Jaded Princess and moved to the door. Hideki followed.

Hideki stepped inside the darkness and moved one step to the right, waiting till his eyes adjusted. Yoshi had taught him that trick. When he could finally see, he moved to the table adjacent to the bar where Aya sat. He took a seat that allowed him to watch the door while he tried to keep the large bartender in his peripheral vision. Hideki noticed the large man stayed within striking distance to the back of his head. Hideki felt vulnerable and adjusted his chair.

"I want a bodyguard," Aya said. "I want you."

"Good timing," Hideki replied. "I need to eat."

"I want you to understand that I want your sword exclusively."

A year ago Hideki would have gone into his wounded pride act, feeling hurt that anyone would question his actions as a samurai. The year was a long time. He no longer felt the need to say or do unnecessary things.

"I cannot guarantee that," he said.

Aya pulled back. "What do you mean? If I am paying your wages, I expect you to work for me alone."

Hideki wondered how he could explain bushido to a female merchant.

"When I pledge my sword to your protection it is as if I did so for a samurai lord. I agree to be part of his organization, to bring no shame to his name and to die for him if need be. But I am still samurai; I still live by the code of bushido. I am still bound by its tenets."

"I do not understand," Aya said, but she was interested now.

"Madam," the bartender injected. "He is saying he will protect you and die doing so, if need be, but just because he works for you does not mean he stops living by his code. If while working for you he sees another in danger, he is bound by his code to lend a hand; to protect the weak; to right a wrong."

Hideki turned to stare at the large man. "You were samurai," he said. It was a statement.

"I have been many things, but now I am a bartender who would give his life for this woman. I expect you will do the same."

Hideki turned back to Aya. "To command such loyalty is more recommendation than normal. I will pledge you my sword for two weeks."

Aya frowned. "It may not be enough."

"It will have to be. I am on a musha shugyo, a warrior's pilgrimage. I can give you no more than two weeks."

"Very well, I shall have to conclude my business by then. I wanted it understood that for those two weeks, you will work for no other, even if they pay you more."

Hideki bit his lip and turned toward the bartender.

"Madam, I know you do not realize it, but those words were an insult to his samurai pride. He has given his word. He will not break it," the bartender said.

Aya's fierce countenance softened. "I apologize. It was foolish of me. I will pay you two ryo a day plus room and board."

Hideki nodded, "If that is what you think your life to be worth."

The bartender smiled. "He will not argue over money. It is beneath him. He is bushi."

Aya looked at her trusted lieutenant and bartender. "I take it you approve?"

The bartender nodded in the affirmative.

"Fine, fetch me the boy that works in the kitchen."

The large man moved around the bar and shredded a way among the tables and into the kitchen at the far wall. He returned with Yasuke in tow, holding a cloth across his mouth. Midori trailed behind.

"I did not send for the cook," Aya said to the bartender.

"I asked her to come," Yasuke said, through the cloth.

"How is your wound?" Hideki asked.

Yasuke just nodded his head up and down.

"It split his upper lip on the right side. I have put spider webs in it and given him a light sedative. It stopped the bleeding. He should be fine tomorrow, but he will have a large scar," Midori said.

"A samisen player, a cook, and a doctor. Now you are acting as his lawyer?" Aya asked.

"No Aya. He asked me to come because he was afraid he could not talk with the wound."

"No matter … I understand you are Ryukyuan. Is that correct?" Aya asked.

Yasuke nodded in the affirmative.

"Do you have connections with anyone in the Ryukyuan compound south of the city?"

Again Yasuke nodded.

"I want a meeting with the head man. Can you take me there? Can you arrange it?" Aya asked.

Yasuke turned to Midori and mumbled something. Midori whispered back and then addressed Aya. "He can do it, but he wants me to come as well," she said.

"Why should I want to take a cook?" Aya asked.

"Normally you wouldn't, but he says he won't go without me."

Aya stared at Yasuke. "Is this the thanks I get for giving you a place to sleep, sell your wares, and learn a new trade?"

"No, he is thankful for all that you have done Aya, but we all sense you need something and that you might put him in harm's way. He just wants someone he can trust by his side," Midori explained.

Aya threw up her arms in surrender. "The yojimbo tells me how and when he'll be my bodyguard; the cook tells me where she is going and with whom. What's next?" She stared at the bartender. "Are you going to tell me how to run the Princess?" The bartender turned around as if having an important task to perform behind the bar. "I want to get started first thing tomorrow. Let's meet here after breakfast and start east. Any complaints?" she asked.

There were none.

XV

Ryukyu Sailors

Aya led the way. Hideki walked one step behind and to her right. A year ago, he would've walked on her left, but he was left-handed these days with his katana on his right hip. It would not do to cut your employer with a fast draw technique from the wrong side.

Midori and Yasuke followed behind. Normally he would be concerned about threats from the rear. But the five families did not hire inferior ninja. Midori was skilled, at least from what Myo had said.

Hideki smiled at the thought of his one and only lover. Where was she now? Was she thinking of him as he did her? Probably not, he had to admit. She was older and more experienced. Maybe he did not mean as much to her as she did to him. No, that was not true. She and the little, noodle-cooking, samisen-strumming kunoichi behind him had broken into the Hatchibori jail and freed a Fox Gang member to follow him to the gang's lair to rescue Hideki. Myo had managed this while the entire government was powerless to act. No, Myo loved him. He was sure of that. He just did not know why. But it did not matter, he told himself. He was lucky to have her and would wait until he saw her again, whenever that might be.

Hideki shook his head to clear it. He could not be thinking of Myo when his giri was to protect the woman who was paying for his sword. He knew from experience that being a yojimbo required an unusual set of skills. It was different from being samurai. Giving one's life for an employer was not much different than the duty expected of a vassal to his lord, but the similarities between samurai and yojimbo duties ended there. Most lords could protect themselves. And why not? They learned swordsmanship from the best teachers in the land. Aya was not samurai. She was not gumi either. When he had been a bodyguard for the Gumsumgumi, he had been protecting dangerous men—men who could be relied upon to join the fray and protect themselves. Aya could do neither, at least physically. She was a merchant-class woman. She had no knowledge of weapons or tactics. That made his job harder. He did not know how she would react when danger came. Would she attack? Would she run away? And most importantly, would she listen to him? There were just too many variables right now. She was vulnerable to everything. He would have to force himself to be alert on this job.

"Thinking of someone?" Midori asked. Hideki physically flinched. "Oh, I am sorry to startle you. But you look like a man thinking of better times."

Hideki chose his words carefully. Both Aya and Yasuke were close enough to hear.

"Yes Midori, I was thinking of better times."

Aya changed the subject. "Yasuke, what are these Ryukyu people like?"

Yasuke paused for a moment. "They are like me."

"I know that much already," Aya said. "Tell me something I do not know."

"Madam, from our very brief meeting, I think there are a great many things you do not know. To which one are you referring?"

Aya spun and focused a killing stare at the young flute maker. "Be careful how you talk to me."

Hideki eyed the young man as well and saw no guile. "I believe he is responding with the truth."

"Then be careful of the truth you speak, peasant. You do not want to upset me," Aya threatened.

"No Madam, I do not."

"And you do not want to upset him, or you may not have the introduction you seek," Hideki reminded.

"You would do well to mind your place also, yojimbo. I

146

could buy dozens of men like you on the docks," Aya warned.

"We all know that is not true; otherwise, they would be here and not Hideki," Midori corrected.

"Now I'm being corrected by the cook. Does anyone know their place?"

"Obviously not," Hideki said. "But judging from the surroundings, we need to stay alert."

It was true. As they had traveled south on the main road, the further away from the center of town they walked, the seedier the neighborhood became. There were no grand buildings here. The homes looked like hovels of claptrap boards, tree limbs, and baked mud thrown together in a hodgepodge of creativeness. Everyone looked different and everyone looked bad. But soon even these poor hovels dissipated until there were no buildings at all.

Yasuke began where he'd left off. "Madam, the Ryukyu people are led by a headman named Hachiro."

"Do you know this headman?" Aya asked.

"I do not know him personally, but I believe he knows me," Yasuke said.

"Why would a headman know you, but you not know him?" Aya asked. "You had better not be bragging, boy, or I'll have you flogged."

Yasuke's head went down. "Oh no, madam; I am not bragging. He must have known my parents because it is Hachiro that would visit the temple where I lived and pay for my education. That is what both the head priest and Chiyo said."

"Chiyo? Who is this Chiyo?" Aya asked.

Yasuke beamed. "Chiyo was a young girl my age. Her parents worked in the temple. We grew up together. I was going to marry her before the bad priests came and made my priests and Chiyo's family disappear," Yasuke said, frowning again.

"Do you have any idea what happened to Chiyo's family or the priests?" Midori asked.

Yasuke shook his head. "Whole families have been disappearing. At first, we thought it was the work of the tengu. But he has targeted Kirishitans. Chiyo's family was Buddhist. Most of the families disappearing in the night are Buddhists."

"So, you are going to introduce me to a man you have never met," Aya lamented. "This just keeps getting better and better."

"It was you that asked for his help. If you do not want it anymore, Midori can take him back to the Jaded Princess," Hideki pointed out.

"I am paying you for your sword, not your advice," Aya threatened.

"True, ma'am, but one normally comes with the other."

"I will bear that in mind. You may have a short career as my yojimbo," Aya threatened.

"You need to relax woman," Hideki suggested. "No one here is your enemy."

Aya stopped and turned toward the three, her hands on her hips. Then she took her hands down and let out a long breath. "I have no other way to meet the headman. We will proceed."

As she turned and continued to walk away, Hideki looked at Yasuke. "That is as close to an apology as you are likely to get."

Yasuke bowed slightly to Hideki. "I know. It is fine. She does not mean to be cruel."

Hideki focused on Aya's back as he walked to catch up. "I am not so sure."

Hideki noticed there was almost no foot traffic now. There was an occasional ragged man carrying large hooks with wooden handles that he had seen the stevedores use to unload ships at Deshima Point in the center of town. But other than that, the road was abandoned.

"How much further, boy?" Aya asked.

"The stand of trees up ahead leads down to the Ryukyu quarters," Yasuke answered.

Hideki noticed the path to the right leading toward the ocean. It was partially hidden by the foliage of beautiful fukugi trees. There were trees throughout Nagasaki, but not this close to shore. Most trees were among the hills as one moved away from the city and up to the mountains above. Most of those were crytomeria mixed with white hydrangea sprinkled with Garcinia and sago palms. Hideki wondered if the densely leafed fukugi trees were imported.

The group turned off the main road and moved beneath the trees and into the shadows of the leaves. The only sound Hideki could hear was their feet moving on a sandy track. Try as he might, he could hear no other sounds. The trees must block the light as well as sound, he thought.

Aya broke the silence. "Are we close, boy?"

"If I remember right, and it has been a while since I have been here, it is just at the end of this path."

They all looked to the end and heard waves break. At the same time, they saw the blue of the bay framed in the window at the end of the trees.

They stepped through the opening to the coast and were amazed. Completely cut off from the rest of Nagasaki was a small village of fifty buildings reaching down to the beach. As they walked toward what appeared to be the central building, eyes turned toward them from every direction.

They never made it to the main building. They were met by a group of men. "They look like a gang of Etas," Hideki thought. They were dressed in black kimonos with only undergarments beneath. The white of their fundoshis showed as a thin white line where their kimono top met in front and between their legs. They had tucked the hem of the kimonos into the obi at the small of their backs. This gave them freedom of movement, but also gave them freedom to swing the assortment of oars, boes and nuchakus they had draped over their shoulders. He moved his left hand instinctively to his katana and stepped in front of Aya.

"Nandiga naichagwa?" one of the men asked as they fanned out in front of Hideki. "Ma-ke-ga?"

"Do you understand him Yasuke?" Hideki asked over his shoulder. "His ben is too thick for me to understand."

"Hai, samurai-sama; I understand. He is speaking Hogen, the Ryukyu language. He has called you a not-so-nice name reserved for mainland Japanese and asked where you are going."

Before Hideki could respond, Aya took over. "Tell them we come in peace to discuss matters of business with the head man."

Hideki knew if she were speaking to samurai, such an out-burst by a woman would be ignored at best but probably incite blades being drawn as a sign of disrespect. He started drifting into mushin as Yasuke translated.

It was Midori who interrupted him. "You can relax samurai-sama; it seems they honor women here."

Hideki controlled his breathing and noticed the line of men had parted and they were being pointed toward the Main building once again.

The main building was the only one Hideki could see that displayed permanence. Unlike the thatch roofs surrounding it, the main building had red tile on its roof with a little, red, clay dog perched atop, crouching toward the entrance. The heavy roof was supported by five stout tree trunks shaved of all bark. And unlike the other structures that used woven bamboo leaves for walls, the main building displayed sliding wood-en walls that moved like tokonoma in a Japanese house, but without paper windows to let in light. Hideki noticed that each home was like a self-contained castle, complete with a hinpun or fence in front to provide privacy. But Hideki also noticed the yashiki gakoi made of rock block, shaped coral and stones and bamboo with shrubs growing through it to add stability. It was one hell of a fence surrounding the building.

"If I was defending any of these houses," Hideki muttered under his breath, "the staggered gate and hedges would slow the attacker and channel him into a kill zone of my choosing."

"You said something, samurai-sama?" Midori asked.

"No, just admiring their defensive position," Hideki said.

"Yes, and did you notice the covered pig sty to the left, the human benjo adjacent and the vegetable garden in the rear?" Midori asked.

"I did notice that. These Ryukyu people are self-sufficient. They raise their own chickens and pigs, feed them vegetables and internalize defensive tactics in their house design. I like it," Hideki said.

They were led onto the porch of the main building and given wet towels to wash their hands and feet. Leaving their sandals outside, they were taken into the building and sat opposite three older men. The oldest of the three bowed and said, "Tatsu desu."

Hideki bowed as well, but it was Aya who talked.

"I need a boat large enough to brave the oceans."

"Such an undertaking would require Tokugawa permission. If not, death could be your payment," the old man said to no one at all.

"I am in a hurry and have no need for niceties. Do you have a ship that is seaworthy?" Aya asked.

From out of the shadows came an old woman. She was dressed in a simple black kimono, identical to the men. She moved into the circle between the visitors and old men. She stopped in front of Hideki. "You are of noble blood," she said.

"You are mistaken," Hideki said.

"She is nigan; the root kami; she does not make mistakes," the old one said. "She is our priestess."

When she came close, Hideki noticed small tattoos on the back of her hand. He winced. Despite his time with the Gumsumgumi and being exposed to all manner of irazumi, he still had the Japanese aversion to tattoos.

The priestess noticed. "Do not be alarmed; you are in a safe place. These tattoos protect all here. Did you notice the dog on the roof?" she asked.

"Yes," Midori said. "They are on all the houses facing the entrance. What are they?"

"They represent the male spirit. They must remain outside. Were they to come inside, they would want to dominate, and it would be a danger to all gathered. Inside the home, the female spirit dominates. My brother," she said pointing to the older man, "is the ninshu, the root person. He leads the village, but in all things, he consults me first. The gods talk to me. I ask the gods, get an answer, and we proceed. It is the way of things," she said.

"Well, it makes sense to me," Aya said. "Let me ask you then, priestess. Do you have a boat that is ocean ready and able to deliver cargo to the Sung?"

The priestess moved to Aya and squatted. She studied Aya's face. "Answer her, brother."

The old man responded. "We have smaller boats that are

ocean ready. We hide them in plain sight so no one suspects."

"Good, good," Aya said barely containing her joy. "And can you reach the Sung?"

The old man looked at his sister. She nodded. "Yes, we can reach China, but it is very dangerous. Japanese and Ryukyu vessels are forbidden. If we are caught, it is death, and that is just the trip over. When we return, if the governor gets wind of our journey, he will turn us in to the Tokugawa, and that means death. You cannot sail without a permit, and Heizo has the only ones, but he lends the red seals to the Big Noses.

The priestess gazed upon Yasuke for the first time. "Yasuke, you have returned to us?" she asked.

"I did not know I could," Yasuke said.

"Certainly, it is your home. You were born here. Your parents were well thought of," she said. "We sent you to the temple to become educated." Then she shook her head in disgust. "There is great evil loose on the land. The kami will take revenge for all the slayings and kidnappings."

"Do you know what happened to the priests at the temple," Hideki asked.

"No, but the kami will reveal it to me when they are ready."

"What cargo do you ship and in what quantity?" the old man asked.

"Urushi nuri," Aya responded.

"You will not make enough profit to pay the passage. Every village in China has a lacquer ware specialist."

"Do they have anything like this?" Aya asked as she passed a small sake cup toward the old man.

Hideki noticed the markings as coming from Mei's workshop high on the mountain where he and Jubei confronted the tengu.

The old man studied the intricate gold leaf trapped under the hard-shiny black finish. Then he passed it to the men on either side. He returned it to Aya. "No, I have never seen such work, nor can I guess how it was done. I apologize for my earlier comment. You will make a fortune with this cargo."

"I will send the boy to you with final details of the cargo. I anticipate we will be sailing within the fortnight," she said.

I want you to launch while any onlookers will think you are going out to meet the Portuguese ships at anchor in the bay."

The old man looked at each of his companions and then turned back to Aya. "It will be as you say. We will be ready."

"No one else must know about our arrangements. I have people after me now," Aya said.

"Who wishes you harm?" the priestess asked.

"I have many enemies. A key one is the governor. I am married to the Portuguese Procurator Dom Joao Rodriguez. My husband's company owes Heizo many reals of silver and cannot pay. He is attempting to get an audience with the shogun to forgive the usury that Heizo charges, but the governor has blocked every effort. Heizo is trying to drive the Portuguese out so he can welcome the Dutch in at more favorable terms to himself. When Heizo is displeased with you, everyone from his personal concubines to the constable in the street knows about it and wants to give you a tough time. So, I travel with a yojimbo," Aya said.

The priestess eyed Hideki again. "Ah yes, the noble born bodyguard. You favor a grandfather I believe. You have a sister…no… a lover that is common born. Your right hand is damaged, but you have learned to compensate for it. You use two swords and engender great friendships. You live by the light of bushido. You strive to be a true warrior," she said.

"How … " Hideki stumbled, "do you know these things?"

"Listen Hideki and learn. She is nigan; the root kami, she is entrusted with the village and given second sight to protect it," Midori said. "Do not question it. It is like Yoshi's haragai. She can see through the darkness."

Hideki did not understand but had enough faith in Midori and his friend Yoshi to not ask any more questions.

"Okay, now we go visit the Kirishitan church," Aya said.

XVI

Mei's Wares

On the walk back to the city, Aya was uncharacteristically talk-ative. "Boy, I want you to come with me to our next meeting. You were good luck in the Ryukyu meeting. I believe in luck and in continuing to play a winning hand. Now I'm going to need all the luck I can muster at the next stop if I am to close this deal." Then she stopped and looked at Midori. "I suppose this means we will have the cook's presence as well?"

It took Yasuke a few moments to realize he was being addressed. But Midori answered, "I guess I am relegated his protector for the evening."

"You might be helpful as well. The priestess seems to like you. We will be dealing with women at the Kirishitan church. Maybe you will be useful for their sake as well."

After an hour of walking, they stopped in front of a mar-velous building. "I have never seen such a structure," Hideki said. "Not even the castle in Edo can match its construction. The walls look as if they are racing to the sky."

"Yes, my husband's people know how to build churches. Now if they could only live the principles that are espoused here."

Hideki looked at her. "Are you not Kirishitan?"

"Oh yes, it was a requirement my husband made before our marriage. But that does not mean that I believe the concepts. I find that people call upon the gods when they are in trouble or hurt. The Kirishitans are no better than the Buddhist monks who are pious in public then slip into my gambling hall after hours. We all have three faces: a public face, a private face, and a secret face. The one we show depends on our circumstances. The Kirishitans are pious one day a week then turn into cutthroat businessmen and whoremongers the other six. No yojimbo, my life has taught me that religion is a tool to be used by ambitious men to create wealth and deceive the masses, nothing more."

Hideki marveled at the polished, white stone walls. The entrance was immense to carry the weight of the massive wooden doors that would fit the grandest Edo's mansion main gate.

As he moved to the entrance, Hideki took the lead position and put his right hand on his short sword. One of the first lessons Musashi had taught him was awareness of the surroundings. Drawing the longsword indoors could be a recipe for disaster.

He stepped from the light of the street into the darkness of the building and moved immediately to the right, so his back was against the inside wall. It was habit now.

"It is all right Hideki. Only friends here," a voice from the shadows of the huge church said.

"Jubei?" Hideki mouthed and released his grip on the short sword. "Where have you been?"

"He has been protecting us," Momo said. "And doing an excellent job of it I might add."

"Yes, samurai-sama, Jubei-sama has protected us with his life," Mei stated.

Jubei's one good eye gave nothing away. It was as cold as the metal patch over the opposite eye.

"You had trouble?" Hideki asked.

"He kept the governor's musket men from killing Mei and taking all our lacquer ware," Momo said.

"It was no trouble," Jubei said

"And how did you overcome the muskets?" Hideki asked.

"The same way you overcame the tengu—the yumi," Jubei stated.

Hideki nodded his head in understanding. He had seen his friend Jubei shoot the yumi before. Few men were his equal with the bow and arrow.

"Are you fugitives now?" Hideki asked.

"Unknown," Jubei replied.

"Aya-san," a male voice behind Jubei called. "Welcome home!"

Aya stepped back in front of Hideki and moved to meet the brown-robed man who had spoken.

"Father Sebastian," Aya said to the Japanese Kirishitan priest before her. "Thank you for arranging this meeting." Aya dropped to one knee and genuflected.

"It was nothing my child. Any enterprise that will help two daughters of the church and hurt that excommunicated wretch Heizo is doubly attractive."

The priest turned to Momo. "Momo, this is Aya. Aya, this is Momo and her daughter Mei. Mei is the artisan of the family now. Momo lost her husband to that spawn of Satan, the tengu."

"I am sorry for your loss, both of you. Where are your wares?" Aya asked.

Momo had trouble recovering. It was father Sebastian who answered. "The wares are safe in the barn in back."

"How much did you bring?" Aya asked.

"You are a very direct woman," Momo noted. "We brought our entire stock, all 200 items."

"I apologize, but we must conclude our business quickly. The longer the pieces are here, the greater the likelihood the governor's spies will discover them and we will lose everything," Aya said.

"What do you intend to do with the pieces?" Momo asked.

"That is none of your concern, Momo," Aya countered. "What you should be asking is how many I will buy; that is, once you have given me a price for all two hundred pieces."

Momo and Mei put their heads together and then turned to Father Sebastian. Aya overheard their conversation.

"Aya is a shrewd businesswoman. But I have always found her to be fair in her dealings," Father Sebastian said.

Momo turned to Aya, "Is one ryo too much?" she asked.

Aya smiled. "I am dealing with babes," she said. No, one ryo is not too much. But it is too little. If the rest of the cargo is as good as the sample Father Sebastian provided, I will pay

157

you four ryo. I do not cheat my partners. And I so want to be your partner."

"Truly," Momo asked.

"Truly, and I will want all the new pieces you can make. I also think you should stay in Nagasaki until the problems with the tengu are resolved," she said. "Do you know anyone here you can stay with?"

"We know several people, but none that could put us up."

"If you do not mind rooms in a waterfront hotel with soiled doves, drinking, gambling and a nosy cook," Aya said, looking at Midori, "I can find you rooms in the Jaded Princess free of charge. I can guarantee you will not be bothered. My men see that our hotel customers are not bothered by anything that happens on the main level."

Momo turned to Father Sebastian. "I will find them lodging in the rectory."

Momo smiled until Aya spoke. "Can you protect them from Bad Heizo? As soon as he gets wind of Mei's presence in Nagasaki, he will send his police, his militia, and maybe the tengu after her. He wants the revenue she can generate and will stop at nothing to get it."

"Do you really think he is responsible for the tengu?" Momo asked.

"I would not put it past him," Father Sebastian said. "I have never seen such an amoral person."

"Aya is correct, Momo. I would recommend the hotel. Aya's men are there as are Jubei and I. You and Mei will be better protected," Hideki said. "You should know I have hired out my sword to Aya for two weeks," Hideki continued to Jubei. Jubei's one good eye showed no surprise.

"I am sure you are both skilled, but Heizo has a militia as well as a police force to draw from. What can two swords do?" Father Sebastian asked.

"Oh Father, I asked the same question when yamabushi attacked the inn. Hideki-sama dispatched them as if they were boys, and they were very large and powerful," Momo said.

"Yes, and Jubei-sama defeated Heizo's musket militia sent to collect our wares. The leader started to beat me," Mei said.

"What happened?" Father Sebastian asked.

Jubei-sama killed several and wounded all but one with the Yumi," Mei said.

Hideki looked at his friend. "Keeping a low profile, are we?" Then before Jubei could answer, "Yes, I know. Disrespect will not be tolerated."

"Exactly," Jubei said.

"It is settled then. With the militia able to recognize their attacker, we are better off in the Jaded Princess," Hideki said.

Jubei moved to Hidcki's side where the others could not hear. "We are getting very involved here."

"Are you worried about winding up in jail again?" Hideki asked quietly.

"Not really; I am worried about your identity being discovered and your death being used in this game of politics and commerce everyone seems to be playing," Jubei said.

"Well, you are not advocating me breaking my contract to Aya and leaving these women to the tender mercies of this Heizo character, are you?"

"No, Hideki, I am not. To do either would break your vows of bushido. I just want you to realize that your name now holds power, and unscrupulous men will want to use you if they can," Jubei admonished.

"You are a good friend, Jubei. I will heed your advice and attempt to stay above the fray. I just find this Nagasaki terrifying and interesting at the same time."

"Why?"

"Because it is based totally on commerce and trade and making a profit. The very foundations of our society are turned on their head here. All that we know and honor as samurai means nothing here. I have to see if I can find a place for myself in this strange new land."

"Why?"

Hideki took a few moments to look around the room at the Kirishitans that he knew. "Because if I cannot, I am afraid I will have to join my brother, my grandfather, and you in destroying it all."

Jubei nodded his understanding. "So, you do see it?"

"Oh, yes. I see it. This upside-down world is a threat the Tokugawa do not see coming. In fact, they are complicit in tolerating it by allowing men like Heizo to continue in power. The Kirishitans may be a threat long term, but the luxuries these merchants bring with them bring something much worse than a new religion."

"What do you see more threatening?" Jubei asked.

"A merchant class at the head of government," Hideki said.

Jubei considered Hideki's face with his one good eye. "You may be right. We need to find a way to meet this Bad Heizo."

"Yojimbo," Aya called. Both Jubei and Hideki turned. "Have your ferocious one-eyed friend take Mei and her people to the Jaded Princess." Then, turning to Father Sebastian, "And make sure all the lacquer ware accompanies them. You and I must go pay our respects to my husband and that mad dog he runs with."

Jubei turned to Hideki, "Cherry blossoms."

"Seems like," Hideki agreed.

XVII

Deshima

Hideki followed Aya through the busy port section of Nagasaki. He stayed one step behind, so he could head off any danger. He did not know how old she was, but she seemed young enough to gracefully dodge the many stevedore pushcarts that zipped past in the noonday heat on their way from ships to the various storage facilities along the far side of the wide, hard-packed, dirt road that was the main artery of Nagasaki. Hideki had to move quickly to keep pace.

"Yojimbo," Aya called over her shoulder.

"Yes, Ma'am?" Hideki answered.

"Drop the Ma'am. I am Aya."

Yes, Ma … Aya," Hideki caught himself.

"When we get to Deshima Point and my husband's office, you may see things that will trouble you. You must ignore them."

"What sort of things?" Hideki inquired.

"Just keep your temper and your sword in check," she said.

"I will try," Hideki said.

"See that you do," Aya said.

"Aya, I am samurai. I live by bushido. There are some things I cannot ignore."

Aya stopped and turned. "Maybe it was wrong to bring you along. I do not want to start trouble unnecessarily."

"I do not look for trouble myself, but if my blade can keep injustice from happening, I must interfere," Hideki explained.

Aya just shook her head. "You ronin are more trouble than

you are worth. If I was not fearful for my life, I would leave you behind."

Hideki smiled his best smile. "Exactly."

Aya spun toward Deshima and picked up the pace.

They arrived at a small finger of land jutting into the bay. There was one access road running toward the point. Several smaller streets, almost completely covered by two- and three-story buildings, radiated from the main road. Once he was standing at the intersection, Hideki could see that these cross streets were dwarfed by two large Portuguese ships on either side of the narrow point.

Aya saw the direction of his stare. "Both ships arrived last night. The black one on the right is my husband's. It is the fastest, but it is not the largest. Two much larger vessels are at anchor in the bay. Deshima is deep enough for these midsized frigates, but the large galleons cannot get in close. They must be offloaded at anchor by lighters. You can just make out the lighters down by the point. They are tied up at the quay," Aya said, warming to her task as guide.

Hideki nodded, "They are impressive," he managed.

"Yes, they are quite advanced in many ways and quite primitive in others." Hideki smiled and gazed across the intersection. Aya's head turned to see what was of interest. "Those are some of the governor's thugs. They call themselves militia, but they are guttersnipes. They prey on the weak. Extortion and intimidation is their game."

Six men in a dizzying array of dirty kimonos, most with hiked hems into their belts so their fundoshi showed, ringed an unfortunate little man squatting beside his wooden medicine chest. The reason for their altercation became apparent when the leader bellowed for all to hear, "You do not have a permit. That means the governor does not sanction your business."

The leader's fists grabbed the lapels of his kimono. "You will have to pay," he said, looking down at the little man squatting before an old, wooden medicine chest.

Hideki knew the real audience was the five subordinates. Bullies always liked to crow about their work.

The little man mouthed his reply, but was too far away for Hideki to hear.

"I wonder what he said," Aya mouthed aloud.

"Oh, something about he had not sold anything, so there was no harm done," Hideki said.

"How could you know?" Aya demanded.

"I do not." Hideki said. "I am only guessing."

Aya frowned. "Yojimbo, you disappoint me. I did not figure you for the type of man to watch someone beaten for sport."

"I am not. I am the type of man who likes to see bullies get their due."

"Due? The stupid little man will be killed," Aya said.

"Possibly, but I will bet my wages that will not happen."

"You would bet your wages on the outcome of a sure thing. Are you stupid?" Aya asked.

"Take my bet and see," Hideki teased.

"I will take your bet, samurai. No wonder there are so many unemployed ronin in the city. You just don't know anything about money and risk."

"You may be right about the money part, but I do know about risk," Hideki corrected. "Let us watch and see what happens."

Aya frowned, staring across the street at the little man. "You must help him. That little man will be lucky if he lives," Aya stated almost to herself.

"Little, maybe. Helpless, I do not believe so. Besides you hired me as your yojimbo. Protecting others costs more," Hideki said. "I am surprised that a business woman like you had not thought of the extra expense."

"I suppose you are correct. He is nothing to me. I just hate to see the governor win anything. He takes a bite out of everyone. There is not an enterprise in the city that he does not have a piece of," she said. Then looking over her shoulder at her bodyguard, "We should go."

"Chotto matte kudasai," Hideki requested.

"Why should we wait even a moment more? The outcome is inevitable."

"Maybe not, I have a feeling this little man can handle himself."

"Just a minute," Aya snapped. "Do you know that man?"

"We met last year on the Tokaido," Hideki said.

"Is he what he appears to be, a traveling medicine man?" she asked.

"He certainly travels much of the time," Hideki confided.

"Then our bet is void," Aya said. "You have unfair knowledge."

"Oh, I am sorry. Do you not make your living with unfair knowledge of others?" Hideki said.

"By the Buddha, I have a feeling that I have been tricked and by a lowly ronin," Aya cried. "Very well, a bet is a bet; our wager stands. Besides there are six of them, they are big, and he is but one and very small at that. I think my money is safe, but I would almost pay just to see a different outcome."

"Maybe we will both get what we want," Hideki said quietly.

Aya gave a sharp intake of breath as a ruffian behind the little medicine man tried to kick him in the back of the head. From his squatting position the little man leaned his body to the left and the kick missed by inches. As a foot moved past the little man's head, his right hand raised a short staff directly into the attacker's crotch. The attacker's forward momentum took care of the rest. Aya flinched as the attacker's primal scream echoed off the high building walls. The attacker dropped to the ground holding his private parts still screaming.

The other five were not sure what had happened. Their gazes were fixed on their writhing comrade. As their attention was drawn elsewhere, the little man moved out of his squat with lightning speed, striking an instep, slashing a kneecap, thrusting into a throat, and reversing the bo's trajectory to crack a skull or two. In the blink of an eye, all six were in the dirt screaming, groaning or unconscious.

Aya turned to Hideki. "What was that?"

"That, my dear businesswoman, was a jo master holding class," Hideki said smugly. "You would be hard-pressed to find it done better anywhere."

As Aya watched, the little man returned to his medicine chest, closed the drawers and slipped everything onto his back. With his jo in his right hand, he moved across the street toward

Hideki. He stopped short of Hideki and Aya and bowed. "The gray one sends his greetings and wishes your return," the little man said.

"Aya, let me introduce Yoshi. Yoshi this is Aya. She is my present employer. I have hired out my sword so that I may eat," Hideki said.

Yoshi bowed to Aya. "Yoshi desu, domo yoroshiku."

Aya returned the bow. "Pleased to meet you as well, Yoshi. That was amazing."

Yoshi looked back across the street. "They were not trained well. They were overconfident."

Hideki pointed to the alley off the intersection with his chin. "It might be time for you to become someone else and accompany us on our mission. We are off to see the governor, whose men you just rendered useless."

The little man nodded and bowed to Hideki and then Aya and trudged off towards the alley.

"Are you crazy? He cannot come."

"Why not?" Hideki asked.

"He is totally unacceptable. He is a street urchin. I cannot show up with him; besides, he fights with sticks. We may likely be facing swords. He would be a liability, not an asset," Aya explained.

"I have fought alongside him against many swords; he is formidable."

"This is your area of expertise bodyguard. I will bow to your judgment," Aya conceded. "But he is so unkempt!"

"You have seen what he can do. Do you really want to reject his capabilities because of the way he looks?" Hideki asked.

Aya thought about it a moment. "No. I would feel better if he was with us," Aya said. "I have seen you defeat five men with two flutes and he just subdued six militiamen with his stick. Do you have any more impressive demonstrations planned for me?"

"No, I so hope everything is peaceful from here on out."

At that moment, Yoshi emerged from the alley dressed in a blue silk kimono and dark purple hakama. His dark hair was tied back with a red silk cord and he wore a light-green, happa outer coat, the sign of the merchant class.

Aya was shocked. "Yoshi, surely you are a magician. Where did you find the new clothes?" she asked.

Yoshi did a half turn as if displaying his finery. "These old things? I just found them lying around," he said to Hideki's snigger.

Aya led the way through the strange-looking buildings that anchored either side of the streets of Deshima Point. This was different than the bustling scenes of Edo's warehouse area. Nagasaki was much smaller. The geography compacted all the action into a very small place. Edo was built on a large swamp that edged gently into the large bay. Nagasaki was precariously perched on the side of a mountain ridge that plunged into a rolling ocean.

Hideki looked up as a seahawk screamed overhead, scattering the ubiquitous seagulls. "This place has lots of faults," he said to no one. "But it has blue skies, deep water and a robustness I did not feel in Edo."

"You are from Edo?"

"I am from Kii province, but visited Edo recently."

"What about you, Yoshi? Are you from Edo?" she asked.

"No Aya-san. My work requires that I travel there sometimes," Yoshi said.

"I am curious about that. What kind of work do you do exactly?" Aya asked.

Yoshi looked to Hideki. Hideki shook his head slightly.

"I travel a good deal," Yoshi said.

"You trade in medicines?" She asked.

"Yes, among other things."

"So you are a healer traveling from town to town?" Aya persisted.

"Mostly, but I have lately developed a desire to settle down."

"What prompted you to give up the freedom of the road?" she asked.

Yoshi looked at Hideki again. "I found a dream opportunity in Edo," he said.

"A dream opportunity? How lucky for you. Is there good profit in it?" Aya asked.

"It seems so," Yoshi responded.

"I am always looking for opportunity. How might we help each other?" she asked as she stopped at a large two-story warehouse painted a garish red.

"What a strange color for a building," Hideki commented.

"You will get used to the Portuguese use of colors. If you think this strange, wait until you visit the Chinese part of town with their reds and yellows, or the Malays. We Japanese are drab by comparison," Aya stated.

The trio stopped at the large entrance to the red building. Stevedores moved in and out of the wide opening with handcarts loaded and unloaded. Yoshi noticed the different garb. "I am seeing colors I have never seen before," he noted.

"Yes, Nagasaki is a window on the world for us Japanese. Through this port pass all the goods that Japanese men of power and women of distinction must have," Aya said proudly.

"The smells, the noises, and the sites almost overcome the senses," Hideki said.

"You will see things today that delight and disgust you at the same time, bodyguard. I need both of you to use restraint." Then, changing the subject, "I am not paying extra for you am I, Yoshi?" Aya asked.

"No, Yoshi earns his own money. He will accompany us because we are friends. I will take care of his end," Hideki said.

"That is the Hideki we all know and love," Yoshi said.

"Good, you cannot make profit if you give too much away. Let that be a lesson to you samurai," Aya said. "Always negotiate from advantage. That is the way you become rich."

"I suppose," Hideki said. "But it is also the reason you need a bodyguard."

As the trio entered the huge building, Yoshi and Hideki flanked Aya and stayed one pace behind so they could spot and intercept any threats. But so far, the men of Deshima Point were too busy carrying, stacking, unstacking, and lifting all manner of boxes and crates to give any attention to a woman of the merchant class and her bodyguard. The only danger Hideki discerned was from the heavily loaded, two-wheel handcarts moving at break-neck speed everywhere. Hideki wondered if there was someone in charge somewhere making sense of all the confusion.

"Merchants make no sense to me," he said to no one.

Aya turned her head towards Hideki as she managed to sidestep a short stack of iron rods in the dirt. "That is because you belong to an archaic class. Samurais' days are numbered," Aya said.

"News to me."

"Shouldn't be," Aya said, looking ahead. "We are in Tokugawa peace years. There is no longer a need for a warrior class. Who do you practice to fight?" she asked.

"Unknown," Hideki said. "But there are enemies everywhere that want to plunge us back into the warring-states period."

"I do not doubt that there are evil men that plot the demise of the Tokugawa. But your real enemy is not other samurai," she said.

"Who then?" Hideki asked.

"Your real enemies are men like Heizo the governor. He is a merchant, with the merchant's eye for profit but the resources of samurai. He knows the strengths and weaknesses of every class and how to exploit them," she said.

"You exaggerate," Hideki accused.

Aya stopped in her purposeful stride and turned to Hideki. "Do I? Who benefits from the goods Heizo imports and exports through Nagasaki?" she asked.

"Everyone, I guess," Hideki said.

"No, not everyone. The government in Edo and the daimyo in the countryside benefit. To fill their desire for foreign things, they give away their power to men like Heizo and lose their soul in the process," she accused.

"What kind of nonsense are you speaking? Heizo is the governor of Nagasaki. He serves at the pleasure of the Tokugawa in Edo. He has no power beyond this city," Hideki corrected.

Aya looked at him sadly. "Your demise will come sooner than I thought, bodyguard. How can you and your kind be so blind?"

"Why don't you open my eyes?" Hideki challenged.

"Why is Heizo in power in Nagasaki? He is a merchant."

"I suppose because he keeps goods flowing," Hideki said.

"Excellent, maybe there is hope for you after all. He keeps the goods flowing. And what does he take for his efforts?" she asked.

"I do not know, maybe 20,000 koku," Hideki guessed.

"You think he takes his pay in rice? Do you think him as stupid as the samurai?"

Hideki had no answer for that. He just glared at her.

"He takes his pay in gold and silver and jewels. He uses hard currency to pay his network of merchants and traders in every port in Japan. Heizo knows what is available and what is in demand before the shogun does. He sets the prices for Japanese goods being traded all over the world. He can rake off as big a profit as he desires, and no one is the wiser. The stupid government does not monitor his transactions. They just benefit from them in the way of goods and services."

"So what is the problem?" Hideki asked. "Everyone is happy."

"You poor fool. You samurai have placed tremendous power in the hands of a villain."

"Heizo is a villain?" Hideki asked.

"Why do you think they call him Bad Heizo?"

"I am new here, Aya. What is so bad about the governor?"

"Walk beside me, yojimbo, and I will complete your education."

Hideki moved up to her right side. Being a left-handed swordsman did have some benefits.

"The huge sums he makes from controlling the price of goods, he puts into the coffers of his extended family throughout Japan," Aya began.

"So, he is a good family man," Hideki said.

"No, you idiot! The money does not go back into the city or the central government in Edo. Do you see an abundance of schools, orphanages, new roads, health clinics? How about temples? Do you see them? No! Heizo helps himself. There are taxes here on everything and Heizo controls all. He gets richer and everything and everyone else suffers." Aya complained.

"You seem to be doing well," Hideki mentioned.

Aya just shook her head in disbelief. "It's not about me. It is about the country. We have had one hundred years of wars. You samurai made a shambles of the country. Now we have been at peace for approximately 33 years, if you don't count the Osaka Castle incident, and what have you done for unification? Not much. With all your power and control, you managed to put a lying, xenophobic, self-absorbed bastard of an embarrassment like Heizo in power so he can cheat the government, cheat the city, and cheat everyone down to the beggar in the streets."

Hideki was struck by her passion. "Yes, I just learned you fine beggars here."

"Why do I bother teaching business to a samurai? I am talking about a huge evil, and you are talking about beggars?" Aya said throwing up her hands and moved back towards the center of the building.

"I appreciate the education Aya. But what of the beggars? Is it true the Govenor fines them?" Hideki persisted.

Aya stopped again. "There is a city ordinance against it. Beggars are rounded up by the militia. They are fined. If the beggar has a family, everyone is sold into slavery on board a foreign ship. They bring a pretty penny in the slave markets of Manila, Malacca, or Chosin. Bad Heizo never misses a chance to make money."

Hideki was having trouble speaking. "Japanese citizens are being sold as slaves in foreign ports?" he stammered.

"Do not act so naïve, samurai. They are only poor beggars. What do you care?" She asked.

"I am young and learning the ways of the world, but selling people into slavery seems evil to me," Hideki opined.

"Really? Have you samurai not administered a system whereby farmers starve in bad years and have to sell their daughters into sexual slavery, so the rest of the family might survive?" Aya demanded.

Hideki stumbled to find the words. "I do not know."

"No, you do not. I do. I have firsthand knowledge of the righteousness of samurai rule. During all the time I was being passed around as a plaything for rich merchants and then dirty sailors and finally the big noses, I never lost sight of my goal."

Hideki had no words.

"My goal was survival. I swore I would not die no matter the degradation or injury. I would survive to earn enough money one day to ensure no one could hurt me again." Then stopping and looking Hideki in the eye. "I am almost there. A few more days and I will have arrived. Do not mess this up for me, yojimbo. Neither you nor your funny-looking, medicine-toting jo master. Do you understand me?"

"We both understand you Aya. We will do nothing to hurt you or your enterprises unless I deem it hurtful to others. Yours is truly a sad story," Hideki said.

"I do not want your sympathy, samurai. I want your sword to protect me long enough to enjoy my planning and sacrificing. Beyond that, we have nothing in common. You samurai are the reason the country is so corrupt."

"It is not supposed to be this way," Hideki said.

"Well, it is this way. Japanese become slaves because you samurai tolerate a crook like Heizo."

"Bushido is supposed to protect the week. A samurai's sword is to ensure there is justice for all," Hideki said.

"Those with power have better justice, yojimbo. And I am amazed that you are just learning this. Where have you been?" I asked.

Hideki was quiet, so Aya turned her attention to Yoshi. "You are a merchant. Surely you know what I'm saying is true."

Yoshi produced a crooked smile. "I am more aware than my samurai friend, but it is his unawareness that intrigues me. His whole family believes what he just said. In fact, it is his grandfather that says, 'No right to small to defend and no wrong too small to right.' They pretty much live by that motto."

"There must not be many in his family," Aya surmised.

"No, they are few," Yoshi conceded.

"I thought so," she said.

XVIII

The Portugese

"I think he is for the pit, Lobo," Dom Joao said with a smile, looking at his wife.

Aya returned the smile and translated his words for Hideki and Yoshi's sake. Then she said in Portuguese, "Be careful husband. He is not like your lap dog's normal opponents. He is strong."

Both Dom Joao and his companion's eyebrows arched. "He does not look strong, little one," Lobo said moving around a large teak desk. "And he has a bad right hand. I do not think he would be much of a problem in the pit."

"Lobo is correct Aya. You have chosen poorly," Dom Joao said. "Let me get you a bodyguard from Lobo's students. They know how to protect a woman."

"No thank you, husband. I am aware of Kuro Lobo's way of protecting women. I'll take my chances with the samurai with the bad hand."

Hideki did not understand the exchange, but he registered the threat of the dark, little man approaching Aya. His left hand on the hilt of his rapier on his left hip was all Hideki needed to see. If the man drew his sword with his left hand, it would be an upside-down draw, but Hideki was not familiar with the strange sword so assumed the draw and strike could be accomplished.

Hideki moved between the man and Aya. Lobo stopped. The smile stopped as well. Then his right hand replaced his left on the rapier's handle. Hideki's hands were full of sword handles as well.

"Lobo, stand down. We do not want unpleasantness in front of my wife," Dom Joao said.

A sneer appeared on Lobo's face. "It is no problem Dom Joao. I would cut this slant-eyed monkey before he could get his clumsy blade out. Besides, you found this wife in a brothel. She has no honor to protect."

Aya translated the exchange into Japanese. Neither Hideki's nor Yoshi's expression changed.

"That is for me to decide, Lobo. While she has humble beginnings, she is the only one in this god-forsaken country who can rival the governor in trade negotiations. I need her," Dom Joao said. Then Dom Joao added. "Correction, we need her."

Dom Joao stepped around the desk and placed himself between Hideki and Lobo, facing Lobo. "There is no need for aggression here. We all serve the same purpose."

Aya translated for Hideki's benefit.

"I do not know what purpose is being served," Hideki said matter-of-factly, "But if this man does not back up and take his hand off his sword, his next step will be his last."

Hideki watched the dark, little man's eyes as they darted from person to person as Aya translated the warning.

"You impudent monkey," Lobo screeched when Aya's translation ended. "I'll skewer you like a Malacca satay," he shouted as he yanked his sword upward.

Dom Joao's hand stopped the rapier's upward movement.

"Now, now, Lobo. Please step back," Dom Joao requested.

"Step back? Why?"

Dom Joao's voice became stern. "Because I asked you to. It should be enough."

"I would like to open the gut of this monkey," Lobo screeched. "It will happen, I swear it." The little man shook with anger, but the rapier returned to its scabbard and the dark man stepped back removing his right hand from the hilt.

Hideki noticed he kept his left hand behind his back.

"Why do you bring bodyguards with you here, my dear wife?" Dom Joao asked.

"For the same reason you keep this dog on a leash,"

Aya replied, pointing to Lobo with her chin.

The vicious, little man pointed a slim finger at her. "I am a Wolf! Not a dog. You would do well to remember that."

"If you say so. Wolf, dog, it does not matter. You are still a beast. Women and children are not safe around you."

Lobo stepped forward again and grasped his rapier with his right hand. "You little whore. I will teach you to address your betters."

Hideki reached for his two swords and stepped back in front of Aya.

Lobo screamed and jumped back, a five-bladed shuriken sticking out the back of his left hand. All eyes turned to Yoshi.

"You were both posturing. I decided to end it. The grown-ups have business to discuss," Yoshi said.

Lobo pulled the throwing star out of his hand and reach for a cloth scarf to bind his wound. As he was doing so, he fixed is black eyes on Yoshi. "You will die for this, you little monkey."

Aya translated.

"Go back to the ship and get that dressed," Dom Joao said. "Hurry back. We are expected at the governor's."

Lobo sneered at Yoshi and turned his gaze to Hideki. His stare conveyed the hatred in his heart. Hideki stared back. Yoshi ignored him. Holding his wounded hand, Lobo strode past Aya toward the stairs.

"A thoroughly unpleasant man," Yoshi observed.

"He will try to kill you the next time he sees you," Aya warned.

"He will try," Hideki said. "He will not succeed." Then, turning to Yoshi, "You need not have interfered. I had it in hand."

Yoshi nodded. "I am sure you did, but I get paid for providing assurances to the Gray One."

"It was not needed. I could've handled it without bloodshed," Hideki insisted.

"Then just be thankful it was me and not Jubei. How much attention would a headless foreigner bring?"

Hideki mulled that thought over for a moment. "I

apologize. You are correct in your actions. Any involvement with a foreigner on my part would not be welcome. Thank you."

"It is nothing. You are samurai and not expected to think quickly. I, on the other hand, am a merchant and expected to think of and act on all contingencies," Yoshi said winking at Aya.

Aya smiled her approval. "That has been my point exactly during recent discussions."

"We will both have to work on him if we are going to elevate his thinking above the animal kingdom," Yoshi said.

"Oh, I like the way you think Yoshi very much," Aya said as she looked at Hideki, happy with the new direction of the conversation.

Pointing his finger at Yoshi, "I am used to this dolt taking sides against me," Hideki said. "But I did not expect my employer to be prejudiced against me."

"I am not. I arrived at my position after careful consideration of your idiotic ruminations," Aya said.

"What is all the jabbering about?" Dom Joao inquired.

Aya turned toward her husband and bowed. "The monkeys were commenting on how easy it was to defeat your pet wolf, husband."

Dom Joao snorted his disgust. "That fancy, little, multi-bladed knife the skinny one threw will not protect them in the pit."

"You value them too little, husband. They may surprise you."

"Nothing has surprised me about Nippon except the greed of the governor," Dom Joao said. "You are supposed to be my adviser. How do I get Bad Heizo off my back?"

Aya did not translate any of this for Hideki and Yoshi.

"Your spies have let you down. Maybe they know your days are numbered here and have decided to wait for your Dutch replacements."

"Do not bait me woman. We are beyond that. How long will your business enterprises last if I am no longer Heizo's partner? He will crush you like a bug. You will be back working the brothels."

"Think what you will, husband. But your fall from power will open up trade opportunities for me," Aya said calmly.

"Ha!" Dom Joao laughed. "I cannot imagine who would do business with you. You have the ear of no one and the ire of everyone. Women have less status in Nippon than foreigners."

"I will let you worry about that. But for old times' sake and because it suits my purpose, I will give you an alternate means to communicate with Edo."

"What do you mean? What do you know?" Dom Joao almost pleaded, then changed his demeanor again. "Tell me now or your descent onto your knees in a brothel will be imminent."

"Do not threaten me, Dom Joao. The days when I quaked at the sound of your voice and the swish of your riding crop are long gone. You use hollow threats in your desperation. So, I take it your attempt to get an audience with the shogun has fallen on deaf ears?"

"They always will, wife. I have to go through the governor to get to Edo. He has little incentive to help. I already owe him more than I can repay," Dom Joao complained. "Who would have thought that irritating monkey would be so shrewd?"

"Then you need to find another conduit to the Tokugawa," Aya said.

"I'd love one; unfortunately, I know of no other. We are now confined to the Nagasaki area. I can no longer mount an expedition to Edo without government sanction. To do so would be to risk death."

"The new bugyo might offer an avenue."

"We have a new bugyo from Edo? Have you met him? Can you introduce me?" Dom Joao asked a new hope in his voice.

"I have seen him, but not met him. My bodyguard, however, whom you so cavalierly disregard, has been offered employment by the new magistrate."

"But how does that help us? Edo is months away."

"Not by boat. Twice a month, a coastal ship belonging neither to you nor to Heizo docks in Nagasaki. It was the same one that brought the new magistrate. To date, they have offloaded provisions for approximately one hundred men and horses for one season. I would say that Nagasaki will soon have a regional police force from Edo, independent and able to roam the countryside," Aya said calmly.

Dom Joao thought this over for a full minute. "So how does this help me with my original problem?"

"Fire your spies now. They are worthless," Aya suggested.

"Provide me with a solution, and I will fire them immediately."

"The magistrate for Nagasaki, like all magistrates in all cities, is appointed by the Roju, the lower house of Tokugawa government. The magistrates report directly to the newest member of the Roju. The newest member was appointed to the Roju last year. He is an old man named Yoshinobu or something. He is the uncle of the shogun. Get the new magistrate to pass your message to his boss, and it is one step to the shogun and you've completely by-passed the governor."

Dom Joao was laughing now. "My, my, but you are a sharp one. It is no wonder that I plucked you from that brothel and made you respectable."

"You made me respectable because I advance your profits in Nippon ... nothing else."

"Come little one," Dom Joao teased. "Do you not have a little love left over from the brief time we shared a futon?"

"No my husband, you take your pleasure in other's pain. It is heaven's will that I survived our brief time together. But you did give me the opportunity to make us both rich, so I will give you one last tidbit of advice."

"And what else could I learn from you today, wife?" Dom Joao asked.

"I do not care if Lobo dies, but do not cross swords with this one," Aya said turning toward Hideki. "I have it on good authority that his skills are of the highest order."

"How sweet. Despite your disclaimer, you still have feelings for me."

"No, your death now would cause me an inconvenience. So try to stay alive for awhile anyway."

Dom Joao smiled again. "I see. Maybe the Pit will have to

wait. Why don't you show these fine gentlemen the sights while I retrieve Lobo? We'll meet you at the foot of the steps," Dom Joao said, bowing to Aya. Pulling on his gloves and tying on his cape he exited past Yoshi toward the stairs.

XIX

The Pit

Yoshi crinkled his nose. "These are some very strange smells."

"Are you referring to the smells of trade or the traders?" Aya asked.

"Both, I think," Yoshi said, smiling as Dom Joao's cape disappeared down the stairs.

"There are goods and spices from around the world here," Aya said, then pointed to crates stacked higher than Hideki's head. "Those are oranges from Madagascar. In that section over there are all manner of spices from Sumatra. There are teas from the Malaccas." Aya pointed to the opposite wall. "This section contains everything from lychee from China to durian from Siam."

Yoshi held his nose. "What is that awful smell?"

Aya laughed. "That is the heavenly fruit, durian."

"Heavenly fruit my fundoshi. It stinks like an open benjo."

Aya continued to giggle at Yoshi's discomfort. "In the Chinese section of the city, it is becoming a necessity, and we only introduced it last year. The Malays and the Malaccans cannot get enough of it. We clear one ryu for each basket sold," Aya bragged.

"Someone pays one ryu for a basket of fruit? Who in their right mind would do such a thing?" Hideki asked.

"I just told you yojimbo, people who are used to it in their own country and cannot get it any longer," Aya said. Then as if trying to explain something important to a slow child, "Despite the smell, the fruit is rather sweet with a slight taste of sake.

Dom Joao says it is the sulfur that gives it its sweet taste as well as its distasteful odor. Whatever it is, for those who like it, it is addictive, and it is a moneymaker for those thoughtful enough bring it in from foreign lands."

"Let us get out of here. I cannot stand the odor much longer or I'll lose my breakfast," Yoshi said.

"Too bad," Aya teased. "A real merchant, like you, should take notice of a fruit with such high profit value."

"I just pity the poor sailors who had to ride the ocean with that wretched smell," Yoshi said.

Then Yoshi froze. "What is that smell?"

"I told you, durian," Aya said.

"No, the sweet smell. It is faint, but steady."

The three stopped to sniff. "It is coming from over here," Hideki said pointing to the corner.

Aya looked at the bin of brown rolled bark. "Oh, that is cinnamon from Malacca. It is a spice."

"What is it used for?" Yoshi asked.

"I believe it is used for flavoring various dishes. It is also used as medicine for bad chi, or so the Portuguese doctors say. Why? Is it a problem?"

"No," Yoshi said. "I have just run across it in some unusual places."

"It is not an uncommon commodity. The Mughals and Bengalis use it extensively I think," Aya speculated.

"Please tell me as we exit this place. That durian is overpowering," Yoshi said.

The trio moved through the side-door exit. Yoshi stopped to take several very deep breaths. When he regained his composure, he turned to Hideki. "I have only been around such a disgusting smell one other time in my life. Both are now associated with you."

"I remember. You were visiting a warehouse such as this at night if I recall correctly. You hid in a vat of night soil."

"So you do recall," Yoshi said.

"Oh yes. Someone remarked you smelled like a pine tree dragged through a benjo."

"That wasn't funny then, and it is not funny now. I was just making idle comment on the fact that I wind up in some very smelly situations when I accompany you."

"What are you two mumbling about?" Aya asked.

"Nothing. We were just remembering embarrassing moments in Edo last year," Hideki said.

"Step through here. I'll show you what passes for male entertainment in Nagasaki," Aya instructed.

"Women?" Yoshi asked.

"No. For that you must visit the Inns. Here I am talking about death," she said. "I find it disgusting and very sad, but I have been brought here many times to see Kuro Lobo and his students kill samurai."

"I have heard of this place. It is called the Pit," Hideki said.

"You are correct. This is where samurai come to die," Aya said.

"I am troubled by this Destreza that seems to triumph over kenjitsu. It does not seem possible," Hideki said.

"It is possible, and it is quite legal," Aya said. "The dead all volunteer."

"A very strange kind of entertainment," Hideki said.

"It is not entertainment for the samurai; it is desperation that drives them," Aya mused.

"Desperation?"

"Use your head, yojimbo. Why did you agree to sell me your sword as my bodyguard?"

Hideki nodded his head in understanding. "So I could eat?"

"It is the same with the ronin in the pit."

Hideki moved behind Aya and entered a garish red building.

"By the Buddha, I was not expecting this," Yoshi said.

"Nor I," Hideki said.

The center of the warehouse was a large earthen pit about ten strides across and fifteen strides long. It was cut about waist deep into the dirt. There were two sets of wooden steps on either end. The area closest to the side doors, through which they had just entered, was bare packed earth. The floor of the pit displayed two large circles. The inner circle was about a man's arm length in diameter. The outer ring was maybe three times as large. Both circles were intersected by straight lines that emanated from one of the steps and spread out to end on the far side of the outer circle. The far side of the pit was filled with an elevated seating section that tapered upward. The last row of the seating almost touched the rafters of the large wooden warehouse. The seating was sectioned into threes by wooden steps starting at the pit lip going up to the last row.

Yoshi did some calculations. "About five hundred people," he said.

"Very good, Yoshi, you are a merchant after all. I was beginning to wonder," Aya said.

"These are the circles of Destreza?" Hideki asked, pointing at the white chaulk on the floor of the pit.

"I don't know. It is Lobo's doing. He says it is part of the Destreza fighting system they practice," Aya said.

"I did not realize the barbarians had fighting styles. Thank you for letting me see this," Hideki said.

"Does seeing this help?" Aya asked.

"It does not hurt," Hideki said.

"Why?"

Yoshi answered. "Because if the Portuguese fight with a style, it will have weaknesses."

Hideki changed the subject. "So, you charge for entry to watch samurai die at the hands of Kuro Lobo?"

"No, my husband does not charge a fee to enter. That is not how the real money is made," Aya said.

"Real money?" Hideki asked.

"She is talking about wagering, Hideki. The spectators gamble on the outcome of the match," Yoshi explained.

"Not just the outcome. They bet on everything. Nothing is off limits. They bet on the length of time one contestant will survive. They bet on how many strokes or thrusts it will take to kill an opponent. I have seen them betting on the amount of blood to be spilled. It is all quite disgusting," Aya said. "But it is the one place in Nagasaki where everyone can come and bet as equals. In those stands up there sit all kinds of people."

"I would imagine it gets loud and very rowdy," Hideki suggested.

"Yes, some nights the fights in the stands are better than the fights in the pits," Aya agreed.

"I guess I never realized how violent this city can be. I never saw anything like this in Edo. How can the governor allow this to go on?" Hideki asked.

"Have you not been hearing anything I have said, samurai? The governor and my husband are the ones who host the pit. This is one of the governor's warehouses. It is his militia that keeps some semblance of order in the stands."

"Would it be possible to see some of the action in the pit?" Hideki asked.

"Possible? It is very likely that Lobo will want to get both of you into the pit and onto the end of his sword," Aya speculated.

"When do the games begin?"

"They start killing each other about an hour after sundown. Everyone will have had their evening meal, probably a few drinks, and all will be looking forward to a night of gambling," Aya said. "It often lasts into the late night."

"There cannot be enough Portuguese sailors in port to allow a spectacle like this every night," Hideki surmised.

"No, the duels between the ronin and Lobo's men are reserved until the end. The rest of the time is taken up with challenges between Chinese Tongs and Malaccan kris fighters or Siam boxers. I have even seen little Ryukyuan stevedores out there trying to make some money using farm implements."

"How do they fare?" Hideki wanted to know.

"Surprisingly well for smaller men without any real weapons to speak of," Aya said.

"Does your Mister Wolf fight more than one duel a night?" Hideki asked.

"He fights once a night. All of his followers fight once as well."

"It seems your Mister Wolf is to be avoided," Hideki said.

"If you are in your right mind you avoid him," Aya responded. "He enjoys killing."

"He enjoys it?" Yoshi asked.

"Oh yes, he says it is better than sex. With him I could believe it," Aya said.

"If I had known that, I would have struck him with something more substantial," Yoshi said.

"Maybe a durian," Hideki suggested.

"Most assuredly a durian," Yoshi replied.

XX

Cages

"Let us proceed to the steps," Aya suggested. "We have a long way to climb to get to the governor's palace and you can see my husband's menagerie as we go."

"Your husband owns those strange beasts we saw earlier?" Yoshi asked.

"Yes, he hopes to convince the Tokugawa to get rid of governor Heizo."

"Do you think it will work?" Hideki asked.

"Who knows? The Tokugawa are far away and they pay little attention to us most of the time."

"I have a feeling that is about to change," Yoshi said.

"How would you know something like that?" Aya asked.

"How can they not? You have a tengu running wild killing Kirishitans, somebody kidnapping whole Buddhist families and now some kind of demon is butchering Sung Buddhists in their temples. I'd say the new magistrate was sent here to get to the bottom of it all," Yoshi stated.

"I know of the tengu, and I have heard of the kidnappings, but what are these killings in the temples?" Aya asked.

Yoshi looked at Hideki. "Tell her. She lives here and has a right to know what goes on in her backyard," Hideki said.

"Tell me what?" Aya demanded.

"Tell you that both the Hikawa Shrine on Mount Tara and Obaku Zen Temple here in Nagasaki have been the victim of some demented killing machine," Yoshi said.

187

"That cannot be. I would have heard," Aya denied.

"It can be and is," Yoshi stated.

"How many were killed?" Aya demanded.

"I did not stop to count, but by the blood, everyone. And the daimyo's troops had been to Hikawa Shrine. It was roped off and barriers up," Yoshi said.

"Yoshi came through there," Hideki provided.

"This cannot be. Why would the governor keep something like this secret?"

"Probably to keep everyone from panic," Yoshi said. "There is great evil loose in your city."

The trio moved through the giant warehouse and out the end. It led them through two more side streets lined with multi-storied structures of equally garish colors and then onto the main thoroughfare of Nagasaki. "At least I know where I am now," Hideki commented.

Aya pointed south. "The Jaded Princess is that way. Where are you staying the night, Yoshi?"

Yoshi looked to Hideki, who shrugged his ignorance.

"You can stay at the Jaded Princess. I always keep some rooms open. We can talk about your connections throughout the country. We may be able to do some business together. I'm always looking for more distribution outlets."

"That should be interesting," Hideki said, rolling his eyes.

"Yes, I thought so too, yojimbo," Aya said, missing the sarcasm.

"Thank you, Aya," Yoshi said.

Aya led the way across the wide, dirt thoroughfare that marked the southern border of the city running along the shoreline. They walked toward the mountains that reached skyward from the sea. A line of foothills paralleling the thoroughfare made lateral urban sprawl eastward impossible. The first level of the city was jammed into the narrow swath between the thoroughfare and the vertical face of the foothills.

From Deshima westward, port business was king. The area contained warehouses, custom buildings, and businesses furnishing tools, parts, vessels, transportation and all manner of items to keep a port city moving at full speed. From

Deshima eastward retail reigned. There you would find the drinking establishments, brothels, restaurants, inns, tatami weavers, sandal repairmen, noodle vendors and other enterprises that sustained the citizenry. The city grew seaward east of Deshima Point as the thoroughfare moved inland.

The second level of the city was perched atop the first line of foothills. All were man-made structures, even the wooden and stone steps that scarred the vertical green of the almost vertical cliffs. The first row of foothills leveled off at about 1000 shaku elevation. Hideki glanced up the long stairways, catching a glimpse of large dwellings immediately surrounding the open area for which they were heading. That was the climb they had to look forward to sometime soon. The governor's mansion was up there someplace.

Directly across from Deshima Point was an open area in the foothill wall that formed a perfect bowl flowing out onto the main thoroughfare and the docks beyond. The center of the bowl was a large, flat, grassy area with several large, barn-like structures. These were a far cry from the warehouses on Deshima. These were of traditional unpainted, rough-board, Japanese design with thatch roofing. Instead of the constant clanging and shouting that permeated every inch of Deshima, a very different din emanated from the opening. There was plenty of commotion, just like Deshima, but here the noise was totally foreign.

A steady stream of peasants carried large water pots and baskets filled with straw, leafy greens, grass, melons, and sides of raw, butchered meat to one of the three large buildings in the center of the area. The ragged, dirty, and sweating laborers carried their burdens on their backs or in two-wheeled pushcarts and returned with loads of dung mixed with straw, uneaten bone, and undigested regurgitation. The smell was awful.

Yoshi and Hideki stopped to watch the steady stream of returning waste carried back across the wide, dirt road and over to the landing on the south side of the point. Here the laborers veered towards the flat lighters. Once there, they would lift their smelly cargoes onto their shoulders, careful to navigate the precariously placed planks connecting land and vessel. Once on board, a sideways shuffle began atop the narrow gunwales until the worker spotted an appropriate location. Then, smelly contents were unceremoniously poured out onto the deck.

"I would surely hate to sail that barge," Yoshi said. "The smells alone around here are enough to kill a man."

Aya stopped and looked back in the direction of the lighters. "Nothing goes to waste. That lighter sets sail in twenty-four hours for the rice fields of Shikoku."

"That is a hard way to make a living," Hideki said.

"You must be referring to the pirates," Aya said.

"Pirates? What pirates?"

"The Wako Pirates of course. They raid from the inland sea South to Shikoku and all the way north to China. No cargo is safe from them. They are devils."

"Surely you jest. Who would pirate a ship full of dung?" Hideki asked.

Aya just looked at the samurai. "You really are a babe in the woods, aren't you?"

"It was a simple question," Hideki said.

Yoshi cut in. "You do see all the hard work going into loading the barges, don't you?"

"Sure, it looks like demanding work," Hideki responded.

"It is," Yoshi said. "That is why the Pirates wait until the hard work is done and the danger almost over before they seize the ship and cargo."

"But who is going to rob a lighter full of dung and straw?" Hideki persisted.

"You must first ask yourself who was going to buy the cargo in the first place," Yoshi urged.

"Farmers from Shikoku will buy it?" Hideki attempted.

"Farmers do not have enough money to buy anything," Aya said. "It is the landowners that buy the load."

"You mean samurai buy pirated dung?" Hideki asked.

"Why not?" Aya continued. "The pirates sell it cheaper than Heizo."

"But doing business with pirates is against the law."

"The pirates do not sell directly to the samurai, Hideki," Yoshi said patiently. "They sell to middlemen who have some semblance of respectability. Those merchants then sell to the samurai, usually at inflated rates."

"So samurai pay extra for pirated goods," Hideki ventured.

"They probably don't know they are purchasing pirated goods. But most of the goods traded from foreign lands are pirated in one way or another."

Hideki shook his head. "I grew up thinking the world ran a certain way. Now that I'm older I see was mistaken. I wonder what else I was mistaken about?"

"Do not let it bother you samurai," Aya said. "At least you are learning how the real world operates; most of your kind are not interested."

Hideki looked into her eyes. "We had better get interested or we will be extinct."

As they neared the clearing, a cacophony of strange sounds and smells assaulted them. "That would be the animals your husband wants to send the shogun," Hideki guessed.

"Yes, he is very proud of them."

As they approached the large open area, wheeled wagons encased in heavy, wooden bars were parked in various patterns around the area. The contents of the cages were large, pacing cats of various sizes and shapes. Aya and company wandered from cage to cage gawking at the sites. Over in one corner of the clearing, far away from the cats, were huge elephants being bathed by trainers with rag hats on their heads. In another corner were huge-necked giraffes bending down to drink from elevated buckets on pushcarts.

Two carts by themselves near the stairs up the hillside made Yoshi stop. On top of the cage, a person in a turban was dropping raw meat to the animal below while loud growls and snarls came from within the wheeled cart. Yoshi moved closer.

"What is the matter, Yoshi?" Aya asked.

"I am interested in this animal. What is it?"

The trainer climbed down the front of the cart where no sharp claws could slice open his legs.

Aya addressed him in Portuguese.

"He says it is a Bengal tiger and a very large one."

"Can I see his eyes?" Yoshi asked.

"His eyes? Why?"

"I'll explain later. Can I see his eyes?"

Aya relayed the request.

"He says they are feeding now and nothing takes them away from feeding. Besides, this one has been ill. They were afraid they were going to lose him earlier, but he seems to have rejoined the living. He says to come back tomorrow."

Yoshi stepped very close to the cage and spoke to the tiger. "Hey there demon. Remember me?"

The tiger heard Yoshi's voice and came off his feed. He launched himself at Yoshi and tried to bite and claw through the wooden bars. If Yoshi had not had lightning reflexes he would have been mortally wounded. But the tiger did not make only one pass. He kept at it, trying everything in his arsenal to get at the little merchant.

The trainer came to Yoshi and pushed him back and rattled off his complaints.

"He says you are upsetting the tiger and wants you to leave and not come back," Aya said.

"I will leave if he will answer three questions for me."

Aya translated.

"He has agreed," Aya said, "but I do not understand."

"There is no reason you should. Please just translate back and forth as best you can."

"Very well, I'll try."

"Question one: Can these tigers be trained to respond to smells?" Yoshi asked.

Aya just looked at Yoshi. Finally, she translated.

"He says yes."

"Okay, question two: what color are their eyes at night?"

Aya did not even pause, just asked the question.

"He says as yellow as two ripe bananas."

"Okay, last question: Is he the only trainer?"

"No, he says he is relatively new. The old trainers are on the ship meeting with Mr. Lobo."

"Thank him for me and thank you, Aya," Yoshi said.

While Aya thanked the trainer, Yoshi and Hideki moved toward the stairs. "I take it you discovered something?" Hideki inquired.

In hushed tones, "The tiger was trained to kill the Sung Buddhists. I smelled cinnamon at both butcher sites and when that damn animal almost killed me last night. He was sick today because I shot him full of fugu poison last night," Yoshi said.

Hideki watched Aya approach. "Then we have identified some of the major evil in this town that must be dealt with one way or another," Hideki said.

"Yes, but I'd feel better if I knew where Jubei was. We're a little outnumbered here."

Hideki grinned. "We usually are."

XXI

Governor's Audience

Hideki and Yoshi followed Aya who walked a pace behind her husband and Lobo. The five trudged up the series of stone steps that led to the governor's mansion high above Deshima Point. Aya was unusually quiet in the presence of the two crazily dressed men. Unlike most Japanese women, Aya refused to look down. Her gaze was focused on the backs of each man's head. She was intently listening to the strange-sounding language each spoke. Hideki was ill at ease. The brightly colored waist coats squeezed their upper bodies but their pants billowed like the sails of their ships. From the knees to the leather shoes they wore on their feet, they had silk stockings that showed the outlines of their calves. The only thing more disturbing was their smell.

"I do not mean to be offensive," Hideki said, "but why do they smell so?"

"You are not offensive. They do not bathe like we do, and their diet is full of meat. Even if they did bathe, they would still smell bad."

"I'm confused. How can such an advanced society with their great sailing machines, cannons, and muskets be so primitive as not to bathe?" Hideki's head came up to see if the men understood his question.

"Do not worry Hideki, they only understand a few words in our language. They are so arrogant they think we should learn theirs."

"How could anyone learn a language made up of a series of grunts and songs that would better fit with Midori's samisen?"

"I have learned their language. Necessity drives us to many accomplishments."

"Yes, I was very impressed with your language earlier today. So, you can understand all that they say?"

"Yes, I understand their language very well. They are right now discussing you."

"Really, and what do they have to say?"

"They are wondering why I chose a cripple as a bodyguard. They think my money would have been better spent on somebody older with two good hands."

"That again?" Hideki said.

"They do not think that you could hold your own in a battle."

"I do not know if I could. I have never been in a major battle."

Now Aya stopped and turned to Hideki. "What? You have never crossed swords with anyone?"

Hideki looked her in the eye. "I did not say that. I have killed many men with the sword. I said I have never been in a major battle. The last major battle fought in Japan was Sekigahara thirty-three years ago. My grandfather fought in that. Both my brother and I were too young for the siege of Osaka castle also. So, neither one of us have participated in a major battle."

They both turned and started walking up the steps again. "Oh, I see. You samurai make a distinction between a battle and killing on the street. I did not know," Aya said.

"The samurai makes his living with the sword. If he follows bushido, he will try to use it for justice and protection of the weak. If he does not, he is a menace to society and must be stopped. We samurai live to ensure peace in the land."

"You are one very strange young man."

"You can say that again," Yoshi mumbled.

"Why?" Hideki asked Aya.

"Because you do not fit in society here. Your principles are archaic and old-fashioned, if they were ever in fashion at all. In this world, you must claw and scrape your way to the top. I started out being sold into prostitution by my loving parents. I don't blame them. By selling me, they and my brothers and sister could survive. I was not beautiful, so I was sent to service the foul-smelling big noses on Deshima Point. It was supposed to be a death sentence. If the pigs do not beat you to death, their pox takes you slowly. But I was lucky. Dom Joao took an interest in me because I picked up his language quickly. He needed someone in Nagasaki he could trust to watch over his interests. I became that someone, and he married me."

"I'm sorry, it sounds like you had a very difficult life."

"Do not be sorry for me, yojimbo. By learning his language, and, more importantly, how business is done, I have become a very rich woman."

"But how can you stand to be with such foul-smelling people?" Hideki asked.

"This is as close as I have to get to them now. I once shared the great Dom Joao's bed, but he tired of me quickly and turned to others less fortunate. But he always kept me around to translate on the waterfront. Besides, he has wives in every port," Aya said, and then smiled at Hideki's wide-open mouth.

"Do not look so surprised samurai. It is the way the barbarians do business. I'm sure he has wives in Macau, Sung, Ayutthaya and probably Manila. You see, they look at us as a child might a toy," Aya explained.

They reached the top of the stairs and found the long noses waiting for them. Aya paused to catch her breath and to listen.

"They are talking about you again," she whispered. "Something about a quick thrust with dirk." Then, "Yojimbo, I do believe they are planning your demise. Which would mean my loving husband and his pet assassin are thinking ahead to mine as well. But first they will want to take advantage of your relationship with the new magistrate."

"But I have no relationship with the new magistrate."

"Yes, but I told Dom Joao that the new magistrate offered you a job."

"He did," Hideki confirmed. "But I took yours instead."

"My husband wants an audience with the shogun. Heizo blocks it at every turn. That is because my husband's request will be to get rid of Heizo," Aya explained.

"I see. Dom Joao wants me to carry the message to the magistrate, so he can send it back to Edo via the Roju," Hideki said.

"You are wise in the ways of government Hideki. Yes, that is what my husband wants."

"So, he wants a favor from me and at the same time he's plotting both our demises?" Hideki asked.

"Now you know how business is done in the real world," Aya said.

"This is how business is done in the Portuguese world," Hideki said.

Hideki kept a smile on his face, but angled himself to keep both the smelly long noses in his vision. "Why would they want your death?"

Aya matched his smile. "They may think the meeting with the governor will go poorly and their petition to the Tokugawa in Edo may be denied. You are their last hope. If they can't by-pass Heizo via you and the magistrate, it would mean the end of the Portuguese in this country."

"But you said you knew where all his holdings were, and he did not. Killing you would mean losing them," Hideki said.

"Oh, he would not kill me quickly. I am sure he would turn me over to Lobo. Lobo will want to take my head."

"I will not let that happen, Aya," Hideki pledged.

"You are considerate, yojimbo, and you probably believe what you just pledged, but Lobo is a dangerous man. He loves his nickname. He thinks it makes him even more dangerous."

"What is dangerous about a name?"

"Nothing. It is what the name implies. Notice that he is darker than my husband."

"Yes, I did notice that," Hideki said.

"That is the kuro part. The wolf part implies his cunning.."

"You have seen him fight?" Hideki asked.

"Oh, yes. He uses the rapier and a large knife. He is amazingly quick. He uses the long sword as a distraction and thrusts with the large knife to the side. He likes disemboweling his opponents."

"I shall keep an eye on the black wolf," Hideki promised.

"As well you should. He has promised Dom Joao to kill you."

Hideki turned back to Yoshi. "Did you hear that?"

Yoshi stopped climbing, thankful for a chance to catch his breath. "Yes, I have thought of it a few times myself. You have that effect on people."

"Quit clowning, Yoshi. What should we do?" Hideki asked.

"Do? I think we should be very careful and promise the smelly big noses whatever they want to hear. That should give us enough time to determine our priority of evil. There is certainly enough around that we will have to prioritize before we begin eradicating it."

Yoshi looked back the way he had come. "That is a long way down."

"Yes, but it is worth the view, don't you think?" Aya asked.

Hideki had to admit, the view was fine. Off to their right was the governor's compound. It was a grand structure with a white wall encasing it and multi-storied structures behind the wall. A squad of mean-looking militia stood at the gate. Dom Joao and Lobo were waved past the gate. Aya received hard glances and a few vulgar comments, but was allowed to pass as well. Not so Hideki and Yoshi.

"No Japanese allowed inside with weapons," one of the guards called out. Two more stood and blocked Hideki's path.

"I am the lady's yojimbo," Hideki explained.

"I don't care who you are. No weapons for Japanese beyond this gate," the spokesman contended.

Dom Joao and Lobo had stopped to see how Hideki would conduct himself.

"I see," Hideki said. "How am I supposed to protect the lady without my swords?"

"Not our problem," the spokesman said. "Now get back down the steps or drop your swords with me."

"How many more of you inside the compound?" Yoshi asked.

"That is none of your concern, midget. But why do you want to know?"

"I'm just trying to get an idea of whether we can cripple

several of you or if we'll have to kill a few," Yoshi said deadpan.

The spokesman wasn't sure he'd heard Yoshi correctly. "What the hell are you talking about? You don't even have a weapon."

"Oh, I try never to carry weapons," Yoshi said.

"Then you should be more careful how you speak to the governor's own guard."

"Oh, I don't carry weapons because I can always obtain a weapon when needed," Yoshi said.

"I'm getting tired of you, little man. I have changed my mind. There is no way you are going anywhere but down," the spokesman said as he reached to grab Yoshi.

Yoshi twisted his upper body and tapped on the extended right elbow so that the reaching hands moved past his body. At the same time with his right hand he reached across the adversary's body and withdrew his wakazashi. With one swift motion, before the man could retract his reach, Yoshi cut his right Achilles tendon. The man dropped to the ground screaming, never to walk without a limp again.

Yoshi never stopped moving. He went right into the thick of the grouped guards and kicked one between the legs. He went down retching. Another he sliced on the top of his right hand as it reached for his sword. A third he elbowed in the throat. He went down trying to suck air through his crushed trachea.

Hideki had his sword out as the spokesman had reached for Yoshi. He reversed the blade and struck right and left cracking two skulls. He parried a thrust from a sword and struck the attacker across the knee. He screamed and dropped his sword grabbing his destroyed leg. Then there were no more opponents.

Lobo clapped his leather gloves together in appreciation.

Dom Joao spoke to Aya. "I understand your warning now, little one. I will make much money on him in the pit."

A black-clad samurai wearing a black sling on his right arm charged out to the gate. He was followed by four armed militia.

"What goes on here?" he demanded.

Yoshi dropped the wakazashi. "Just correcting rude behavior. The gentlemen you see in recline were trying to cancel our appointment with the governor."

"Those men are the governor's militia. To strike them is death," the injured man said.

"We are not militia, so we did not kill anyone," Yoshi said. "We just showed them the error of their ways."

"Tahei, these men are my bodyguards. We have an appointment with governor Heizo. Your men were trying to interfere," Aya said.

Hideki returned his sword to its scabbard.

"I could have four muskets here in a second and have you both shot," Tahei said.

"One slight problem with that," Hideki pointed out stepping close to Tahei.

"What would that be?"

"Your head will be off your shoulders before you can finish the sentence."

Tahei looked Hideki over. "Your iai that good?"

"Please don't test me. I have cut no one today. I do not want to start now."

Tahei turned toward the four behind him. "Get these men attended to and replace them at this gate." The four scrambled to obey.

"Follow me," Tahei said to the group.

Dom Joao, Lobo and Aya sat at the ornate rosewood western table. Hideki and Yoshi sat in western chairs behind the three. The governor sat across the table from Aya. The black-clad, injured samurai sat behind the governor. There were four more militia placed throughout the room.

"Remind me to practice a way to fight out of these contraptions," Hideki said.

"It is a little strange, isn't it?"

"Strange, my legs are already asleep," Hideki said. "How about you?"

"No, I am fine."

"How do you do it?" Hideki asked.

"You would not understand. You are samurai, used to an

easy lifestyle. I am a merchant, used to the hardships of life."

"Alright, don't tell me."

"Shsss," Yoshi hushed Hideki. "The governor is about to speak."

Both turned their attention to the big table.

"So, Dom Joao, how was the trading season?" the governor asked.

Aya translated. "About as expected," she replied for her husband.

"I hope that means you are able to pay off a sizable portion of your debt," the governor said.

"No. Without some relief from your usury, this will be our last trip."

"Usury? You were willing enough to take my silver teals when we started several years ago. Now you owe me the agreed interest and you say you cannot pay. In almost every country I know, that is considered a default on a contract and is grounds for dissolution," the governor said.

"That is why I am seeking redress from the shogun. But that is not in your best interest, so you continue to refuse to advance my request to the Tokugawa. Your stinginess will jeopardize the trade within Japan," Aya translated.

"Oh I doubt your withdrawal from Nagasaki will leave a void for long. We have already had inquiries from other nations to fill your spot on Deshima Island," the governor said.

"That would be from the godless heathens, the Dutch?"

"Well, you call us Japanese godless. And at least in dealing with the Dutch we don't have to put up with you trying to incite rebellion via your church. At least with my dealings with the Dutch in Hirado, they honor their debts. All in all, so far it looks like a good trade."

"The Dutch do not have access to all of our ports of call. The trade of goods that you and the samurai have grown so used to will dry up."

The governor looked directly at Aya. "Is that true Aya?" he asked.

All eyes went to Aya. "It may be true for some period of time. But business hates a vacuum. If Japan needs an item, I imagine we will figure out a way to supply it eventually. It is what businessmen do," Aya said. Then Aya translated what she had said for the Portuguese. Both became agitated.

"You crooked whore," Lobo yelled. "You will die for this treachery."

Aya translated the outburst. Hideki moved his katana into his left hand.

"Gentlemen, let us try to be civil," the governor said. "You owe me 150,000 silver teals. You want to continue to do business in Japan. I cannot allow that without you paying me at least one half of what you owe me."

"Where would I get 75,000 silver teals?" Dom Joao asked.

"Probably from within the holds of your three ships."

"I do not have 75,000 silver teals in my three ships," Dom Joao protested.

"Then you will not mind if Tahei takes a look tomorrow," the governor said.

"I mind immensely. Those ships are sovereign Portuguese soil. I will not be boarded by your militia," Dom Joao said.

"What if I send my militia anyway?" The governor Asked.

"Then I would send a lot of them," Lobo said.

"You would threaten me?" the governor asked.

"No threat. A promise. You try to seize any of my ships and I will blow this city off the map," Lobo said.

The governor smiled and turned to Dom Joao. "I would have thought you would try to get word to the Tokugawa via the new magistrate."

"I have not yet met the man," Dom Joao said. "But that might be a good idea."

"Do not rely on it too much, my friend. I have spies everywhere. If you attempt anything with the magistrate I will know," the governor said.

"So you are not going to do your job and forward my request to the shogun?" Dom Joao asked.

"There is no need. You can no longer roam free in Japan. You and your church are forbidden from proselytizing, so you must rely on the shogun's representative in Kyushu to get your request seen. That would be me. You owe me money. Frankly, I feel no reason to help you," the governor said.

"You are an evil little monkey! I will take pleasure in opening your guts!" Lobo shouted, smacking the highly polished walnut tabletop.

Aya did not translate.

"I take it Mr. Lobo has just threatened me and called me a name," the governor said.

Aya did translate this.

Dom Joao let out a long sigh. "We seem to be at an impasse. What do you want?"

The governor placed his elbows on the table top and rested his chin on his hands. "Finally, a sensible response. You owe me money. I want at least one half now to continue our trading relationship. Otherwise, I will seize your cargo and ships in the harbor and all your assets in Nagasaki. You will be tried as treasonous foreigners and probably boiled alive in the Hot Springs of Shimabara."

Dom Joao smiled. "You think you can seize our ships?"

"I have a militia of 200. I can hire just as many ronin at a moment's notice. You have three ships in port with a total of 100 men. What do you think?" The governor asked.

"I think you have never attempted something like this," Lobo said. "You have no idea what we can do."

"Possibly, but I have many samurai on the payroll, and as they are always reminding me, they do know warfare," the governor countered.

"They know nothing. We prove our superiority every night in the pit. Your samurai are paper tigers," Lobo taunted.

The governor turned his face to Aya. "Aya, what do you think of our current situation?"

"I think you both have made up your minds that relationships going forward will be strained at best. Each will make less money as a result. Governor, you will eventually restrict profits to a degree that you will get what you want, new Dutch trading partners to replace my husband," she said.

"But do we have the capability to seize their ships?" the governor asked.

"I do not know. That is a question best left to a samurai. I would defer to my yojimbo."

All eyes went to Hideki.

Hideki conferred in whispers with Yoshi. "Why do you consult with a merchant?" the governor asked.

"He is well traveled and wise beyond his station, and is a trusted friend. I value his judgment," Hideki said.

"We want a military point of view, not a merchant's," The governor said.

"That is shortsighted of you, governor. As the Tokugawa representative in Nagasaki, I thought you would have more sense."

Surprise showed on the governor's face. Hideki continued.

"You have enough men to seize the ship docked at Deshima, but no way of capturing the ships at anchor. As soon as you attack the docked ship, the ships at anchor will loose their canon onto your warehouses and your attacking men. You run the risk of everything being destroyed. While you might survive the attack, you will lose your trade goods in the city, and your tenure as governor would be over," Hideki predicted.

"Who would dare fire me?" the governor asked. "The Portuguese would be held responsible."

"The Lord Matsukara, daimyo of Shimabara, would be here in a flash, probably to put you to death for allowing such destruction and placing his position in jeopardy with the Tokugawa," Hideki said.

"Preposterous," the governor laughed.

Aya looked at Hideki for a long time. "Very good, yojimbo; very good indeed."

Hideki bowed slightly to her compliment.

The governor changed the subject. "So, tell me Aya, how is your attempt at cornering the latest market in urushi nuri progressing? My latest attempt at getting into it did not fare well," he said, staring at an obviously uncomfortable Tahei in his sling.

"I believe it to be progressing," Aya said.

"You know, I could make you a very wealthy lady if you allow me access to the artisan and her wares. The market is very exciting right now."

"I am flattered that you would be interested, Governor,

but I am working on a very tight profit margin. Maybe next time," Aya apologized.

"Too bad. If my information is correct, it could be worth a lot of silver," the governor said.

"How much silver?" Dom Joao asked.

The governor's eyes narrowed. "Are you a player in this enterprise?"

"I could be," Dom Joao said, "for the right price."

The governor thought for a moment, trying to weigh all options. "About 75,000 in silver I suspect."

Aya was agitated. "Where would you get urushi nuri?" she asked her husband, fearing she already knew the answer.

"I suspect the same place as you, dear wife," Dom Joao said.

Lobo's laugh is an ugly thing. "You did not remember we represent the church here in these heathen lands?" he taunted. "Father Sebastian answers to us. By now our men have all of Mei's wares on board the docked ship."

Aya visibly deflated. Then she translated.

Hideki leaned forward and whispered to her. "How many men did Lobo send?"

Aya wasn't paying attention. Hideki repeated the question. "How many men did they send?" this time loud enough for Yoshi to hear.

Aya turned her head toward Hideki. "What difference does it make?"

"It makes all the difference in the world to you," Hideki said.

"Ask the question," Yoshi chimed in.

Aya asked the question.

"My husband says Lobo dispatched four of his best."

Yoshi and Hideki smiled at each other.

"Why are you smiling, yojimbo? I have just lost everything to the dishonesty of the Kirishitan church," Aya said.

"Do not translate this. We are smiling because they did not send enough," Hideki said quietly.

"What do you mean?" Aya asked.

"We mean your cargo of urushi nuri is at the Jaded Princess."

"That cannot be. Lobo's men are very skilled," Aya said. "They only had one samurai with them and he had only one eye."

"Trust us," Yoshi said softly. "The cargo is still yours. Your husband just does not know it yet."

Aya tried to force a smile. "Can this be true?"

"Continue translating and act like Lobo has beaten you. I am confident the outcome will not be to their liking," Hideki said.

"Tell him," Dom Joao demanded, attempting to get Aya's attention.

Aya turned back toward the table and her husband. "Tell who, what?" she asked.

"Tell the governor I'll provide the urushi nuri for 70,000 silver teals worth of direct debt forgiveness and renewed trading rights for one year," Dom Joao demanded.

Aya translated the offer.

"Well, maybe you have bought yourself a year, Dom Joao. But if I were you, I would be planning my exit from these islands at the end of next year," the governor warned.

Don Joao smiled. "Of course. Governor, why don't we exchange the cargo for the vermillion licenses of the Tokugawa?"

"See, you can be reasonable," the governor said.

"Oh yes, we can be reasonable, but I would be careful were I you. Your attempt to drive out the church and attack Kirishitans could backfire," Dom Joao challenged.

The governor leered at the words. "Always the threat of a Kirishitan uprising. Don't you have any new threats?"

"You and the daimyo tax them beyond endurance, boil their missionaries in hot springs and hunt them with a monstrous goblin. What do you expect but revolt?"

"Any revolt will be put down without mercy. Your trading would cease," the governor warned.

"But you would lose your post and your head," Lobo laughed. "Just ask this crippled bodyguard," he said pointing toward Hideki.

"Tahei," the governor said to his wounded militia leader. "See our guests out." Then, as an afterthought, "Dom Joao, bring the urushi nuri to me within two days. I will have the licenses ready by then," the governor said rising, having lost all interest in further discussion.

XXII

Shiro

The trio started down the vertical steps toward Nagasaki below. Yoshi paused to admire the view.

"I think we should find Mei quickly," Hideki suggested.

"And I think you should always look before you leap," Yoshi said.

Hideki stepped up next to his friend. "Okay Eagle Eye, what do you see?"

"I see a large crowd gathering just outside the cages below."

Hideki strained his eyes in the dusk. "I see them now. Any idea who they are?"

Aya stepped up as well. "From way up here, they look like normal town folk. But they could be Kirishitans protesting to the governor."

"What do they have against Bad Heizo?" Hideki asked.

"Just about everything. Taxes are high and there are no improvements in the city. What really has everybody frightened is the tengu."

"And the Kirishitans suspect the governor?" Hideki asked.

"He is an easy target, especially since he became a Shinto priest," Aya speculated.

"That appears to be a pretty aggressive mob," Yoshi pointed out.

"Yes," Hideki agreed. "There are more protesters than militia. When we get down there, Aya, you stay behind me."

"But I am one of them. They would not hurt me."

209

"He is correct," Yoshi said. "Mobs are unpredictable."

"And you have to factor in the militia. They are nothing but a bunch of untrained thugs. Anything could happen," Hideki said.

The steepness of the stairs required Hideki to remove his katana from his Obi, to keep the saya from bouncing on the steps. He carried the sword and scabbard in his right hand and led the way down. When they reached the clearing below, the noise from the clamoring crowd combined with the sounds of the frightened animals made normal conversation impossible.

"It looks like their ranks have swelled," Aya yelled to be heard.

"With the end of the workday, I would imagine they have been joined by laborers and dockworkers," Yoshi said.

The militia of forty men was spread out across the mouth of the open area protecting the access to the governor's mansion. Twenty men armed with jutte in their belts and striking with rokushaku bo were enough to cover the area. A second rank provided support, ready to step into an empty spot if the mob gained the upper hand. The first rank was led by a yoriki standing on a handcart bellowing orders that no one could hear over the din of the mob.

"The militia is too close together to use a bo effectively," Yoshi said.

"Yes, they are getting in each other's way," Hideki agreed. "They can only poke and strike down."

"I do not see any women or children," Aya said. "At least none will be hurt."

"I see one youth," Hideki corrected.

"Where?" Aya asked straining to see in the failing light.

"Their leader," Hideki said.

Aya caught a glimpse of him. "Oh, that is Shiro. He is pretty famous among the Kirishitans for disagreeing with the governor."

"He has to be my age or younger," Hideki said of the young man running back and forth on the front line of the mob giving encouragement and instruction.

"He commands hundreds," Yoshi observed. "Does it

make you long for the days in Kii Province?"

"Shut up, Yoshi!" Hideki said. "You talk too much."

"It is a trait in demand amongst us merchants," Yoshi said.

"Tell me about this youthful leader of the rebellion," Hideki requested.

"He is from samurai stock. I have heard he was a son of a Konishi clan retainer. There are rumors among some that he is the illegitimate son of Hideyoshi, but most of us think as much of that as we do of the miracles attributed to him," Aya said.

"Miracles?" Yoshi said. "What kind of miracles?"

"I do not know. I am a businesswoman. I deal in reality, not make-believe. All I know is he is called Heaven's Messenger by some of Father Sebastian's flock."

"He does not wear the two swords of his class," Yoshi observed.

"If he keeps leading protests, he may need to," Hideki said.

"How do you plan to get Aya through this?" Yoshi asked. "It will be nice if we got through in one piece as well."

"I take it you do not think slashing our way through is a good idea?" Hideki said.

Yoshi turned his head sideways and smiled. "Wait here," and disappeared back toward the animal cages.

"Where did he go?" Aya asked. "One moment he was here and the next he was gone."

"He does that a lot. You get used to it after a while," Hideki said. "But he usually comes up with good ideas."

The screams of the angry mob and the cursing of the militia grew louder and louder. The mob outnumbered the militia three to one. The second rank of the militia was now blended with the first rank and barely keeping them out of the entrance into the flat area leading to the stairway to the governor's mansion. Hideki looked back towards the area where Yoshi had disappeared but could see only darkness now. He switched his gaze back to the excited mob and started to tell Aya to move back towards the stairs.

An eardrum-bursting shriek blasted out of the darkness, dwarfing the sounds of the mob and the militia. Everyone froze. The protesters stopped pushing and the militia turned toward the ungodly scream. The blast from the darkness trumpeted again. This time a huge creature emerged. It was several men high, had a long nose from which it screamed, and, protruding from below its head, two upward-sweeping, ivory fangs. As it walked and screamed, the earth shook. It was as if the earth had opened and a demon from below was being thrust upon them.

Everyone panicked.

Now the militia was in a foot race with the protesters to find safety somewhere else.

Hideki started to draw his sword but realized its uselessness against such a behemoth. For all of its rage and head shaking and trumpeting, the animal stopped at the opening to the main road and calmed. Now that it was between Hideki and the moon, he could see two men sitting upon the monster's neck. The monster knelt down on its front knees, and one of the men carefully stepped down and came toward Hideki and Aya.

As soon as Yoshi stepped down, the huge animal raised back on all fours, turned calmly around and moved slowly back into the bowl area.

"Who are you?" Aya asked both men.

"Just a simple merchant like you making a simple business transaction," Yoshi said.

"I'm beginning to believe that neither of you is what you seem," she said.

"You should be pleased. It worked. The entire mob is dispersed along with the militia," Hideki said. "I told you he had good ideas."

"Well, not the entire crowd," Yoshi added.

Hideki turned to find the youthful leader of the mob coming in their direction. He stopped and bowed to Aya and then to Hideki.

"I never thought I would have to compete with an elephant," Shiro said.

"What did you hope to achieve Shiro?" Aya asked.

"I had hoped to get the new magistrate's attention. We

Kirishitans are being persecuted daily. We are loyal subjects to the shogun. Why do they kill us?"

"The shogun is killing Kirishitans?" Yoshi asked.

"Something is and I do not believe in tengus," Shiro said.

"Right now, you only have to deal with Bad Heizo. If you keep up the protests, the Tokugawa will take note," Hideki warned.

"That is what we want. Our government must step in and make changes here," Shiro said.

As the four moved south on the main road towards the Jaded Princess, Hideki saw that Shiro was younger than he had thought. He was closer to Yasuke's age than his own.

"Why do you do this?" Hideki asked.

"Someone has to. It is not right to allow evil in our midst," Shiro said.

"If you continue, I would suggest hiring your own yojimbo. The governor will realize killing you might solve some of his problems," Yoshi opined.

"I do not have money for a yojimbo, and Jesu will protect me."

Hideki snorted his disbelief. "If you get the attention you crave from the Tokugawa, you may meet one of their assassins. They do not take kindly to insurrection."

"If they come, we will pray for them and reason with them. We are loyal. We have nothing to fear," Shiro said.

"I was once like you. I placed all my faith in my sword and bushido. I thought that as long as I had right on my side I would prevail. I have since learned the hard way that evil people will win every time if the odds are great enough. Having enough friends on your side, good tactics, and the right weapons are more important to success. You, Shiro, have numbers, but your weapons, tactics, and naiveté will get you killed," Hideki said.

"Who are you, sir? You do not speak like the yojimbos I have seen," Shiro asked.

"I am just a ronin from Kii Province who has seen a little more of the world than you," Hideki said. "I would hate to see a young man with your obvious leadership skills killed too early."

"Be careful, Shiro. What my yojimbo says is true. Come back to the Jaded Princes with us until this dies down. You will be safe there," Aya said.

"Thank you Aya. Has your cook gotten any better?" Shiro asked with a grin on his face.

Aya laughed. "Yes, she is quite good."

"She? That is an improvement. I shall partake of your hospitality. Thank you," Shiro said.

"Just do not let any of the girls take you upstairs. They think sleeping with a handsome young man brings good luck," Aya teased.

Shiro blushed.

Hideki wondered if he could blush anymore. Much had happened in a year. He felt like that seventeen-year-old youth who wanted to see Edo so bad a year ago had turned into an old man at eighteen.

"The crowd has dispersed and the moon is providing enough light that we can get back easily. I'll take the left. Yoshi you take the right. Let us go talk to one of those Tokugawa assassins," Hideki said.

Hideki could not see the surprised look on Aya's and Shiro's faces.

XXIII

Okeari

Aya had barely placed one foot into the Jaded Princess when individual shouts of "Okaeri" started in the front and echoed throughout the building. When the last distant shout died, Aya bowed to all her employees acknowledging her return and their welcome.

"They like you," Hideki said.

"That is probably true," Yoshi said. "But now everyone throughout the establishment, from the burly bartender to the lowest prostitute upstairs knows the oyabun has returned."

"Observant of you, Yoshi," Shiro said. "Combined with that elephant trick, I am starting to wonder if you are a mere merchant."

"Oh, I am more than a mere merchant. I am an unusually good merchant," Yoshi said.

"Quit showing off Yoshi," Hideki said.

"Oh, he is not showing off. Only a real merchant would know we use the 'welcome back' greeting to alert all to the boss's return. If you had let him continue, he would have told you I now know who is on duty and available throughout the building," Aya said.

Hideki rolled his eyes. "You make yourselves sound like ninja."

Aya placed her index finger beside her nose. "We may have much in common, but I have no firsthand knowledge of the Shinobi no mono. Ninja are not something we merchants know much about. But like us, they camouflage their real intent to confuse their adversary. Also like us, they are adept in their own styles of communication to baffle the competition. And lastly, stealth and deception are their tools. So I guess you could say real merchants are very much like ninja."

"If you say so," Hideki said watching the huge smile on Yoshi's face. "Aya, ask your people where Mei is," Hideki said.

"More importantly, ask him where your urushi nuri is located," Yoshi added.

Aya's eyebrows raised in hope. "Really?"

"Just ask him," Hideki said again.

Yoshi nodded his agreement. Aya moved to confer with her bartender.

She was smiling broadly when she returned. "I do not know how you did it, but Mei's wares are safe in my vault. Thank you so much."

"Do not thank me," Hideki said. "Let us thank the one responsible."

As the four made their way upstairs and down the hall, the sounds of male patrons being catered to emanated from behind the paper-thin walls used by Jaded Princess prostitutes.

The end of the hall opened into a great room. It was almost twenty tatami wide and forty tatami deep. But the only tatami was a raised portion placed in the center on the polished hardwood floor. Sitting on one side of the tatami were gamblers from various walks of life. Some were merchants clad in the finest silks. Some were laborers still wet from their toil on the docks. Some were ronin clutching their remaining short sword, their katana checked with the bartender before moving upstairs in desperate hope they would guess correctly and win enough to eat tonight. All paid little mind to anything but the scantily clad and heavily tattooed dice man opposite them.

The dice man sat on folded knees clad only in white undergarments. In one hand he held a leather cup, the mouth facing the players, so they could see the empty maw. In his right hand were two dice, one held between his index finger and his middle finger. The second di was between his middle finger and his ring finger. His palms faced outward in a display of openness.

Next to the dice man sat the barker. He was similarly

dressed and would control the game. On either side of the two were two rough-looking toughs in old and worn kimonos clutching cheap swords. They rounded out the Jaded Princess' employees and would step in if the losers became rowdy.

"Place your bets. Don't be shy. If you don't bet, you can't win," the barker called in a song-like chant.

When it looked like the gamblers were finished placing their wood placards onto the tatami, the barker continued. "Everybody have their bets in? Good! Make sure your placards represent your bet. Even is parallel to the tatami, odd is perpendicular."

The barker nodded to the dealer. The dealer nodded back and made a grand ceremony of dropping the dice into the open cup. He rotated the leather cup in his left hand so that all could hear the ivory dice clicking against each other in the confines of the leather. Then he slammed the leather cup onto the cloth-covered tatami in the center and let them rest there unseen. He removed both his hands and sat back on his legs.

The barker took over. "All right gentlemen, what do you bet now on, even or odd? Last chance to change your bets. Turn your placards parallel to the tatami edge for even and perpendicular for odd. Bet now."

Once movement stopped on the other side of the tatami, the barker nodded to the dealer again. He reached forward and removed the leather cup. The dots on the ivory dice added up to an even number.

"Even!"

There was moaning from the men seated opposite the dealer. One let out a whoop. "I won, I won!" one of the laborers said.

The banker turned to a wooden strong box by his side. He counted out the exact number of placards in front of the winner. These he shoved across to the winner using a wooden rake. The losers had their placards collected by the two toughs using the same type of wooden rake.

"Easy come, easy go," Yoshi said as he walked behind the banker and slid back a door to reveal a smaller room behind with Mei, Momo, Jubei, and Gon eating an evening meal. Jubei's katana was by his side.

As the four entered the room, the women seemed happy to see Aya and exchanged pleasantries. Jubei nodded to Hideki and Yoshi and went back to eating.

The burly bartender moved up beside Aya. She turned to him. "Why is he still armed?" she asked.

"Because I have no one capable of disarming him," Tatsu said. "But if you want to lose a lot of men trying, I'll give it a go."

Aya looked from the one-eyed ronin in black to her yojimbo at her side. "No, do not bother. I have it on good authority that he is every bit as dangerous as you surmised."

Midori and Yasuke followed into the room, both holding two trays each. These they sat down next to Mei and Momo. "I thought you might like your meal up here," Midori said.

"Good idea," Aya said. "Why don't you both stay so we don't have to repeat ourselves?"

Midori and Yasuke knelt behind Hideki as he, Yoshi, Aya, and Shiro sat on folded legs and admired the small, grilled fish with a steaming lump of rice and lesser amounts of chopped radish as a side dish. Steaming cups of tea provided the liquid.

"Ita da ke masu," Yoshi said as he picked up a chunk of fish with his ohashi and plopped it on his tongue. "Oishi."

"Well, there you have it. Our traveling merchant has pronounced our food edible. Now we can eat," Hideki said.

Midori turned to Yasuke. "See, they like it."

Yasuke nodded.

No one spoke as they ate their meal. Upon completion, Midori and Yasuke removed the dirty dishes and returned as directed by Aya.

"I assume I have you to thank for getting my cargo," Aya said to Jubei.

Jubei's one good eye stared at Aya. He said nothing.

"He does not speak much. But your assumption is correct. That is why at the governor's mansion we asked your husband how many men he had sent to intercept Mei's wares. We knew it was not enough," Yoshi said.

"Obviously you defeated all four. What did you think of their tactics?" Hideki continued.

"Not much," Jubei mumbled.

"What about their Western fencing? Did you find it difficult to deal with?" Yoshi asked.

Jubei just stared at the little man.

Yoshi continued. "I guess not. But we have heard it is superior to Japanese kenjitsu."

Jubei snorted. "You are misinformed."

Mei felt compelled to pick up Jubei's end of the conversation. "Jubei-sama is quite correct. As soon as the men rushed into the church, they drew their fat swords and came for me. Jubei was among them instantly. He killed them all in a matter of moments. I have never seen anything so horrific or so heroic at the same time."

Tatsu whispered in Aya's ear. "I told you so!"

Aya nodded then moved to Jubei. "Domo arigato. You saved our future."

Jubei grunted and belched. "Good fish."

"What is your next move oyabun?" Hideki asked Aya.

"What do you mean?" Aya asked.

"Shortly, if not already, your husband is going to realize he has no urushi nuri to pay his debts or to leverage one more year of trading. He is going to come for this cargo with everything he has," Yoshi said.

"That is not all," Hideki added.

"Yes, the governor will know soon and will deploy his substantial resources to obtain Mei's wares before Dom Joao does. He would save a lot of money and headaches if he gets his hands on it first," Yoshi said.

"Can you get a fair price from the governor?" Hideki asked.

Aya laughed. "You have not heard a word I have spoken all day."

"Then you must deploy Yasuke and Midori immediately to the Ryukyu village with word to set sail tonight," Hideki advised.

Doubtful, Aya turned to Tatsu. "What do you think?"

"I think your yojimbo is correct. Normally, I would say

with so many seeking the cargo, I would make a deal with the strongest for the best price. But all the players seem desperate, and that makes trading very difficult. You cannot trust any one of the normal players," Tatsu said.

"But if we move it out of the vault, we could lose it all," Aya countered.

"If either your husband or the governor decides you have the cargo, it is as good as lost. We cannot hold off either one of them. And if the triads learn there is precious cargo here, we will lose it immediately."

"Who are the triads?" Momo asked.

"Ancient Chinese gangs," Yoshi said. "They come with every port. Triads are very corrupt and very powerful and always dangerous."

"Then you think the longer we stay here, the more tenuous our position?" Aya asked her lieutenant.

"Yes ma'am," Tatsu said. Then looking around the room, "With your yojimbo and the man in black over there and whoever and whatever this little make-believe merchant is, you have a chance to get the cargo to the Ryukyu village tonight and at sea. But as your yojimbo says, you must put the steps in motion now and not hesitate. Beyond that, I do not have a clue."

"Thank you, Tatsu. I respect your counsel as always," Aya said. Then she turned to Hideki. "Will you and your two friends continue to help?"

Hideki put down his cup of tea. "I pledged my sword to you for two weeks. I do not control my friends. You must ask them yourself."

Aya turned toward Yoshi and then Jubei. "Will you assist in our quest?"

Jubei nodded toward Hideki. "I follow him."

Yoshi smiled. "These two dim-witted samurai must have the wisdom of us merchants to keep them out of trouble. I will follow Hideki as well."

Before Aya could open her mouth, Tatsu grabbed her arm. "Do not offer them money, ma'am. It is obvious to me they are guided by something else."

Aya closed her mouth and nodded, then offered simple thanks. "Mina san, domo arigato goziamus."

"Midori," Hideki ordered.

"Hai," Midori answered.

"Get Yasuke to the Ryukyuan village as quickly as possible. Alert them to the impending arrival of the cargo and the possibility of trouble from both the Portuguese and the governor. Be careful getting there. Do not get caught."

"Hai," Midori answered and grabbed Yasuke by the arm and pulled him through the door.

Aya then looked toward Mei and Momo. "Ladies, I will pay you now for your wares. I will take them off your hands and their safety becomes my burden."

Both bowed to Aya. "Domo," Momo said.

"Please stay as long as you wish at the Jaded Princess. I will have your cart returned to you tomorrow. You can shop in the city before returning to the mountain if that is what you desire."

"You are very kind," Mei said. "We would like that. We are in no hurry to return to the mountain with that tengu still out there."

"Tengu?" Aya said. "That is just a myth, isn't it?"

"It is no myth that killed my husband," Momo said.

"No, it is real enough," Hideki said. "I managed to get an arrow into it. It is an awesome creature, but it does bleed."

"I heard it only attacks Kirishitans. Is that true?" Aya asked.

"So far, that is what I have heard also. But Jubei and I are no Kirishitans and it attacked Momo's inn with us in it."

Aya shook her goose bumps away. "That is for another night. Tonight, we must defeat less demonic forces."

Aya looked at the departing backs of Midori and Yasuke. "Will they be safe on the roads tonight?" she asked.

It was Jubei that answered. "Safer than you know."

XXIV

Ryukyuans

Midori moved with Yasuke following behind. She did not move down the center of the street. She chose the darkness instead, moving quickly from building shadow to alleyway void then into the black of a spreading tree.

"Who are you, Midori san?" Yasuke asked.

"Quiet," she whispered. "Follow in my footsteps and keep up."

Midori was dressed like a commoner. Her kisode was brown with the bottom tucked up into her obi to allow her more freedom of movement. Her legs were covered in a dark blue pant-like momo hike. Both colors faded quickly in darkness. The legs were tucked into kyahon that protected her shins. Her tabi socks were black and fit perfectly into straw sandals. Her last bit of attire was a conical straw hat that she carried in her hands.

"Try not to make so much noise," Midori whispered.

Yasuke nodded and shrugged his shoulders in the dark.

They were moving behind the buildings along the main street of Nagasaki. Yasuke was feeling his way in the black when someone grabbed his sleeve and yanked him down. His first instinct was to knock the grabbing arm away with an outside karate block using the inside of his left wrist. It was like striking a post.

"SShhh!" Midori warned.

Then Yasuke heard the voices approaching and saw the light of their torches.

"Close your eyes," Midori whispered. "They won't see the reflection in your eyes."

Yasuke did as he was told. This woman who he thought of

223

as a cooking mentor seemed to know a great many things.

A group of twenty militia hurried past to some appointment back toward the center of town. They were armed with spears and swords.

When the last one passed, Midori released her grip. "Open your eyes. If you are having trouble seeing, hang onto this," she said and placed the end of her walking stick in his hand. She then stood, turned, and moved off into the darkness with Yasuke in tow.

They moved slowly through the rest of the town, but upon reaching the outskirts, picked up the pace. Yasuke's eyes adapted to the darkness the further they traveled from town. The stars, and the three-quarter moon reflecting off the dirt road as well as the sound of the ocean crashing somewhere to the right kept them on track.

As they moved in the moonlight, Midori asked a question loudly. "Yasuke, have you heard anything from your girlfriend and her family?"

"Why are you speaking so loudly?" Yasuke asked.

In the same loud voice, she answered. "I don't want to surprise anyone in the dark. It has been my experience that those on watch at night have a tendency to be jumpy."

"I don't think there is any need for worry, Midori-san," Yasuke said.

"You base that on your years of experience dealing with sentries, do you?"

"No," Yasuke said. "I base it on the courier I sent before we left. He is related to me and said he would alert the village."

Midori stopped and reassessed her protégé. "You are a man of many surprises Yasuke-san. I will not underestimate you again."

"Good," Yasuke said as he moved around his friend and mentor. "Does that mean I'll be making more money preparing the noodles?"

Midori addressed the back of his head as he moved down the trail. "No!"

As they made their way toward the sound of the crashing ocean, the fire from the village lighted their path. They rounded the last turn, and the fukuji trees gave way to a large clearing and many lesser houses staggered around a large one with a red tile roof. Yasuke and Midori headed straight for it. This time they were not impeded.

The headman and his sister greeted them. The village was anything but sleepy tonight. Everyone seemed to be moving.

"We have brought advanced word that the cargo will arrive soon and must ship tonight," Midori proclaimed as they sat on folded legs in the large house.

"Yes, Yasuke's warning prepared us," the old priestess said.

"We are provisioning two boats now," Hachiro said. "How many handcarts worth of wares do we ship?"

"I do not know," Midori confessed.

"One handcart and two crates," Yasuke said, then smiling at Midori, "We saw them in the church, remember?"

"Clever boy," Midori said.

"When will it arrive?" Hachiro asked. "We must catch this tide or have to wait another day and night."

"Aya understands the urgency. The Portuguese are looking for the cargo now. But if we have to wait another day or two, Heizo will have his militia out looking for it also," Midori said.

"How many of the big noses will come?" Hachiro asked.

Midori shook her head. "I do not know."

Yasuke answered for her. "No more than fifteen or twenty. There will be two officers, four or five able-bodied seamen armed with short, wide blades they call cutlasses and a few hangers-on from the dock armed with clubs. The big noses pose the greatest threat. Any officer will be armed with long rapiers and nasty little knives in their belts worn in the back."

All eyes turned to Yasuke. "What did they teach you at that Temple school?" the priestess asked.

"This I learned from dodging their patrols in town as I tried to sell my flutes. They are an arrogant people and very mean-spirited," Yasuke said.

"Brother," the priestess directed, "send two to the Nagasaki Road."

"You want to stave off an attack?" the old man asked.

"No, let the attackers in and let no one out," the old woman said. "Send your best. They will be contending with runners bearing requests for help back to the city."

The old man nodded his head. "It will be as you say nigan." Then he turned to direct two men. They picked up two roku shaku bos and departed for the main road at a run.

"What of the defenses?" the headman asked.

"How will the urushi nuri arrive?" the priestess asked Midori.

It was Yasuke who answered. "One pushcart to overflowing covered in waterproof oilskins." Midori nodded her agreement.

The old woman walked to the edge of the central structure and gazed on the courtyard center of the village. "Unload the cargo and place it on the two vessels upon arrival. Return the pushcart to this open area. Put straw under the oilskins."

"They will think it the cargo," the headman said.

"Yes, we will kill them here. No one must remain alive," the priestess said.

"Bodies to the sea?" the headman asked.

"Of course," the priestess said. "The fish must eat too."

XXV

Attack by the Sea

Hideki, Jubei, Yoshi, and Aya arrived with several of Aya's men from the Jaded Princess pushing and pulling a wheeled cart heavily laden with Mei's treasures.

"Mei did not come?" Yasuke asked.

"No, there was no need. The urushi nuri belongs to Aya now," Hideki said.

The headman turned to Aya. "Normally I would purchase the cargo from you and take my chances in the markets overseas. But I don't have that luxury today. I will have to act as your agent with the Sung," he said.

"That is acceptable," Aya said. "But to add incentive to your enterprise, I will pay an extra one bu for each piece that reaches the Sung market."

"Very generous," the priestess said. "But we need to know the sale price of the goods to know how generous."

"Sell the plain pieces for no less than four bu. The inlaid will go for one ryu," Aya said.

"That is a very high price. They may not sell." "Half of salesmanship is setting the perceived value. If I start the price high, our next trip will be just as lucrative," Aya said.

The old woman smiled. When she brought her tattooed hands to her chin Hideki thought the blue emblems danced with the firelight.

"Two bu per piece seems more generous," the old priestess suggested.

Aya smiled. "I would have gone as high as three. But two it is."

Yasuke looked surprised. "Are they not supposed to sign something?" he asked Midori.

"I believe they both want to do future business, so they will live up to their agreement," Midori said.

"We must hurry," Jubei said. "Either the governor's men or the Portuguese will figure out where we have gone."

Hideki turned to the headman. "Do you need our assistance?"

The old priestess answered. "I do not believe so, noble one. We have been protecting ourselves for generations."

Jubei moved next to Hideki as the old woman moved off. "By the Buddha, she said that with such confidence I almost believe her."

"Have you ever trained with or fought against Shuri or Naha Te?" Hideki asked.

"Not knowingly."

"Jii insisted my brother Naga and I learn all manner of martial arts. He brought in masters to teach us in Kii province. I have had some introduction in Ryukyuan empty hand techniques as well as some of their weapons they call Kobudo," Hideki said.

"Kobudo; like kobu as in fist?" Jubei asked.

"Yes, just like the word for fist. It is strange is it not? Their weapons system takes on the name for the way of the fist. I never understood it. But that may be because they have their own language and our words may not translate well," Hideki said. "I believe they call their language Hogen."

"I do not care what they call it, just so they can handle whatever trouble comes down that dirt road tonight," Jubei said.

"Having second thoughts about this musha shugyo?" Yoshi asked.

"By the Buddha, Yoshi, do you have to always sneak up on people?" Hideki asked.

"I thought I was making enough noise for even two dull samurai to hear. Maybe I should start wearing a bell?"

"No, no bell. There are times when your ninja stealth serves me well. And no, I am not having second thoughts about my swordsman's pilgrimage. Although this place gets more dangerous by the minute," Hideki said.

"I am not sure it is any safer in Edo," Yoshi said.

"What do you mean? Do you have news?" Jubei asked.

"Is my grandfather okay? Are my brother and his family safe?" Hideki asked.

Yoshi put both hands up to silence the two. "Your grandfather is well. He stays busy at the Roju when he is not playing the fool at your brother's place," Yoshi said.

"What do you mean, playing the fool?" Hideki demanded. "Is something wrong with my grandfather?"

Jubei moved in close to hear Yoshi's response.

"There is nothing wrong with the gray one that does not come with being a great grandfather and playing with his latest offspring," Yoshi explained.

Hideki looked relieved. Jubei's expression did not change.

"What word of the shogun?" Jubei asked.

"He is in very poor health from all that I have heard," Yoshi said.

"If Hidetada dies, we start the feud between Iemitsu and his younger brother Tadanaga in earnest," Hideki said. "It is no longer a game played by the Shogun Hidetada as it was last year."

Hideki prompted Yoshi further. "Out with it Yoshi. What other unwelcome news do you have?"

"The Bird Woman is back."

"What? How can that be? She was confined to a nunnery by the shogun himself," Hideki said.

"Yes, but the shogun is very ill. The heir apparent is Iemitsu, the oldest brother. He is already giving orders as if he will be shogun soon. One of his first was to break O'Fuku out of the nunnery and put her back in the Ooku running the concubines in the inner palace. She tends to Iemitsu daily," Yoshi said.

"That is not good," Hideki commented.

"Are you referring to your actions being the cause for banishment or your jutte strike crippling her arm?" Yoshi asked.

Hideki did not respond to the barb. Jubei looked at Hideki.

"If there is a power struggle, my father will need my sword," Jubei said.

"I know my grandfather will need protection as well. O'Fuku is a sore that will not heal," Hideki said. Then looking at both friends, "We should make plans to return to Edo as soon as my contract is up with Aya."

"I am relieved to hear you say that. I do not like the structure of this town and the evil men that run it. I have had doubts about just what type of evil we were facing ever since my night in the trees on Mount Tara," Yoshi said.

"Speak plainly ninja. What are you saying?" Jubei asked.

"Man-made evil is easily dealt with. Conjured evil is something else again," Yoshi said.

"What are you talking about? Are you saying the tengu we fought is conjured evil?" Jubei asked.

"I do not know. The cries I heard on Mount Tara frightened me. I am not easily frightened. I resorted to conjuring to counter it," Yoshi said.

"What did you conjure?" Jubei asked.

"I do not know. I have yet to see it materialize. But I know it will," Yoshi said.

"Will you be able to recognize your handiwork when it appears?" Hideki asked.

"I think so, but I am not certain. I have not used the black arts in this fashion before," Yoshi said.

"Great," Jubei said. "Now instead of a seven-foot tengu, we will be facing a two-headed dragon."

"Laugh if you like. But I know the power of the arts. I will see something soon," Yoshi said.

"I hope we see some reinforcements soon," Hideki said looking into the dark of the ocean.

"You are correct. The Ryukyuans are preparing for an attack from land. The Portuguese will most likely come from the sea as well," Jubei said.

As if on cue, a group of fifteen Portuguese sailors and another six dock rats noisily moved into the central open area of the village from the city road. All were armed, one of them with the rapier of an officer. A large, bearded man wearing a dark waistcoat and large, billowing pants tucked into knee-high, leather boots waved his rapier and gave orders. Two dressed in a like manner pushed the common sailors around and held much shorter but wider blades into position around the wheeled handcart.

"I think we should allow the villagers to handle the land assault. We should reposition in case anything comes from the sea," Jubei said.

"Excellent idea," Hideki said. "Yoshi, you get out front and let us know what you see." Yoshi turned and disappeared.

The three turned towards the pounding surf. They had not gone ten paces when they could make out a large, strange-looking boat being pulled onto the sand.

"I count another ten," Jubei said. "But I cannot see everything."

"You see any firearms?" Hideki asked.

"Not yet," Jubei said. "But I do not have a clear view."

Yoshi dropped out of the tree right next to the two. Both Hideki and Jubei were startled.

"I see two muskets, one officer with the long sword of the big noses. The rest appear to be sailors with short, wide blades called cutlasses," Yoshi said. "There are no more than fifteen total."

"This is the only path to the village from the sea and it is narrow here. Jubei and I will make our stand here. Yoshi can you take care of the muskets?" Hideki asked.

Yoshi was already reversing his garments and head wrap. Where he had appeared gray a few moments ago, he was now black from head to toe and already moving to the shadows.

Hideki and Jubei moved to a position on the path that was bordered by steep rock walls. They automatically moved to this position without consulting with each other, Hideki on the left and Jubei on the right.

When they came, the lead sailor carried a cutlass in one hand and a lantern in the other. They suddenly halted when they saw the two samurai in their path.

Jubei shifted his katana to his left hand and withdrew a short throwing knife from his saya. He threw it swiftly. The knife lodged itself deeply in the sailor's chest. He toppled over. When the lantern hit the sand, the light extinguished.

"Masterful," Hideki said.

"They cannot get more than four abreast here. If Yoshi takes care of the muskets, this little corridor may work in our favor," Jubei said.

One of the sailors pushed the first group toward the samurai standing in their path with drawn swords. The sailors moved tentatively at first, but when the samurai offered no aggression, they charged. Two moved toward Hideki and two toward Jubei. As soon as the first wave attacked, a second wave filled the void.

The cutlasses were half the length of the katana, but the width of the blades was twice that of the Japanese swords. They were butcher's weapons made for cleaving and chopping through meat and bone. But the Portuguese had to get in close to use them.

Hideki judged the one on his right was just slightly in front of his partner. Both sailors had their cutlasses high, ready for the downward chop that would sever bone and muscle and chop off arms at the wrist. Hideki stepped to his right and brought the katana up high in his left hand. He started a shomen downward strike but dropped his left fist to the right side of his body, moving the tip of the sword to the left. At the last minute he whipped the tip of the sword back to the right by dragging his fist in a horizontal plane to the left. The tip followed and sliced deeply into the sailor's midsection. The dying sailor dropped his cutlass and tried to gather his intestines back into his body. Hideki let the tip continue to the left and deflected the cutlass from the sailor there. With the wakazashi in Hideki's right hand he shuffled forward and stabbed the second sailor high in the chest.

Hideki had no time to look to his right to see how Jubei was doing. The next two cutlass-wielding sailors were upon him. The one on the right was already in mid strike. Hideki brought up both swords and caught the downward motion in a scissor block using both his swords. He used the katana to deflect the strike down and to the left, keeping the tip up and pointed to the opponent on the left. With the wakazashi in his right hand, Hideki drove the razor sharp short sword into the enemy's midsection and pushed the dying body into the path of the sailor on the left. The second sailor hesitated for just an instant. It gave Hideki enough time to shuffle forward and drive the point of his katana into his opponent's throat. The sailor fell to his knees trying to stem the flow of blood spilling out onto his chest. Hideki stepped forward and brought the wakazashi on top of the sailor's head. It split the skull and the man fell sideways without a sound. Both were dead before they hit the sand.

Now Hideki looked to his right. There were four dead bodies at Jubei's feet. Hideki smiled and brought his attention back to the path.

The Portuguese with the rapier was giving orders. The remaining sailors did not attack.

"I sure hope Yoshi got those muskets," Hideki said.

The remaining seven sailors grouped into a circle. The officer with the rapier kept looking back toward the sea. What he saw he did not expect. A metal ball spewing sparks dropped into their midst. The sailors knew what it was. They use it to drop onto enemy ships they were boarding, hoping to ignite a powder magazine. They started to move in all directions away from the grenade. But the fuse had been cut just right. They had taken no more than one step when it exploded. All the remaining Portuguese were knocked off their feet. Some died instantly. Others were knocked unconscious by the blast.

Without compassion Jubei and Hideki moved among them extinguishing every life.

"I am getting more like you every day," Hideki said.

"This is necessary. Besides, they came to kill. It is karma," Jubei said.

"Yes, but I am still troubled by it," Hidkei said.

"Killing these foreign devils should not trouble you," Jubei said.

"That is not what troubles me," Hideki said.

"Then what?" Jubei asked.

"It is troubling that taking a life is getting easier and easier," Hideki said.

"Lamenting the loss of your youthful innocence?"

"Maybe. But killing other men does not seem to bother me as it once did," Hideki said. "It just seems like it ought to somehow."

"Think about the lives of the Ryukyuans you just saved. I doubt they would have survived attacks from two directions," Jubei said.

"I know you are right, Jubei. It is just we make decisions in the moment as to what is right or wrong, and someone often dies as a result. I'm getting used to thinking I'm right with every decision, and that cannot be the case," Hideki said.

"If you are looking to me to be your conscience, look elsewhere. These long noses came here to kill. Now they are dead. That is a good ending to me," Jubei said.

Yoshi found his two friends waiting for him. He carried two muskets.

"Anyone at the boats?" Hideki asked.

"No one alive," Yoshi said.

"Stupid question," Hideki said.

"You are learning," Yoshi said. "It looked like you two were having a discussion on tactics."

"No, our young friend was having an attack of conscience, wondering if all the killing he is doing is good or not," Jubei said as he wiped the blood off his katana.

"Is that all? Well, if it helps, think about all the villages around the world these barbarians have raided using just these tactics to rape, plunder, and enslave others. Save your sympathy for the Yoshinobu if the Bird Woman gets her way," Yoshi said.

"Good point my ninja friend," Jubei said. "If she is back and in power, all of our killing skills may not be enough to save the Yoshinobu or the Yagyu.

Hideki, Jubei, and Yoshi returned to the village. When they came to the center clearing, it was littered with the bodies of the foreigners.

The headman and the priestess stepped into the light.

"Don't tell me you slayed these big noses with just your farming tools," Jubei said.

"Some," the priestess said. "But for the most part we relied on tinbe-rochon, nunte-bo and eku."

"Are they weapons or people?" Jubei asked.

The priestess laughed. "They are weapons, Mr. Sword Master. You helped us today down by the beach. Now I will return the favor in case you see these weapons in an opponent."

"Wouldn't that mean I was fighting one of your people?" Jubei asked.

"Most likely," the priestess said. "But it cannot be helped. Husband, have the three weapons brought here."

The headman bowed and called out three men's names. They trotted forward into the firelight. "Each of you show these three your weapons and how you wield them," the Priestess said. The three bowed and stepped in front of the three friends.

"Now I understand," Jubei said. "The dual tanged nunte adds another shaku to the length of the bo and I suppose the two tangs allow for trapping the opponents blade."

"Correct, Mr. Sword Master. In the hands of an expert, a swordsman like you would find himself impaled on the tip just moments after he's lost his sword, the Priestess said.

"How would I defend against this?" Jubei asked.

"Oh Mr. Sword Master, we owe you a debt, but not that much. You will have to work out a defense for yourself," the Priestess said.

"Sort of looks like a bo with a jutte sticking out of the end, does it not? Yoshi asked.

Jubei looked up. "You are not far wrong. It is much like a naginata in that regard except there is no blade for slicing. The tangs, one going forward and the other to the rear are for trapping the sword and the sharp spike is for stabbing."

"Wait until you see this weapon. It is called tinbe-rochin. The turtle shell is reinforced and acts as a shield. The rochin is held in the right hand and is used for thrusting. The Portuguese would be at a distinct disadvantage banging on the tinbe with a cutlass, leaving themselves open for a lethal thrust from the rochin," Yoshi said. "I like it."

"I would never suspect an oar could be used as a weapon," Hideki said.

"Anything can be used as a weapon if you know how to employ it," Yoshi said.

"We are fishermen, Prince of the Yoshinobu. We use the items available to us. The eku or oar is one of the most fundamental tools we have," the priestess said.

"They all have one thing in common," Yoshi said.

"Yes, they provide the reach advantage over swords and cutlasses," Jubei said.

"Especially cutlasses," Hideki agreed.

The priestess dismissed the three Ryukyuan warriors and called for Yasuke. He reported and bowed to the priestess.

"Have all the bodies loaded into the Portuguese boat at the beach. Take enough men with you to row their boat out into the bay. Tether one of our boats to theirs. When you are far enough out to catch the receding tide, scuttle their boat and return in ours. I do not want any bodies washing up on shore here," the priestess directed.

Yasuke responded with a word Hideki had not heard before.

The Priestess turned to Aya, who had joined the circle. "While Yasuke is cleaning up, I will have your shipment move on the tide."

Aya smiled. "At last," she said. "I hope this means profit and freedom for everyone."

"Where to now?" Hideki asked Aya.

"I do not think Nagasaki will be safe for any of us for a few days. I have been planning a trip to my village for some time. Now seems like an appropriate time as any to start," Aya said.

Aya turned and summoned her men. She gave them instructions and rejoined Hideki. "I have given instructions for supplies to catch up with us tomorrow. I suggest we depart tonight toward Unzen. That way we by-pass the city and Heizo's patrols. We can spend the night at the Chinese temple that just reopened."

"I think we should spend the night here and depart in the morning," Yoshi said.

"With Heizo and my husband both searching for this cargo? Do not be stupid," Aya said.

"Yes, merchant, where is your sense of adventure and closing the deal?" Jubei asked.

Aya turned to give more orders, the decision made, leaving Hideki, Jubei, and Yoshi standing alone.

"If you must know Sword Master, my sense of adventure has been somewhat sated of late by a huge tengu and a fierce, black demon who climbs trees almost as good as me and has yellow eyes," Yoshi said.

Hideki and Jubei set off to follow Aya. Jubei turned his head to address Yoshi. "Come ninja. The big, bad samurai will protect you."

"If only you could," Yoshi mumbled under his breath. Then he stepped off in trace of his friends.

XXVI

Slavers and Pirates

"Keep moving. We do not have all night," Jobu said.
"If you want your shochu and rice you had better have this
miserable lot bedded down by first light."

"What is the rush Jobu?" Asked Yama. "No one is looking
for us and these peasants will not be missed for some time."

"The Osprey wants to set sail the day after tomorrow. That
means this lot and the sorry buggers in the barn have to be
moved and stowed aboard tomorrow," Jobu said.

In a hushed tone Doi asked, "Why the hurry boss? Does
the Osprey know something we do not?"

"He is the Osprey, stupid. Of course he knows things
we do not. You don't get to be the leader of the Wako pirates
without knowing things," Jobu said. "How do you think he's
managed to stay alive with both the Chinese and Japanese
governments wanting his head?"

"Still, we have come a long way and the men are tired. We
are all looking forward to some drinks and breaking in some of
these young girls," Doi said.

Jobu surveyed the struggling band of stumbling rabble
behind him. They were a conglomerate of all ages from
children to wizened old people of both sexes. There were
two rows, each human bound neck to neck to the person in
front by large hemp ropes, the kind found on ships. They had
all been uprooted by a raid on their village earlier that night.
Those not taken captive were put to the sword. Wako left no
witnesses. If they complained, they felt the lash of the cat-of-

nine tails Doi and the two rear guards Imo and Yama carried.

"There is one or two in this bunch that might be worth a poke," Jobu said.

Doi grinned. "There are three. One is fixed up like a boy, but I saw her right off. I cannot wait to get my hands on her."

"That is only if I do not fancy her myself. I might just exercise my privilege as leader," Jobu said.

Doi's glare was murderous. "You do and I'll stick a knife in your gizzard while you sleep," he said.

"You would threaten your better?" asked Jobu.

"You are no better than me. You forget we were both raised on the same boat. I know you better than you know yourself," Doi said.

"Makes no difference anyway," Jobu said. "Aika may take them away from us. She has done it before."

"That's rotten. Why does the Osprey let her do that? And what does she do with the young girls she takes?" Doi asked.

"Do not know," Jobu said. "Why not ask the Osprey or Aika the next time you see them?"

Doi shook his head from side to side. "No thanks. I have seen that she-devil carve a man's innards with that jeweled knife she always carries. It was not a pretty sight."

Jobu turned around facing the captives and walked backwards as he shouted to the two guards in the rear, "Keep pushing them. If one falls, kill them where they fall," he said, spinning back to the front.

"I do not think the Osprey nor Aika will be pleased if we kill the slaves," Doi said.

"They will be less pleased if we do not have them processed and on board tomorrow," Jobu said and picked up the pace.

The soon-to-be slaves tried to keep up as they moaned and groaned against the harsh treatment and tried to keep the rough hemp off their already raw necks.

"The supplies will join us tomorrow morning at the Chinese temple," Aya said.

"How will the supplies be delivered?" Jubei asked.

"I have hired a teamster and his horse," Aya said.

"Convenient," Jubei said.

"But a little noisy if we are trying to stay silent on this road," Hideki said.

"You think the horse will give us away to Heizo or my husband?"

"Or to a large tengu that preys on Kirishitans," Jubei said.

Aya looked around as they walked. "You don't think we'll run into that thing do you?"

"I don't know," Hideki said. "At first it only attacked lone Kirishitans on mountain roads. Then it killed Momo's husband when it was still light out. Next it attacked Momo's inn with several people inside, us included. It would appear it is getting less and less discriminate in its targeting."

Yoshi put up his hand to call the group to a silent halt. Jubei and Hideki placed their hands on their swords.

"What is it?" Aya asked. "I did not hear anything."

Hideki shushed her with a finger to his lips.

Yoshi placed his hands to his mouth and let out a light melodic bird call that was distinct but delicate.

Almost immediately the same call came from somewhere off to their right.

"It is fine," Yoshi said. "It is Midori catching up with us."

"I still do not hear anything," Aya said.

"That is because you do not listen," Midori said as she seemed to pop out of thin air.

"Where is Yasuke?" Hideki asked.

"That would be him crashing through the brush," Yoshi said.

"Oh, now I hear," Aya said as the sound of tree branches swishing and twigs snapping reached everyone. They all turned to the right as Yasuke slid down the little embankment onto the road.

"Midori, you left me behind," Yasuke complained.

"I could not take all the noise, Yasuke. You really are a city boy."

"The Ryukyuan village all tidied up?" Hideki asked.

"Yes," said Yasuke. "Just as the nigan commanded."

241

"My wares got loaded and left on the tide?" Aya asked.

"Yes," Yasuke said, bowing slightly to his employer.

"Good," Aya said. "Then my future should be more secure."

"Let us get started," Hideki said. "That temple may not take in travelers after a certain time."

They had been traveling uphill for several ri when Yoshi held up his hand again. This time he waved everyone off the road and into the trees.

"What is going on?" Aya asked.

Hideki shushed her again more violently with his index finger to his lips.

"Do not shush me, yojimbo. You work for me," she said.

"Not if you are dead," Jubei said.

She could not see his face clearly, but could make out the tsuba covering his bad eye. The image sent a chill up her spine. She complied quickly.

Midori appeared in their midst. "I make them out as Wako pirates. They have about twenty captives of all ages. There are only four pirates. What are your orders," she asked Hideki.

Aya looked at Hideki and started to say something but decided against it.

"We could easily overtake them and free the captives. I believe them to be on their way to a Portuguese slave market somewhere. Or we could just follow them and see where they go." Yoshi offered.

"Or we could overpower them and question them as to their destination and who is behind the slavery and let the captives return home," Jubei said.

"Let us pursue Jubei's suggestion," Hideki said. "How are they arrayed?"

"Two in the rear armed with cutlasses and whips. One in the front armed with a cutlass who seems to be the leader and a fourth roving armed as the two in the rear," Midori said.

"Who are you people?" Aya asked.

She was ignored.

"Tactics?" Hideki asked.

"Midori and I will take care of the two in the rear. The

sword-master and you can handle the leader and the rover," Yoshi said. "That is if the sword-master here can refrain from killing his opponent."

"Look who is talking," Jubei said. "I think your body count was higher than both of ours on the beach."

"And it was a good thing it was," Hideki said. "Yoshi, execute your plan. We will continue down the road and take them from the front."

"This is exactly the thing I knew you would do," Aya said. "I pay you good money to be my yojimbo and you place me in danger at the first sign of trouble."

"The only danger you will be in is if you keep talking," Jubei said.

Aya stopped talking and sought shelter behind Hideki.

"I told you bushido will not allow me to turn a blind eye to evil. I can think of nothing more evil than slavery," Hideki said. "Besides, I want to know what those pirates know."

Aya did not reply. She just kept a weather eye on Jubei.

Hideki smiled. "He is not going to hurt you. He has already risked his life several times on your behalf. He just gets peevish at times."

Aya nodded, but kept Hideki between herself and Jubei.

They heard the pirates coming from a ri down the road. The laughter of the guards juxtapositioned against the cries and moans of the captives made for a strange set of sounds.

"Hold up!" Jobu called to the group, holding his hand high.

"What is it?" Doi asked running to the front of the halted mass.

"I'm not sure," Jobu said. "Looks like two samurai standing in the middle of the road. Tell Imo and Yama to be alert."

Doi nodded his consent and turned to shuffle to the rear. He came back quickly.

"They are not there!" Doi said.

"Who is not there?" Jobu asked.

"Imo and Yama," Doi said.

Jobu turned his gaze to the two samurai in the road. "I

would imagine they had something to do with that."

"What are we going to do?" Doi asked.

"I'd say that was up to them," Jobu said.

Hideki and Jubei moved toward the two pirates.

"Little late for a walk, is it not?" Hideki asked.

Hideki and Jubei stopped within striking distance of the two.

"We are militia from the governor of Nagasaki. These people are criminals," Jobu said.

Hideki looked behind Jobu. "All of them?"

"Yes, all of them. Do not interfere with the law unless you want trouble," Jobu said.

"Even the little children are criminals?" asked Hideki.

"Yes, all of them. Now clear off," Jobu said, placing his hand on his cutlass.

"I do not think you are militia. I do not think you represent the law, unless it is Wako law. I ... "

Hideki did not get to finish his sentence. Jobu started to pull his cutlass from his belt. He never got it out.

Hideki's instinct took over. Using his right hand, he grasped the saya holding his katana on his right side and reversed it 180 degrees. With his left hand he grasped the handle of his katana and started a sky to earth cut. But now the blade was reversed so the non-cutting back of the sword was down when striking and the cutting edge of the blade up. He struck Jobu on his collar bone at the juncture of neck and right shoulder. Jobu screamed, let go of his cutlass and collapsed in the dirt road, kicking to get away from the pain.

Doi saw what happened to his friend and reached for his cutlass. "That would be a mistake," Jubei said. "I only use one side of my sword."

Doi hesitated for just an instant then tried to pull his cutlass from his leather belt.

Jubei grasped his saya with his left hand and pulled his katana as he lunged forward with is right foot. Jubei executed a perfect iai draw where the last third of his blade struck Doi in the throat and cut through skin, vocal cords, and vertebrae and kept going until his sword and right arm were extended. Jubei then recovered by stepping forward, flicking the blood off his sword and retuning it to his scabbard. The corpse sank to the dirt road and spewed blood for several seconds. The head rolled toward the tied captives. They recoiled away from it.

The captives now huddled on the far side of the road, away from the two samurai. They did not notice Yoshi and Midori moving among them. They did notice when the ropes fell away. Most sat down where they were. Yasuke, Midori, and Yoshi gave them water which they guzzled greedily.

Aya moved among them asking questions. "They are from a village not far from mine. The pirates raided them and killed many. They are not sure if anyone is left alive."

"Can they find their way back?" Hideki asked.

"Most assuredly," Aya said. "It may take a little time for the old ones."

"Get them started as soon as you can. Yoshi, give them some money to help rebuild," Hideki said.

"Why do the merchants have to carry the samurai? Why not give them your own money?" Yoshi said.

"I don't have any money," Hideki said. "I had to take a job as a yojimbo."

Yoshi opened his purse after determining who the headman of the village was now, and then returned.

"You are recognized as their savior from the pirates and an undetermined fate. I am recognized as their savior from starvation. Once again the merchant class saves the day," Yoshi said.

"Do you always obey him?" Aya asked.

Yoshi looked at her. "Only when he's right," Yoshi said.

"Is he ever wrong?" she asked.

"Not very often," Jubei said.

The former captives started moving back down the road.

"Will they go by the Chinese temple?" Hideki asked.

"No," Aya said. There is a fork in the road that goes west. They will take it. We will continue on toward Unzen."

"Let's not get too far behind them in case they run into that tengu," Hideki said. "Yoshi, who do you think should stay with the pirate to ring the truth out of him?"

Yoshi looked to Midori. She nodded. "With pleasure. What do you want done with him after he talks?"

"How do you know he'll talk?" Aya asked.

They all looked at her and then continued as if she had said nothing.

"Finish him off and leave him for the animals," Hideki said.

"Hai," Midori said and moved off. Yasuke started to follow her.

"Not you, Yasuke," Hideki said. "Midori will be traveling fast after she is finished here and you would only endanger her or slow her down."

Yasuke nodded his agreement.

"Who are you people?" Aya asked as they all turned to proceed to the Chinese temple. "You are much colder than I thought. One minute you are freeing slaves and giving them money, and the next you are torturing and killing your captive."

"Do not worry too much about that pirate," Jubei said. "We have to kill him to ensure your safety."

"My safety? What do I have to worry about?" Aya asked.

"What was the first ploy the pirate used?" Hideki asked.

"He was militia for the governor," Aya said.

"Exactly," Yoshi said. "If we let him live, where does he report?"

"Either to the pirates or to Bad Heizo," Aya said. "Oh!"

"Oh, indeed," Jubei said.

XXVII

Hideki Commits

Hideki, Jubei, Yoshi, and Yasuke followed behind the captives until they turned east at the fork.

"Well, we cannot protect them forever," Yoshi said.

"No, we cannot," Hideki agreed. "If we continue on this path, will we come to the Chinese temple that was the scene of the massacre?" he asked Aya.

"Yes," Aya said. "I am told the Sung have cleansed it and restarted operations."

Hideki looked at Yoshi. "You think they will be less than cordial to night travelers?"

"Would you be?" Yoshi asked.

"Probably," Hideki said. "Why don't you take a look ahead?"

"What? And take on that tengu alone?" Yoshi asked.

"You are a big, bad merchant, smarter than we samurai. Surely you can handle one tengu," Jubei said.

"Do not wander too far," Hideki said. "I just want some advance warning on either a tengu or Chinese vigilantes."

Yoshi bowed slightly, picked up the hem of his kimono, tucked it into the back of his obi and moved down the dark road.

"Is that wise?" Aya asked. "You are possibly wasting a valuable man's life. Why not send a warrior," her head nodded toward Jubei on her right, "to do a warrior's work?"

Jubei answered for Hideki, "Because Yoshi is many things when he has to be, but the best thing he is is invisible. We will know well in advance if anyone approaches us from above."

Aya turned toward Hideki. "That is close to what you said about him earlier. So what is he? Is he a merchant, a warrior, or something else?"

Hideki smiled, but Aya could not see his teeth as the moon went behind a cloud.

"He is all those things and more. But above all, he is a friend," Hideki said.

"I have been wondering about that. You are a ronin, yet a master swordsman," she said nodding her head toward Jubei, "a mysterious man who is either a merchant, a medicine peddler or a ghost and a multi-talented cook, samisen player, and torturer all follow your every direction. Why is that?"

"Woman, you ask too many questions," Jubei said. "Just be glad that we do follow him. That way you get more profit. Isn't that what you are all about?"

"Oh, I am glad. I just do not understand it. And what I do not understand gives me pause. It makes me think there is some rationale I have not contemplated and therefore some way I can be harmed."

Hideki addressed Jubei as if Aya was not there. "You were correct Jubei. This allegiance to profit blinds people to basic good. It may need eradicating."

"What? Eradicate profit? Are you two crazy? You could no more eradicate profit than stop the tide," Aya said. "The entire country runs on the goods that flow through Nagasaki. You try to eradicate profit and there will be riots everywhere."

"Do you think the shogun has not thought of replacing everyone with samurai?" Jubei asked.

"The shogun does not think of us at all, unless the shipments of goods slow down," Aya said.

"You have a high opinion of yourself, merchant," Jubei said. "The shogun has sent a magistrate to survey the situation."

"Yes, and the governor is still Bad Heizo, a commoner, who is still in power because he keeps the goods flowing from ports abroad, through the pirates and down thousands of tributaries and over highways and foot paths across Japan.

Who is going to ensure the goods flow if you get rid of him?"
Aya asked.

As they trudged upward their pace slowed.

"You have a good point Aya," Hideki said. "If he is
eliminated who should replace him?"

"The best replacement would be me," Aya said without
hesitation.

"I saw that one coming," Jubei said. "Just what we need,
a female governor, former prostitute, wife of a big nose and
current brothel owner."

"But for obvious reasons," Aya continued as if not
interrupted, "that is not possible. So you would have to replace
him with someone that knows most of what he does."

"Is that his second in command with the wounded arm,
Tahei, I believe?" Hideki asked.

"Heavens no," Aya said. "Tahei is samurai. He could not
put together a deal with a poxed prostitute. He is good for
killing Heizo's enemies and running slaves."

"You think Midori will find out that Heizo is involved in
putting his own countrymen into slavery?" Hideki asked.

"Of course," Aya said. "The Wako pirates have a larger
fleet than the shogun. How do you think the goods flow
without allowing them a slice of the profits?"

Hideki stopped walking. Jubei was all ears now as well.

"You mean to say that you know Heizo is involved in
slavery?" Hideki asked.

"You samurai are even dumber than I thought. Of course
he is. Why do you think he's called Bad Heizo? There is no
deal, no matter how small or how illegal that Heizo does not
get a cut on. He controls everything," Aya said.

"Why would he risk everything to sell slaves?" Jubei asked.

"Risk is what he lives for. I guess it is the same rush
you must get from killing some poor soul. Heizo gets a rush
when he completes a deal and makes profit. The higher the
risk, usually the higher the reward. But I suspect he has other
motives," Aya said.

"What other motives could he have?" Jubei asked.

"What does Heizo want?" Aya asked.

"More profit," Jubei ventured.

"Surely, but what are his political goals at present?"

"To get the Portuguese out of Nagasaki and the Dutch in," Hideki said.

"Correct, yojimbo," Aya said. "By driving fear into the population via a tengu and pirate raids the Kirishitans are outraged and riot in the streets and the Buddhist population panics when whole villages are carried off into the night."

"If you are correct, Heizo has earned his name of Bad Heizo," Jubei said.

Hideki continued to walk but placed his hands behind his back.

"Aya if you wanted to break up this slave trading and bring Bad Heizo down at the same time, what would you do?" Hideki asked.

"It is not in my best interest to bring him down," Aya said. "I am still plugged into the trading that goes on in the city. If the distribution of the goods coming and going in the port is disrupted, so are my profits and my plans for the future."

"After tonight, I don't think you are plugged in anymore. Both Bad Heizo and your husband will feel outwitted at best, but most likely betrayed," Jubei said.

"Let us broaden the scenario," Hideki said while walking. "How would you go about stopping the slavers, getting rid of Bad Heizo, and keep the goods flowing, while getting rid of your own husband and elevating yourself to have the power of the governor if not the title?"

"Why would a ronin even contemplate such a question?" Aya asked.

"Let us say we are curious men looking to pass the time solving problems," Jubei said.

"Not good enough. I have told you I find your stories implausible just by the power you wield here," Aya said. "Now you want me to think of changing the government and kill my husband. I do not think so."

"Think of the profit," Jubei said.

"Profit is no good to dead people," Aya said.

"What if we could offer you protection?" Hideki asked.

"You are supposed to be my yojimbo now. Yet you abandon me to free slaves. Your track record in protecting people is poor," Aya said.

"I suppose that is true," Hideki said. "However, all of us have used our swords to help you achieve your ends. That should buy us some good will."

"Oh, it does. I am very appreciative," Aya said. "But you are talking about a very different level of risk. Do not get me wrong. Just contemplating a coup of Heizo is appealing on many levels, but he is a devil with eyes and ears everywhere. Give me some time to think over your quandary."

"Do not take too much time or we will have to think of an alternative plan," Jubei said.

"Do you have that kind of power?" Aya asked.

Jubei looked at Hideki. "Maybe," Jubei said.

"*Maybe* does not cut it. If I am to stick my neck out on an enterprise that may change things forever in Nagasaki, I will need greater assurances," Aya said. "Without them, I could lose everything."

"You may lose everything anyway," Jubei said. "If Bad Heizo has the Portuguese thrown out of Nagasaki in favor of the Dutch, now in Hirado, you will be his next target. You are living on borrowed time."

"I have thought of that," Aya said. "And I have no solution. I have nowhere to run."

"Then you should be motivated to find a solution to my quandary," Hideki said.

"And you should be willing to give me better assurances," Aya said.

The three walked up the incline on the road. Hideki nodded to Jubei. "Tell her who you are," Hideki said.

"I am Yagyu Jubei," Jubei said.

"I know that already," Aya said.

"Maybe you do and maybe you do not," Hideki said. "What do you know of the Yagyu family?"

"I do not know anything," Aya said.

"Jubei is the heir to the Shinkage-ryu sword fighting school."

"How wonderful for him," Aya said. "He's a master

swordsman with a school he'll inherit someday."

"Not just any school. The Shinkage-ryu school has only one student, the shogun. Jubei was the sword instructor to the shogun until other duties called him away," Hideki said.

Aya stopped walking. "If you are that important, why do you take orders from Hideki?" she asked.

"Gives you pause, does it not?" Jubei said. "Work it out yourself, you are a smart business woman. If the Yagyu owe allegiance to only one family, who is that family?"

Aya's facial expression did not betray her. Her voice did. "Am I supposed to bow down on this road?" Then, "Are you really a Tokugawa?" she uttered, all arrogance gone from her voice, now replaced with fear.

"No to the bowing part. I do not want anyone to hear us." Hideki said. "I am Yoshinobu Hideki, cousin to the current shogun, brother to the magistrate of Edo, grandson to Yoshinobu Masashige (whom I call Jii), a member of the Roju."

Aya was in shock. She could barely squeak out her next question. "May I ask why you are here?" adding, "samurai-sama."

"Aya, do not call me that. Do not change your attitude towards me. Just keep thinking of me as your yojimbo," he said.

"That is too much to ask," she said.

"All right, then I must ask you to elevate yourself. You and I and Jubei and Yoshi and Midori are now all co-conspirators. I want us all to act as equals. We must keep the act of ronin and brothel keeper going."

"But I am a brothel keeper," she said.

"Yes and I am a ronin on a musha shugyo. I actually came down here to sharpen my sword skills. I was injured last year and my master recommended this pilgrimage to make up for what I lost," Hideki said.

"Your hand?" she asked.

"Yes, my hand. And Jubei and I have discovered Nagasaki is corrupt from top to bottom. Pirates are complicit with the governor selling Japanese into slavery; a tengu is killing only

Kirishitans; another creature kills Chinese Buddhists; the governor uses his militia to enforce his insatiable appetite for profit; taxes go to his private coffers and not the public good; and most egregious of all, the governor fixes tariffs on goods both coming and going with no regulation or oversight and keeps everything for himself. Does that about sum up the situation?"

In a whisper she replied, "Yes."

"Do you agree all of this is wrong?" Hideki asked.

"I do not know about right and wrong," she said. "I know it perpetuates poverty and ignorance and desperation and death."

"Do you want to help change it?" Hideki asked.

Aya paused as if thinking.

"She is trying to figure her profit," Jubei said.

Aya looked at Jubei. "You are closer than you know master swordsman. But what I was really thinking was how much better off the world would be if the profit was shared with the poor without me having to give all mine away. I was also thinking what an oddity it is to see a compassionate samurai caring about others."

Jubei shrugged his shoulders. "Yes he gets us all with his childlike adherence to bushido."

Aya started to turn back to the path.

"You have not answered my question Aya," Hideki said.

Aya smiled. This time both samurai saw it as the moon moved from behind the clouds just-in-time.

"Yes, I want to change it. Yes, I want to stop Bad Heizo and seize his power, even if I'm a figurehead. And yes, I will help you."

"Good," Hideki said. "Now we are on equal footing with Heizo."

"We are still outnumbered," Jubei pointed out.

"Maybe not," Hideki said. "When we three are reunited with Midori we will hatch a plan."

"You have something in mind already?" Jubei asked.

"Yes, but it is too early. We need to get Aya's obligation satisfied first."

"Oh no, I could never hold you to that now," Aya said.

"I insist. Ever since you told me where your parents reside, I have been anxious to visit," Hideki said.

"You are anxious to visit my parents?" Aya asked.

"Not really. I am anxious to visit the daimyo of the area. Your parents happen to live close by."

"You plan to visit Matsukawa-tono?" Aya asked.

"Yes, if I can think of a way to get to him," Hideki said.

"You will find a way," Jubei said. "You always do."

With that, Jubei put his hands inside his sleeves, tucked them inside his kimono and turned to resume the trek up the dirt road.

They trudged on for another ri when the night was interrupted by the call of a nightingale.

Jubei and Hideki froze. Hideki whispered to Aya, "Get off the road. Pull back into the trees on the right."

Jubei turned and ensured Yasuke moved into the trees as well.

Aya's curiosity got the better of her. "What is it? What did you see?" She whispered.

"He did not see anything," Jubei answered. "He heard a Nightingale."

"So what? Nightingales sing at night," she said.

You ever hear one singing the same song three times?" Hideki asked.

"No, I do not think so. They are known for their elaborate singing," Aya said.

"This one did," Hideki said.

"It was Yoshi," Jubei said. "That little monkey surprises even me with his skills."

Everyone was crouched down under the tall pine trees.

"Where is he?" Aya asked. "It has been too long."

From his kneeling position Jubei spun on one knee drawing his sword in one motion.

"You will get yourself killed like that one of these days, Yoshi," Jubei said.

Both Aya and Hideki turned to see Yoshi moving up behind them almost hidden as he moved from tree to tree. Jubei returned his sword to his saya as Yoshi approached.

"I gave you warning. Did you not hear?" Yoshi asked.

"We heard," Hideki said. "What is our status?"

"The Sung have re-opened the temple. It is heavily guarded. They were opening the gates for night travelers, but all are being checked before entering," Yoshi said.

Hideki turned to Aya. "You are known to the Sung, are you not?"

"Yes, but we are competitors, not friends," Aya said.

"Time to get friendly," Hideki said. "Let's go."

As they approached the temple Yoshi pointed. "See that tall camphor tree near the wall?"

"Yes," Jubei said.

"I spent a very fearful few hours there on my way into Nagasaki."

"Fearful?" Jubei asked.

"Terrified is more like it. I was treed by a yellow-eyed, tree-climbing monster."

"A tengu?" Aya asked.

"I do not now think so. I did at first because it was a dark night, and all I could see of him was those almond shaped yellow-eyes. When it jumped about eighteen shaku to get at me, I almost fell out of the tree in surprise."

"How did you escape?" Aya asked.

"I had a blowgun in my medicine chest and my wife had supplied me with fugu poison. I darted him in one of those devilish yellow eyes. It screamed and took off towards Nagasaki."

"Nagasaki? Are you sure?" Hideki asked

"Yes, strange is it not? But stranger yet was a smell of blood and cinnamon I found inside the temple. I could not place the smell above the blood until Aya took us on that tour of those foul-smelling fruits dockside in Nagasaki."

"You got inside the temple even though it was locked?" Aya asked.

Yoshi ignored her. "What is even more interesting is the fact that one of the large cats the Portuguese plan gifting to the shogun almost died that evening."

"Yes and it went crazy when he smelled you by his cage."

"Just something to remember if you talk to the Sung about an alliance," Yoshi said.

Hideki bowed deeply toward Yoshi. "You are one very smart man."

Yoshi smiled. "Your grandfather seems to think so."

They moved to the temple gate and Aya handled the request for shelter for the night. The head guard knew her and let them pass.

After baths and an evening meal of rice covered by a tasty fish soup, Aya joined Yoshi, Jubei, Yasuke, and Hideki in their room.

"Midori just arrived," Aya said.

"Good, tell her to bring her food in here after bathing," Hideki said.

"I already did," Aya said

Hideki smiled. "Already thinking ahead, huh?"

"Always. It is how I get ahead."

Jubei continued to oil his sword. When he was finished, Midori stepped in and bowed to Hideki. "Pardon the delay," she said.

"Report," Yoshi said.

"The Pirates are indeed slavers. They transport their slaves to a large barn north of Nagasaki. They make raids about once every few months but recently have stepped up the tempo," Midori said.

"Who are they?" Yoshi asked.

"Wako Pirates, as you suspected. He was especially proud of that."

"How can they raid with impunity?" Jubei asked.

"It is as Aya said. Heizo's deputy meets them at the barn and takes his cut either in silver or girls," Midori said.

"That is a very damning statement against our governor," Yoshi said.

"Maybe," Hideki said. "Are you sure he was telling you the truth?"

"She knows her business," Yoshi said.

Hideki bowed to Midori, realizing his mistake. "Sorry, I was not thinking."

"No problem," Midori said. "He will raid no more villages," she said.

"Perfect," Jubei said. "My kind of woman."

Midori bowed to Hideki, signaling her report was finished. She turned toward Jubei and winked before sitting down to eat.

Hideki spoke to Yasuke. "I am sorry about your girlfriend and her family. There is nothing we can do for them. Maybe we can keep it from happening again. Are you interested in joining us?"

Yasuke looked into Hideki's eyes. "Yes, I want to kill them all," he said.

"Killing is the easy part," Hideki said. "Right now we need your brain. I have asked Aya to formulate a plan to bring down Heizo, keep the goods flowing, and stop the slavery. Do you have anything to contribute?"

"How can we do this? We are but five," Yasuke asked.

"No, I believe with your help we might enlist the Ryukyuan settlement. I also have hopes of getting the Sung to come on board with us in some fashion. That might change things," Hideki said.

"That still will not be enough yojimbo," Aya said.

"Maybe not," Hideki said. "But the trip to your parents' village may change that."

"You want to enlist the aid of my parents' village? They are just farmers," she said.

"I am not interested in them. I am interested in the daimyo who lives near them," Hideki said.

"You want an audience with Daimyo Matsukawa?" Aya asked.

"If possible," Hideki said. "I would very much like one."

Yoshi interrupted the ruminations. "So what have you come up with, Aya?"

"The easiest way is to kill Heizo," Jubei said.

"No Sword Master it is not," Aya said. "He keeps all his contacts and all his payoffs on scrolls in his home. They are hidden in a strong room off his sleeping quarters. He claims to sleep with the key around his neck, and that room is guarded day and night. Only after we seize the scrolls can you even think of killing Heizo. There is no way to break in with guards on duty every hour of the day and night."

Jubei turned to Yoshi. "What do you think?"

"It is not up to me. It is up to the one who must execute. What are your thoughts Midori?" Yoshi asked. "A diversion perhaps?"

"That might work. But I would rather infiltrate and see if we can steal the scrolls without killing innocents," Midori said.

"Midori, you have let the young master's ideals rub off on you," Yoshi said.

"More probably the young master's lover," Midori said.

"Yojimbo, you have a lover?" Aya asked.

"Yes, but I have not seen her in three months."

"So that is why you never coupled with any of my girls," Aya speculated.

"I suppose, but let us turn our attention to the plan. Yoshi, how do we execute?"

Yoshi nodded to Midori. "Your skills are first rate. You will be on your own unless you can rally some of the five families. I will let you tell them how you will execute this," Yoshi said.

"I will try to infiltrate the compound. I will either enter as a prostitute for one of Heizo's nights of debauchery or as a stealer in after one of his sessions of wine and women."

"Stealer in? Do you mean as a thief?" Aya asked.

"Yoshi is a valued member of the Yoshinobu family. He is its strategic counselor. Midori is a valued lieutenant to the head of the Five Families Ninja group working exclusively for the Yoshinobu," Hideki said.

"Ninja? No wonder you two fooled me," Aya said.

"Midori, you are carrying the most important part of this plan. Can you get the help you need, and can you accomplish the mission?" Hideki asked.

"I believe I can," she said. "I will depart tonight for Nagasaki to work on this and to gather evidence against Heizo."

"Very well. I will work on the daimyo. Let's get a good night's sleep and push on early in the morning," Hideki said.

"When do you plan to approach the Sung?" Yoshi asked.

"I will have to wait for the right time. I really know little about them and their relationship to Heizo. They might not support an attempt to replace him," Hideki said. "It may have to wait until we pass this way again."

Yoshi shrugged. Aya took that as a reason to depart.

"What about me?" Yasuke asked.

"That is for Midori to decide," Hideki said.

"He is no ninja. He has a warrior spirit. Take him with you young master," Midori said.

"What about it, Yasuke? You want to learn how to fight tengu and pirates?" Hideki asked.

"Absolutely," Yasuke said. There was no smile on his young face.

XXVIII

The Sung

The fat man in Chinese clothing smoked from a long-stemmed pipe. He sat in a straight-back chair with his feet on a cushion. Two young serving girls were taking the remnants of his evening meal back to the kitchen when a deep voice behind the sliding door spoke.

"Reporting," the voice said in Chinese.

The fat man took the pipe from his mouth. "Enter," he said. Then he clapped his hands to dismiss the girls from the room. They bowed and scurried out as soon as the man entered. They stayed out of his way. They knew of him and his reputation.

The messenger was slender and tall. He, too, was attired in long, Chinese silk robes. His long, black hair was tied behind at the nape of his neck. Around his waist was a wide, red sash. In front, two hatchets were tucked into the sash with only the head and tip of the handle showing. He bowed to the fat man.

"What have you learned?" The fat man asked.

"The yojimbo leads them. They are hatching a plan to bring down governor Heizo. They want to enlist the help of the Ryukyuans, the daimyo in Shimabara, and eventually us."

"Who is he?" The fat man asked.

"Uncertain. They are sending a woman to steal Heizo's accounting books," the slender man said.

"A woman? Very interesting. How?" The fat man asked.

"She said she would either enter as a prostitute or a stealer in," the slender man said.

"So the yojimbo has ninja at his disposal. That changes

things and makes a visit with the daimyo possible. I believe a shogun spy or emissary has come to visit," the fat man said.

"Orders?" the slender man asked.

"I need to think this through. We already know how Heizo operates. Even if he pays good money for this information, ultimately our station will not improve. We have seen how he treats his partners the Portuguese. On the other hand, if we participate in Heizo's overthrow, what can we expect in return?"

"What do you wish to have happen?" the slender man asked.

"That is the question, is it not? The Chinese ban on direct trade with Japan is still in force. It was punishment for the Wako pirates leading raids on Chinese soil. Heizo has ensured the Wako Pirates are as strong as ever, so I do not foresee any change politically on that front," the fat man said while packing his clay pipe. "The Wako will remain dangerous for years to come."

"What if we received permission to do our own trading?" the slender man said.

"Good thinking, but highly unlikely," the fat man said. "We don't have the shipping, and we are not officials to the imperial court. So, what is our strength?" the fat man asked.

The slender man thought for a moment. "We are a secret society sworn to loyalty. We exist in the shadows and we are in every port."

"Very well put," the fat man said. "So we need to think on a larger scale."

"Sorry master, this is not an arena I usually frequent," the slender man said.

"On the contrary Hai Yang," the fat man said. "You are the leader of the Golden Edge Tong. Your accomplishments have kept you in that position for several years. It is time you develop a strategic eye so you can move up."

"Master, there is no place for me to go," the slender man said, "unless you step down."

"Oh, I am not stepping down. But I may step up," the fat man said.

"How?"

"If the young ronin is successful in bringing Heizo down, who steps into the void?"

The slender man thought for a moment. "I imagine the Portuguese will want to strike a new deal with the Tokugawa," he said.

"But will the Tokugawa let that happen?" The fat man asked.

"Why wouldn't they?"

"Two reasons. First, the Portuguese come with their church. The Tokugawa are more and more restrictive of the Kirishitans. The riots that are cropping up with some regularity scare them. The fact that the Dutch are in Hirado up north attests to the Portuguese's days being numbered," the fat man said.

"What is number two?"

"Number two is the Portuguese are involved in slavery. I believe most of the missing Japanese families can be laid at their doorstep," the fat man said.

"The Portuguese are stealing Japanese families and selling them into slavery?" the slender man asked.

"Probably not. I imagine Heizo is targeting Buddhist families to seize what he needs for his new Shinto trappings. He is probably using his private connections for that, but it is the Portuguese that transport them to the slave auctions of Malacca and westward."

"Even enemies make money together," the slender man said.

"Of course, but when it becomes public knowledge the Portuguese will be out," the fat man said.

"So you think that the Dutch will be brought down to fill the void left by the Portuguese?"

"Yes," the fat man said.

"Then how does that help us?" The slender man asked.

"The Portuguese own Macau and Manila. They will not want to give up the flow of trade to and from Japan. They will need someone in Nagasaki to act as their representative. We have legitimate enterprises throughout the world. I think you need to send some agents to Hirado. Find out who is in charge.

Find out how they operate. What are their weaknesses? Curry their favor; spend some money. Do what you are good at. This young ronin could be good for us on many levels. Keep an eye on him. I would not want anything to happen to him just yet," the fat man said.

"Yes, master! It will be as you asked," the slender man said.

"I think it is time for me to start buying warehouse property in Nagasaki. I believe we are going to need it," the fat man said to no one in particular.

XXIX

Aya's Village

"I trust your stay was pleasant," the Chinese fat man said.

"Much more pleasant than sleeping out in the open," Hideki replied.

"Our furnishings are scant. It is, after all, a temple," the fat man said.

"They were sufficient to our needs sir and much appreciated," Hideki said as he bowed.

"Then perhaps we can be of assistance in a future enterprise," the fat man said.

"Possibly," Hideki said fully alert now. "Would this future enterprise have anything to do with pirates and their leader?"

"Very much so," the fat man said. "We would look forward to supporting that enterprise in any way possible."

"That is very good to know," Hideki said. "I plan to pass this way again in a few days. Perhaps we can speak then?"

"Perhaps," the fat man said.

"Before we take our leave I would like to pass on some information that you may find interesting," Hideki said.

"And what would that be?"

"I have it on good authority that the massacres of your temples may have been carried out by the second in command of the Portuguese," Hideki said.

"I am less than surprised. Lobo likes to kill. But why would he target our temples?"

"An acquaintance of mine who is knowledgeable in these things says one of the large tigers currently in holding pens in

Nagasaki was trained to follow the scent of cinnamon. The trail was left to the temple's doorstep and then each room dusted with the stuff," Hideki said. "I am sorry that is all I can give you."

"It is enough," the fat man said. "When you pass this way again, please stop and talk."

Hideki bowed. "It would be my pleasure."

"What did the Sung fat man want?" Yoshi asked as he and Jubei strolled up.

"You should speak more nicely of our host," Hideki said.

"He did not look like any temple priest I have ever seen," Yoshi said.

"Oh he is not. Unless I miss my guess, he is the leader of the Triad in Nagasaki," Hideki said.

"Yes," Yoshi said. "That explanation fits his description. What did he have to say?"

"He said we should stop and talk to him about our new enterprise upon our return," Hideki said.

"So you were correct," Jubei said. "They were listening to everything we said."

"It appears so," Hideki said. "He was interested in your information about the tigers."

"As well he should be," Yoshi said. "It takes a special kind of evil to slaughter monks and priests in their temple."

"And they might have gotten away with it," Jubei said. "If it were not for your ninja skills no one would have been the wiser."

"Why sword master, was that a compliment?" Yoshi asked.

"Yes, but do not let it go to your head, monkey," Jubei warned.

Aya and Yasuke approached, followed by a pack horse led by a teamster.

"Who is a monkey?" Aya asked.

"Never mind," Hideki said. "Your traveling companions were exchanging verbal barbs."

"They do that all the time," Aya said. She turned to the horse. "My supplies arrived."

"Those are a lot of supplies," Yoshi said.

"Yes, but we may need them," Aya said. "Breakfast was certainly scant."

"But the price was right," Yoshi added.

"Chinese Buddhist temples are known for their austerity. We should be thankful for the shelter," Hideki said.

"Oh, I am grateful. But we will be able to eat well on the road," she said, pointing to the horse packed high with supplies. "So which is it to be today, my Lord or yojimbo?"

"A little of both, I think," Hideki said. "You will have to lead us from here. How far is it to your village?"

"We should be there by noon," Aya said. "If we do not linger long at the village, we can be to the daimyo's castle and Shimabara before dark."

"Good, I don't mind telling you that I do not like traveling at night with that thing still running around, even if you did manage to put an arrow into it," Yoshi said.

"You battled the tengu and lived." Aya asked. "I did not think that possible. You must be as skilled as my bartender thinks and twice as lucky."

"It was not much of a battle. We were inside and he on the other side of some wooden walls," Hideki said.

"I heard walls could not hold him. I heard he could scale high walls and smash down houses," Aya said.

"I cannot speak to those things. I just know he was very large and very loud," Hideki said.

"But you wounded it?"

"I got an arrow into it. Whether it was wounded or not remains to be seen," Hideki said.

"It let out a loud howl when Hideki let fly. It then tried to smash down the walls in earnest. Then it shuffled off," Jubei said. "I would still like to know more about it."

"Oh no, Jubei-sama. To meet that thing is to invite death," Aya said.

"Why does it attack only Kirishitans?" Jubei asked aloud.

"No one knows," Aya said. "But if I were to guess, I would say it was the result of some old Shinto evil spell."

"More like Shugendō," Yoshi said.

"Shugendō?" Jubei asked. "Were they not the fathers of Yamabushi and ninja?"

Now Yoshi had everyone's attention. "Yes," he said. "They were the early aesthetics. They broke off from the Shinto and retreated to the mountains. They felt the religion had become too diluted. They went to the mountains to regain their spirituality. They wanted to commune with the kami, the gods of the mountain. Some say they are still up in the mountains."

"Are you saying all this because we have fought with Yamabushi recently?" Jubei asked.

"No, I am saying it because Aya brought it up and it was the Shugendō who invented the dark arts. They were the ones who cast spells, not the Shinto."

"I have never seen a Shugendō priest," Jubei said. "I thought they were part of ancient history."

"Maybe, maybe not," Yoshi said.

"Why not?" Hideki said. "We have seen everything else on this trip."

"What do they look like?" Aya asked.

"As I recall from my father's stories," Yoshi said, "they dressed all in white. They shaved their heads and carried a large naginata. They were able to conjure superhuman strength when needed."

"If they have superhuman strength, I hope one shows up on our side," Aya said.

"That may be a problem," Yoshi said. "No one ever knows for sure when one is summoned if it will fight on your side or not."

"We are just talking old wife's tales. Aya repeated some gossip she's heard to scare young children into eating their vegetables, and now we are worrying about potentially fighting a Shugendō priest. We have enough enemies now. Let's not make some up," Hideki said.

"I am afraid that warning may come a little too late," Yoshi said.

"What have you done, monkey?" Jubei asked.

"I was traveling across Taro Mountain and got lost. I heard the tengu roar. It was dark and I heard a human death scream that was close. The next tengu roar was very close indeed. I climbed a large tree that only a bear could follow and before I fell asleep applied some of the dark arts to summon help," Yoshi said.

"We have Portuguese swordsmen killing samurai, a tengu killing Kirishitans, Yoshi's cat killing Chinese Buddhist priests, a governor sponsoring killer Yamabushi and the governor and the Portuguese knee-deep in slavery. Now we may have to face a Shugendō priest from the distant past summoned by one of our own. This trip keeps getting better and better," Hideki said.

"Good job, monkey," Jubei said. "If this Shugendō priest kills one of us, I'm killing you."

"We have not seen the Shugendō priest yet. He probably does not exist. He is probably just a fairy tale," Hideki said. "Besides, if he's real we have a 50/50 chance he fights with us and not against us, right Yoshi?"

"That is the way I remember it," Yoshi said.

Jubei looked at Hideki. "It may all be a fairy tale. You forget I have trained with ninja. I have seen some very strange things that I could not explain brought about by present-day ninja. Yoshi is considered old school by all that know him. He uses haragai. He sees through the darkness. Everyone thought that art was dead. But how often has he saved us with it?" Jubei asked. "If Yoshi thinks there is a chance we may meet this Shugendō priest, I for one will be thinking about how to defeat it."

"Okay, okay. Maybe it will work for us. I hope so. We could certainly use some good luck," Hideki said.

"We did not see Midori this morning," Aya said.

"She left last night," Yoshi said.

"She did not even say goodbye," Aya said.

"You will see her again. She says you still owe her for two nights of noodles and samisen playing," Yoshi said.

"That is one bill I guess I had better pay," Aya said.

"Worry about that later. Let's get moving. Aya, you are leading us," Hideki said.

Mount Taro was far off to the northwest and Mount Unzen was to the immediate east. The trail moved upward ever so slightly. It was an easy trek. They arrived at Aya's village before noon.

They moved into the center of the mostly deserted village. Hideki was struck by the poverty. He had been caretaker of the Yoshinobu lands and had at one time or another been in the huts of every peasant on his grandfather's estate. This village reeked of desperation. The paths were not well kept. Weeds grew everywhere. There were no gardens. The thatch on the roofs was old, and large holes could be seen in each.

Because it was close to noon, the farmers were returning to their homes for the noon meal. The appearance of samurai and a horse struck fear into the men and women as they returned. They bowed low and scampered into their huts.

Finally, the village headman approached, bowing low at the waist. "Honorable samurai-sama, we have already paid our taxes to Lord Matsukawa. We have nothing else to give," he said.

"Hello, Ichi," Aya said. "You are the headman now?"

Ichi bowed again and again. He could see no way in which this would end well for him. "Yes, my lady. But we have nothing to give."

"You don't recognize me, Ichi?" Aya asked.

Ichi's head came up ever so slightly, just enough to see Aya's expensive kimono.

"No my lady, I am sure we have never met." Ichi said.

"How about a 13-year-old girl sold to the talent scouts some fifteen years ago from Gotou and Hasebe's hut?" Aya asked.

Ichi's head came up slowly until he could see Aya's face. Then he fell on his knees and prostrated himself. "Forgive us. Please do not take revenge. We have so little," he pleaded.

"Be at peace Ichi. I come to give, not to take. Are Gotou and Hasebe still alive?" Aya asked.

Glad to be conveying good news, Ichi rose to his knees. "Oh yes. They have two sons and two daughters grown. All are married. Their hut is crowded during festivals."

"Go about your business Ichi. My yojimbo and his men will accompany me," Aya said.

Ichi bowed low again. "Yes my lady."

Aya motioned for all to follow her. They arrived at a disheveled thatch hut. There was smoke coming out of the eaves of the structure, so someone was present.

"There will not be room for all," Aya said. "I will go in first."

"No," Hideki said. "Your yojimbo will go in first. You come behind."

Aya fell in behind Hideki. Both stooped low to enter at the only opening.

Yoshi looked at Jubei. "You have never been in a dirt floor hovel before, have you sword master?" Jubei did not respond to the taunt. "Okay," Yoshi said. "We will stay out here and keep our eye on the plunder."

Jubei found a tree stump and sat down after pulling his katana from his obi. Yoshi went to an opening in the thatch wall and peaked in.

Hideki straightened as he entered the dim lighted and smoky hut. He moved to the right to keep from being illuminated by the daylight.

Aya stood as well and moved toward the bowing figures gathered on the far side of the iroi fire pit in the center of the hut.

"Otosan, Okasan, do you not recognize your daughter?" Aya asked.

All heads came up suspiciously. An old hag with no teeth strained eyes to see Aya's face. An old man with one good eye moved his head from his wife's face to that of Aya's.

One of the grown men spoke first. "My lady, we are but poor farmers. We have nothing for you here. Please be good to us."

"So, you speak as the man of the house do you Akio?" Aya asked.

The man looked stunned. "How do you know my name, my lady?"

"I was not lying, Akio. I am your sister. I was sold to talent scouts fifteen years ago. I have returned from that hell to greet my loving family," Aya said.

All prostrated themselves again each in supplication to

Aya, asking to be forgiven and spared. In the little hut, the noise was deafening.

Hideki stepped forward. "Quiet!" he shouted. Instantly the room became still except for the crying of the women.

"I have thought long and hard about what I would say to you upon my return. I thought about killing you all when I was being raped and manhandled and whipped for wanting to go home. But an interesting thing happened. Turns out I have a tongue for something besides the sex trade. I can learn other languages. And I did. And I went from being the toy of a sadistic foreigner to being his wife and managing all his accounts in Japan. In other words, I am now a rich woman. And my new friends here have taught me that there is more to life than making money," Aya said.

Aya looked at Hideki. Hideki shrugged. "There is a horse outside. It is weighed down with gifts that will make you rich in this village and ensure an easy life for all here. I give it freely if you can answer one question," Aya said.

"What is the question?" This from the dirty woman at Akio's side.

"The voice of reason belongs to a woman. Very well, I want to know if Gotou and Hasebe, my loving father and mother, knew what kind of life they were selling me into fifteen years ago?" Aya said.

Akio conferred with two other men and their wives.

"We are afraid your yojimbo will kill us no matter how we answer," Akio said.

Aya nodded. "Fair enough; you need not answer. I prefer to believe you did not. I must get on with my life, so I cannot tarry in the warm bosom of my family. The gifts on the horse are yours," Aya said as she turned and fled.

Hideki was caught by surprise. He bowed and bent down to follow her out.

Aya was already giving instructions to the teamster counting out his coins when Hideki caught up to her.

"That was quick," Hideki said.

"You saw them. I am but a fleeting memory to them. I wanted to rub their noses in my success and in their desperation, but could not. They have nothing except their offspring. They probably would not have that if they had not sold me," Aya said.

"Do I detect a beating heart instead of a change purse?" Hideki asked.

"Who knows? If I fall prey to crazy ronin schemes, maybe I'm losing my mind as well as my grip on reality," Aya said.

"Or maybe you are human after all," Yoshi said.

"Are we moving?" Jubei asked from the stump.

Yes," Hideki said. "You are leading the way again, Aya."

"Follow me Prince of the Yoshinobu. It is an easy walk."

XXX

Damsels in Distress

The movement to Unzen town was easy. The road was a dark volcanic sand pounded by years of travel. It sloped downward to the left, away from Mount Unzen far off to the right. Trees and scrub on either side of the road hid the terrain, but it did not take a topographer to realize to the right the ground sloped up to the summit of the treeless and hellish looking mountain. The volcanic cone spewing hot gases and the barrenness of the whole mountain top gave it a sinister and inhospitable look. But it was several ri to the east. To the left the ground sloped off quickly to what Hideki suspected was Shimabara Bay. He could not see the water, but felt its presence.

Yoshi was the first to react. He froze. So did Jubei and Hideki. Aya kept walking until Jubei whispered, "Freeze."

"Sounds of battle and women screaming," Yoshi said.

"How far?" Jubei asked.

"Not far," Yoshi said, cupping his hands to his ears.

"I do not hear anything," Aya said.

"That is why my family does not employ you as a ninja," Hideki said.

"Can you tell how many?" Jubei asked.

"No, but I can tell that swords and something larger are involved," Yoshi said.

"Let us hurry. Someone may need our help. Stay on the road, Aya. Keep her safe Yasuke," Hideki said as he started to shuffle ahead. Jubei and Yoshi kept pace.

Aya moved slowly after the men, Yasuke in tow.

"Just what I suspected he would do, abandon me," Aya said.

"But he did not abandon you. I am here," Yasuke said.

Aya turned to her protector. "And I thank you for it, Yasuke. Yesterday you were just an assistant noodle cook that I let sell flutes in front of the Jaded Princess and sleep with the chickens. Now my life may depend on you. No, I do not blame you. I blame those fool samurai. They rush off full tilt into danger without any thought as to what the odds may be. At least Jubei had the sense to ask how many they face. Hooking my star to this kind of recklessness may need some rethinking," Aya said, almost to herself.

When Aya and Yasuke reached the rise, they saw the scene laid before them in a grassy pasture. The road split the pasture from top to bottom and a stream from right to left. A small footbridge allowed the road to traverse the stream. Off the road and on the side of the footbridge were two women. One wore the garb of a Buddhist nun. The other wore the bright kimono of a samurai girl. Three samurai were engaging six yamabushi dressed in an attire Aya had never seen before. Hideki, Jubei and Yoshi were shuffling quickly to reach the scene.

"Who are they?" Aya asked.

"They are called yamabushi and have something to do with the Shinto religion. I think they killed my masters at the Buddhist temple where I stayed. I dislike them almost as much as pirates," Yasuke said.

"It does not look good for the samurai," Aya said. "Look, one is already wounded and lying in the road."

"You have not seen our three fight, have you?" Yasuke asked.

"I saw Hideki beat the stuffing out of some deputies with your flutes," Aya said.

"That was child's play for him. I have a feeling if we watch closely, you will see some expert swordsmanship from Hideki-sama and Jubei-sama."

Aya turned her head toward Yasuke. "You like them, don't you?" she asked.

Yasuke did not look at her. He kept his eyes focused on

the area by the bridge. "*Like* may not be the right word. I respect them both. Neither says much, but when they do you need to listen. They are both strong men doing right when they can. I think I would like to be like them when I am older," Yasuke said.

Aya kept staring at the side of Yasuke's face. "I believe you already are like them."

Yasuke kept staring into the pasture. "That is a good thing."

Aya joined Yasuke staring at the battle below.

The six monks had the three remaining samurai surrounded with their backs to the stream and the women between them and the water. It looked desperate for the samurai.

Aya watched as Yoshi, Jubei, and Hideki move up behind the yamabushi. There they hesitated. She did not know why. She stopped breathing, completely captivated by the scene of brutality that was about to unfold. She was too far away to hear what was being said.

"I am telling you, there is greater danger from the trees on the left," Yoshi said.

"Haragai?" Jubei asked.

"Yes, and it is sounding a very large bell in my head," Yoshi said.

They hesitated for only an instant. "The evil is in front of us now. It is what we will deal with first. Yoshi, get to the women and protect them. Jubei and I will deal with the yamabushi."

Continuing to move forward, Hideki drew both swords. "We are Ronin on a musha shugyo. We will assist," Hideki yelled.

Drawing hope from those words, the samurai shouted back their understanding and attacked the yamabushi with a renewed vigor.

Yoshi approached the two women and bowed. "I am Yoshi, friend of the two ronin, and I am here to help."

"What can a merchant do to help?" The young girl asked, as she drew the tonto from her obi.

"Akane," the old woman said. "Be polite."

"Yes, obasan," the girl bowed her head but did not take her eyes off Yoshi.

Yoshi took off his medicine chest and withdrew his bedroll from the top. From within he pulled his ninja sword and placed himself in front of the women with his back toward them.

"Maybe you are not a merchant after all," the girl said.

"I am what I need to be my lady. But unless I miss my guess, our real threat will emerge from those trees over there just as soon as my comrades terminate those fools with the shaved heads."

"Do you really think so?" the old nun asked.

"I am sure of it. Just watch and listen," Yoshi said.

Three of the yamabushi turned towards the new threat of Hideki and Jubei. The remaining three pressed their attack on the three samurai.

One large yamabushi gave a bloodcurdling cry, raised his naginata over his head and charged Jubei. Jubei surprised Hideki by charging at the same yamabushi. Hideki was surprised for two reasons. First, charging was not a standard swordsmanship tactic. Secondly, that left two yamabushi for Hideki to fight.

The large yamabushi timed his attack well and brought the large blade down with both hands and both feet planted amid a loud shout. Only Jubei was not there. At the last moment Jubei angled to his right and lunged inside the arc of the blade. Jubei's own blade moved from the scabbard in a lightning iai draw that found flesh as soon as it cleared the scabbard. The large yamabushi collapsed in a heap of bright blood and intestines. Jubei had just executed a flawless cut from navel to armpit and did not stop. Jubei let his momentum carry him to the nearest yamabushi fighting a samurai, taking him from behind by turning his blade and executing a right to left yokomen cut. The monk yelled and collapsed at his opponent's feet.

Jubei turned to the two remaining yamabushi. They both divided their attention between the samurai opponents and this new fierce threat. When they did, the samurai struck them down. One fell all the way to the ground and the other to a kneeling position. Today was not a day for forgiveness. The one-eyed sword demon dressed in black had set the stage for ferocity. The samurai finished off their wounded opponents.

Jubei flicked the blood from his sword and returned to its scabbard in a flourish. He then turned to watch his protégé.

The two to challenge Hideki were now even with him. The deaths of their comrades made them cautious. They moved to either side of Hideki. One raised his naginata and the other had his blade aimed at Hideki's head.

"Aren't you going to help him?" One of the samurai asked Jubei.

Jubei did not answer. He just folded his hands on his swords and watched.

The girl asked Yoshi, "Can he survive?"

"I do not know. Fighting is always a chancy thing at best. But he is lucky," Yoshi said.

"It will take more than luck. It is quite clear that one means to distract him while the other spears him," the girl said.

"Possibly," Yoshi said.

As the overhead strike came from his left, Hideki moved towards the lunge from his right. When he started his spin to the right he brought his right hand up and outside with his short sword. The wakazashi bit into the long naginata blade and deflected it to the right and down. With the completion of the spin he was away from the kill zone of the overhead strike from his left and now inside the attacker's vulnerable zone from the lunge. With the momentum of the lunge deflected, the attacker almost ran onto Hideki's katana in his left hand. Hideki thrust it through his throat and out the back of his neck. The attacker dropped to his knees releasing the naginata and coughing up blood.

Hideki let him fall by yanking his sword free and spinning to the second attacker—only he was not there. With the killing of all his comrades, the last yamabushi had had enough. He was several steps toward the trees before Hideki realized there was no longer a threat.

Hideki cleaned both blades using folded paper carried inside his kimono and moved toward Jubei.

"You keep letting them go and you will see them again."

"You go chase him down if you wish," Hideki said. "But do not forget the threat from the trees."

The samurai introduced themselves and thanked Jubei and Hideki. Yoshi moved to help the wounded samurai using his medicine box.

When introductions were done, the women moved up. "We thank you young men for helping," the old woman said.

"Why would yamabushi attack you?" Hideki asked.

The old woman continued answering for the group. "We do not know. My granddaughter and I were making a pilgrimage to the baths at Unzen when they attacked with no warning."

"Where have you come from?" Hideki asked.

"Shimabara," the old woman answered.

"That is the third time we have run into them. Before this trip, I had never seen a yamabushi," Hideki said.

"Where are you from?" the young girl asked.

"Jubei is from Edo. I am from Kiai province. We all met on the road," Hideki said.

"You all seem to be very good friends to have met on the road," the young girl proposed.

"Akane," the old woman warned. "Do not pry."

"I just find it interesting that these two with such combat skills and the magic merchant over there just happen along on the Unzen/Shimabara road when we need it."

"You would prefer if we waited a while?" Hideki asked.

"Of course not," the old woman said. "Please forgive my granddaughter; she has been raised among rough men."

Yoshi moved back to the group. "He will need a litter to be moved anywhere."

"One of our entourage raced back to Shimabara when we were attacked. I am sure help will arrive shortly," the old woman said.

"And who might they be," one of the samurai asked, watching Aya and Yasuke come down the road.

"She is with us," Hideki said. "She is the reason we are on this road."

Aya moved up and bowed to all. "Aya desu," she said.

Yasuke moved up and did likewise. "Yasuke desu."

"I hate to break up the reunion," Yoshi said. "But those trees are still a threat."

Everyone turned toward the trees. "Are you expecting more yamabushi?" The old woman asked.

"Something else," Yoshi said. "Something much larger I think."

Then the loud howl that Hideki and Jubei heard on the mountain filled the pasture and struck fear into everybody's hearts.

"By the Buddha, what is that?" the old nun asked, clutching at the robes at her throat.

"That is what the people of Mount Taro call a tengu," Jubei said.

"A tengu—are there really such things?" the girl asked.

"We do not know. We have not seen one in daylight. We know it is real, comes out at night, is quite powerful, and so far, has killed only Kirishitans."

"Kirishitans; there are no Kirishitans here," the girl said.

"Maybe it is expanding," Hideki said looking at Aya.

"What should we do?" The old nun asked.

Hideki stared at the far tree line. "We have a dilemma," he said, pointing to the wounded samurai. "We cannot move him without risking further injury. We could leave him to the tengu's tender mercies, but it hasn't been very merciful so far."

"No, we will not abandon him," the young girl said. "I will stay with him. You help my grandmother to Shimabara."

"It is a type of madness, is it not, this samurai thing?" Aya said to no one.

"Close to it," Yoshi said.

"What do you mean?" the old nun asked.

"You make decisions counter to sanity. Common sense and self-preservation are not high on your list for defining actions."

"What would be the best course of action if a sane person was deciding?" the girl asked.

"Leave the injured man, hurry back with help but with enough men to turn the tables on this tengu," Aya said. "Save as many lives as possible."

"You may choose that course if you wish," Yoshi said.

"Two days ago, I would have been the first to do so. The insanity must be contagious. Now I find myself dreading what I know is coming but looking forward to it as well," Aya said.

"Interesting, is it not?" Yoshi said.

"You, of all people, know better. But still you follow this do-gooder around the country from one adventure to the next against overwhelming odds and act like it's natural," Aya accused.

"Yes, Hideki does grow on you," Yoshi said.

"I find him an acquired taste," Jubei offered.

Aya ignored him. Instead, she turned to the girl. "Hideki, Jubei, and Yoshi will no more allow the wounded samurai to remain here alone than they would abandon me, and the Buddha knows I have given them reason," Aya said. "So, let us skip the theatrics and hear what we are really going to do."

"Another convert," Yoshi said.

"Welcome to our little band of lunatics," Jubei said.

Aya nodded. All eyes went to Hideki. "My lady," Hideki said looking to the old nun. "I am really not in charge. They just humor me usually in a situation like this where we talk out a tactic if there is time, and anyone with the best idea acts as leader," Hideki stated.

"Agreed," the girl answered for her grandmother. All looked to Hideki.

Hideki nodded agreement. "It will be dark in an hour. The tengu supposedly hunts at night. We cannot count on it, however. A rescue may be in the works. I cannot imagine a samurai lord not moving heaven and earth to ensure the safety of his mother and daughter. So, we just have to hang on until relief arrives. That may be several hours or sometime tomorrow. Either way, we must contend with a known murderer of gigantic size who may be intent on our demise," Hideki said. He then paused to see if there were any comments. There were none.

"Okay, I suggest we gather as much wood as we can and build huge bonfires around our position between the road and the stream. We need enough wood in case we are here all night. We pool our supplies and even sleep in shifts. The last time Jubei and I tangled with the tengu, it scared me. It is large and powerful. I do not believe it is agile. And we know it bleeds," Hideki said.

"How do you know that?" the girl asked.

"Hideki got an arrow into it. It roared, and we found the blood trail the next morning," Jubei said.

"I have a question," the girl said. "Do we fight the tengu in front of the fire or behind it?"

The three Shimabara samurai nodded their heads acknowledging a good question.

"What do you suggest?" Hideki asked.

"I think behind it. If we fight in front we will be illuminated against the flame. If we fight behind the flame the illumination favors no one," she said.

Hideki looked at Jubei. Jubei nodded his agreement. Hideki turned to Yoshi. Yoshi shrugged.

"We are fine with your tactics. We will stay behind the fire. Are you going to evacuate your grandmother?" Hideki asked.

"Just try it young man," the old nun said.

"We three have fought together many times, and you three Shimabara samurai are a team. Let us keep the teams together. We will go gather firewood while you man the first watch," Hideki said.

"Agreed," the girl said.

"I suggest we gather wood on this side of the road," Yoshi said.

"Really?" Jubei asked.

Aya and Yasuke joined them.

XXXI

Fighting a Tengu

By the time the shadows extended across the road, three bonfires were stoked along its length. Behind the fires were large piles of dry branches, enough for the night. Directly behind the fuel for the fires were the collected naginata from the slain yamabushi. The corpses had been dragged away from the defense site toward the dreaded tree line.

"How is the haragai Yoshi?" Jubei asked.

"Still there," Yoshi replied. "He is in the trees."

"It should not be long now," Hideki said.

"I am scared," Aya admitted.

"Everyone gets scared," Jubei said. "It is what you do about that fear that counts. You stayed."

Aya tried to smile but did not quite make it. Jubei stepped next to her and removed his wakazashi with scabbard intact. This he extended with palm down to her. "Unlike our young friend, I fight Shinkage-ryu style. We only use one sword. Use this if you have to keep yourself safe," Jubei said.

"I do not know what to say or do. I do not know how to use it," Aya said.

"It is deadly sharp. Keep it in the scabbard unless you feel threatened. If you must draw it just cut down whatever is troubling you," Jubei said.

Aya took the weapon gingerly in both hands and Jubei turned away.

The girl and her grandmother moved to Aya's side. "That

285

is no small gift he bestows on you," the girl said. "A samurai's sword is his soul."

"I do not know what to do with it," Aya said.

"Here, let me help," the old nun said, taking the wakazashi from Aya and placing it into her Obi on the left side. "This is how we samurai women wear our tantos. Your wakazashi is larger, but is carried there."

"Thank you. But I am not a samurai," Aya confessed.

"No matter dear," the old nun said. "After tonight you may be."

Aya managed to smile. "I am a merchant and a brothel and gambling-house owner and have been worse. You are not supposed to talk to my kind."

"Aya," the girl said. "If you are good enough for these warriors and my grandmother to accept, you are good enough for anyone."

Aya knelt down on the grass and started to cry.

"Why is she crying?" Hideki asked Yoshi.

"Who knows?" Yoshi said. "I would try it myself if I thought it would help our cause tonight."

Everyone froze at the sound of a huge howl emanating from the direction of the far trees. With the darkness, no one could see the trees anymore. Their vision was reduced to a short distance beyond the fires. From the crashing and stomping in the trees beyond, it was certain the tengu was coming.

"Does anyone have an idea on how to fight this thing?" the girl asked.

"He wields a two-bladed naginata. He is very large, so I assume powerful. If you try to clash with, him you will die. Stay away from the blades and work on his wrists and legs is my best guess," Jubei said.

"Not bad, sword master," Yoshi teased.

"I meant it for the real warriors. Use whatever dirty tricks you are comfortable with," Jubei said.

"Boys, behave," Hideki said.

"Do not venture beyond the road," Yoshi yelled as he cast objects into the grass beyond.

"What were those?" the girl asked.

Yoshi showed her one. "It is called a tetsu-bishi. It consists of three spikes. No matter where or how I throw it, one of the spikes will point up," Yoshi said.

"Amazing," the girl said.

Then he was there. He looked huge. The firelight illuminated his fiery red face with white stripes and long nose. He was clad in a flowing white robe pulled off his massive black shoulders hanging on his back, like wings. His white hakama, white leggings and white tabi set off the blackness of his arms and chest. In his massive right hand, he held a two-bladed naginata.

"How did he miss the tetsu-bishi?" Akane asked.

"Look at his feet. He is wearing gettas," Yoshi said. "The wooden clogs are impervious to the spikes."

The tengu stepped closer to the center fire and swung the dual bladed naginata into the flames. Half-burned logs and tree limbs blasted toward the samurai.

"Look out!" Hideki cried as he barely dodged flaming embers streaking directly at him.

"Yoshi," Jubei yelled. "Do you have darts?"

"Hai," yelled Yoshi moving closer to the flames.

Jubei joined him, pulling a kogatana from his scabbard. "He appears right handed. Aim for his right shoulder."

Both let their small weapons fly. Both struck him deeply in the shoulder area. The beast let out a massive roar of pain and anger and reached for the kogatana and dart with his left hand. He did not let go of the naginata. When he pulled out the kogatana, red blood pumped out over his white kimono. He attempted to do the same for the dart but had difficulty grasping it due to the blood. This made him madder as evidenced by bloodcurdling roars. When it did remove the dart, more blood flowed.

"Well, it still bleeds," Hideki said.

"Yes, and if it bleeds, we can kill it," Jubei said. "I just hope we damaged it enough so it cannot wield its weapon."

The beast picked up the naginata with both hands and elevated the blades high above his head. He let the weapon drop of its own momentum to the right rear. As the blades moved down, the beast stepped forward, bringing his momentum toward the fire. The blades crashed into the burning logs sending them and a million embers toward the stream.

Yoshi and Jubei dove in opposite directions to miss the fiery wood headed their way.

Hideki jumped up and stepped into the center with both swords drawn. "I think we will have to cross blades with this thing."

The center fire was dispersed and was not a deterrent any longer. The tengu held the naginata at center shaft in front of his body, blades angled between his head and right shoulder. He plodded straight towards Hideki.

Hideki stood his ground. Yoshi and Jubei moved back to flank Hideki on both sides. There was plenty of illumination from the other two fires. When the beast was within striking distance he pushed the blades high with his right hand and guided the weapon down upon Hideki.

Hideki stayed planted as long as he dared, then dove to his left front. He completed the roll on his feet as the impact of the two blades striking the ground where he had been sounded throughout the pasture.

The two blades cut deeply into the sod. Three things happened at once. Yoshi jumped on the head of the naginata, keeping it from being extracted. Hideki sliced the tengu above the knee of his leading right leg. Jubei took two running steps and jumped at the beast. He slashed at its face with a two-handed overhead strike.

The beast screamed with the new pain in its leg and fell back just in time to make Jubei miss its head. But Jubei seldom misses completely. The wooden white and red mask with the long nose split and fell away

Everyone was stunned. The tengu mask was at least familiar in Japanese lore. The real face of the tengu was not. It was as black as the torso. It had wide lips and a flat nose and tattoos all along its face. The beast used his opponent's stunned inaction to release the naginata and reach behind him in his flowing robe to retrieve a nodachi. This long sword he swung at Jubei's head. Jubei parried the blow with his katana, but the power behind the blow knocked Jubei sideways and onto the ground. The black giant would have followed up with the finishing blow to Jubei except Hideki sliced his right buttock with his katana.

The giant screamed and spun on Hideki with an overhead strike. Hideki's training was almost his undoing. He used an X block consisting of both his katana and wakazashi.

The shock of the blow drove Hideki to his knees. He knew he could not withstand another. The giant retracted the blade and screamed his anger as he brought it down again at Hideki.

"By the Buddha," Hideki thought. "Is this how it ends?" He would never see Myo again. He would never see his new nephew. He would never hold the sword again. His eighteen years did not pass before his eyes. Instead, he wondered why he could not make his body dive sideways and evade the attack. He forced his swords up using sheer will power, but he knew he could not stop the blades this time. They had stopped the tengu and unmasked it. They had cut it. They had made it bleed. Now it wanted revenge.

Hideki watched the long-bladed nodachi as it started toward him. Then a slicing naginata blade passed over Hideki's swords moving from his left. For an instant Hideki wondered who had saved him. Yoshi was still a step behind and to the right, too far away to mount a defense. Jubei was still reeling from the massive strike that had pummeled him to the ground. Recognition dawned as a single blade naginata struck the black giant in the chest at the same time a high pitched kiai pierced the pasture. Yasuke had entered the fray.

The tengu roared again and shifted back as he took the impact of the blade in the center of its chest. One of the six pom poms made from conch shells sewn into the yui-gesa on its torso took the full impact. The rest of the blow was dissipated by the Hirataka-nenju prayer beads hung from its neck. The blow moved the giant back a step, but it recovered quickly. It brought the nodachi down in a one-handed arc aimed at his latest tormentor. The long-bladed sword sliced into the shaft of Yasuke's naginata and into his upper arm. Yasuke screamed and went down rolling in the grass away from the beast.

Hideki slowly came to his feet and wondered if the young Ryukyuan who had just saved his life would survive the wound. He hoped so, but he had other things to worry about. The black giant had turned back to Hideki, wanting another opportunity to cut him in half.

Yoshi moved to his side and Jubei was now to the right of Yoshi.

"Damn thing will not go down," Yoshi said.

"We just have not cut it enough," Jubei said.

"Any ideas on how we accomplish that?" Hideki asked as he shook feeling back into his arms.

The three Shimabara samurai now took up positions behind the three. "We have company," Yoshi noted.

"They are most welcome," Hideki said. "But I don't see how we are going to defeat this thing and come out alive."

"That is your weakness, prince," Jubei said. "You must go into battle expecting nothing. mushin, remember? Without the naginata this is just a sword fight."

Hideki did remember. The giant stepped toward Hideki and started a right to left yokomen slash with the long sword meant to sever Hideki's head from his shoulders.

Hideki slipped into mushin. He automatically dropped by bending his knees and bringing his sword up, handle down, to deflect the blow to his right using the giant's momentum. As he did this Hideki leaped forward into the giant and stabbed his wakazashi into the large black stomach with his right hand.

The giant screamed and leapt back, placing his left hand on Hideki's short sword now lodged in his gut. He dropped to his knees. The giant brought up his nodachi and pointed it at Hideki. He came to one knee.

"By the Buddha," Yoshi said. "What do you have to do to kill one of these things?"

The answer came in the form of a white-robed yamabushi leaping over the sobbing and prostrate body of Yasuke. The newcomer landed beside the black giant and brought down a single bladed naginata on the back of the giant's neck. The black head tumbled to the grass and rolled forward to stop in front of Yoshi. The tengu corpse fell over sideways away from the newcomer and pumped blood into the grass.

Yoshi moved to his fiend's side. Jubei joined them. All three turned to look at the silent yamabushi. He was clothed almost as the tengu had been, but everything was white. Somehow, the fountain of blood spewing from the giant's neck had missed him.

The newcomer was taller than Hideki or his friends, but still shorter than the giant had been. He looked at Yoshi and bowed. Then he turned and moved back into the darkness.

"Wait," Yoshi cried. The darkness did not answer.

XXXII

Shimabara

Yoshi worked on Yasuke's arm. "How is he? Hideki asked.

"He will live," Yoshi said. "I've given him something for the pain, but the damage should not be permanent."

Akane and her grandmother moved up. "What was that white-robed monk?" Akane asked.

"I have no idea," Hideki said.

"Me either," Jubei said. "But he may have saved our lives. That was as good a use of the naginata as I have ever seen."

"Very timely too," Akane said.

"Yes," Hideki agreed. "I had met my match. In fact, I'd probably be dead now if Yasuke hadn't taken a hand."

"I do not agree," Jubei said. "Your use of mushin allowed you to deliver a fatal blow."

"I do not know," Hideki said. "It looked like he was getting up to come after me. I'm just as happy that Yoshi's friend showed up and put an end to it."

"Let's be clear," Yoshi said. "We now have two mysteries. What was that black giant and who was that white yamabushi."

"If he was no friend, who was he?" Akane asked. No one had any answers.

The old nun approached the dead giant. "I have never seen anything like this. It is what nightmares are made of."

"I have," Aya said.

All eyes turned to her.

"In Nagasaki the Portuguese bring slaves from the Africas. I have seen these features and tattoos before. I have never

293

seen any this large, but I would bet it was brought here by the Portuguese and sold to Heizo, if I had to guess."

"The govenor?" Akane asked.

"Yes, the same," Aya said.

"For what purpose?" The old nun asked.

"He is feuding with the Portuguese. They owe him money and they cannot pay. He wants to create unrest among the Kirishitans and provoke the shogun to cast the Portuguese out and bring down the Dutch from Hirado," Aya said.

"You seem very well informed," Akane said.

"She is," Hideki said. "She is married to the Portuguese Procurator, Dom Joao. Nothing happens in Nagasaki that she is not aware of."

"Interesting," Akane said. "You are obviously more than a brothel owner."

"She is much more," Hideki said. "She is our friend."

"Yoshi," Jubei said. "Did you conjure that white yamabushi?"

Yoshi shrugged.

"I do not believe he was yamabushi," the old nun said. "I have seen his dress once before, years ago, when I was a little girl at the foot of Mount Omine. I believe him to be Shugenja."

"Shugendō?" Yoshi asked.

"Yes," the old nun said.

"I do not care who he is or where he sprang up from. I owe him a life," Hideki said.

"We all do," Akane said.

"Horses," Yoshi said, "coming fast from the direction of Shimabara."

"I do not hear anything," Akane said.

"That is why you are not ninja," Aya said.

"Ninja?" Akane said. "Ninja, yamabushi, tengu and Shugenja; I have to go to the baths more often."

They all heard the horses now. They came thundering into the pasture and surrounded everyone with their swords drawn. Yoshi, Jubei, and Hideki raised their hands, palms outward to show no dangerous intent.

"Are you harmed?" One of the leaders asked Akane.

"No, but we have one wounded that will require a litter or a cart."

"Who are you?" The same man demanded looking at Jubei.

Hideki spoke. "We are ronin traveling to Shimabara who aided the women when attacked."

"Hideki?" A voice from the rear asked.

"Hai," Hideki responded.

The man moved his horse forward. All moved out of his way. The samurai leader bowed to him.

"Saito?" Hideki asked.

"Hai," Saito answered. "I see you have met my sister and grandmother."

"I have," Hideki said bowing to the women, "and enjoyed their company."

"This young man and his friends saved us all," the old nun said. "We were attacked by yamabushi."

"What the hell is this?" Saito asked, pointing to the headless corpse.

"This is the tengu that has been killing Kirishitans," Hideki said.

"Did you kill it?" Saito asked.

"No," Hideki said. "I helped, as did we all, but a very timely appearance by a Shugendō monk saved us and killed the killer," Hideki said.

"Shugendō monk? Are you sure?" Saito asked.

"No," Hideki said. "But your grandmother is."

"Lower your weapons, commander," Saito said. "We are among friends."

"I did not realize your home was Shimabara," Hideki said.

"It is. My father will want to thank you himself." Then, turning to his grandmother, "Do you want to camp here tonight or start home immediately?"

It was Akane who answered. "Commander, as soon as you make a litter, put the wounded man on it and let us return to Shimabara. We do not want to spend another moment here."

"Bossy is she not?" Saito said.

"I had not noticed," Hideki said.

It won him a smile from Akane.

"Cherry blossoms, neh?" Yoshi said.

"Shut up Yoshi," Hideki said. Then, "If you did conjure the Shugendō monk, thanks."

They were seated on cushions in the great room having breakfast across from the lord of Shimabara castle. Lord Matsukara was seated at the kamiza in front of the family shrine. His was the place of honor, raised slightly above the rest of the room. His wife, mother, and daughter set next to the raised area on the main floor to his right facing inward. His son sat opposite on his left side also facing inward. The fourth side of the square was completed by Hideki and Jubei facing the lord of the castle. Behind them were Aya, Yoshi, and Yasuke with his right arm in a sling valiantly trying to eat with his left hand. Everyone ate in silence until the lord spoke.

"My women have been regaling me with your bravery, Hideki," Lord Matsukara said.

Hideki stopped eating and placed his bowl and watabashi on the tray before him. "I do not believe I was brave, Lord. Most of the time I was frightened."

"That is what bravery is: facing your fears and acting anyway. It is the essence of bushido," lord Matsukara said.

"The real bravery was demonstrated by my friends. If Yoshi had not jumped on that two-bladed naginata when it struck the ground, my days on this earth would have ended there," Hideki said.

"Yes, Akane cites that act as most remarkable," noted Lord Matsukara.

"Jubei's willingness to almost jump into the tengu's lap also kept me from dying. So all in all, they are the brave ones," Hideki said.

"Yes, my mother mentioned that leap was magnificent," Lord Matsukara said.

"They were all magnificent. Even Aya refused to abandon us," the old nun said.

Lord Matsukara looked over Hideki's shoulder. "I

understand you are a businesswoman, Aya," he said.

Aya bowed low from her seated position. "Yes, my Lord."

"And you own a brothel? Is that true?" Lord Matsukara asked.

"The Jaded Princess is a waterfront tavern for waterfront workers of Nagasaki. We provide comfort, food, entertainment, gambling and, yes, girls. But I run a clean establishment and none of the girls are there against their will," she said.

"Interesting," Lord Matsukara said. "You have any other business outside of the Jaded Princess?"

Aya hesitated and shifted her eyes around the room as if in a trap.

"Go ahead and answer the lord truthfully, Aya," Hideki said.

"Very well; I have many holdings. In my name, I own two warehouses, a pottery factory, a repair dock and two farms that grow the food for the Jaded Princess. Also in my name, but co-owned by my husband Dom Joao, are three more warehouses, two lighter companies with ten ship-to-shore craft, a postal business for distributing goods and a courier service throughout Kyushu. There is much more, but too much to mention here," she said.

"By the Buddha," the old nun said. "I had no idea."

"Aya, you are a woman of many accomplishments," Lord Matsukara said. "Why have you thrown your lot in with these three adventurers?"

Aya shifted her head to the side. "That is a hard question to answer. I started out looking for a yojimbo."

"Yojimbo? You need a bodyguard?" Akane asked.

"Yes, but I did not want one that could be bought by a higher bidder. I wanted one that was loyal. Hideki fit that bill," Aya said.

"Why did you need a yojimbo?" Akane asked.

"Many reasons. First, my husband is a cruel man. I was his plaything until I started to learn his language," Aya said.

"You speak the big noses' language?" The old nun asked.

"Yes. Dom Joao, although a leader in his Kirishitan church, has wives in every port. He chooses them for their desperate situation and their ability to speak his. He feels when he marries them and entrusts them with his holdings while he is away, they will hang on his every word and always do his bidding," Aya said.

"And you do not?" Lord Matsukara asked.

"I look after his holdings the best I can, lord. But I also realized a man that has wives in every port has no loyalty to me. One of these days when he is displeased with me, he will have me killed by his assassin, Lobo," Aya said.

"Who is this Lobo?" Lord Matsukara asked, looking at Saito.

"A very talented swordsman who kills ronin regularly in the Destreza Pit for money," Saito said.

"There is a Portuguese swordsman who bests samurai?" Lord Matsukara asked.

"He does not fight the best," Saito explained. "He fights the most desperate."

"Perhaps he should be introduced to the best," Lord Matsukara said.

"He will be," Jubei said.

All eyes turned to Jubei but he spoke no more.

"Hideki, tell me about yourself," Lord Matsukara said.

"My parents died when I was young. My grandfather raised both myself and my older brother in Kiai province. I met Yoshi on the Tokaido last year and Jubei in Edo shortly thereafter," Hideki said.

"And you are a ronin now?" Lord Matsukara asked.

"Jubei and I started out on a musha shugyo. My previous sword mentor told me it was the best way to reach my goal," Hideki said.

"And what is that goal?" The lord asked.

"I always wanted to be the best swordsman in Japan," Hideki said. Then holding up his right hand, "but an accident shattered that dream. So now I strive to be the best man I can be."

"Lofty goals both," Lord Matsukara said. "Are you married, Hideki?"

All the women's eyes turned to Hideki.

"No lord, I am not," Hideki said.

"So how did you find my daughter, Akane?" Lord Matsukara asked.

There were no protests from the women, so Hideki answered. "I found her charming, easy to look at with an amazing grasp of tactics," Hideki said.

"Not bossy or overbearing?" Saito asked.

"Shut up, Saito," Akane said, and then blushed.

"We will come back to that. I am still interested in how a young ronin commands such respect from three followers obviously older and worldlier," Lord Matsukara said.

Yoshi responded. "Lord Matsukara, it is because we are more mature and worldly that we are drawn to his pure heart, his willingness to do the right thing every time despite the consequences and his childlike adherence to bushido."

"Could that be all?" Lord Matsukara asked.

Jubei did not speak. Seeing that Aya wanted to, the lord encouraged her. "Go ahead Aya. What do you have to say?"

"It was that simple for me. I am a businesswoman who has experienced what a bad life has to offer. I have survived and thrived by playing the odds and looking for profit at every turn. Pragmatism is my life. These three turn that on its head. They are loyal to each other and whomever they are fighting for and will face certain death if right is on their side. Hideki has given me hope for a better future in Nagasaki," Aya said.

"What is wrong with Nagasaki?" Lord Matsukara asked.

"Everything," Aya said. "But it all begins and ends with Heizo. He controls everything."

"That is what governors do," Lord Matsukara said.

"Not good governors," Hideki said. "There are no schools in Nagasaki. There are no hospitals. There is no infrastructure at all. Imagine how life in this castle would be if there were no rules for sanitation, no rules for when flames must be extinguished, no firemen and most importantly no justice."

"I see your point. Heizo has been lax in his responsibilities," Lord Matsukara said.

"No, Lord. Heizo likes it that way," Hideki said. "It is part of his plan. Heizo controls everything. He sets prices on all goods coming and going and spends nothing on infrastructure beyond his own group of thugs who extort most of their wages from the townspeople and farmers. I believe him to be behind the tengu that attacked these ladies. I know him to be behind the yamabushi, and I am gathering evidence that he is behind human slavery of Japanese citizens."

Lord Matsukara's head came up quickly. "What?" The lord turned to Saito. "Is this true?"

"I do not know father," Saito said turning to Hideki. "You have proof?"

"I have seen it with my own eyes, Saito. But I'm gathering proof as we speak."

"This is very serious, indeed," Lord Matsukara said. "Can he be that stupid?"

"I believe it to be part of Heizo's plan to create trouble with the Kirishitans via the tengu. If he can get the Kirishitans to revolt, he is a large step closer to getting rid of the Portuguese in favor of the Dutch. If slavery of Japanese families can be laid at the doorstep of the Portuguese, it is almost certain they will be expelled. If either of these two things happen and becomes known in Edo, the Portuguese will be out and your position here would be tenuous," Hideki said.

"How could a simple ronin know all this?" Lord Matsukara asked.

"I have informed friends," Hideki said. "And I listen."

"We have been laying the Kirishitan problem at Shiro's feet," Saito said.

"He is definitely their charismatic leader," Hideki said.

"You have met him?" Akane asked.

"Yes," Hideki said. "He is very young, but commands respect among the Kirishitans."

"What is he like?" Akane asked. "Is he a firebrand full of hate and threats of his god Jesu?"

"Quite the contrary. He is soft spoken and quite engaging. But I have only met him once. Aya is a friend of his," Hideki said.

All eyes turned to Aya.

"I have known Shiro for many years. He is a quiet young

man who has been thrust onto the local stage due to his faithfulness and natural leadership. Some attribute miracles to him, but I have never seen that side of him," Aya said.

"This is getting out of hand. First Kirishitan uprisings and now slavery; I thought I could put down any insurrection if I could capture the leader. Now you tell me it may be part of Heizo's plan to foster unrest for his own political ends. I am afraid if the gatherings get any larger, I must take some action," Lord Matsukara said.

"Talk to Yoshi about that, Lord. He put one down single-handedly. Well, he and an elephant," Hideki said.

"That was you?" Saito asked.

"Guilty," Yoshi said.

"Impressive," Akane said. "I have more respect for ninja now."

"Ninja?" Saito said.

Lord Matsukara interrupted his son. "This is more of an enigma. How does a ronin command the respect of the ninja? Is this how you are gathering evidence against Heizo?"

"It is one way we are gathering information."

"Hideki, you are either a liar or a shogun spy," Lord Matsukara accused.

The tenor in the room changed.

"I am no liar. Neither am I a shogun spy. I am on a musha shugyo with my friends," Hideki said.

"Then declare yourself. What is your full name," Lord Matsukara demanded.

Hideki hesitated. "Very well, I am Yoshinobu Hideki. My brother is Yoshinobu Nagamasa, magistrate of Edo. My grandfather is Yoshinobu Masashige, currently a member of the Roju. The shogun is my first cousin. Iemitsu is my second cousin. One of them is now shogun. I just do not know which one because we have been traveling."

Everyone was in shock. Then the women bowed low. Saito bowed low as well.

"I suppose you can prove all this?" Lord Matsukara asked. Before Hideki could answer, Jubei reached into his kimono and produced a Tonto with a golden Hollyhock Crest on the sheath. He held the knife above his head for all to see. No one would dare display the mon of the Tokugawa. To do so falsely meant death.

Lord Matsukara saw the emblem of the shogun's family and rushed to come off the raised tatami onto the main floor. Then he bowed low. "Please accept my apologies Lord Yoshinobu."

"Please, everyone rise. I am not Lord Yoshinobu. That is my grandfather. I am plain Hideki. I am on a musha shugyo as I explained. Everything else I said was the truth. But Aya was correct. Our family motto is 'No wrong too small to right, no right too small to defend.' I cannot let evil exist without trying to correct it."

"Then we are on the same side," Lord Matsukara said.

"That is my distinct wish, Lord Matsukara, and the reason I wanted to meet you," Hideki said. "Please return to your rightful position Lord."

Lord Matsukara moved back to his cushion on the raised portion of the tatami.

"Father, if word of the slavery gets back to Edo, we will be lucky to escape with our lives," Saito said.

"Oh," the old nun said as if just realizing the gravity.

"We will try to keep that from happening," Hideki said.

"You know we will have to arrest Heizo," Lord Matsukara said.

"I do not believe that to be prudent," Hideki said.

"Why not?" Lord Matsukara asked.

"Because many people owe him their livelihood," Aya said. "He must die, and it must look like natural causes."

The lord thought on this for several minutes and whispered with Saito.

"I think you are right," Lord Matsukara said. "We cannot allow him to survive and continue to plague the land."

"We are working on that," Hideki said.

Aya spoke again without being asked, taking strength from Hideki's revealed position. "He must be killed. He knows too much not to blackmail those in higher places," she said. "Besides, he could buy his safety from the Portuguese or the Wako pirates."

"You have qualms about killing him Hideki? If so, you do not have to do it," Saito said. "We can find someone."

"No, we have contemplated it because he is an evil man, and I just told you I cannot abide evil," Hideki said.

"If he dies, who replaces him?" Yoshi asked.

"He was put in power by my predecessor, the Kirishitan daimyo," Lord Matsukara said. "I guess it is up to me to appoint one of my retainers."

"You could do that, but do you have one who understands business and how things are done not only in Nagasaki but all ports of call in other lands?" Hideki asked.

"No one," Saito said. "Do you have a suggestion?"

"Yes, Aya!" Hideki said.

All eyes went Aya. "But she is a woman," Lord Matsukara said. "She is a brothel owner and she is of the merchant class."

"Heizo is of the merchant class, so that should be no barrier. But I agree, it would be better to have a samurai in that position. I propose Aya's bartender," said Hideki.

"Tatsu?" Aya asked. "He does not know anything about business."

"I think he knows a lot more than he lets on. But that isn't the reason I nominated him," Hideki said.

"Why then?" Aya asked.

"Because he is in love with you," Hideki said.

"What?" Aya asked.

"It is true. He will do whatever you ask when he becomes governor, but you will be the power behind him. You keep the goods flowing to and from Japan. Lord Matsukara supports you and Tatsu. Everyone looks good. Edo is happy. You work with the new magistrate to pump justice into Nagasaki, establish fair custom prices and divert money to Lord Matsukara for the upkeep of the territory and give Edo its due. Everyone's happy," Hideki said.

"Sounds too easy," Lord Matsukara said. "But it would mean I could alleviate some of the taxes on the peasants, possibly Kirishitans. That might placate them."

"If we do all this," Saito asked, "what do you need from us?"

"I'm glad you asked," Hideki said. "We have been war

gaming this among ourselves. It is high time we got the input of the people whose lives will be most impacted."

The planning began.

XXXIII

Marriage Offer

"When will you return to the city?" Akane asked.

Hideki turned at the sound of the feminine voice. "Probably tomorrow," he said.

"So soon? Why not stay and go and with my brother in a day or two?" Akane asked.

"I want to be around to provide support to another member of our team as well as tie up some loose ends with our Chinese friends," Hideki said. "Besides, Aya may need some protection from her husband and Heizo."

"I had some plans for you Hideki. At least until I found out who you really were," Akane admitted.

"Oh, what kind?" Hideki asked.

"You heard my father. I put him up to proposing a marriage," she said.

"You put him up to proposing?" Hideki asked. "That is a little forward, is it not?"

"Not at all. I am a woman who knows what she wants."

"And am I what you want?" he asked.

"Maybe," she said. "I would have to get to know you a little more, but from what I have seen so far, I think you fit."

"I am pleased to find I measure up. Your standards cannot be too high considering a handicap Ronin as your partner," Hideki said.

"You think so little of me to think I have had no suitors?" she asked.

"No, I think quite highly of you. I have seen you under

great strain and watched you make good decisions. You are quite impressive," Hideki said. "Besides, you are also pleasant to look upon."

"I too have seen you under stress. Your bravery is commendable, and that hand did not slow you from attacking and slaying those insolent yamabushi, nor did it hinder you in taking on a tengu," she said.

Hideki smiled. He had to admit he enjoyed this young lady's company. There was not the explosive fire he felt when around Myo. But he had not seen Myo in several months. Would the fire still be there? He hoped so. But he also felt like he could talk for hours with this girl. He felt a certain kinship with her. He felt they had much in common.

"As you remember, I was not alone in fighting the tengu, and he turned out not to be a tengu at all," Hideki said.

"That is another point in your favor. You do not seem to have the arrogance I see so much of in young men these days," Akane said.

"I appreciate the compliment, but it is uncalled for. I find my foolish pride places me and my friends in jeopardy more often than I would like," Hideki said.

"That is another thing. I have never seen such loyalty in retainers," she said.

"That may be because they are not retainers. They are my friends," Hideki said.

"What an unusual mix of friends. A master swordsman, a brothel owner, a ninja, and a young Ryukyuan boy look to you as their leader."

Hideki laughed. "Yes, we are a diverse lot. And you have not met Midori yet."

"Who is she?"

"She works with Yoshi. She has saved my life twice that I know of," Hideki said.

"Is she your lover?" Akane asked.

"You are bold," Hideki said.

"It is how I learn. But you did not answer, so maybe that is an answer in itself," she said.

"No, Midori is not my lover," he said.

"Then who is?" she asked.

"This conversation digs deeper and deeper," Hideki said.

"You may avoid answering if the subject is too sensitive for you," she said.

"You have a way of challenging and calming at the same time my lady," Hideki said.

"You may call me Akane and I shall call you Hideki, if you will permit it," she said.

"Again, calming followed by a challenge. All right, I shall call you Akane and you may address me as Hideki or ronin or anything you wish," he said.

"So who is your lover? Surely you are not celibate?" She asked.

"I have had only one," he said.

"Who?" She insisted.

"Her name is Myo and she resides in Edo," Hideki said.

"Oh, a big city lady," Akane said. "Is she from a noble family?"

"No, she is not," Hideki said.

"So you took advantage of a commoner? Shame on you," she said.

"I took advantage of no one. While it is true she is no samurai, she is quite accomplished," Hideki said.

"How accomplished?" Akane asked.

Hideki reddened. "She runs her father's courier service."

"Another businesswoman? You seem to be drawn to them," she said, looking around.

"No, Aya is my employer. I am acting as her yojimbo," Hideki said.

"Maybe you do not measure up. Most samurai would not sell their sword," Akane said.

"You may be correct," Hideki said. "My first sword master would not approve. But I decided I needed to eat. If that makes me unacceptable, I will have to live with it," Hideki said.

Akane smiled. "I see something else. In some ways you do not seem to be a slave to tradition. In other ways you are. You are practical when it is called for, such as selling your sword. But you are traditional in your adherence to bushido. You are very unusual for a young man. How old are you?"

"Lately I have felt very old. But I am now eighteen years."

"Eighteen only? You look older," she said.

"Travel ages you I guess," he said.

"Am I embarrassing you?" Akane asked.

"Maybe a little," he said.

"Then I shall quit questioning you," she said.

"Please do not stop. Despite your disarming nature and direct questions I find I enjoy your presence," Hideki said.

"Does that mean I still have a chance?" She asked.

"I have to return to Edo when this is all over. My brother and grandfather are at risk," he said.

"At risk from whom?" she asked.

"There are old enemies now in power," he said.

"Is it the new shogun?" she asked.

"I hope not, but probably so," he said.

"Then maybe I do not want to wait for you. You may be a pariah," she said.

"Such would be a safe choice," Hideki said.

"But samurai wives have to be ready for adversity. Their husbands can fall out of favor and lose their heads and lands at any time."

Hideki was enjoying the exchange. She was disconcerting yet engaging. She was disarming yet enchanting. This was a new experience for him.

"I have no response. You have bested me again," he admitted.

"Again? When have I bested you before?" she asked.

"You came up with the best idea for the defense against the tengu," Hideki said. "It was impressive."

"That was nothing. It was common sense. What was impressive was a suggestion from a woman taken seriously by such fierce warriors," she said.

"The best idea should overcome everything else. You would not believe where some of our best ideas come from."

"Again, you are most unusual. Perhaps I will wait for you," she said.

"I can promise you nothing. My heart belongs to another."

"Then we will have to wait and see how things turn out. I wish you luck in your endeavors, Hideki," she said.

"Thank you, Akane. I also wish you well," Hideki said. Then he turned and walked off to find Jubei and Yoshi.

XXXIV

Cannons

"I have had unofficial word that Hidetada is dead and Iemitsu is the new shogun," Heizo said.

Father Sebastian translated for the benefit of Dom Joao and Lobo.

"What does that mean to us?" Lobo asked.

"Unknown," Heizo said, "except he appears to favor the Dutch over your foul Kirishitan church."

"A foul church that has made you rich," Dom Joao pointed out.

"I made myself rich," Heizo said. "But it is just as well. I also got word the tengu was killed yesterday. Now maybe your people will be safe to walk the streets at night."

"Was it really a tengu?" Lobo asked.

"No, it was a large black slave brought into the country. I am afraid suspicion is cast upon you, Dom Joao," Heizo said.

"That is ridiculous," Dom Joao said. "There is no slave market in Japan. Any slaves here were given as a gift to the shogun."

"Nevertheless," Heizo said, "everyone is pointing fingers at Deshima."

"You bastard," said Lobo. "You kept one back for your own purposes. You trained him and made him into a tengu to stir up the Kirishitans hoping Edo would run us off and bring down the accursed Dutch."

"No need to get hostile Lobo. You unleashed attacks on the Buddhist temple with your trained tiger. How do you think that will sit with the new shogun?" Heizo asked. "Whether we like it or not, we are in this together."

"Except we are not trying to get rid of you," Dom Joao said.

"Really? And what message would you convey to the new shogun should you meet him and give him all those exotic pets?"

"We would convey his Holiness' welcome and hope for continued success for both countries," Dom Joao said.

"Most assuredly," Heizo said. "Your platitudes would be accompanied with a desire to get rid of me and your debts."

"Rest assured, if we are driven out, your sins will be made known to Edo," Dom Joao warned.

"The tengu? Edo does not care about the Kirishitans. That is the main reason they want to get rid of you," Heizo said. "Besides, your alliance with the Wako pirates is enough to condemn you."

"You really are a bastard. You are as much involved in slave trading and the pirates as we. It is you who picks the raid sites," Lobo said.

"Yes, but I do not have any direct links to them. You do," Heizo reminded. "But who is going to believe a big-nose foreigner over the governor of Nagasaki?"

"They will believe proof," Dom Joao said.

"Oh, you have proof, do you?" Heizo asked.

"This is not our first alliance of convenience. Of course we have proof, and it will be delivered to the proper authorities if we are banned," Dom Joao said.

"Speaking of foreign trade, how did you fair against your wife's lacquer ware enterprise?" Heizo asked.

"Not well," Lobo said. "She has outflanked us and used the Ryukyuans to launch her trade business."

"And you let that happen? How sloppy," Heizo said.

"They must have had help. We dispatched a longboat to the Ryukyuan village," Lobo said.

"What was the outcome?" Heizo asked.

"We never heard from it again. Even the boat disappeared," Lobo said.

"That is unfortunate," Heizo said. "I must place one of you under arrest until I am paid."

"Do not be a fool, Heizo," Dom Joao said. "You don't think we have ventured up to your compound without some insurance?"

"What possible insurance could you have?" Hideki asked.

Dom Joao stood up. As he did so, four militiamen and Tahei stepped forward with hands on swords. Heizo waved them off. Dom Joao moved to the opening at the south end of the room. The sliding doors were already open. The view of Nagasaki Harbor and the bay was breathtaking. Dom Joao waved his yellow scarf overhead. He then returned to his seat.

"That was impressive," Heizo said.

"Are any of your militia in the barracks next door?" Dom Joao asked. "Get them out."

Heizo waved Tahei to check.

Tahei returned and bent to the governor's ear.

"Just a sick man and the maintenance staff," Heizo reported.

"Unfortunate," Dom Joao said.

The sound of cannon fire from the bay bounced off the building. Moments later, the whoosh of incoming cannon fire could be heard, followed immediately by the exploding of the militiamen's barracks.

Heizo jumped under the table. The militiamen and Tahei went to all fours. Dom Joao and Lobo remained seated. Father Sebastian hunched low in his chair and muttered prayers.

There were a total of seven explosions. When all was quiet, Heizo crawled out from under the table. "You are a real bastard yourself," he said.

Heizo then barked orders to Tahei. He ran out of the room. He returned walking slowly. He did not whisper in the governor's ear this time. "Gone; all gone. There is nothing and no one left," he said. Father Sebastian interpreted.

"Just a taste of what will happen if we are not back aboard our ship by noon," Dom Joao said.

"Thank you for that demonstration," Heizo said. "Now both of you go and allow us to put out the fires and care for our dead."

The two Portuguese and Father Sebastian stood and left. On the way down the steps to the harbor, Father Sebastian asked, "Would you have bombarded the governor's mansion with all of us in there?"

"No, Father," Lobo answered. "There is no way to survive such a bombardment."

"Then how would we have gotten out if Heizo had not surrendered?" Father Sebastian asked.

"Lobo would have dispatched his bodyguards, and I would have had to think about killing Heizo," Dom Joao said.

"You are certain that Mr. Lobo would slay five men?" the Father asked.

"Certainly," Lobo answered. "You Japanese do not have the science of sword fighting. You do not know Destreza. With the samurai, it is all brute force. I kill them weekly in the pit."

"Father Sebastian, you may come with us if you like," Dom Joao said.

"You are leaving?" the father asked.

"Yes. Heizo is too dangerous for us to remain here. We will cast off my ship from the dock by the end of the week," Dom Joao said. "The new shogun may try to turn you into a martyr."

"Thank you, but my job is here," the father said.

"Good, I am glad to hear it. We will need someone to communicate with here in Nagasaki," Dom Joao said.

"You will be back?" Father Sebastian asked.

"Most assuredly," Dom Joao said. "I believe Heizo is too greedy and Edo too stupid to stop persecution of your flock. Eventually they will rise up. When they do, we will support them with arms and ships," Dom Joao said.

"But that will bring the shogun into the fray. He will have to put down any insurrection," Father Sebastian said.

"What if our side wins?" Dom Joao asked.

"Then God is truly on our side," Father Sebastian said.

"Yes, and we will be in a position to expel the Dutch and negotiate from strength with Edo," Dom Joao said.

"What do you want me to do?" Father Sebastian asked.

"Just keep on doing what you do Father. Protect your flock

and develop good relations with this boy, Shiro. He may be key to an uprising," Dom Joao said.

"It will be as you say," Father Sebastian said.

"We will send messengers to you from time to time with instructions from the Church. You will recognize them by their ability to identify the color of scarf I waved to commence the bombardment," Dom Joao said.

"Yellow?"

"Precisely," Dom Joao said at the foot of the steps.

"What will you do with all the animals and men that tend them?" Father Sebastian asked.

"Leave them," Dom Joao said. "They are all heathen anyway."

315

XXXV

Preparations

"You are crazy," Tatsu said.

"Hear him out Tatsu," Aya said.

"I have not been a samurai for over ten years," Tatsu said.

They were seated in an upstairs room of the Jaded Princess. Tatsu had posted guards around the room to ensure privacy and give the alert if militia or Portuguese sailors appeared.

"It will come back to you," Jubei said.

"But I do not want to be governor. I like it here," Tatsu said.

"It is because I trust you, Tatsu, that this offer is being made. I would consider it the highest favor to me personally if you would accept," Aya said.

"But I do not know anything about being governor," Tatsu complained.

"You do not need to know much. I will teach you. I plan to be your brains for this endeavor," Aya said.

"You and I will be working closely?" Tatsu asked.

"More closely than now, dear Tatsu," Aya said.

"If it helps you my lady, I will do it," Tatsu said.

"Good," Hideki said. "That's a major part of the puzzle completed."

"Do you want to use your old samurai name or create a new one?" Saito asked.

Tatsu smiled for the first time. "I shall use my old name again. I am Shunichi Tatsuyo."

"A fine name," Midori said.

"Yes," Aya agreed. "A fine name."

"I will have the declarations drawn up and presented in a day's time," Saito said.

"Where is Yasuke?" Hideki asked.

"He is preparing noodles for tonight," Midori said. "He had been taking the loss of his fiancée and her family hard. But the new girl has taken the sting out, I believe. He is young and will love again."

"Loss of your first love is always hard," Tatsu said.

"Yes," Yoshi agreed. "Is he talented enough to continue working here with that arm in a sling?"

"I believe he is, especially with the new girl assisting," Midori said. "But I think that is up to Aya."

"I certainly do not want to upset my new trading partners. Yasuke has a job here if he keeps the patrons happy. Besides, he thinks he is my new yojimbo," Aya said.

"Maybe he is. Okay," Hideki said. "A second problem solved. Midori, do we have any proof to link Heizo with the slavery?"

"Yes," Midori answered. "While you were slaying the tengu, I set a trap for Heizo's right-hand man, Tahei. He's in our custody and singing like a bird."

"That puts them in the stew," Saito said.

"Where is he?" Yoshi asked.

"He is currently residing in a pit behind the Ryukyuan village. He cannot get out, and it seems the villagers have no love for Heizo and his lieutenant," Midori said.

"Will he be alive to testify?" Yoshi asked.

"The priestess gave her word that not only will he be alive, but he will be talkative," Midori said.

"That is good enough for me," Hideki said. "Then there are several things left to deal with. First are Heizo's scrolls. Second is getting the Chinese on board. Third is the magistrate and lastly the Portuguese."

"You have forgotten one," Yoshi said.

"Which one?" Hideki asked.

"The one you remembered but do not want to think about. Killing Heizo," Yoshi said.

"The monkey is right," Jubei said. "We cannot leave him alive."

"I do not know how the magistrate will take to us killing the governor during his first week on the job," Hideki said.

"He will have to get over it," Saito said.

"We cannot kill Heizo until we have those scrolls in hand," Aya said.

Hideki looked at Midori. "Can you do both?"

"I have been checking. Heizo does not send for prostitutes as often as he used to. But he does once a week. He draws from the new girls delivered to his brothels in town. A militiaman reports to three inns Heizo owns and collects the girls. He brings them up the stairs to Heizo's quarters. All I have to do is replace one," Midori said.

"They will let you in?" Saito asked. "Marvelous. What happens once you are up there?"

Midori reached into her sleeve and produced a folding fan. She snapped it open covering most of her face and took on a new personality. "Oh samurai-sama, you should not ask the shy courtesan such a personal question."

"By the Buddha, you people are dangerous," Saito said. "I have heard prostitutes speak in just such a manner."

Midori resumed her regular demeanor. "I have been spending some time with the girls down the hall. They have been very helpful."

"Midori, are you okay with the assignment?" Hideki asked.

"Get the scrolls. Kill Heizo. Come back with the scrolls. Yes, I am comfortable," Midori said.

"Okay, now what about the Chinese?" Hideki asked.

"That should not be too hard. They have been shadowing us since we slept in their temple," Yoshi said.

"Can you get word to them?" Hideki asked.

Yoshi looked at him like he was a child. "Of course. I will put it in a note and pretend to drop it. They will pick it up."

"Smart," Saito said.

"Good," Hideki said. "Now the magistrate. I think Jubei and I and Saito should handle that."

"What is your plan?" Jubei asked.

"I do not have one. We will just go talk to him," Hideki said.

"I mean your plan for when the magistrate throws you in jail," Jubei said.

"Oh that," Hideki said. "You can flash your Hollyhock, and all will be well."

"I do not think so," Jubei said.

"Then what is your plan?" Hideki asked.

"To keep the magistrate in the dark," Jubei said.

"Not tell him?" Hideki asked. "How does he deal with the death of the governor?"

"Just like any other death. Depending on how it is done, he may rule death by natural causes," Jubei said, looking at Midori.

Midori nodded to Jubei.

"The sword master is correct," Yoshi said. "What do we hope to gain by involving him?"

"I hope to stay out of jail and off Sado Island," Hideki said.

"He will have nothing to connect you to anything. He certainly isn't going to find anything on Midori or the rest of us. Besides, the real investigation will rest with Saito's father, the daimyo. Let us keep as many people as we can in the dark about all this," Yoshi said.

"Good counsel," Jubei said.

"Yes, that is what my grandfather pays him for," Hideki said. "Okay, no magistrate. Now what should we do about the Portuguese?"

"What do you want to do with them? I hear they will be gone by the end of the week. Blowing up the militia barracks certainly did not heal wounds between Heizo and Dom Joao," Aya said.

"They will be back," Hideki said.

"Yes, but there is little that can be done about that," Aya pointed out. "I recommend one of the first things the new governor do upon the death of Heizo is restrict all foreigner movements to Deshima."

"How do you propose to do that, string a fence across the point?" Saito asked.

"A fence might work, but I was thinking about the first public works for the new governor. Build a canal across the point with only one bridge spanning it. Man the bridge with customs police. No foreigners out and all goods coming and going inspected and proper tariffs paid," Aya said.

"Smart," Saito said.

"The public works keeps unemployment rates down. Good idea, Aya," Hideki said. He then turned to Midori. "A lot of this hinges on you. I know how capable you are. What do you need from us?"

Midori thought a minute. "I need nothing, Lord. This is a one-woman job."

"How do you plan to pass as a young girl? Don't get me wrong, you are not old, far from it. But you are not sixteen either," Tatsu said.

"It is all in the lighting, makeup and attitude Tatsuo-sama," Midori said. "Unfortunately, most men are willing to see what they want to believe."

"When does Heizo call for his next batch of women," Yoshi asked.

"Tonight," Midori said.

"Then you should go and make preparations," Yoshi said.

"Hai," Midori said and bowed and stood and moved through the sliding door.

"You people are just plain scary," Saito said.

"Not to good people," Hideki said. "We are scary only to the evil ones."

"So what do the rest of us do while Midori is deciding the fate of Nagasaki?" Aya asked.

"I think we should visit the Portuguese sword-fighting pit," Jubei said.

"Really?" Hideki asked.

"Really," Jubei said. "I have heard Lobo is fighting tonight."

XXXVI

The Pit

This time the Pit was crowded. The spectators populated the seats and benches that started at floor level and moved away, almost reaching the rafters on three sides. The competitors stood or squatted on the floor level on the fourth side. The attitude of the crowd was boisterous. It was the only form of entertainment most could afford. Entrance was free. No saki or shochu was sold. Meat on a stick, bowls of noodles and various sweets were hawked by enterprising vendors carrying most of their wares on their backs. Louder than the vendors were the bookmakers, most of them Chinese, who wandered the three-sided venue taking bets once the contestants were matched.

Yoshi sat in the bleachers just below the Chinese section beside Aya. "Will you be betting?" Aya asked.

"I believe so," Yoshi said. "I know what both can do."

"I do not usually bet. My money has always come too hard to lose it on things I cannot control," Aya said.

"Understandable," Yoshi said.

Hideki and Jubei wore numbers pinned to the back of their kimonos. Hideki was number eight and Jubei was number ten. Lobo was number five. There were three other Portuguese in the competition. "They all appear to be students of Lobo, given the way they deferred to him," Hideki said aloud.

The rest of the competitors were running down on their luck, trying to make enough money in the pit to survive.

"What do you know about this Destreza?" Jubei asked.

"Nothing," Hideki said.

323

"See the circles in the pit?" Jubei asked.

"Yes and there are lines through them," Hideki said.

"The idea, I believe, is to move around your opponent until you find an opening and then move closer using the inner circle," Jubei said. "Just be careful in the inner circle. That is when they will reach for the dirk at their back and try to disembowel you."

"Yes, I see how they hold the rapier in one hand and place their other hand on the opposite hip. It is not much of a reach to slip the hand from the hip rearward and grasp the dirk."

"Mind you watch that. I do not want to have to explain your death to your grandfather," Jubei said. "And this is to the death. Expect no mercy."

"Remind me why we are doing this?" Hideki asked.

"It is an opportunity to kill several snakes," Jubei said. "And what better way to test your skills on a musha shugyo and against foreign swords?"

"Remind me to find a more lax instructor," Hideki said.

"Try to use mushin. It will help you," Jubei said.

"If it comes, I will use it," Hideki promised.

It was up to the contestants to choose their opponents. Lobo made a beeline to an old ronin in a ragged kimono. A Japanese merchant translated.

"Mr. Lobo chooses you. Do you accept?"

Before the ronin could reply, Jubei made his own challenge. "That is much like the Portuguese dog to challenge the old. You have no honor, and I will take great pleasure extinguishing your life, Mr. Dog."

After the translation, Lobo spun to face Jubei. "Oh, it is the yojimbo and his protector. I did not know you had the guts to show here. I accept your challenge. I will have my best student fight the yojimbo," Lobo said bowing slightly and moving off towards his disciples.

"I usually do not let emotion enter into a killing, but I am going to enjoy cutting that smelly dog," Jubei said.

"Just mind that you do. I cannot afford to lose another mentor," Hideki said.

Once the contestants had been decided, the names were

written in black letters in kanji on white canvas and pulled toward the rafters on pulleys for all to see. When this happened, bookmakers went into the crowd. Each wore a number as well. Most moved towards the Chinese section immediately. The betting was fast and furious.

"What are the odds on Jubei?" Yoshi asked the bookmaker.

"10 to 1 against. He is fighting Lobo. Lobo has never lost," the bookmaker said.

"I will wager two ryu," Yoshi said.

"On who?" The bookmaker asked.

"Jubei to win," Yoshi said.

"That is a lot of money. What do you know?" The bookmaker asked.

"I know you will either take the bet or move on. There are many other bookmakers here," Yoshi said.

"By the Buddha, you are a pushy one. I will take that bet," the man said. "Where are the ryo?"

Yoshi reached inside his kimono and produce the two gold coins. The bookmaker took the coins and bit into each. Satisfied, he wrote a receipt and handed it to Yoshi.

"You must think he can win," Aya said.

"Of course. He is one of the best swordsmen in Japan."

"Who is the best?" Aya asked.

"That would-be Hideki's first mentor, Myamoto Musashi," Yoshi said.

"Then Hideki must be very good himself," Aya said.

"He is very good. I would wager money on him, but his conscience might get in the way. He is just as likely to walk away from the contest if he is facing another ronin. A man with a conscience is a tricky thing for a gambler," Yoshi said.

"I see your point," Aya said.

The crowd grew restless and booed in many languages. Finally, the first match was called. It was a young ronin against a Portuguese sailor. The sailor began by flicking his rapier at the face of the ronin while he crossed-stepped to the right following the white lines of the outer circle.

"How is he doing?" Aya asked.

"He is doing well in deflecting the repeated thrusts of the rapier, but he has failed to recognize the thrusts are setting up the dirk."

"What do you mean?" Aya asked.

"Notice the large circle in the dirt?" Yoshi said.

"Of course, I see it and a smaller inner circle," Aya said.

"Where did they both start?" Yoshi asked.

"The outer circle I think," Aya said.

"Exactly. Where are they now?" Asked Yoshi.

"They are both standing on the inner circle," Aya said.

"Yes. The Portuguese has used the thrusts to close the distance. Like most samurai, the young ronin has trained to use one sword, the katana. He has had to contend with only one sword, the rapier. But now that the Portuguese has closed the distance to the inner circle, he will soon move his left hand from his left hip and move it to the small of his back where the dirk awaits. The ronin has only moments to live," Yoshi said.

"How do you know all this?" Aya asked.

"Easy, I am a merchant," Yoshi said.

"You are no more a merchant than I am a samurai," Aya said.

"I watched a samurai of some distinction give you a sword," Yoshi said.

"Yes he did. And it is my most cherished possession," Aya said.

As she spoke, the rapier tip dropped, the ronin took the bait and stepped in to thrust. The sailor raised his rapier tip and deflected the thrust to his right while pivoting to his left, the dirk in his left hand, which he thrust into his opponent's side. Screaming in pain, the ronin dropped his weapon and fell to the dirt floor holding his right side. He looked up at his opponent with tears in his eyes from the pain. The Portuguese sailor smiled and thrust the rapier into the young Ronin's heart. A cheer went up from the crowd.

"Too bad," Yoshi said. "But at least it will drive up the odds."

The next three fights were between ronin.

"Are they any good?" Aya asked.

"No," Yoshi said. These are provincial samurai who have lost their post and come to Nagasaki to look for work. The swords are a symbol of their status, but they are not tools of their trade."

"So they are not as good as Hideki or Jubei?" she asked.

Yoshi turned and looked at her. "You have seen both fight in real combat. Did you not see?"

"It all happened so fast," Aya said. "One minute there were yamabushi everywhere, and the next minute they were all dead."

"That should give you some clue," Yoshi said. "Hideki's next."

Hideki climbed down the steps and turned toward the pit. He bowed and moved up to the outer circle, his katana in his left hand. His Portuguese opponent was much darker skinned than Hideki, a condition highlighted by the frilly white shirt he wore tucked into skintight, deep-brown lower garments that disappeared into thigh-high leather boots folded down just below the knee. The fact that his opponent's manhood area was prominent in the skintight clothing seemed vulgar and embarrassed Hideki.

"Center yourself," Hideki said to himself. "Take deep breaths."

As he exhaled, the command "Hajime" started the contest. The Portuguese sailor raised his rapier and started moving to Hideki's left along the outer white circle.

The sailor thrust the tip of the rapier at Hideki's eyes. Hideki ignored it. His mind had already calculated the distance needed to strike each other.

"Distance is life," Musashi would say.

The sailor made a mistake. Musashi had been correct.

"Become a left-handed swordsman until your right hand has recovered," Musashi once said over Hideki's complaints that a left-handed swordsman was a freak.

"I fought a left-handed swordsman once," Musashi said. "He almost killed me. Everything is backwards. You train for years and come to expect certain movements from your opponents. You cannot expect that from a left-handed swordsman."

They move differently. Become a left-handed swordsman."
Hideki had obeyed.

The mistake was not realizing Hideki was left-handed. His leather, buckled shoes had stepped across each other to his right as he had done a thousand times in the pit. But he was moving to Hideki's left. The sailor was moving into Hideki's sword hand.

"Stupid," Yoshi said in the stands.

"Hideki?" Aya asked.

"No, the sailor," Yoshi said. Then getting the attention of the bookmaker, "Sumi masen, what are the odds on this fight?"

"20 to 1 on the sailor," the bookmaker said.

Yoshi held up more gold coins. Three bookmakers raced to get to him. The first one there snatched up the coins and wrote Yoshi a receipt. The other two turned away disgusted.

When the bookmakers departed, Aya asked her question. "What did he do wrong?"

"He has not registered that Hideki's left handed, and what's more important is his coach and his friends have not either," Yoshi said.

"That is good for Hideki?" Aya asked.

"If he uses it, it could be very good," Yoshi said.

Hideki made himself relax. He could feel mushin coming on.

Again the rapier tip flipped quickly back up towards Hideki's eyes. Hideki did not move. He was in a left-foot-forward chudan no kamae with his sword at mid-level, the tip pointed at the sailor's eyes. The rapier's tip stopped just a hand's width from Hideki's face.

Hideki registered all this but was not thinking about it. He was in mushin.

"That's it," Yoshi said.

"What happened?" Aya asked.

"Hideki has slipped into mushin," Yoshi said.

"What is that? Is it good?" she asked.

"Very good. When warriors practice hours and hours for years and years, only a few will be able to forget everything. They no longer think about what they are doing.

Their body takes over. Mushin is 'no mind,'" Yoshi said.

"And young Hideki can do this?" Aya asked.

"Oh yes. He is a prodigy," Yoshi said.

With each cross-step the sailor took, he made small circles with the tip of the rapier. He also stepped closer to Hideki as he moved.

"The fool missed something else," Yoshi said.

"What?" Aya asked.

"How many hands do most samurai use on their sword?" Yoshi asked.

"Two I believe," Aya said. "At least all we have seen to-night use two hands."

"Right. How many hands does Hideki have on his kata-na?" Yoshi asked.

"One," Aya said. "That is odd."

"Very odd for a samurai. The advantage the Portuguese have is that their usual opponents are not skilled swordsmen and their style is to always have two hands on the katana. Mu-sashi taught Hideki his style of Niten Ichi Ryu," Yoshi said.

"Niten Ichi Ryu?" Aya asked. "Two heavens as one?"

"Yes, also two swords, one mind," Yoshi said. "Watch closely. It should not be long now. I think the Portuguese are going to be one sailor short and I'm going to be many gold coins richer. I'm going to be a wealthy man," Yoshi said. "I may need some advice on investing."

As the sailor got closer, Hideki retracted his arm slightly to lull his opponent into a closer striking distance. When the sailor's toes touched the inner circle he spun the tip of the ra-pier in small circles at eye level to distract Hideki, then lunged off his back foot with a thrust at Hideki's head. But he kept his momentum coming with a pivot on his forward foot bringing his left foot around and closing the distance. As he completed the pivot, his left hand held a dirk. To his surprise, Hideki was no longer there.

When the thrust to his eyes came, Hideki did not think about it. He shuffled to the outside of his opponent's right foot making the thrust miss high and to the right. Then his free right hand moved for the wakazashi in the front of his

Obi. Hideki's shuffle and the sailor's pivot forward did the rest. Hideki's wakazashi sunk into the sailor's stomach and stopped at his backbone. Hideki released his grip on the short sword and spun on his left foot, bringing his katana down behind the neck of the now bent over sailor. Hideki decapitated him. The sailor's head hit the dirt with the thump. Blood spewed high in the pit. The corpse collapsed in the dirt, turning the inner circle a dark black.

Hideki retrieved his wakazashi, bowed to his deceased opponent and climbed the three steps to the main floor with a sword in each hand. He took the wakazashi in his teeth and cleaned his katana with the paper sheet from within his kimono. Then he returned the katana to its saya. He did the same with the wakazashi.

Jubei moved to his side. Both watched the Portuguese contingent, who were like the rest of the crowd—deep in a stunned silence.

"They are not used to samurai winning," Jubei said. "Good job. I really want you to teach me that mushin."

The clapping started in the bleachers, then spread right and left, and soon the place erupted in cheers and yelling, "Go kudo."

"See, now they agree with me. They are reinforcing my comment about a good job," Jubei said.

"Please take care of Mr. Dog quickly, and let's get back to the Jaded Princess. I am not sure how many friends we have made here," Hideki said.

"Do not worry, friend Hideki. I am very confident," Jubei said.

"I have no doubt in your swordsmanship. I do not trust Mr. Lobo. Be ready for anything," Hideki said.

"I am ready," Jubei said. He turned and stepped into the pit as soon as a maintenance crew had removed the corpse, spread and tamped down new dirt and refilled the white rings of the circles.

The crowd still had not settled down. They had seen the unexpected. They wanted more despite losing money on Hideki. Pride was taking precedence over greed.

Jubei drew his katana and toed the outer white circle. Lobo drew his rapier. Unlike his student, he was clad in a white, longsleeved shirt and waistcoat. Like his student, he wore black pants tucked into the leather boots that came above the knee. His left hand was on his left hip, his right side toward Jubei. The rapier was in his right hand.

"Hajime" sounded. Jubei was in a right-foot-forward chudan no kamae with the sword tip pointed mid-level.

When Lobo crossed-stepped, Jubei shifted his rear foot to the right to keep the sword tip on his opponent.

Just as Lobo was about to cross-step again, Jubei stepped forward into Hasso no kamae. Jubei brought his rear left foot all the way forward and raised his sword high. Now his left side was forward and somewhat vulnerable, and the distance was cut down considerably.

Lobo smiled. He lunged toward Jubei's left side with the tip of the rapier aimed at the heart. Jubei brought his hands down and deflected the thrust to the outside with his blade just above the tsuba. Then he dropped the tip to his opponent's throat level. Lobo had started his pivot on the front foot, bringing his rear foot around with his left hand holding the dirk but froze when he saw the tip of Jubei's katana dangerously close to his throat. He backpedaled quickly.

Now Lobo faced Jubei with a weapon in each hand. Jubei pressed him. He lunged forward toward Lobo's middle. Lobo deflected it with the rapier as Jubei knew he must. Jubei let the tip of his katana go to his right, but instead of coming back to a guard position, he dropped the tip and brought it back across Lobo's right thigh. A dark line appeared against the black pants as he let out a yelp. Fear appeared in his eyes.

Jubei was having none of it. He brought his katana up, faking at a slash intersecting Lobo's right shoulder and head. Lobo brought his rapier up to deflect the slash to his right. Unfortunately for Lobo he could not bring the rapier back in time to stop a lightning change of direction that brought Jubei's katana down across Lobo's stomach from left to right. The white shirt split and a crimson sash appeared. Lobo jumped back, clutching the cut as best he could with the hand holding the dirk.

Lobo looked into Jubei's one good eye and saw death. He spun and ran to the steps. The crowd booed. Jubei took two long strides across the pit, raised his katana as he moved and slashed Lobo from right shoulder to left hip. The Portuguese screamed and dropped to the floor of the pit where his screaming turned to sobs.

Jubei knew he had dealt a killing blow. He flicked blood from his sword and returned it to his saya. Then he stepped directly on top of the dying Portuguese captain, leaving a foot print on the white shirt, climbed the steps and joined Hideki.

A chant started in the crowd and grew until it was deafening. "Jubei, Jubei, Jubei," they chanted.

"We did well," Aya said.

"Yes, and when I find those two bookmakers we will do better," Yoshi said.

"Come, I will show you where they hang out."

"You are a very good person to know in Nagasaki," Yoshi said. "Let us collect our money and our samurai and return to the Jaded Princess, where I think it might be wise to double the guard."

A fat Chinese spectator moved to Yoshi's side.

"A most auspicious beginning," he said.

Yoshi remembered him from the temple. "Yes, indeed," Yoshi said.

"The matters you left in the note will be accomplished," the fat man said.

"Glad to hear it," Yoshi said.

The fat man turned and moved off with the crowd.

"Trouble?" Aya asked.

"No, no, far from it," Yoshi said. "We were just planning your future."

"My future?" Aya asked.

"Oh yes, my dear, and that of the city's," Yoshi said. "Now let's go and get my money."

XXXVII

Midori Steals In

From the entrance of one of Heizo's brothels, Midori could see the militiaman descending the steps from Heizo's mansion. The madam and the farm girl she had picked for Heizo tonight were both in back trying to decide which end to stick in the benjo ditch first. The women's discomfort was the effect of something Midori had placed in their tea.

When the militia men arrived at the entrance, Midori blocked his way. "I am the one you are looking for," she said hiding behind the fan.

"Get out of the way whore. I deal with the madam only," he said.

"The madam sent me. She is indisposed," Midori said speaking a higher pitch than normal.

"Indisposed? I am on the governor's business. What can she be doing that is more important?" he demanded.

"I believe she is sick," Midori said. "I don't know if it is catchy."

One of the things everyone feared in a port town was the plague.

"Never mind," he said. "Let us get going. Say, you sound older than he usually likes. How old are you?"

"Oh samurai-sama, the madam said the governor wanted someone with enough experience to teach these girls something this time. I guess that was me. Where are we going next?" Midori asked.

"We have two more stops. Keep up," he said.

They picked up two frightened, very young girls. Then they started up the long steps to Heizo's mansion. By the time they reached the top of the steep hill, it was dark. At the top they were checked somewhat roughly by a security detail and shown into the mansion. They were escorted into a large room that was the governor's sleeping quarters.

"Use that room off these quarters. Strip off all your clothes and bathe. Put on the silk kimonos provided. There are no obis. Let the kimono hang open. When the governor arrives, you will be lying on his futon. He will tell you what he wants. Be sure to give it to him if you want to live to see tomorrow," the militiaman said.

The three did as they were told and bathed. They then slipped into the silk kimonos and moved to the large futon in the sleeping quarters. The young girls barely spoke. They were both shy. Neither girl noticed Midori palm two glass vials. One she placed beneath the edge of the futon. The other she kept in her hand.

"Here, dab this on either side of your nose. You will smell sweet for days," Midori said.

"What is it?" one girl asked.

"It is perfume from China," she said. "Here, smell it."

One girl did. "Oh, it is sweet. I will try."

She dabbed it on either side of her nose. The other girl got curious. Midori held it for her. Then she dabbed two spots on either side of her nose.

The sliding doors moved open and the governor walked in, turning to close the door behind him.

"Good evening my lovelies. What sort of the bliss do you have planned for your governor tonight? Let's get a good look at you," he said.

The two girls standing at the foot of the large futon bowed at the waist trying to hold the kimono together with their hands.

Midori was at the head of the futon standing straight, the front of her kimono hanging and exposing her body to full view.

The governor moved past the two girls and stopped to

admire the beautiful partial nude before him. "My, my, my; you are a lovely creature. But you appear older than most of my girls," he said.

In her best young voice, "Oh Governor-sama, the madam thought you could use some experience to help with the pleasure and to bring the new girls along."

"Interesting idea. Why don't you undress me? What is your name?" he asked.

"I am Midori." She said and began undressing the fat, little man. She was most interested in the key he had on a chain around his neck, but she was too professional to stare at it.

Midori forced the governor slightly down onto the bedding and noticed the two girls were already sound asleep. The perfume was time delayed. The governor had not noticed as Midori was busy rubbing her hands over his chest and his fat, little belly.

"If you enjoy this, you should really like what's coming next," she said.

"Bring it on, my sweet Midori."

So, Midori clamped her left hand across the governor's mouth and ran a long needle through his right eye into his brain. He kicked and lurched for a moment and then lay still. Because he was lying down there was very little bleeding. But he was dead just the same.

Midori pulled the two girls over to his body and staged them as if they were performing sex acts. She discarded the silk kimono, put on her own clothing and started hunting for the safe. It did not take her long. It was hidden behind a Western wooden closet. The cabinet pulled away from the wall to reveal a strongroom behind with iron bars and a great lock. Midori used the key to open the lock and started pouring over the various scrolls. She ignored the gold and treasures lying everywhere. She found three scrolls that showed payments to various entities, from Wako pirate captains to Edo officials. Another detailed how distribution was made throughout Japan on incoming goods.

Midori placed the scrolls in hidden folds of her kimono and started out of the strongroom. She stopped to scoop up a handful of gold coins and put them in another pocket. Then she took the vile from under the futon and held it under the girls' noses. They came around slowly. They both looked at the naked governor on the bed.

"Is he dead?" one asked.

"No, no, just sleeping. I am afraid I wore him out," Midori said.

"Did I … Did we?" one girl started.

"No, no. I was the only one," Midori said. "You girls are still virgins. Let us go down the hill."

When the girls got clothed, they started out of the mansion. No one in the house challenged them. When they started to traverse the compound, they were stopped by the security detail.

"You are leaving early," the commander of the guard said.

"Oh samurai-sama, it was not us. It was the governor. He finished ahead of us," she said.

The guard laughed. "So, you made him happy?"

"So happy he gave us one of these," Midori said holding up one gold coin.

The guard snatched the coin out of Midori's hand. "Whores have no need of a gold coin. Go on, get down the hill where you belong," he said.

Midori frowned as the guards laughed at her loss and their gain but led the girls down the hill to safety. "Men are so predictable," she said to herself.

At the bottom of the hill, Midori turned to the girls. "If you want out of the brothel life, come with me. I can get you back to your families or started on new lives, either one. But if you go back to the brothels, you will be dead by tomorrow."

Neither wanted to return. "Follow me to your new life," Midori said.

They entered the Jaded Princess, and Midori left the girls in Tatsu's care. She went upstairs and saw Yoshi. She found him eating a light meal with Hideki, Jubei and Aya.

Midori handed the three scrolls to Yoshi as well as a key to the governor's safe room. "It went well, but I picked up two virgins destined to be deflowered by Heizo. They are down with Tatsu now. I promise them they would be returned to their families for new lives."

She produced several gold coins. "I lifted this from the governor's vault to help the girls on their way. They cannot go back to the brothels when word of the governor's death spreads. They will be the first suspects," Midori said.

"We will have to get them out of Nagasaki tonight," Aya said. "I will take care of that first." She stood and went downstairs.

When she returned, she said, "Let me have the gold. One has opted to return home. She will do so triumphantly. I have a group leaving tonight that will divert to the girl's village and drop her off."

"She will receive the money?" Midori asked.

"Yes. They both will. You can trust my man and myself," Aya said.

Yoshi passed the scrolls to Aya. "Can you use these?"

Aya opened the scrolls and poured over them. It took several moments. "This is all I need to keep the city running and the goods flowing," Aya said. "These are better than gold." She then turned to Midori. "Are you sure Heizo is dead?"

Jubei answered for Midori. "She says it, it is so."

Midori looked at Jubei. "Why Jubei, how sweet of you."

Jubei grunted.

"Is Saito still in his room?" Hideki asked.

"Yes," Aya said.

"Alert him to Heizo's demise. But tell him to take no action until he has heard of the death on the streets," Hideki said.

"Aren't you the wily one?" Yoshi said.

"Not that wily. I have killed two men in 24 hours, once by my sword and once by decree. I sure hope I did the right thing."

XXXVIII

Death of a Procurator

Dom Joao watched Lobo die. He had mixed emotions. The very first thing he thought was of the enormous increase of the ships' stores that would be his. The second thing he thought was that he had lost a large bet on Lobo's swordsmanship. As far back as he could remember, Destreza had been superior to the samurai style of sword fighting. Yet that one-eyed vagabond had made Lobo look defenseless. What really galled him was the fact that Lobo died a coward. In the end, all his posturing and past victories meant nothing. Maybe the samurai swordsmanship was superior. He did not know and did not care. He had to think fast.

The death of Lobo in the pit was humiliating. But the rumor of Heizo's death was something else again. If true, he had to make up his mind as to his next course of action. His sources told him the governor died of natural causes. But Dom Joao doubted that. Too much was at stake. Were the Dutch behind it? Was the new Shogun behind it? Or were there new players in the game? He did not have enough information and enough time to gather any.

He had two options: stay or go. If he stayed, he might have a better chance convincing the new shogun and his people that the Portuguese offered the best distribution for Japanese exports as well as being the obvious choice for imports. Portuguese sailors were at home in most ports throughout the world.

If he stayed, what were the dangers? Was there a new enemy? Was the new magistrate a threat? Could he now get word to the new shogun through the magistrate? What about Aya?

Could he trust her? She had betrayed him on the urushi nuri, but he did not really blame her. She sniffed the opportunity and exploited it, just as he had trained her to do.

Aya must be back in Nagasaki. Her yojimbo fought in the Pit tonight and seemed very friendly with the one-eyed devil that butchered Lobo. Would they come for him next? Probably not. He had dispatched two boatloads of sailors to retrieve the urushi nuri from the Ryukyuan camp, but they had disappeared. The search party he sent later did not even find one boat. He suspected the Ryukyuans had interfered, but he had no proof. It was likely that Aya had been at the Ryukyuan camp when his sailors arrived; therefore, her yojimbo had probably taken part in their disappearance. Was that provocation for revenge? He hoped not. He knew he did not want to cross swords with the yojimbo or his one-eyed friend. Aya had been right in her warnings. Her yojimbo was strong.

He was not sure about the general population of Nagasaki. If the governor was dead, would the townspeople rise up and start looting? Would they stop at Japanese-owned businesses? He thought not. On board his ship was enough silver and gold and jewels to buy a small country. Should he put to sea to protect it? The only other people that might pose a threat to him were the Sung. He had no direct dealings with them. He was aware of their propensity for violence. He visited every port in Asia, so he knew that the triads were active in Nagasaki.

Then it dawned on him. Lobo and that trained tiger had wiped out two Chinese Buddhist temples. Those killings were enough to make the triads want revenge. They were his biggest threat now.

It was decided. He had to leave. Dom Joao made a beeline for the quay and his ship. He did not even slow down at the gangplank. He raced up the wooden structure and shouted commands at the officer of the deck.

"Prepare to cast off; I want to be underway on the tide," Dom Joao said.

The officer of the deck touched his plumed hat, signifying he understood and would obey, but Dom Joao did not notice. He was still moving quickly towards his quarters. Before he entered, he looked forward and aft. There were still many ragged stevedores coming and going and loading. The sailors would get rid of them soon enough. Dom Joao grasped the handle of his captain's cabin but paused to look at the sea state. The tide had not turned yet. They would be underway soon.

Dom Joao stepped down into his large cabin, took off his sword and hung it on the bulkhead. Then he turned to pick up a flintlock pistol on a small counter. He checked the powder pan to ensure there was enough to ignite a round. There was. He let the hammer move slowly back into place and stuck the loaded pistol into his wide, leather belt.

Dom Joao spun at the voice. "You will live a few moments longer if you keep your hand away from that pistol," the tall, slender man said in passable Portuguese.

"Who are you?" Dom Joao asked.

"I am the avenger for the lost souls of our two temples you destroyed," the tall man said.

"I had nothing to do with that," Dom Joao said.

"Please stop moving your hand toward your pistol," the tall man said.

Dom Joao stopped "How did you get in here?"

"I am the leader of the Golden Hatchet triad. We come and go as we please," the slender man said.

"What do you want with me? Dom Joao asked.

"I came to settle the score," the man said.

"That was Lobo's doing. Not mine."

"Lobo has paid for his sins; now an example must be made," the slender man said.

Dom Joao moved his right hand to his belt and felt the familiar wooden grip as a golden hatchet blade sliced into his forehead. He was dead before he hit the floor.

The slender man retrieved his weapon from Dom Joao's head and made three heavy chops to the back of the corpse's neck. When the head was severed, he placed it in a small canvas bag and departed.

XXXIX

To Edo

"Place seems deserted without the Portuguese ships," Yoshi commented.

"Does seem quiet," Hideki mentioned.

"Oh, it will get busy again when the inter-coastal shipping starts pulling in to fill up," Aya said.

"Yes, but no more huge Portuguese ships," Yoshi said as he turned to Aya. "Aya, you have my sincerest condolences on the death of your husband."

"I'm afraid I can shed no tears for the man," Aya said. "But how did you know? I just got word of his death at the hands of a mutinous sailor from the magistrate this morning?"

"We merchants have our sources," Yoshi said.

"Was it the same source that put an end to our governor?" Aya asked turning to face Midori.

Midori turned her palms outward and shook her head in the negative.

"No, Aya. No one in our entourage killed your husband, Dom Joao. My sources, like the magistrate's, say it was a disgruntled Portuguese sailor who was not happy with his share after Lobo and his student lost their lives in the Pit," Yoshi said.

Aya nodded her acceptance of the explanation and bowed slightly to Midori.

"I hope we have mild weather," Jubei said.

"You are not an all-weather sailor, Jubei-sama?" Tatsuo asked.

Jubei grunted.

"I believe that may be the reason we walked all the way here," Hideki said.

"We walked all the way here so I could sharpen your sword skills and you not embarrass me on your musha shugyo," Jubei said.

"Well, how did you do as an instructor?" Hideki asked.

"Nicely laid verbal trap," Saito said.

"Yes," Yoshi seconded. "Now the pressure is on Jubei to either accept the fact that you did not embarrass him or that he was a poor instructor."

All eyes went to Jubei.

"You are still alive, aren't you?" Jubei asked.

Yoshi clapped his hands. "Another perfect answer from the sword master."

"You might want to consider we will be on this small junk for several weeks, monkey. It is very hard to hide on such a ship," Jubei said.

"Boys, both of you behave," Hideki said. "Any moment now the captain of the ship will signal us to board. Let us depart on our new adventure in harmony."

Jubei looked at Yoshi with his one good eye and winked.

Yoshi nodded.

Saito looked at Hideki. "My sister sends her regrets."

"Is Akane not well?" Aya asked.

"No, I think she is fine, but her message to you was a little cryptic. She said 'Goodbye and if it was meant to be you will see each other again.'"

Midori considered Hideki's eyes. Hideki stared back.

"Please tell your sister that I greatly respect her and value her as a trusted friend. But she knows my heart belongs to another. I wish her the best," Hideki said.

Midori smiled.

"In case I forgot to thank you all, thank you!" Aya said.

"You have nothing to thank us for," Hideki said.

"Yes, I know. 'No wrong too small to right and no right too small to defend … 'or some such. But thank you anyway. All of you."

"Aya, you can do one thing for me," Hideki said.

"Anything, yojimbo," Aya responded.

"Meet with Shiro and explain everything. Let him know that continued uprisings will be dealt with harshly. I would hate to see what we have set in motion be destroyed due to religious fervor," Hideki said. "I know the Portuguese are gone, but I doubt their agents have left. Tell him to be vigilant if he does not want to become a martyr."

"Hai, Hideki. I will help him," Aya said.

"And I guess with Saito and his father's backing, it should not be hard for your new shipping enterprise to obtain a red seal," Hideki said.

"That will be a banner day," Aya said.

"Don't worry, Hideki," Saito said. "It is already in the works. She will be trading with the authority of the Tokugawa very soon."

"Is this trouble coming?" Yoshi asked.

"Is your haragai sounding the alarm, monkey?" Jubei asked, turning to face the long street.

"No sword master. Strangely it is not," Yoshi said.

The discernable sound of Jubei slamming his sword back into the saya made everyone turn toward him.

Jubei shrugged. "I have learned to trust the monkey's skills."

Everyone turned back to watch the lone horseman walking his mount down the major street of Deshima Point. The helmet on his head announced his position. As he passed the various warehouses on the Point, it became obvious he was armed with only his kodachi and a riding crop.

"At least he did not come with yoriki," Yoshi said. "So we must not be under arrest."

The magistrate stopped his horse near the group where he could be heard but did not dismount.

"I heard you were leaving us," the magistrate said.

"Yes," Hideki said.

"And you are going to Edo?" the magistrate asked.

Hideki looked to the golden hollyhock painted on the side of the ship forward.

"Yes, again," Hideki said.

"You have undoubtedly heard the big news," the magistrate said.

"The governor's death is big news? There is little else talked about on the streets, and every corner has a group of Saito's father's men," Hideki said. "It would be hard not to hear. How did he die?"

"He appears to have died of natural causes. He had just spent an evening with three young prostitutes. He must have had a stroke. One of his eyes was very bloodshot. There were no other marks on his body," the magistrate said.

"Who is the new governor?" Yoshi asked.

"Ask your friend there. Saito's father picked her bartender as the new governor," the magistrate said.

"Strange choice," Hideki said.

"Not so strange when you consider he gets Aya's business acumen," the magistrate said. "Turns out he was a former samurai and has been returned to that status."

"Lucky him," Hideki said.

"Yes, wasn't it? I have to ask, did you and your friends here have a hand in any of this?" the magistrate asked.

"I do not know what you mean magistrate. I told you I was here on the musha shugyo. I came to sharpen my sword skills."

"Yes, but I have the old governor's right-hand man in custody. He was found on my doorstep this morning with a confession pinned to his chest. He didn't seem much the worse for wear, but he flinches at the smallest movement. I think someone scared him. But he has certainly put the last governor in the hot seat. It is almost as if it was a good thing Heizo died when he did. Otherwise he would be facing charges."

"Nice story magistrate, but again, why are you telling me this?" Hideki asked.

"What about your eclectic group of friends?"

"They are just that, friends. They try to keep me out of trouble," Hideki said.

"That is not what I heard," the magistrate said.

"What did you hear magistrate, and who did you hear it from?" Hideki asked.

"Two more yoriki came into port yesterday on the ship behind you. They had been part of the Gumsumgumi that were turned into a police force last year in Edo. The whole country is talking about it still. They mentioned they were trained by the younger brother of the Edo magistrate, master swordsmen Myamoto Musashi and Yagyu Jubei as well as a funny little man who defeated samurai with ease and had a beautiful wife. He also had the habit of materializing and disappearing almost magically," the magistrate said.

"Interesting story, but what does it have to do with us?" Hideki asked.

"I believe you to be Yoshinobu Hideki; your one-eyed friend is Yagyu Jubei, and the one dressed as a medicine peddler must have a beautiful wife," the magistrate said.

"How will you use this information magistrate?" Hideki asked.

"Now that you are leaving, I will not use it. It is why I came alone. I just wanted you to know any future vigilante efforts in Nagasaki will not be tolerated," the magistrate said.

"Is that all?" Hideki asked.

"No, I also wanted you to know that I could have handled the situation, given enough time," the magistrate said.

"I am sure you would have magistrate. Is there anything else?" Hideki asked.

"Yes, since you are going to Edo, would you deliver this packet to the Roju?" The magistrate asked, pulling a sealed packet from within his kimono.

"Magistrate, I will be happy provide the captain of the ship with such instructions. But I am a lowly ronin and would have difficulty providing anything to the Roju," Hideki said.

"Very well, please pass it on to the captain with those instructions. Have a safe journey," the magistrate said and turned his horse and left.

"He has a rather high opinion of his capabilities," Aya said.

"Over inflated, I would say," provided Saito.

"Be that as it may, you both will have to work with him. So, learn to play nice," Hideki said.

Jubei moved up beside Hideki. "Is that our savior coming down the street?" he asked.

Hideki turned toward the direction Jubei pointed. Coming at them was the tall, white clothed monk they had last seen on the night of the tengu's slaying. He walked right up and spoke to Yoshi.

"So you are leaving?" the tall monk asked.

"I did not think you talked," Yoshi said.

"I talk when it is necessary," the monk said.

"I wish to thank you for saving our lives," Hideki said.

"You are welcome Prince of the Yoshinobu," the monk said.

"How do you know who I am?" Hideki asked.

"We have been on Mount Omine since the founding of our sect hundreds of years ago. Do you not think we keep track of our neighbors?" the monk asked.

"Then you are Shugenja," Yoshi said.

"Yes. We received word a tengu was killing Kirishitans and yamabushi were killing Buddhists and taking over temples. By the way, there are no more yamabushi in Nagasaki," the monk said.

"You are very well informed for a monk," Yoshi said.

"We listen. Just as we heard the governor had died. That saved me a job. Our sect cannot have tengu and yamabushi killing innocents. It reflects badly upon us all," the monk explained. "Anyway, I wanted to warn you that Iemitsu is now the shogun, or at least acting like it and the Yoshinobu are no longer in favor. I imagine the bird woman will send the Iga and Koga after you soon."

"I am amazed at your knowledge and skills," Hideki said.

"How do you think this one learned his skills?" The monk asked, pointing to Yoshi. "We started it." He then moved his hands together in very strange manipulations and chanted, "RIN; HYO; TOH;" here Yoshi joined in and mimicking each hand movement and chanted, "SHA; KAI; JIN; RETAN; ZAI; ZEN."

When he had finished he brought his hands down. "It is good to see one who practices the old ways." He then turned and moved up the street.

"So, you did not conjure him?" Jubei asked Yoshi.

348

Everyone stared at the strange monk as people got out of his way.

"I have no idea," Yoshi said.

"Cherry blossoms, then?" Hideki asked.

"Cherry blossoms, indeed," agreed Yoshi.

The four friends boarded the ship for Edo as Aya, Tatsuo and Saito waved goodbye.

To be continued in Death Among Brothers, Book Three: The New Shogun.

Glossary

Arami: The oil from the urushi tree used to make nuri lacquer ware.

Bachi: A plectrum used to strike the strings of the samisen.

Benjo: Ancient open sewer system of Japanese cities.

Bokken: A Japanese wooden sword used for training.

Bu: Slang expression for Ichibuban, a small silver coin.

Bugyo: A magistrate appointed by Edo.

Bunraku: Famous Japanese puppet theater.

Bushi: Forerunners of the samurai. Skilled warriors in many forms of combat.

Bushido: The ideals of an ethical life practiced by bushi warriors of Japan, forerunners of samurai.

Chosin: Edo era reference to Korea.

Choto matte kudasai: Japanese for wait a moment please.

Conbanwa: Good Evening in Japanese.

Daimyo: Overseers of vast domains appointed by the Edo government.

Deshima Point: A small point of land jutting into Nagasaki Bay with docks for deep-water vessels.

Dojo: Martial arts hall for training.

Fugu: Japanese puffer fish with a toxic poison in its inner organs.

Geta: A form of traditional Japanese footwear that resemble both clogs and flip-flops.

Gomen nasai: Sorry; an apology.

Habu: Black, venomous pit viper from southern Japan normally found in the Ryukyus.

Hachi maki: Japanese term for headband.

Hai: Yes.

Hakama: A pant-like type of traditional Japanese clothing.

Hakata: A seaport city in northern Kyushu, Japan.

Han-gappa: Outer coat worn by commoners in Edo period Japan.

Haori: Traditional hip-to-thigh length, kimono-like jacket.

Haragai: A sixth sense allowing the practitioner to "see through the darkness."

Hikawa Shrine: A Kyushu, Japan Buddhist shrine established for seamen in Kyushu, Japan.

Irashimasu: Means "Welcome" (normally used in shops/restaurants) in Japanese.

Jii: Japanese slang for grandfather.

Jiyu Waza: A free form of martial art sparring.

Kamae: A Japanese martial word for posture, implies correct distance.

Kamishimo: Kamishimo is the set made of the Kataginu (sleeveless top) and Hakama, worn by Samurai and courtiers during the Edo period.

Katana: A long, single-edged sword used by Japanese samurai.

Kirishitan: Japanese pronunciation of Christian.

Kuji kuri: Nine symbols cutting; finger weaves used with mudras or chants to open energy centers for the ninja; considered the black arts by some.

Majutsuhi: A magician associated with finger weaving and the black arts.

Mamushi: Brown, camouflaged, venomous pit viper found in southern Japan.

Master: One of a higher station; in martial arts, "master" could be Soke or head of the system.

Matsukara: Family name of Daimyo in charge of all of Kyushu in 1633.

Matte: A Japanese word used in martial arts to signal a halt or to wait.

Metsuke: Edo era government spies; secret police.

Mon: A small, bronze coin formally known as Kan'ei tsuho; A mon can also be a family crest or emblem.

Mt Tara: Mountain in Northern Kyushu, Japan.

Munenori Yagyu: Father to Jubei, counselor to the first three Tokugawa shoguns.

Musha Shugyo: A warrior's pilgrimage by budding swordsmen traveling the country side looking for challenges and improvement of their skills with a sword.

Mushin: A mental state into which trained martial artists are said to enter during combat.

Myamoto Musashi: A famous Japanese swordsman, believed to have been one of the most skilled swordsmen in history. He founded the Hyoho Niten Ichi-ryu or Nito Ryu style of swordsmanship and wrote Go Rin No Sho (The Book of Five Rings), a classic work on strategy, tactics, and philosophy.

Nagasaki: A seaport city in southern Kyushu, Japan, established by the Portuguese.

Naginata: Halberd-like weapon with a sharp blade on one end.

Oba-san: Honorific for an older woman.

Ofudo: A Japanese word for bath.

Oishii: A Japanese word for describing food that is good.

Okasan: Mother.

Otosan: Father.

Roju: Lower house of Edo government consisting of six to seven men responsible for keeping the country running.

Ronin: A samurai who has no master; literally wave man.

Samisen: Three-stringed musical instrument resembling a banjo.

Shinkage-ryū: A school of sword fighting founded by the Yagyu family and favored by the Tokugawa shoguns.

Sumi masen: Japanese word for "excuse me."

Tabi: Japanese socks with a separate area for the big toe.

Taira: Upper house of Edo government consisting of two men responsible for advising the shogun.

Tanto: Japanese knife.

Tengu: A type of legendary creature found in Japanese folk religion, also considered a type of Shinto god.

Tsuba: Hand protector on a Japanese sword.

Udon: Japanese thick, wheat noodle dish; often served hot in soup.

Urusai: Japanese word for "noisy."

Urushi: A tree whose sap provides the base of urushi nuri lacquer ware.

Wajima: A city on the Japan Sea know for it Wajima nuri lacquer ware.

Wakazashi: Shorter sword of the dual set worn as a badge of samurai status.

Watabashi: Common stick-like eating utensil for Japanese unlike lacquer ware ohashi.

Yagyū Jubei: One of the most famous and romanticized of the samurai in Japan's feudal era.

Yamabushi: Mountain warriors, usually monks of a Shinto order.

Yojimbo: Edo-era Japanese word for bodyguard.

Yumi: Traditional asymmetrical Japanese bow for shooting arrows.

About the Author

William Marcus Charles II (Marc) is the author of *Simplified Self-defense for Women*, published by the Marine Corps Association. He has been published in the *Marine Corps Gazette* and in *Ensign*, a global monthly of the LDS Church.

Born in Murfreesboro, Tennessee, Marc spent his formative years in Warren, Michigan. He graduated from boot camp in San Diego at nineteen and for the next twenty-four years wore the Eagle, Globe, and Anchor proudly until retirement as a Lieutenant Colonel of Marines.

He spent much of his military career in Asia where he studied martial arts. He is a Roku-dan (sixth degree black belt) in Okinawan Kenpo Karate and a Roku-dan in Kobudo (the weapons of Okinawa). He has trained in Aikido, Jujitsu, American Kenpo, Shorinryu, Judo and other lesser known styles. He has founded three martial arts schools in the United States.

Marc graduated with honors from Park College with a BS in Management and Finance and has an MBA from National University.

He and Sako currently reside in Encinitas, California.